THE DREAM OF GOTAMA

Written and illustrated by

Walter A Elliott

With best wishes
Walter A Elliott

First published 2002 by
Edward Gaskell publishers
6 Grenville Street
Bideford
Devon
EX39 2EA

isbn: 1-898546-53-3

THE DREAM OF GOTAMA

Printed and bound by
Lazarus Press
Unit 7 Caddsdown Business Park
Bideford
Devon
EX39 3DX

With all my fondest love to Beryl my wife
who I miss more than words can ever say.

To see the trees against the sky as I walk by.
To see raindrops on a window pane, to hear a sigh.
To watch the corn blow in the wind whilst strolling
To watch the clouds across the sky, billows rolling.
To feel the breeze upon my cheek as I walk by,
To hear the ripples of the brook, as birds fly by.
To see a million diamonds sparkle in the stream,
Reflecting fragments of the sun. I sit and dream
Of picnics in the waving grass and nights so free
Under stars that float and shimmer in a cosmic sea.
To say I love them and everyone is very true,
But truer and more important still, is my love for you.

Walter Elliott

INTRODUCTION

Old wives' tales and good meals are often best taken with a pinch of salt. This is equally true with some more serious subjects such as Philosophy, Politics, Society and the Sciences. The condiments of humour, with a smattering of the sceptic and satirist, can sometimes help us digest that which frequently seems to be intellectually or emotionally indigestible. Moreover, the condiment of humour, in particular, can perhaps be the best vaccination against the ills of falsity and fanaticism so often prevalent in contemporary society.

I've written *The Dream of Gotama* in the hope that people who enjoy reading about some of the deeper questions of life may be entertained. I've endeavoured to include a number of intriguing and thought provoking subjects in the story, which tempers serious topics with some tongue in cheek humour. I have, at times, leaned towards a more surreal humour, as this seemed appropriate for the type of *avant-garde* tale I wished to tell and, hopefully, carried the implication that we should never take life, or ourselves, too seriously. I also wanted to make implicit the question of whether people will finally be future masters or slaves of their clever creations, one of the more important being artificial intelligence.

As an artist, I'm familiar with painting subjects in contrasting shapes, tones and colours. Similarly, in this book I have tried to combine and contrast a little seriousness with some splashes of humour, in a recipe that, hopefully, will occasionally bring on a smile and, if I'm lucky, even an outright laugh. The story has also been illustrated with a few of my paintings. So, if my reader enjoys just some of the story and humour, or some my illustrative paintings, I'll feel my efforts have not been wasted. But, if my reader finds enjoyment in the story, the smatterings of humour and *also* looking at my illustrative paintings, I'll consider myself very fortunate indeed, because there are few things to match being able to give enjoyment as we travel life's highway.

My grateful thanks to Edward Gaskell and Jenny Capern for all their advice and encouragement in the publishing of this book.

Contents

Illustrations:

N.B. Many of the following illustrations are seen by Gotama in the Great Hall and have been indiviudually described within the text – bold page numbers. – while others are simply representative of the many other images Gotama sees.

THE DREAM OF GOTAMA

We're only ripples on a stream,
Flickers of light gone as they begin,
Insubstantial in continual change,
Fleeting things of thought and mind.

Walter A Elliott

Gotama Mann, admired politician and scientist was flying to New York to attend a United Nations debate prior to voting on an important resolution. There was at this time considerable unrest in the world with an increasing threat of war between many nations. There had been an alarming increase in the number of countries possessing the nuclear bomb and new types of nerve gas; this was particularly worrying with the worldwide increase in terrorism and the possibility that some of these groups also possessed nuclear, biological and chemical weapons. Global warming and many other ecological threats to the stability of the natural world were also causing alarm. Moreover, the economic state of many nations was now at a very low ebb and many people were starving. The time had come when something urgent had to be done to avoid world catastrophe and the extinction of the human race.

A motion had been put forward by members of the UN who considered that world government in some form was now an urgent necessity, not only to mitigate threats of global terrorism, nuclear war and world pollution, but also to benefit the underdeveloped regions of the world and particularly the poorer communities. There had been an increasing clamour among UN bodies for a general debate and vote on the subject. Gotama Mann was in every way a fine politician, but he had been dogmatically anti world government or coalition in any form. There were too many different ideals and ways of life to satisfy. He was positive in his opinion that such a government could never be made to function as a global administrative body.

Most people behind the scenes at the UN were of the opinion that the motion as proposed didn't stand a chance of being adopted if Gotama spoke against it. He was in fact a very persuasive speaker. It was therefore almost a foregone conclusion that the new proposals for world government or coalition of countries would come to nothing. Some even considered it pointless to attend such a debate. It was almost as if Gotama had the casting vote in the palm of his hand. He had some inkling of this during preliminary discussions with colleagues, but it had not troubled him to any extent. There were times when Gotama could be rather dogmatic and unbending, like most politicians.

He was now comfortably relaxed in the aircraft seat. The faint drone of the engines, the soft background conversations of the passengers and the recent late nights spent entertaining, gradually instilled in him an overwhelming drowsiness. At last he slipped imperceptibly into a deep sleep. High above, from somewhere in outer space he heard a voice that seemed to ring and echo across the galaxies.

THE DIMENSIONAUTS

Man is eternity cloaked in Time

Walter A Elliott

"What's this?" the dimensionaut asked.

"Don't know exactly," replied his colleague. "I picked him up in a crevice of Space/Time, a tiny backwater of only three dimensions."

"Three dimensions!" The first dimensionaut laughed. "I vaguely remember passing briefly through there during my early apprenticeship. I was a nine X grade dimensionaut then and didn't have much idea how it would be to experience twenty or more dimensions." He laughed again as he peered curiously at the figure laid out on an operating table in the centre of the curved laboratory glowing with countless green and orange lights. "He's a real museum piece. How did you ever manage to find him?"

The second dimensionaut chuckled. "It was during a time reversal experiment that I suddenly noticed him floating in the low 3D space/time grade."

The first dimensionaut stroked his antennae, which seemed more satisfying than stroking his head. "He looks particularly scruffy. He still has a few remnants of very early dimensional grades. Look at those bits of hair in odd places. Leftovers from apish beginnings, I shouldn't wonder. What are those two things there?"

"Fish eyes, I think, of the type used once or twice on primitive planets, but not very long lasting and extremely limited in range and vision. Must have originated on a planet like Earth, I should think. Definitely biochemical in origin. Very primitive indeed."

"Let's have a look with the interface scrutiniser!" The first dimensionaut moved quietly towards a flashing instrument panel. He muttered an incoherent sound that incurred a buzzing sound above them. Thereupon a shiny cylinder, like an X-ray machine, lowered itself towards the inert body. "Take it up to twenty thousand million acuvoltus first time then turn the scrutiniser to the bio-chemical cul-de-saco condition."

"Have done!" replied the other dimensionaut. "Phase one holographic encelographs for one two and three dimensions. Registering now," he said.

"Negative! He's no reptilian that's for sure. His scales are different. Switch to phase three, nine W. Contact now. Getting funny blips on the chart recorders. Ooooog, whatever are they?" (Ooooog, it should be said, was the alien version of 'oh God', but it had an Ooogi Ooogi sound that was particularly expressive and could break windows and wine glasses if any were around.) The dimensionaut turned his head through one hundred and eighty degrees, a novel alien ability, in order to view the new data streaming in behind him. "He must be a parasite of some kind. Surely not! ! No, he's his own destroyer, actively biochemical.

Take the phasing deeper. Ego visions very strong, several million more than expected for safety. He's definitely a second-degree amphibian of some kind, I'm sure. Look at that." The dimensionaut pointed to several screens, on which holographic data appeared. "Probably just at the start of their time/space dimensional drift as a minor sequence planet. Just beginning space orientation, like the earlier amphibians first struggled out of the primordial sea. This time they're struggling out into the ocean of Space and Time."

The other dimensionaut also had a scratch of his antennae. It seemed not only satisfying, but also conducive to concentration. "Probably," he muttered "Couldn't have evolved for very long into the second phase because his behavioural responses and ideologies are very ego and planetary orientated. Suffering from aggressive over compensation strategies. Nuclear derivative syndromes show up plainly. Obviously from a very primitive world that needs a few million more years of simmering in the evolutionary pot in order to create anything of lasting value. Critical evaluation indicates phase two evolution with maximum danger levels. Also out of phase conditions between intelligence and emotional advance. Ethical valuations show sharp reversals and little growth whilst intelligence wave structures are strongly in the ascendant. With the nuclear position at danger level and the uncertain judgement coefficients, biological evolution could go forward or move directly into extinction. Poor devils!"

The dimensionauts stood for a few moments, like two clones, unable to decide what course of action to take. Suddenly a soft clicking noise interrupted their reveries.

"Check motivation bias modulator." The voice came from nowhere and everywhere in the cabin. Both dimensionauts leapt swiftly into action. "Recorder data coming in now, via intergalactic scanners. Distinctive biological behavioural patterns evolving."

One dimensionaut let out a strange echoing screech of astonishment. "What strange patterns they are too! Take the probe scrutiniser deeper into the unconscious memory banks. Link in with his attitude synthesisers. Perhaps we can get to the cause of his plight. Detailed reports coming through now. Switch on atomic recorders and analysers and tap into manual access loud sensory speakers for the five senses only. See if you can tap into a generalised attitude level."

Suddenly, without warning, an voice of a human man could be heard, mellow and booming, as the loudspeakers transmitted the prone man's thoughts as spoken words. "Man, in his present plane of experience is doing everything possible to adjust his behavioural patterns so that he can obtain maximum rewards with a minimum of effort and a minimum of penalties." The voice struggled amidst considerable interference. "He craves for more pleasure and less pain, more power more easily, more gratification of sensual desire."

Both dimensionauts raised their ear lobes simultaneously in surprise. "Sounds as though it's a hedonistic world that this species is creating. More data coming in."

The human type voice boomed again. "Man has a new orientation, ostensibly labelled "progress." Vast sums of money are spent on 'pop' worship, footballers, racing drivers, tennis and snooker stars. Such heroes are honoured with wealth beyond the wildest dreams of ordinary people and starving children are born to die in loneliness, squalor and despair only a few hours flight time away. Progress, progress, we must have progress, the voice shouted frantically. All these things are done in the name of progress."

One of the dimensionauts moved to another monitor. "Second phase instrumentation showing warning beacon."

The other dimensionaut left his own instrument panel to join his colleague. "What do you think?"

The voice boomed again. "The progress of Mankind is marvellous to witness. He has invented the H-bomb and the pill. He now has the ability and knowledge to cure countless diseases that have plagued the world for centuries. He spends billions of pounds every year, developing more and more lethal weapons, which can destroy the world countless times over. More and more terrorists use them to kill, injure and maim. Greed, hate, fear and ignorance motivate individuals and nations. More and more people are expecting a world catastrophe – a holocaust."

Suddenly there was silence again. One dimensionaut turned to the other. "What do you think it is?" he asked.

"Ooooooog knows! Could be a second phase amphibian reaching a critical nuclear phase. May even be extermination by more subtle means. Recorder analyser shows a recent upgrading in information technology and international communication. This could have reached critical conditioning levels so that processor networks may have overridden people's individual biological intelligence. It's a more subtle and creeping type of extermination that the nuclear type, but can be equally effective."

"No, I don't think it's that! More likely to be the internal blows to mind and body delivered to people by each other. Look at the low peaks in the man's character scope analysis. Much of his energy has been used aggressively. He may be high in the intelligence quotients, but he appears to be low in terms of inter-human compassionate behaviour. Just look at those black spots indicative of riots, wars and civil disturbances. Poor devil! He's so progressively intelligent, yet so conspicuously blind to the evils of his own making. Race discrimination level also at warning peak spectrum. Black, white, yellow and hot radiant positions. Tolerance levels proportionately low. Superficial and poor judgement activity at record peak."

One of the dimensionauts blew quietly through his suckers. "Just look at that pattern of 'Mara' and ignorance developing. Pity the human race can't see itself objectively from the outside. They might curl up in laughter or collapse in tears if they knew what was in store for them. How easy to avoid catastrophe, yet how difficult for them to see, chained as they are in the tight web of their own karmic condition."

"More data coming in. Looks like a global catastrophe is on the horizon. Threatened by the destruction of the planet's natural wealth. Freshwater life in the rivers and lakes has been halved in only 25 years. 30% of the marine ecosystems have been lost in the same period and over 10% of the Earth's forests destroyed. It looks as though the devastation caused by pollution is increasing at an alarming rate and all nature could be killed off in another 50 years. Pollution by cars and factories has increased by 100%. Even the seas, lakes and rivers are drying up, like the Aral in Asia, which has lost 70% of its water. The human population is now using more than half the available fresh water. Up to 60% of over 200 species of freshwater fish, birds, reptiles and mammals are declining. Carbon dioxide emissions from cars and industry have more than doubled since the 1960s and are now at danger levels. It's doubtful if the planet will be able to reabsorb them. The Earth people seem to have a voracious appetite for plundering the globe's natural resources. Marine fish consumption has more than doubled to 84 million tons since 1960 and 60% of the world's fish resources are now either fully exploited or in dangerous decline. It looks as though the world-wide consumption pressure is growing at an alarming rate at about 5% a year. Fish and meat consumption and carbon dioxide emissions will reach unsustainable levels in just a few years. The ozone layer is deteriorating and global warming is at a dangerous level. Soon the polar ice caps will melt resulting in terrible flooding. Drastic climatic changes are imminent that will reap havoc and death across the length and breadth of the planet. The Earth's natural ecosystems are suffering a terrible sickness and mankind is responsible. Time is running out. If the Earth is to remain a living planet, drastic changes in attitude are now urgently required, particularly of governments. The planet is obviously dying and something must be done about it."

"What's this new data coming in. Periodic mass hysteria and fanaticism developing into international madness, which they call wars. Strange how 'ego' is so tightly enmeshed in people's motivations. Selfishness is rife. Even more strange how Man has managed to evolve along progressive lines and has formed such large regulated communities when he is fundamentally flawed and wrapped up in so much selfishness."

The dimensionauts turned towards a large monitor in which appeared a continuous flow of multi-dimensional holographs, which were accompanied by the booming human voice. "Man's addiction to pleasure and his frantic efforts to obtain it, is reminiscent of a poor drunk drowning in his sorrows. He will do almost anything just to taste pleasure's sweet intoxicating wine. Or to smell the fragrance of pleasure's flowers that wilt and die so quickly in the noise, grime and ugliness of civilised living. He is addicted to the chase and shouts 'who but a fool would give it up?'

Suddenly a short verse appeared on the monitor screen, accompanied by the voice.

"Man, a blend of trite sage and Bunyan,
Ham and ecstasy,
Sweet and sour. Whine and spirit,
Scrambled ecstasies on boast,
Prune pie and lie please,
Coffee and Goonhill,
He is but a mortal portal,
A pale shadow, a brass clown,
Reflecting an image. A sad comedy."

"The receptivity frequency seems to be changing," one of the dimensionauts muttered half to himself.

Just at that moment a door at the far end of the white laboratory cabin opened to reveal a figure carrying a large brief case. "Good light year, sir," the two dimensionauts said, momentarily stiffening to acknowledge the presence of their superior.

"How are you both?" retorted the new entrant. "I haven't seen you for centuries, since we were all at that party in Andromeda. I remember it was a brilliant Nova occasion when we investigated the case of our friend 'flash Harry' and his binary systems." The two dimensionauts smiled. "I came as soon as I could," the new entrant said.

The newcomer looked quite aged in comparison with the two dimensionauts. Yet he emanated a sparkle of manner that endowed him with a special kind of youthfulness. It was a combination of wisdom that comes with age and a sprightliness of youth. He had a rugged, yet kindly face out of which two eyes gleamed like twinkling stars and a long green bedraggled beard lay on his chest. The most odd part about him was his spectacles, which appeared to be constructed of numerous layers of glass. Despite the depth of the various lenses, his bright blue eyes could be plainly seen. They were like blue peacocks twinkling with kindness and humour. He had a thin body attired with a robe of scintillating colours. His head was a mass of curly ultramarine and white hair that stood up, like some frothing wave in an ocean storm. Although his proper name was unpronounceable in human terms, he had been assigned a simpler one that most life forms of primitive intelligence, like the human, could understand. It was 'Ooopsantensag,' a name that his superiors, in the galactic quadrant, thought would suitably describe him, because he often tripped over his antennae, which had a nasty habit of collapsing without warning, like a couple of drooping elongated string beans. It usually happened when he was slightly stressed doing jobs that required special concentration, like deflecting a planet away from a super-nova or a black hole, or making one a suitable habitat for life, the latter being especially tricky. Setting down his briefcase with an air of modest authority, he moved towards the light speckled indicators and instruments. "Had any further results?" he said.

"We've managed to get an overall picture of the species," commented one of the dimensionauts. "Processor intelligent instrumentation indicate that he's a member of mankind from planet Earth."

The old alien stroked his beard. It was softer and easier to reach than his antennae. "I didn't think the humans would imperil themselves quite so soon," he muttered. "Wasn't long ago they were given their divinity transplant. Mind you, I did think at the time that the ape was a difficult subject for such a specialised grafting. I remember he had several nasty relapses and once or twice we didn't think he would make it, in the face of the competition, meteor and comet impacts and volcanic upheavals. It looks as though it might be a case of rejection of the transplant again. It's not the first time, of course. Not long ago, only a couple of sec-flashes of time dimension, when Man was in the cul-de-sac condition, the Roman era to be exact, we had to inject a special kind of restorative to try to bring him round. It was, in fact a brilliant move on the part of the 'Beyond' to filter some of his radiant medication through to the earth's primitives. But alas they nailed it to a wooden cross. That wasn't the only instance either. Only a spec of time previously another one of our special agents called Socrates was given hemlock for his efforts to enlighten. And so it was with the Gandhi type implant and many others sent to try to lift the stupid creatures out of the morass they were drowning themselves in. It was a great disappointment that one of our first nirvana transplant successes, the Buddha, rarely seems to have been repeated without some kind of primitive animal response. Man must be made to learn somehow. We must find a way to cure him of his blindness. We must remove his blinkers, otherwise it will be too late and he will have missed his chance to step into the wider dimensions. The big question is how do we do it?"

Ooopsantensag looked vexed and for a long time remained engrossed in his own thoughts, if thoughts they were. Occasionally he would touch a small pin head size switch on the side of his spectacles as though to alter their focus. Each time he looked in a different direction.

"Looking back through the dimensional records?" one of the dimensionauts enquired. Ooopsantensag waggled his beard and nodded.

"Yes," he replied. "Just taking a few glimpses at similar evolution in other parts of the galaxies and taking in some future time dimensions. I'm also accessing some aspects of the universal intelligence in order to reach a decision. Many have passed through this particular evolutionary phase but few have been faced with the current danger levels. There was the case of Beta-Outovit, the planet in Andromeda that suffered similarly."

One of the dimensionauts had another scratch of his antennae. "Yes, I remember only too well. Blew up like a young Nova in the end. Not much left now to show for all their early efforts. That was nucleonic and pollutionic blight of similar type to phase 2 exit amphibians. Yes, sad business that was. They were so near to reaching the 3rd phase utopian condition too. Very sad indeed."

There was another very long silence as each member ruminated amongst old light year memories that extended across the thresholds of many galaxies. "There must be a way," the old alien muttered as though whispering to himself. After what seemed like an eternity, he suddenly shouted something that sounded very much like 'Geronimo.' I've got it he shrieked as he slapped his hand on his lower universal joint, the equivalent of a human knee. "There's only one thing for it!"

"What's that?" a dimensionaut enquired.

"Another transplant, but with a difference."

The dimensionauts looked sceptical. "But we've tried that several times already without much success. They all suffer from rejection. Humans think that rejection is something to do with replacement hearts, livers and kidneys. They are unaware that they are all dying from a more subtle rejection of the psychic heart. It's a secular society where altruism and love are dirty words. It's almost taboo for the modern man and women to speak of them. Many consider they taint of an outdated age as dead as queen Victoria. For many, the modern age is the age that God died. His replacement is 'self gratification. The main object is to grasp as much as possible in the shortest possible time. It's a race to keep up with the 'Jones' at all costs. Modern man is more impressed by sexual potency pills, the Jumbo jet, football, or an X rated film."

"I know that," retorted Ooopsantensag. It's partly because those who should be reflecting the deeper wisdom, such as the clergy and others with similar vocations have lost contact. Most are too busy with whist drives, coffee mornings, repairing church roofs and trifles at tea parties. The ordinary man in the street just can't stomach them.. They give him severe psychic seizures. He prefers getting back to basics, like screaming at football matches and having sex as often as he can." The old alien thought for a moment, or at least it appeared that he was doing so. There was really no way of knowing whether he was using 'thought' or some other indescribable medium of consciousness that he'd picked up in some far away foreign galaxy.. However, we must assume he was 'thinking' because I, as your 'story teller,' cannot imagine anything else.

Ooopsantensag suddenly awoke from his reveries. "It's such a nuisance," he said. "They've all been misguided by too much dressing up in pompous clothes and fine church hats that they have forgotten the kernel of truth. They see only through physical eyes and not their inner being. The Christians seem to enjoy their singing but have forgotten how to meditate. The Buddhists and wise men of the East seem to have found a way to enlightenment, but we need many more like them if we are to save the planet Earth from catastrophe. And there is so little time!"

At that moment the old alien was interrupted by one of the dimensionauts who was studying thousands of images and figures on an adjacent monitor screen. Although humans boast about their scientific achievements, 'greed' seems to be Man's speciality, not science," he said cynically. It's centred in the depths of human mind and is a more potent destroyer of life and environment than the most powerful bomb. According to our space/time and dimensional scanners, humanity appears to be like a ship lost in the ocean. Plenty of attention is being paid to making the ship materially seaworthy, but little or no attention to the rats and the woodworm inside. Also there doesn't seem to be anyone at the rudder."

The dimensionaut stopped speaking. They all gazed silently and rather disconsolately at the flickering lights on the instrument panels all of which conveyed meanings more complex that I could explain here. "Do you think it would help if one of the advanced extra-terrestrial cultures in the galactic union contacted the human race to advise them where they're going wrong?" queried a dimensionaut.

Old Ooopsantensag hesitated for a moment, stroking his antennae. "It might seem an obvious remedy," he replied. "It could save the planet Earth from total extinction, but would undoubtedly destroy mankind with even more thoroughness than he is destroying himself. Darwinian natural selection is not just confined to the earth species. It also applies to cultures throughout the galaxies. We have found that whenever an exceptionally advanced culture has made contact with a primitive civilisation there has been a complete absence of comprehension by the primitives. It would be rather like a human trying to converse with a worm or an ant. Moreover, contact by Man with a more advanced culture would only enslave him. It would never free him. He would become as extinct as the Dinosaurs. For these reasons the very advanced galactic cultures in the Universe have made it their policy to allow planetary life to incubate and evolve in perfect isolation in order to conserve them in all their uniqueness. Planets are allowed to evolve in their own way with just the occasional spur in the right direction by us if required, as when like naughty children they start to do dangerous things, like blowing themselves to kingdom come. As you know, there are billions of planets where life has advanced to such a degree that they have been able to communicate with other similar planetary systems. These advanced civilisations have joined together to form the 'Galactic Organisation for the Prevention of Meddling into other Planetary Business.' This vast group acts like a syndicate. They enjoy watching planets evolve and making resolutions rather like the United Nations Organisation on planet Earth, except that the U.P.O. resolutions usually carry some weight and mean something."

"One resolution states that there shall be no direct interaction with evolving life on planets until they reach the seventh grade in advancement. The Earth life is only at the second grade, which is far below the limit. Direct interaction at this time would therefore be highly detrimental to the primitive life forms. If we are to assist in human advancement, it must be in such a way that they have no knowledge of any such intervention in their affairs. It must be a particularly subtle mind transplant that will help them to attain the beginnings of a higher transcendent plane of conscious awareness. They have already taken the first faltering step up from the lower biological animal and have created the beginnings of a planetary nerve network they call the Internet. We must now help them to take the next step towards wisdom and enlightenment. It will necessitate the embodiment of the Perseus Mk three million four hundred thousand one hundred and fifty three upgrade for primitive worlds and the Andromeda Mk ten million five hundred thousand nine hundred and fifty four transplant to quicken progress towards a fully integrated living planet. Such a giant step can come with terrible side effects, but it may be our best chance to establish some unity between Earth peoples and save them from extinction. Also, it's most important that a special mission be sent to Earth without delay to alert mankind to all their current dangers. With that the old alien bent down and spoke briefly into unseen instrumentation. "Give me full power on all cosmic quadrant amplifiers and interface with Milky Way and Andromeda galactic processors to obtain phase one universal focus."

One of the dimensionauts registered a look of astonishement. "You're not trying to individualise the universal again?" he said.

Ooopsantensag looked thoughtful. However, whether he was actually entertaining thought was any one's guess. He was probably making use of conscious essences that were far above 'thought' as human thought was above those of the worm. "It's the only true source of harmony and wisdom," the old alien replied. "We should be able to tap a spontaneous answer to our problem that will be in accordance with the overall pattern of universal harmony and which will coincide with the regulations of the galactic unions. Whatever we do must accord with the galactic union's health and safety practices for living planets. It's the one way in which the answer will reflect the universal infinite intelligence inherent within everything. Our galactic processor systems are thousands of times more efficient and sensitive than a biological brain in tapping this source of intelligence. Human's would call it intuitive inspiration, but their form is usually distorted out of all recognition by clumsy primitive intelligence and poor resolution, rather like a defective loudspeaker in an otherwise perfect hi-fi system."

"But even our advanced galactic quadrant pick up system isn't yet perfect," replied the second dimensionaut. "The slightest error on our part could result in an out of phase dimensional sequence of events with catastrophic repercussions."

The old alien revolved his three sensory points. "I've thought about that," he said. It's a risk we shall have to take. It's possible that all we shall get will be a formulated answer to our problem via the high resolution conscious processor relay feedback. On the other hand, if the result is another individualisation of the infinite teleological mode incarnated in human form, then we shall have to watch events very carefully." The old alien looked slightly perplexed, although whether he felt perplexity was anyone's guess. He sat for several minutes, which for him could have been a couple of light years. Occasionally he would press buttons and make strange sounds under the mass of monitors and instrumentation. He would then mutter some incomprehensible jargon as though talking to himself, but with each muttering a change of monitor patterns appeared. Coloured lights twinkled everywhere and a buzzer blurted out strange sounds. Suddenly the lighting in the cabin grew fainter and a peculiar heavy half-light intruded.

"What's happening?" a dimensionaut murmured.

"I think its too much load for the power system. Switch in all available galactic circuits quickly, for Ooooooog's sake, before we turn our space/time inside out and incur a reversed sequence."

For a moment there seemed to be a kind of controlled panic in the cabin as the three aliens operated numerous controls, pressed thousands of buttons and spoke unrecognisable sounds and signals in all kinds of 'beyond sound' frequencies.

"We're drifting into out of phase dimensions," he shouted in his own very special linguistic way that seemed to emulate and improve upon the best of human oaths and blasphemies.

"I can't hold the sequencing of event patterns. There's insufficient power to keep the time drift steady and in line with the Earth's multi-dimensional planes. I've got phase one focus with the universal and curvature is taking place. Curvature from infinite to finite mode increasing and becoming irreversible"

"Have you obtained the correct resolution?" Ooopsantensag said in a tone that seemed to indicate some urgency.

"Yes, but I can't yet tell whether the curvature is correct." The dimensionaut suddenly changed a phosphorescent reddish mauve in colour, the equivalent of 'frightened white' in human terms.

"Is the curvature infinite or finite?" the old alien muttered impatiently.

"Still infinite, according to our Time/Space/Motion and contingent dimension plasma formations."

Ooopsantensag kicked off what appeared to be heavy boots exposing two peculiar fan-like feet. He then took on some kind of weightlessness that enabled him to move much faster in a levitated condition. In fact, he began moving so fast from instrument to instrument that he became a mere blur of his original self. Suddenly all the cabin lights went out with the exception of those in some of the instrumentation.

"Can't hold it for much longer," one of the dimensionauts groaned in a way that seemed to indicate that his personal power source was also fading fast. His voice was deepening like a slowing down record. "All reserve power packs and terminal points connected. Curvature becoming clearer and closing very quickly."

"Is it finite, is it finite?" spluttered the old alien, almost in desperation.

"Curvatures crossing all required dimensions now. All designed forms closing in fast although a bit wobbly. Not sure how they will congeal. Time/Space bubble sequence now in formation. "That's good, good, good," Ooopsantensag whispered softly as he too was rapidly becoming more of a blur and less substantial.

"Can't get more resolution without more power. Doesn't need much. It's no good, we just can't obtain proper phasing unless..."

"The old alien twinkled his antennae. "Unless what?"

"Unless we use all reserves of our dimensional modular capsule."

There was silence for a moment. "If we do that," came the reply, "we could end up anywhere in infinite Space/Time. We could find ourselves in black holes and other universes. Even beyond present, past and future, in a dimensional no-mans-land.

"I know that, but it's a risk we have to take if the mission is to be completed. If it means saving a living planet then we must do it. The old alien made a final few billion searches through countless billions of alternative plans.

"We might never get back," interjected one of the dimensionauts who was suddenly reminded of his ten wives and fifteen hundred offspring waiting for him back in Andromeda. It might mean casting ourselves out of all known time/space sequences and out of the main sequence track for our own galaxies."

Ooopsantensag slowed his blurring image for a moment. "We have started the curvature that in a brief moment will become finite. It is imperative that the full sequence of events now take place." He said firmly. "We all know the risks and we wouldn't be dimensionauts otherwise. We must do what we must." He drew closer to the two dimensionauts. "Do you both agree?"

After a brief moment of silence during which the two dimensionauts seemed to search within themselves for an answer, they both turned to the old alien and nodded one antenna in agreement. "If it has to be done, then we must do it." The three then hugged each other's multi-coloured chest spots as a final gesture of affection.

"Very well. Switch to all energy reserves now." One of the dimensionauts placed his flipper like hands on two tiny levers at one end of the cabin and slowly turned them, at the same time muttering incoherent commands into a huge instrument panel. The cabin grew even dimmer as all available power drained from the vehicle that had brought them safely through countless light years and from other universes but now stood threatened by their altruistic decision to come to the aid of a dying planet called Earth.

Suddenly, without apparent warning, the walls of the cabin appeared to curve outwards and in a flash of light all had disappeared from view. Nothing remained except the vast stretches of stars strewn across the night sky. Below, the blue orb of the Earth spun gently in the infinite stillness, apparently unwatched, but ...

PROGRESS 13 – PRESENT AND PAST

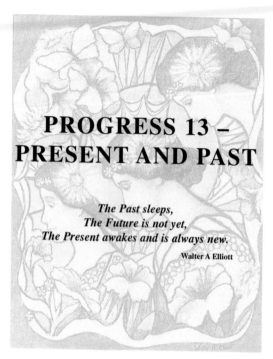

The Past sleeps,
The Future is not yet,
The Present awakes and is always new.

Walter A Elliott

Gotama Mann opened his eyes and peered through the small aircraft windows adjacent to his seat. He must have slept for sometime because the clock at the far end of the aircraft cabin registered early evening. A vague melody, a kind of ethereal anthem repeated itself in his brain, but went almost unnoticed as he became aware of the white wisps of cloud far below. It would be sometime yet before the aircraft arrived at its destination. In the meantime, he was determined to take things easy and he snuggled deeper into the soft enveloping wings of his aircraft seat.

Most of the other passengers slept. Some were being served drinks whilst a few others quietly chatted to their neighbours. It was the first long distance passenger flight of the new Jumbo Jet, which was so fearsomely voluminous that it had been characteristically named 'Progress 13.' The conditioned association of quantity with progress was now generally taken for granted by everyone and to question such a presumption was tantamount to questioning an *a priori* axiomatic truth. Quantity obviously came first; quality followed on as best she could.

Through the windows, Gotama could see the beginnings of the sunset as yellows, reds and pearly greys streaked the sky. Wispy pink clouds flew like fragile angels blending and merging around the great red orb, only partially seen.

It was interesting, Gotama mused, how everything inside the cabin reflected the outside. The giant cabin, the seats, the passengers themselves were all involved in the changing colours as they reflected and ricocheted, one to another in a prismatic wonderland, a microscopic reflection of the macrocosm.

Gotama noticed how the changing colours of the sun cast the passengers in different atmospheres and lights. It was this that made him think about the many other subtle reflections in life that make people what they are. How interesting, he thought, if instead of being born in the western world, a person had been born in India or one of the Asiatic or Middle East countries. His or her ideas, education, interests and character would be quite different. It was possible that even terrorists had part, if not all, of their character moulded by their particular education, upbringing and environment. He tried to imagine himself as a Buddhist working in the paddy fields under a wide brimmed pyramid hat. Ideas were more potent colourisers than any sunrise or sunset. Ideas, thoughts and experiences not only moulded a personality; they could also transfigure the environment. The Taj Mahal, the golden Buddhist shrines, the pyramids, holy mother and child, skyscrapers, jet planes, satellites and computers all originated in Man's mind, yet how different they all were.

He pondered. If ideas were like toys handed out to us at birth, which we merely accepted and made our own, whether they were ideologies or table etiquette, or how we should earn our living, then there was little originality in any of us. We were no better than the bees that altered feeding arrangements of their young in order to produce either a queen or a worker. Was it merely this environmental moulding that made the difference between a Communist and a Conservative, a Buddhist and a Catholic? Were we all manufactured items of the environment and education, reminiscent of Aldous Huxley's test-tube babies? Were we merely test-tube babies in an environmental and educational test tube? If not babies, a kind of test tube moulded prefabrication none-the-less.

How different people would be if provided with different education in different societies. Could there be really be any true originality? Or were we all, together with our values, cast in a determined mould of yesterday, without any alternative but to solidify our ideas into forms already prefabricated for us? However, if life did contain some kind of free impulse, some instinct for spontaneous creativity, then in us too there might be an emergent newness, originality and freedom of will that could perhaps be independent of such deterministic causes and effects.

Gotama laughed to himself. It struck him as rather comical that the giant plane in which he sat, with most of his neighbours asleep for the journey, should be called 'Progress'. To have progress, we must know *from* what and *to* what. Progress of the human race was a mere concept of Man's mind that, like an ephemeral flower, opened its petals to the light of a new day and just for a brief moment held out its promise of wonder, but could wither and fade like so many flowering civilisations had done before. Moreover, evolution in one aspect only led to a corresponding involution somewhere else. Evolution and involution were two sides of the same coin. You couldn't have one without the other. It was just the same with advance and decline. An advance along one front only resulted in decline on another; a kind of compensation as Emerson would have said. Changes, yes, but as to progress, this was a mere human definition, an empty terminology, a local cosmic event probably of little or no importance. Scientists were continually adding new facts and figures to our knowledge of the physical world and universe. They were trying to get nearer and nearer to a final truth, an equation that would explain the final all absorbing truth of all created things. But how did their knowledge of the relative world relate to the meaning of 'ultimate truth' within all things?

A sharp tap on his shoulder brought Gotama back from his reveries. He looked up. The young attractive face of the stewardess looked down at him smiling. "Would you like something to eat or drink, sir?" she asked politely.

"Yes please," he answered. "What would you recommend?

"Most people are addicted to our modern conditioned soup with raison d'être. It's always well advertised on world con-vision. Or there's pop salad with lets, beat and garsley, a favourite with the young. And there's heart with compassionate sauce or heavy heart with grave dressing. In fact we have foods to suit all moods and tastes, the very latest in attitude foods."

Being somewhat surprised by the menu, Gotama asked if he could have something simple like a cheese sandwich.

"Certainly, sir," the stewardess replied. "And if you would like a drink, I can recommend a glass of pure Time Stream. It is the most refreshing drink of all."

There was something in the way she spoke that intrigued Gotama. Also there was something mysterious about her eyes and facial expression. In fact, there was something distinctly odd about the whole situation. He looked at his watch to see how long he had slept, but was shocked to observe that its hands had quite disappeared, and had been replaced by a tiny phosphorescent spot of coloured light in the centre of the dial, from which radiated soft rays in all directions, as though they were from a pearl coloured star. The spot of light was no larger than the point of a pin. Then in a moment it too had disappeared. He looked up to check the time on the main cabin clock, but to his astonishment the clock had also altered its appearance and had suddenly grown a large number of extra hands on its face, replacing the usual two. In fact there were so many hands that it was impossible to tell what time was being registered. He conjectured that it was perhaps indicating different earth time zones. He mentioned the fact to the stewardess who chuckled, her eyes dancing with a mysterious sparkle.

"I can see, you're not accustomed to this type of long distance time travel," she said playfully. "In Progress 13 planes, everyone lives in his or her own 'Now' time, as well as in relative time. Your watch now indicates your own internal time dimension; some call it the eternal 'without time' dimension. It's like a gyroscope: it will never alter or deviate like the relative time clock in the cabin. Deep inside you never age, but outside you always do. Surely, you must have noticed?"

She turned away still laughing, and disappeared along the narrow passageway between the seats. Gotama looked perplexed, especially when he noticed an additional phosphorescent sign that glowed briefly under the cabin clock. It read *'Time Plane now entering critical unpredictable zone 13."* There was also something strange about the stewardess he couldn't quite fathom. It was not only the strangeness of the menu, but also the way she had talked about 'Time.' No one had ever spoken in quite the way she had about relative and absolute 'time.' How ridiculous to say that there was a different time dimension within himself than that experienced in the outside world. Everyone knew that 'Time' was a mere measurement related to motion. Where there was motion, there was time. It was only where there was no motion that there could ever be 'timelessness.' He thought for a few moments about her odd comments. Was it possible that there could be a quality within the depths of him that did not participate in motion and was therefore 'timeless'? If it were so, then that quality, or whatever you liked to call it, would be beyond 'time' and would be eternal.

Another thing he couldn't understand was why he had become so philosophical all of a sudden. He was a practical man and although some of the deeper issues interested him, he was generally too busy with practical matters to entertain such thoughts in the normal course of events, but the odd talk about 'Time' by the stewardess set Gotama thinking. He possessed a strange feeling, almost an intuition, that this was no ordinary plane, but something much more strange and sophisticated.

All did not smell quite right in the precincts of 'Progress 13.' Hamlet's words rang though his head as though in a new setting, yet their meaning still rang true. It wasn't just the unusual smell of strange food now being served, there was something else that Gotama couldn't quite define. The plane in which he sat seemed larger than he had expected. It had several things about it that were unusual to say the least. There was now no noise from the engines for one thing. And there was no vibration. The smoothness was uncanny, almost unreal. Another peculiarity was that he couldn't see any ground below. He knew the plane must be at high altitude, but he had been in aircraft before and you could always discern some ground below between the clouds.

Just at that moment, a voice at his side demanded his attention.

"Is this seat taken?" A a man with a polished square face beamed somewhat inanely down at Gotama, at the same time indicating one of the adjacent seats.

"Not as far as I know," Gotama answered.

The man bowed stiffly and almost looked as though he was about to click his heels in German fashion. Instead, he placed his bowler hat, umbrella and briefcase on the luggage rack. He had a face that looked as though it had been forged in a four wall press tool.

"I've been rather busy," he said breathlessly, "performing some important duties at the other end of the compartment." His chest seemed to swell visibly as he continued. "My name is 'Mr Bureaucrumb. I am responsible for the internal power supplies of 'Progress 13.'

Mr Bureaucrumb bent forward as though he intended to impart a confidential secret. "You see," he said, "Progress 13 depends for its power on my organisation, which consists of dreaming up as much superfluous paperwork and unnecessary documentation in order to keep as many people as possible busy at all times. The specialised art of my ministry strategy is to plan all the right things at the wrong times and all the wrong things at the right time. We have always been good at this for as long as I can remember. I pride myself in the knowledge that using these methods we in the government ministry have created more employment for people than anyone else."

"Progress 13 has an insatiable appetite for my superfluous documents for its special impulse 'bumph' engines, which consume extraordinary quantities of failed government manifestoes, vast quantities of obsolescent ministerial documents, local planning failures and lots and lots of unnecessary red tape. There are of course thousands of V.I.P 'Bureaucrumbs' like myself, all conditioned and prefabricated to precise specifications by stereotyped educational gauging machinery, the result of the miracle age of the latest enlightened education and technology. I'm truly proud to be such an important cog in a society which just can't do without me; just as I can't do without Parkinson's law. Civilisation would surely crumble if it weren't for Bureaucrumbs like me making use of it. We may be just humble Bureaucrumbs, but we can guarantee to make a good meal out of any job." Mr Bureaucrumb swelled like a bullfrog once again as he oozed with pride and conceit at his self confessed achievements.

"How exactly does your organisation operate?" Gotama politely enquired, hardly knowing how to respond to his strange companion.

"It's all very clever," replied Mr Bureaucrumb, his face white, square and gleaming, like clean office walls. "My colleagues and I work in teams. It's the team spirit that matters. We all try to help each other; everyone tries his best to do everyone else's job. We work so efficiently and closely together, that with any move we make we usually manage to step neatly on someone's toes. It's a necessary hazard of the job, but it does assist in creating a great mass of duplicated paperwork and committee meetings, all of which serve to provide more employment for more people. Government ministries love us."

"Our motto is teamwork for the good of the masses. Never mind about leadership, that's an old fashioned relic of the past. It's all very cleverly done," Mr Bureaucrumb went on. "To work well as a team it's all a question of timing. I administrate and organise when I know nothing and when my colleagues really know what to do. Then they administrate and organise when I know all the answers and they know nothing. In that way the work is made far more interesting and you never know from one minute to the next what's going to happen. It's the very latest in organised anarchy, or organised chaos as the scientists call it. There's so many of us helping with someone else's job that most of us eventually dispense with our own jobs and take up the next person's in line."

"People are always tumbling over each other if it means a more prestigious name on the door and a fatter wage packet. We're all for one, and one for himself (or herself), a wonderful new socialist doctrine. And by leaving lots of our jobs to others, we can keep expanding our force, as we constantly need to employ new staff. So it's helping to eradicate unemployment when we're around. Without us there would be no Progress 13." He laughed at his remark, as though it had some humorous implication. His throaty laugh was like a thin veneer of falsity projected from a walking accounting machine. He seemed to Gotama to be a man with an exceedingly large cranium, but with a heart in inverse proportion. His face reflected a mass product, a piece of ingenious computer fodder, machine fed, machine nurtured, reared on synthetics, the ultimate in originality relegation.

Mr Bureaucrumb said no more but simply opened the *Times* in an impressive manner. He gave the newspaper an important flourish to show it who was the master, and with another equally impressive cough he began to study the share prices.

Gotama's mind, once again reactivated by this brief but interesting encounter, engrossed itself with the theory that education beyond a certain point resulted in the dehumanising of Man, reducing him to some kind of computer software. Man could become the mere conditioned interface, the minor link in the giant chain of computerised electronic robots. Was Mr Bureaucrumb really the creator and maintainer of society that he so proudly

27

claimed? Or was he just an end result of a gigantic community process plant built originally by Man for his own betterment but which had turned the tables and made him the slave of his own creation? Was Man really governing the vast complexities of the process, or was he merely being led by it into ways and values that would ultimately imprison him?

Could Man govern and control the extra-computerised limbs he had built for himself, or were they becoming individualised forces on their own account that would eventually create an irreversible and detrimental alteration to things he most valued and loved? Man was a function of his environment, just as the environment was in a sense a function of Man. The two were enwrapped inseparably together. Any alteration in the one, effected changes in the other. Who or what was governing and controlling the social process? Time alone would tell.

Already Man's nuclear deterrent ballistic missiles were under the control of computerised robots, because technology had become so complicated and the time limits for defence decisions had become so short that it was impractical to entertain human intervention in the system. Even if the final decision to fire retaliatory rockets was made by the head of state, such a decision had to be based on 'faith' that the complex warning systems were functioning correctly. People's safety and the world's safety had therefore passed out of the jurisdiction of the human brain and were now tied inseparably in complex electronics. And what if there was a fault somewhere in the system, a wrong detection, and a mistake in recognition whether the electronics had actually picked up approaching missiles? There would be no going back. One mistake, only one, was all that was necessary for the obliteration of the world and its billions of people.

Was Progress 13 a symbol of Man's technological efforts? Gotama looked about him at the vast interior of the extraordinary plane. It seemed almost like a microcosm of the technological macrocosm that Man had created. It had an undisguised impersonality, a coldness of plastic and sheet metal with hard lines that were gaunt and tasteless, poor competitors when compared with mountains, hills and streams in an open countryside. There were lush soft seats and every modern convenience, things definitely to be appreciated, but there was more in the depths of Man's spirit to be satisfied. Material pleasures were necessary but not just as ends in themselves.

The more Gotama examined the plane, the more he experienced certain misgivings about Progress 13 and the authenticity of its design. It was a technological masterpiece; there was no doubt about that. In fact, the immensity and intricacy of its design was enthralling. Yet there was something indefinable that reeked of foulness in an otherwise efficient and perfect design.

Rising from his seat, he decided to investigate some of the other parts of the plane. He scrambled passed Mr Bureaucrumb, accidentally stepping on his toes. This momentarily revealed a square white face from behind the stocks and shares page. "Sorry," said Gotama, apologetically.

"Don't worry, I'm used to it," replied Bureaucrumb as he once again disappeared behind his newspaper.

Gotama turned towards the rear of the plane, but, after a few steps, was confronted by a stewardess in the course of her duties. She was smilingly serving synthetic food by the exotic name of 'Conditioning Commerciale' to a famished passenger who was complaining that it always gave him dyspepsia, pain and panic attacks. The stewardess was patience itself and plied the passenger with seven pills, one for the dyspepsia, one for the pain, another for the panic attacks, and four to remedy the side effects of the first three. "You may need another pill for the side effects later," she said pleasantly, "because it's possible there'll be side effects from the first set of side effect pills. Having delivered her final words of reassurance, the stewardess looked up and noticed Gotama. Edging gracefully to one side to let him pass, she smiled. "Can I help you?" she enquired.

"Is it in order for me to look around the plane?" Gotama asked.

The stewardess looked slightly uncomfortable; slightly hesitant as though she wasn't absolutely sure if it was indeed permissible. Then, regaining her self-assurance, she said, "of course."

She thereupon pointed to a long list of instructions printed in beautiful lettering on the side of the cabin. "You are perfectly free to do just as you please," she said laughingly. "We all believe in the freedom of the individual here. We also believe in the freedom of the press, freedom of speech, freedom of action and free enterprise and we have produced statues of liberty to prove it. You are perfectly free, providing you adhere to the three million laws and regulations; rather more than the original ten commandments. For a complete list you would be advised to refer to the two hundred volumes series called *What Not To Do In Civilisation*. These cover things like not going through red lights, not spitting on buses, not parking on zebra crossings and not knocking anyone down on them. Also, not playing a cacophony of loud music to the whole street so that the residents need ear plugs and doctor's prescriptions. And not trying to catch a train to Cornwall if it's going to Glasgow, and not to expect one to turn up anyway. Not to expect to be free to be a sprinter, if you've had your leg off. Also, if you've only three months to live, not to expect a hospital appointment for at least six months. Other useful tips when enjoying freedom in our society include things like do not pay your Tax Bills if you want to go to prison, do not breed butterflies for bulk food, do not wear ice skates on dry pavements, do not enter by exit doors, do not shout or whistle in libraries, do not whisper at football matches, do not laugh at funerals, do not fall from aeroplanes without a parachute, do not park in the centre of motorways, do not dive into emptied swimming pools, do not kiss crocodiles unless they ask you and even then have second thoughts, do not mess with champion boxers if you don't want dentures, do not forget to pay the mortgage or feed the cat, do not try brain surgery if you're a car mechanic, do not climb Mount Everest in carpet slippers, do not swim with sharks, at least not for very long, do not pick neighbour's flowers, do not wear your overcoat in tropical nudist camps, but you're quite free to live with mother-in-law if you want a quick divorce, but you're not yet free to walk on water. There are a few million other dos, don'ts, cannots and shouldn'ts in civilised living, but we pride ourselves on our being free, in a free society. When looking round the plane, it's advisable not to look too deeply into things," the stewardess said. "If you really want to look into details, I would suggest you wear our specially tinted spectacles with conventionalised lenses. These are essential to obviate the glare of seeing too much truth all at one time. They will also enable you to view things as part of our organised social institution called 'civilised living'. If you wait just a moment I will bring you a pair." With that, she promptly disappeared through an adjacent cabin doorway. She returned after a few minutes, all smiles and laughter. "Here they are. You've been given a very special pair," she said mysteriously. "There's no charge for 'Orthodoxy Spectacles,' they're all included in the Social Standardisation Service, together with some preliminary Aldous Huxley somas and several other aids to conformity.

The spectacles fitted precisely and must have been designed by some ministry accountant. There was some gross distortion when Gotama looked at certain things. The stewardess explained that this was due to a type of polarisation called 'mass conditioners.' These could take various forms according to whether one looked at television ads, social rules and regulations, habits, culture, etiquette, fashion, education, the government, law and order or the church, to name but a few. It was apparent that the 'Orthodoxy Spectacles' with their invisible frames, couldn't be seen by others and in this respect were rather like contact lenses. The stewardess mentioned that nearly everyone was automatically provided with a standard pair at birth, which they wore for the rest of their life, almost without knowing it, because they never had to be removed or replaced. There were different rose coloured shades of lenses to suit the conventions of different people in various types of society. Gotama noticed that the special lenses diffracted and muted many human actions that might otherwise have been quite colourful. Much of the clear brightness was sadly dimmed to a kind of mediocre grey that reflected a rigidity of the orthodox and conventional. All spontaneous branching out was pruned to the roots. However, there were occasions when scenes of warfare and battle were distorted and made to appear quite splendid and gave a curious feeling of patriotic fervour, a sort of 'up with the honour of the regiment' attitude.

The stewardess smiled condescendingly. "To give you some idea of your bearings," she said. "The cabin in which you are now situated is called Present. Towards the rear of the plane you will find the cabins of the Past. Be very careful there, because some of the leading lights are now very dim. It's not a popular set of cabins as many are used merely for deep sleeping and forgotten memories, although a few are quite beautiful and spectacular. The forward cabins are ultra-super-modern and are called Future. New work is always being carried out in them and there is much there that will surprise you. You will find many of the cabins strange but you will soon become acclimatised and adapted to your new surroundings. Is there anything else you would like to know?"

Gotama said there wasn't and thanked her for her assistance. "I think I'll investigate the tail end first," he said, as they parted.

The cabin of the Present seemed enormous, although he seemed to pass through it in a twinkling of an eye. In no time at all he had reached a door at the back of the cabin which presumably led into the rear compartments. It opened into a long corridor, at the end of which was what appeared to be a freight cabin full of sheep, pigs, chickens and other animals, all with extraordinary human expressions. Gotama drew a sudden startled breath. Each animal was neatly encased in its own tight fitting crate and was provided with just sufficient room to reach its food, presumably to keep it in useful productive condition, but not enough to allow it to run off its usefulness. The delicate balance of 'freedom' and 'restriction' seemed to have been arranged to ensure maximum profits with minimum outlay. It reflected a scientific efficiency but little or no humanity. The closer Gotama looked the more the animals appeared and acted like people.

For just a brief moment the endless rows of chicken battery cages seemed suddenly to transform quite magically into countless dismal railway compartments carrying crushed occupants with glazed eyes and absent expressions. Others revealed figures crouched and constricted over desks or glued to telephones and PCs, whilst many sweated in the tedium of unrelenting factory production line conveyors, all tightly bound in gold and silver chains that severely limited their movement and creative options. Moreover, their beautiful wings were harshly clipped and their ankles ringed with a Company number. Yet others stared with gaunt eyes from somewhat brighter windows of box like houses, but told subtler stories of rigid family and mortgage constraints. All the battery cages seemed to provide some security of tenure for the various occupants, in the same way that crushed chickens were provided for, but at what price?

Some sort of mechanical conveyor transported synthetic foods at intervals predetermined by an intricate control feedback system, connected into the animal's behavioural mechanism. It was obvious that the system had been worked out with a great deal of precision and with particular emphasis on the economy. The creatures might just as well have been called the products of economic motivation. What a joke! Walking pounds, shillings and pence. As Gotama peered into the open-sided crates, all with double glazed picture window fronts, he could see that the animals had been housed in a kind of hierarchy according to their economic usefulness. They were not just pounds of weight, but represented pounds, shilling and pence of usefulness. They were utilitarian sheep, no more, no less. Weighed, measured and conditioned from birth, they had adopted Pavlovian impersonalities. Suddenly, as he gazed at the animals all drugged into a strange lethargy, by the synthetic mind and body conditioner food, he thought for one brief moment that he saw the white square face of Mr Bureaucrumb staring out of one of the gold embossed crates. Gotama drew away in horror at the unexpected.

Continuing down the corridor, he came across a door marked 'Past.' The door opened by itself and he was somewhat alarmed to find himself inside a long, low, dark and reeking passage, the walls of which were dank dripping slimy stone. Murky gaslights flickered in the semi-darkness. Water flowed somewhere. It was a cross between a dungeon and a sewer. The initial shock of the spectacle filled him with foreboding. He had never expected to see such an ignoble sight aboard the Progress 13. Then just as he was about to make a hasty retreat, a shrill alarming cry pierced his eardrums and sent cold shivers all over him. He was on the verge of retreating from the scene altogether, but some curiosity in his nature overcame his fear and made him grope along the dark wall towards the point where the horrifying screams had emanated. Without warning, a gruesome crawling figure enmeshed in chains and filth emerged, outlined against one of the flickering gaslights. A gaunt perspiring face with stubbly chin and bloodshot eyes peered at him out of the darkness. "Who the dickens are you?" were the only words that, like a sudden reflex, broke from Gotama's lips.

It was a fearsome sight, the unkempt face twisted in agony. A slippery mouth in the agonised face moved like some shiny eel struggling for its freedom. There was a harsh grating whisper. "Dickens you say, Dickens, Dickens." The voice repeated itself as if gasping for its last ounce of breath. "If you know Dickens, you'll know who I am. I'm the ghost of civilisation past." As he said this he gave a shudder that seemed to make even the solid stone walls participate. After that, he knelt down with his face in his hands and wept pitifully, whilst shaking his wet grimy chains in the squelching filth. Lifting a pale snake-like arm, he pointed into the murky interior of his prison. "Look," he groaned, taking a frenzied glance over his shoulder. "There are my little ghosts of civilisation past." With that he shouted some incoherent command, whereupon Gotama found himself surrounded by hundreds of tiny children with drawn pallid faces and pleading eyes. All were similarly dressed in brown torn and tattered rags. Their little thin legs and feet were bare and bruised. They wore expressions of sad resignation as they tried to cling to Gotama for comfort. There was no hate in their eyes, only sadness and tears.

It was the look of innocence together with the sad smiles of welcome that suddenly brought hot tears of pity and compassion to Gotama's eyes. "What monstrosity has caused this?" he choked. "Why are you all here in this pitiful condition?"

"Why indeed," moaned the creature, almost hidden from view in the murky darkness. "We are all the 'pains of progress;' of struggle for survival; of Man's craving for material wealth and security at any cost." There was silence for a few moments, with only heavy breathing from the dark creature and whimpers from the tiny children. Then the creature began again. "The children of pain have changed little since the dawn of Man's consciousness. Only the context in which their agonies are endured has altered. They have been born, struggled and dropped from exhaustion in fields, mines, factories and cellars throughout the world. They've bled on battlefields and drowned on the high seas. There's scarcely a place you could mention where they haven't suffered at the hands of Man. From Inca ceremonies to Hiroshima exterminations, from terrorist atrocities to community and social abuse, from ignorance, greed and hate, to economic mismanagement, exploitation and dire poverty, all these things and many more have contributed to the creation of these children of woe. Wherever there has been grief, pain and tears; wherever people have hurt, misused, despised or brutalised their fellows, these children have been born and have cried in the hearts of mankind."

"But why are they here in this terrible darkness?"

"Why? Because," the voice muttered slowly, as if in pain. "Because mankind likes to forget these things. Its greed, vanity, pride and hate that generally rule his heart. 'Ego' and greed are the chief culprits. The children of 'pain' are their procreation. Man doesn't want to feel responsible for their birth. So he tries to brush them under the carpet and forget them. That's why we're a secondary consideration in his dream of progress. He may think he thinks of others, but he really thinks of himself. Why! Even the clergyman will frequently think of his own self respect and will do things that will gain him more self respect. Vanity and pride go very deep in people. It's all self motivation, self and self. They're not entirely to blame though. They often struggle to do better. We're just part of their struggle to reach a star that always seems to elude their grasp. But they must go on. There's only struggle and search, search and search for that star. Then perhaps one day people will find a way to bring compassion and healing to these children of their making."

Gotama looked on the scene for a long time, unable to move himself, his inside sick with horror and grief. Spontaneous tears seemed to burn furrows in his cheeks that would leave their mark forever.

The voice continued. "Your tears of compassion are better than molten gold my friend, more precious by far than any earthly treasure. They're the only magic fluids that can save people and their world. Without them there is no hope for planet Earth."

At last Gotama turned to go, kissing the nearest of the children on the forehead as he did so. After retracing his steps, he noticed that the main passageway opened out into a broader area. Before him was an extravagantly ornamented hall of considerable dimensions, adorned in tapestries of magnificent colours. Huge draperies, intricately woven with gold, silver and coloured designs enveloped both walls and ceilings. Soft clouds and angelic figures were gracefully inset on the ceilings between domes of enormous breadth. A huge dance floor receded into the distance on which many hundreds of ladies in crinolines twirled serenely in time to bright music, accompanied by gentlemen smartly attired in the brilliant red and gold jackets of the military. Soldiers' swords glistened under massive chandeliers. Ripples of laughter emanated from charming lips that sipped champagne, smoked cigars or spoke sweet words. Through the blue haze of tobacco smoke a group of musicians were like vague shadows in the distance. It was a hall fit for kings, grand dukes and the highest in feudal nobility.

As Gotama watched, the scene changed as it became increasingly enveloped in a blue haze that slowly melted the edges of everything and everybody in the hall until they became indistinct colours without solidity. Finally, like the baseless fabric of a vision, they dissolved to be replaced by new images. At the same time the tender civilised music was transmuted by some miraculous unseen alchemy into a deafening thunder as a military bugle call sounded. Hardly discernible at first, at least not as solid objects, wild screeching horses made their debut in the strange arena, midst flailing arms, streaking swords and cursing riders.

The ballroom had, in but a moment, become a battlefield. Soldiers, in waving plumes and glistening armour, rushed in from all sides, accompanied by a horrid stench of gunpowder and sweat. A thunderous battle ensued, as horses screamed and riders slashed swords. Huge cannons roared and recoiled. Fires blazed. The earth was red. Men whimpered whilst others raged. If the incredible scene was not a weird kind of memory of some long forgotten Napoleonic battle, then it must be very much akin to such a thing, thought Gotama, who was too surprised and shocked to move.

At that moment, the rattle of a drum gradually subsided and new images began to rear themselves out of the old. As by some emergent magic, people of different races, dressed in strange apparel, slowly materialised to become living solidity and movement, only to finally disperse. Enormous castles formed as a background that subsequently faded to become sailing ships, galleons, cathedrals, coaches and horses, pyramids, temples, even dinosaurs and long extinct creatures. Children, old men and women, kings, queens and emperors, all came and went with their environments. Images appeared and faded like strange evolving patterns that seemed to reflect or re-enact society's past memories; memories long since gone from individual consciousness but somehow retained in a deep group unconscious, like a living fossil beneath some latent mantle of the Earth.

It was difficult to tell the span of time bridged by the swirling images, but it must have been very immense indeed. How long Gotama stood watching he didn't know, but it seemed like many hours. He was most surprised therefore to observe from a clock that only a few minutes had elapsed since he first entered the magical hall. So much had happened in so short a time; all compressed into what had at first been a relatively small space and had grown to great distances to encompass great spectacles and pageantries of the past. It was a kind of three-dimensional play with real plots, real people, real histories displayed over immense time. The whole episode was so extraordinary that Gotama was at a loss to understand how it could have possibly occurred. Almost as though to indicate that the show had ended for the moment, the images made their finale quite abruptly leaving the immense hall comparatively empty.

Gotama walked slowly and somewhat hesitantly towards the central body of figures remaining. One of them had obviously noticed his presence and was coming to meet him. It was a man who looked welcoming enough and quite solid too, except for one very peculiar thing. He walked quite upside down. How he managed to defy the laws of gravity was a mystery. But that he did so was indeed evident enough. Gotama was completely staggered.

"Don't be alarmed," the man said, showing a broad upside down grin that looked a bit grim from the other way up. "I've been walking this way ever since I can remember."

Gotama had witnessed some strange things in his time but they were in quite a different league. This man was not just content to walk upside down, he was levitating at least three feet away from the floor whilst doing it. The man had a shrivelled lined face, out of which shone two of the brightest most luminous eyes Gotama had ever seen. The face was set in a mass of curly white beard with hair that streamed behind him into a pale ectoplasmic mist. Around his neck were vast numbers of trinkets, chains and other glistening paraphernalia. He wore graceful scintillating robes of many folds and undulations, whilst on his feet were open sandals that showed two white feet.

"Good afternoon," said Gotama, a little uncertainly. "Or is it good evening?"

"Good yesterday, more like," replied the old man briskly. "Let me introduce myself. I'm Christian Past. Glad to welcome you to my sanctuary of dreams. I can't come down just now," he went on, looking up from his inverted position. "I like to keep my feet firmly in the clouds, especially when thinking important things, like the compilation of my encyclicals on subjects like birth control and abortion, which I do my best to keep clear of. Any slight reminder of heaviness, gravity or matter seems to give me nausea. However, you mustn't be concerned. I can see everything much clearer this way. I look back to front and inside out, as it were. It takes a lot of concentration and effort at first, but eventually you can see things from above in a sort of special kind of way, a kind of different dimension. Like the Good Samaritan, I like to look the difficult way, whereas most people prefer to look the other way." He peered up at his feet, looking like a weird trussed up chicken. "When I'm in this position, I'm hooked up good and proper," he said with a chuckle that echoed from wall to wall. "But I'm content, more than most I'd say and that's what really matters."

Christian thought for a moment then continued. "If Man didn't wear his orthodoxy spectacles so tightly, he would be a lot better off. I'm not saying that the orthodox churches haven't worn their own special variety for hundreds of years, even with blinkers to match for most of the time and usually with exceptionally powerful conventionalised lenses. The churches have asked for a great many of the troubles they now complain of, such as leaking roofs and being empty. They're rather like the man who insists on stuffing himself with only one type of meal and then complains of indigestion. The churches have been guilty of rigidising, narrowing and conventionalising the 'truth' to such an extent that any living spirit of truth has become buried, leaving only a dead fossil; a fossil reflecting a very blurred and faint imprint of the original. There may be a few churchmen still aware of the truth, but I have yet to find one. The vast majority can't seem to see the wood for the trees. If they met Jesus in the street, they wouldn't know him. They would probably decide he wasn't quite the type of fellow to ask to their current whist drive or afternoon tea party. He would undoubtedly be considered improperly dressed to attend High Mass, or even Low Mass, and especially afternoon teas and jumble sales. You see, my son, people like to idealise Jesus; they've forgotten he was a rebel. He must have been quite a rebel to incite the authorities of the day to execute him. There aren't many so called Christians today who would be prepared to suffer the recriminations of their fellows that he did. Most prefer the neat Sunday pattern of church attendance in best suit with behaviour to match.

However, it's not only the orthodox churches that have fallen under the spell of Lady Convention. In fact, most of the world's peoples and their societies have been flattened and conformed on her ironing board. She also uses her giant steamroller to flatten everything to standardised shapes, and prides herself on her washing. She uses special bleach to reduce everything to Conformist Beige, a shallow mediocre hue that has little individuality or depth. And once everyone's behaviour and outlook has been reduced to the standard conventional colour it's going to be difficult to change back, because all the bright, eccentric, individual colours will have disappeared. And there will be no one around to remember what the old colours and eccentric characters were like.

Conventional behaviour in all societies involves a distortion of 'true seeing'. It's the result of using those orthodoxy spectacles too much. They can be very habit forming. With their orthodox and conventional views, they frequently make you quite dogmatic in thinking you're always right. They create a nasty habit of wanting to see the conventional way and the right way up. But this is not always the best or truest way to view things. Once you know the true secret of life, you can cast away forever your orthodoxy spectacles with their accompanying rigidity of thinking, sensing and seeing."

Christian squinted one eye as though he was imparting some intimate and secret truth. "Once you can forget the symbolic gravitation of the world, with all its vanities, its greed, hate, ignorance and desires for more and more pleasure, you become as free as a bird in the sky. I may look like a bit of a trussed up bird, but at least I've left the ground. I've managed to get transcendentally launched." His grin widened to expose two gorgeous dimples.

"But surely it's uncomfortable to constantly be in that position?" Gotama retorted, as he gazed at the inverted figure. "Besides making the blood rush to your head, you seem to have turned Man's natural pleasure instincts upside down. Your teaching seems to want him to give up the very things he lives for, namely his pleasures. What else has Man got? To remain upside down like you would be very painful for him, to say the least."

"Good God no my boy!" Christian answered. "I'm just like a weightless astronaut and not merely confined to a space/time capsule either." He winked and shrugged his shoulders. "Can't say that I haven't made my own mistakes, though. There's a world of beauty in the sea, sky and earth that I didn't let myself notice until almost too late. I projected my own faults and sins on to Nature's canvas; a canvas that was neither dirty nor clean, but was just a canvas for my own projected ideas. In my projections it became as mud and filth to me."

"Surely a gross error of judgement?" Gotama commented.

"Indeed, indeed! Perhaps, perhaps! Still, past is past and cannot be undone. It will remain unchanged for eternity. I must sleep in my inverted bed according to my Christian philosophy. I and other devotees have conceived it and it must remain part of me." His last words reflected a kind of sadness, as if there were something else he could have wished to add, if only he possessed the ability to bring it within the thresholds of his mind. "We are as our thoughts and actions make us." He muttered gravely, as though a new karmic stream of thinking had suddenly come upon him in surprise.

He surveyed Gotama intently, without speaking. Then, as if arriving at a final conclusion, he said, "See what you have to see here in the past, my boy, but see it quickly and be gone. Rest not in the past; do not rely on future projections, for both are but images, mere concepts of the mind. Only one exists, the eternal 'Now.' See to it that you find it without delay. I bid you adieu and good luck." With a last quick flourish, he vanished like a boy in an Indian rope trick, as an enveloping mist gathered about him.

For a second or two, Gotama, bewildered by the sudden disappearance, remained rooted to the spot. He experienced a vague sensation of timelessness that proved most satisfying. It was an intuitive feeling of neither being nor non-being. How very extraordinary, he thought. I've always tried to imagine what it must be like to be weightless, but have never even considered that it may be possible to experience timelessness.

A loud clanging noise attracted his attention, like a tolling bell. It came from the huge balcony fringing the hall, girdled with beautiful white ornamented balustrades. A wide set of carpeted stairs led from the hall up to a balcony. Gotama mounted them two and three at a time. Arriving on the balcony, he realised there was another vast hall just beyond. Entering through a huge carved doorway, he was immediately confronted by what appeared to be a vast engine room with countless numbers of instrument panels and workshop sections arranged around the periphery. In the centre, towering above everything stood a huge mass of machinery. The placed reeked of heat and fumes.

A man dressed in oil-stained overall approached. "What can I do for you, mate?" he asked, in a kind of cockney accent. He was obviously curious to see one of the Progress 13 passengers in his part of the plane. Gotama explained that he was interested in the plane and would be grateful for the man's help.

The man drew briefly on his cigarette. "Did you want to see the engine room?" he enquired.

"Yes, if I may," replied Gotama.

The man in overalls surveyed him closely. "Very well then. First we'd better get permission from the Chief for you to look round. He deals with all the administrative side of the business. He's called the Time Bender and works for the Super Grand Wizard of the Cosmic Quadrant. If you'll follow me I'll take you to his office."

The man in overalls introduced himself as Mudbelly Jones and led the way across the huge engine room. He seemed friendly enough as he said in a rather husky voice. "The old Time Bender's main job 'ere is bending the 'Infinite' into Time/Space bubbles called parallel universes. 'e uses all sorts of dimensions, but 'is favourite number is eleven and 'e vibrates the Time/Space membranes like strings of a cosmic 'arp. And 'e loves making 'is bubble universes collide wiv a big bang at 'is singularity points, where more bubble universes are spewed out, like some sausage machine gorne beserk. 'e also does a few uvver lickle jobs, like stirring up tiny swirls in time and space and wiggling 'is cosmic strings and branes to make atoms and molecules, so that we can all 'ave bodies to work in. Atoms are 'is speciality. He loves to make 'em do all kinds of fings, from working in brain boxes to blowing up in supernovas. 'es got a real knack for making 'em by bending infinite nuffingness into a finite somefin, so that 'e can make Time and Space for us to live in. He says it's like solidifying lickle waves of a cosmic ocean. In this 'ere engine room 'es also responsible for all the clearin aart from Time Present. Quite a big job really. It's only by incineratin' the rubbish from the Present that 'e can make the impulse into the Future.

He also loves playing 'is super gravity games, bending space and time in all sorts of weird and wonderful shapes and vortexes around things like black 'oles and super-novas. Anuvver favourite is the space/time warp competition between 'is rival forces of gravity and those of black energy and dark matter. It's like a big tug of war wiv black energy curling space and the galaxies outwards towards infinity and 'oo knows where, and gravity trying to pull 'em back again to where they all started in the big bang days.. At the moment 'es giving Man the impression that black energy's winning, cos the galaxies look as though they're moving away from each other faster than a tom cat runs from a policeman, and ole gravity doesn't seem to 'ave the mass of muscle to pull everthin' back agin. Although 'oo knows what'll 'appen in the future when ole Time Bender makes up a new set of rules for the universe, which 'e 'as the 'abit of doing just for the 'ell of it. And 'e also fancies 'imself as a bit of a magician. 'e uses all kinds of cosmic mirrors to make ghost images and reflections of galaxies and stars, just to confoose primitive life forms peering frough telescopes, trying to make sense of it all. Most 'uman scientists fink that everyfing is determined by causes and effects all linked togevver in what they call their bottom up theory, where what 'appens in the smallest determines what 'appens in the largest, but them scientists are in for a few big surprises. The ole Time Bender keeps lots of special secrets up 'is sleeve; secrets that would make your 'air curl and which would put an entirely different complexion on the way the cosmos works, if 'e let those secrets ever be known. 'ave a quick squint at one of the engines before we go to the Time Bender's office," he said jovially.

They walked round the gigantic mass of machinery. "It's a magic engine called Miracle," Mudbelly explained. Our engine bends Infinite Now Time into three dimensional time that 'as a Past, Present and Future. It's these three dimensions that make up Man's lickle world. All foughts, sensations and actions have karmic reactions and are the fuels consoomed in the giant combustion chambers that, like a jet engine, push the Time dimension plane into the future. Ingenious don't you fink? It's only by consoomin' the Present that we can create a Past and make 'eadway into the Future."

"Most intriguing," muttered Gotama, as he read the nameplate in polished pewter on the side of the engine. It read, 'Lewis Carol Karma Special'. Underneath, in smaller font, were the words 'Feed in Chance and Determined Planes smoothly and do not overload Movement and Change relays and always operate with a pinch of salt' There were also two small inscriptions in very fine script. One read -

> Man's mind curves eternity
> Like a bow, from which he
> Shoots the arrow of Time

The second read -

> The cloak of Time covers the eternal
> Like the coat of the invisible man.

"'ere's Mister Time Bender now," Mudbelly said, pointing to a distant figure coming towards them. "We call 'im lucky Frankie the Time-Whittle blower, cos of 'is never ending toones and 'is never ending employment scheme, always whittling away Time wiv 'is miracle jet engine, but 'aving the pleasure of knowing 'e can never whittle it all away. There's just too much of it in that there infinite. 'es a workaholic. 'e works all hours God sends. Never got time to retire!" He laughed. "We can't complain of unemployment 'ere!" As the man approached closer, Mudbelly Jones shouted to him. "Hi, Frank. 'ere, come and meet a bloke oos interested in your Time Jet."

A man with a high forehead, clothed in strange translucent and scintillating colours, wearing headgear of the peacock plumage variety, joined them, giving a nod in half cordial acknowledgement of Gotama's presence. Bright orbs of phosphorescent light, pulsed and shimmered, like Cepheid stars, in a huge halo around him. Images reminiscent of atomic particles, like electrons and protons, together with planets and moons whirled in tight circles, all enmeshed in the vibrant fan-like backdrops that fluted up, like fountains, from his head, for considerable distances, to be lost in misty vagueness somewhere in the topmost reaches of the great engine room. The changing colours of his peacock patterned costume were interspaced with linear images that curled in from distant points to form weird curvatures and vortexes, like concave and convex clock faces. All were quite magnificent and exhilarating to witness. He had about him a presence and energy that were both mysterious and hypnotic, with flashing eyes that shone like pools, indicative of high intelligence.

Mudbelly chimed in again. "This 'ere gent wants to know sumfin abaart 'ow this 'ere place works."

"I see," Mr Time Bender said, without enthusiasm. "If there's anything I can explain that is of particular interest, please feel free to ask."

Gotama bent forward, pointing to the giant generator combustion chambers surrounded by soft coiled pipes that moved like snakes, pulsating valves, strings of spiral globes that reminded him of DNA molecular structures, some flashing lights and peculiar instrument monitors. "I always thought a jet engine had to take in air in addition to fuel." Gotama said, half jokingly, in an effort to break the ice "Where does the equivalent of air come from when travelling through such a rarefied atmosphere as Infinite Time?"

"Not much trouble there mate," Mudbelly chimed in. "The engine uses somefin called Karma fluid and there's plenty of that in the hot air from all 'uman beins in the world, not to mention all those politicians, economists, the bureaucrats, the men from the city, the trade unionists, churchmen and the media in the central cabins. Quite sufficient to keep this 'ere engine runnin' anyways. With all their rubbish, there's plenty for burning, plenty of 'uman thoughts and actions to keep fings changing all the time, but not always for the better."

"Mind you! Some of 'em don't always take kindly to changes. Do you know, not long ago we 'ad a cheeky devil called Charlie Darwin 'oo wanted to change the name of Progress 13 to Evolution! 'e said it was an upgrade for an outdated programme. I'm not saying 'e wasn't right in what 'e said, but it came as a shock to many of the old boys, like Genesis and 'is church people 'oo 'ad spent lifetimes trying to make 'emselves feel nice and secure. They were a bit like old Bureaucrumb and 'is cronies. All thought they 'ad it worked out. Thought they knew it all! Fair put 'em all out it did! They've never been quite the same since. Took the wind right out of their sails. To fink that there might be only Natural Selection of those 'oo somehaaw 'ung on to life better than uvvers did. I tell you mate, the clergy nearly went berserk. Fought their entire world was a crumblin! You see, they 'ad everyfing all planned out nice and neat and to fink that someone else 'igher up 'adn't planned or designed 'em made 'em too lonely for words. You see, they liked to 'ave company in this 'ere big cosmic place. They fort it ought to be like a big National Insurance Scheme, complete wiv a bloke on a throne in the sky 'oo was just there to give 'em security, play nice music wiv 'em and to feed 'em like they was unemployed or somefin. All they really wanted was to live on Cosmic National Assistance. However, they were a bit presumptuous. It was no way to treat a bloke up there anyway. Asking 'im for 'andouts all the blinkin' time. It wants someone like that there Jesus 'ere again. 'e'd stir 'em up for sure. Just like 'e stirred up that uvver lot before. 'Cos they're all the same nowadays yer know. Just the blinkin same! Although, on second foughts, if 'e were to come today, people wouldn't crucify 'im. They'd probably ask 'im to dinner, and hear what 'e 'ad to say and make fun of it!"

It was quite obvious that Frank Time Bender, the original Time and Motion engineer, was becoming somewhat impatient with the lengthy commentary being delivered by Mudbelly Jones. With a sudden gesticulation, he threw up his arms. "Yes, yes, quite so! Perhaps I can leave you both to finish your discussion. When you are ready, perhaps you would like to meet me in my office where I shall be pleased to explain some of the functions of our karmalife future moulding technology and its implications. I look forward to seeing you."

With that he withdrew, leaving Gotama once again alone with Mudbelly who half apologised for Mr Time Bender's quick departure.

"A workaholic 'e is! Never 'as any spare time. Uses every bit 'e can lay 'is 'ands on for this 'ere making of three dimensional Time for sensations and thoughts to live in. 'e can't stop yer know. It's a thing wiv 'im. 'e can't stop or else we'd all slip neatly back into a sort of 'orrible timelessness wivart so much as a blink of an eyeball." Mudbelly Jones laughed. "You've got somefin in store for you when you visit that place in the Future end of this 'ere plane. We've got nuffin 'ere to compare wiv all the fascinatin' fings in those forward cabins. We sometimes get our lighter 'istorical entertainment in these 'ere Past cabins tho', like the uvver day when Lady 'amilton and Cleopatra played a duet togevver called Strumpet Voluntary. And then there was old 'enery the Eighth 'oo spent most of 'is time bedding and de'edding and changed the blinkin church too, just so 'e could marry 'oo 'e wanted. And then there was that there Einstein 'oo, when asked what Relativity was all abart, told us, when a man sits with a pretty girl for an hour, it seems like a minute. But let 'im sit on a 'ot stove for a minute – and it's longer than any hour. That's relativity 'e said. So you see, we do 'ave our moments. Like the bloke 'oo said 'is name was Mr Goon, 'oo read us 'is poem that went something like 'Parding Miss Harding, is our Kitting in your garding, Eating of a mutting bone? No, 'e's gone to Londing. How many miles to Londing? Eleving? I thought it was only seving, Heavings! What a long way from home!' " Old Mudbelly gave a muffled laugh and his rotund tummy shook slightly and rumbled in harmony. "And that reminds me of anuvver bloke 'oo told us 'is life story in a different way. 'E said that when God gave out heads, 'e thought 'e said beds, and 'e asked for a soft one. When God gave out looks, 'e thought 'e said books, and 'e didn't want any. When God gave out noses, 'e thought 'e said roses, and 'e asked for a red one. When God gave out ears, 'e thought 'e said beers, and 'e asked for two big ones. When God gave out chins, 'e thought 'e said gins, and 'e asked for a double. When God gave out brains, 'e thought 'e said trains and 'e said 'e'd take the next one. When God gave out legs, 'e thought 'e said kegs so 'e ordered two fat ones. Since then 'e's been trying to listen better."

Old Mudbelly then shook and vibrated with mirth and could hardly speak. However, in between gurgling giggles, he went on, "My mate 'arold came in the uvver day and said 'ed made up a poem that went sumfin like

"Perhaps the world is crying, 'Oh, dear!'
Perhaps good God is shedding a tear,
Because 'e sees that Man's a lout,
Who keeps on knocking Earth about!
Perhaps the world is just a joke,
To give a laugh to some old bloke,
Who 'adn't much to think about,
Except 'imself, the poor old trout.
Perhaps 'e conjured up the notion
By mistake and brewed a potion
That should 'ave made Man like a God,
But sadly made 'im just a sod"

And 'ere's anuvver tickle-tum rhyme for you,

Old Mr Barrett,
Tripped up on a carrot
And knocked 'is belly
Against the telly.
The telly went bang,
The telephone rang,
Mr Barrett said 'ouch'
And fell back on the couch."

Mudbelly burst into another quake of laughter.

Mudbelly's laughter was so infectious and hard to resist, Gotama laughed too, but then decided to try to change the subject, as he was beginning to tire of the old gossiper. He had noticed some old men standing by some broad wooded benches, filing pieces of metal. Others were using chisels to carve beautiful images in stone and silver. "Who are the old men?" Gotama enquired.

Mudbelly Jones studied them for a few moments. "They're living memorials to the past," he said. "They're the old craftsmen; ooze skill was beyond compare. They lide the farndation for the later technological age that fanked 'em by putting 'em out of work. We've kept 'em 'ere as precious museum pieces." Mudbelly then led the way between several oil stained and marble encrusted workbenches until they stood within a few feet of the old men. They were all white haired and some had beards, but every face was warm and cheerful. Their eyes were bright with intelligence. Each was completely absorbed in his occupation. "You won't find such bright contented faces anywhere," Mudbelly commented. "They're interested you see! They can create somefin from start to finish and take pleasure in the result. Not like some of 'em uvvers you'll come across, packed in modern sardine tins and 'uman battery cages they call efficient working conditions, where each job is timed to the fraction of a second. In the past the craftsmen weren't chained to any conveyor belt where a man or woman aint meant to be, nor can be 'uman." Despite his rough rugged character there was the vaguest suspicion of tears in the eyes of Mudbelly Jones. "Just look at those fings of beauty," he said, his voice sounding as though it choked just for a moment. "All those fings they've made 'ave been lost to the world. All their special craft skills too. Sad, aint it?"

Some of the delicate carvings, tapestries, paintings and sculptures being worked on by the old men possessed a beauty and originality of style that could only be achieved by immediate human contact and inspiration. Only by the strange union between artist and his creation could such masterpieces attain that unique aura of perfection and beauty, attributes so often lost in later ages by the substitution of quantity for quality, machine for the human craftsman. "It's very sad," Mudbelly, continued. He shrugged his shoulders. "Still, what's progress but the laying down of one achievement of Man for anuvver; one ambition for anuvver; one beauty for anuvver. It must go on, it must go on." His voice trailed off into a tremor, as though he was only half convinced of his words. He turned and indicated several paintings on one of the benches. "Aint they beautiful?" he said quietly. "You should see what's 'appened to those scenes now that Technology's taken over. They've been carved up wiv strips of concrete everywhere. Old Bureaucrumb calls 'em necessary for modern commerce and for people's well being. I 'ope 'es right, cos it won't be long before scenic beauty's covered all over wiv 'em. Let's 'ope that his 'necessaries' are good for people, cos they'll be all people will 'ave soon. There'll be no going back to beauty again, when Man decides 'e only 'as time for necessaries."

Just at that moment, a young girl with long black hair approached. Gotama was immediately attracted. She had the trimmest figure and it was obvious from her movements that she was aware of the fact. Her eyes were not just eyes they were saucers of blue. Even the old craftsmen came to life and managed a few whistles as she glided past.

"Mr Time Bender sent me to ask whether you would like to join him in his office for some tea and a chat," she purred, as her dreamy eyes tore into Gotama's heart, like an arrow from Eros's bow. The girl then led the way up several flights of stairs to an office with windows overlooking the engine room. "If you would like to wait here for a moment, Mr Time Bender will be back shortly." She then took a seat at a desk in the corner.

After several minutes the office door was flung open and in strode Mr Time Bender. "I trust you managed to glean some information downstairs in the workshop," the Time and Motion engineer said, his eyes penetrating Gotama's face for an answer. "You probably think this place has been designed by somebody like Lewis Carroll. However, I can assure you that despite the fact that some of the procedures seem akin to the mad hatter's tea party, they have all been designed with a purpose in mind, although not always easy to ferret out. We excuse ourselves for the organised chaos by calling it lateral thinking." Gotama commented that he thought everything looked quite splendid, but that there were many things he didn't understand. He said that there were times when he felt rather like Omar Khayam when he always found himself leaving through the same door as he went in, particularly when looking for a reason for things. Mr Time Bender nodded. "I frequently feel the same," he said, as he turned to the dark haired girl, who was now typing at great speed at her desk. "Miss Chief would you be kind enough to make us some coffee please?" The girl smiled and disappeared through an adjacent door leaving the men to their discussions.

"To make it easier for you to understand all that you see in Progress 13," Mr Time Bender went on. "I must first impress upon you that I and my colleagues, together with the Karma reaction engine, all function on a different plane and at a different material level from what you are used to. You are able to see me as a person only because we have organised it that way and because you have been provided with your special spectacles that help you to objectify things that would normally be beyond the sensory world, like Time and other dimensions for instance. Although you are seeing me as a person, you must consider this as a temporary expedient to enable you to understand things that we consider are especially important for you to know at this critical time in planet Earth's history. Under normal circumstances you would, no doubt, define me as some kind of 'force' or 'energy field' or even as a 'scientific law,' which can effect infinite Time to make it curve upon itself to produce Finite Time. This results in your experiences of past present and future and a continual passage of time. Your sensation of Time running into the past is a fundamental part of your type of consciousness. In brief, we are all Time, Pure Time. We are self-creating through the medium of Mind. Mortals are just congealed Time. Their experience, for the most part, is created by their own Karma, a process whereby every thought, sensation and action breeds its own reaction and result. Just as a mother reproduces her likeness, so do thoughts, concepts and sensations. These are vast breeding grounds that people never see with physical eyes, but which exist nonetheless and are powerful agencies for altering the environment as well as themselves. The vast computer processor systems I shall show you can be likened to those that exist in people's brains and in their complex social activities. The human brain is a breeding ground for Concepts and Sensations. It is a vast network of ideas and feelings that are not only linked with each other inside our brains, but also enable us to communicate with each other in the outside world. It is this subtle communication linking the brain's breeding grounds of concepts with the external links, person to person, that make civilisation what it is. That is why it is so important for the proper constructive concepts to be conceived and bred in each human brain, for it is here that civilised living and true progress begin.

All mortals are a subtle blend of concepts and sensations from which arise notions of 'self' and 'not self,' 'mind' and 'beyond mind.' We all live and breathe not only in a cosmic ocean of space and time but also in an ocean of the unborn and unmanifest. They are both oceans of indescribable immensity, yet which function in the most minute. They are the origins of dimensions and cycles quite beyond human comprehension. All conscious experiences only become so by participating in some of these dimensional cycles that are like tiny movements in the surface of the ocean's swell. Fundamentally, we are the ocean. We possess an inherent power within to bend Timelessness into Time and universal Mind into spatial extension and movement. This is what everyone does spontaneously, without being fully aware of the processes involved. A blind man who suddenly sees again will at first see only vague patterns without extension. It takes sometime before he can create the necessary spatial extension called natural seeing.

The progress of Mankind is fundamentally a progress of human concepts. Human brains analyse sense data, interrelate it and create directives towards the future. These directives trim the controls of the plane we have called Progress 13. The plane has many control feedbacks that act as regulators for both the individual person and for society. They are also to be found in the many compensations and control mechanisms in Nature herself, which some scientists have defined as a Gaia type of self-balancing system. Nature's own system was created aeons of time before Man had an inkling of automatic control systems. Man considers himself a modern genius, but Nature herself invented automatic self-compensation billions of years ago. The type of self balancing automatic control device we are speaking of, can only be successful if the data is processed quickly enough so that corrections can be made to compensate for accumulating errors before they become too great. If conditions in the process control systems of Mankind alter too drastically or too quickly, there may be insufficient time to make corrections to avoid catastrophe. Excessive interference in natural rhythms by modern Man and incorrect human judgements could easily upset Nature's automatic control mechanisms with very serious consequences.

We have quite recently observed that Man's values are being polluted as much as his environment. This is a serious state of affairs. Man's 'values' are his control settings for the maintenance of stability within his society. If these control settings are disrupted or eliminated, it means that the very foundations of society might crumble. There are all sorts of behaviour patterns in the animal world that have evolved in the struggle for survival. We should, therefore, never be dogmatic in thinking that only one pattern is ultimately 'right' for future society. Such rigidity of thinking could result in mankind going the same way as the Dinosaurs. However, although changes in values and behaviour aren't necessarily bad, there are some that could seriously harm a population and even bring it to extinction. Unfortunately, we have begun to see a number of these dangerous changes taking place in the human condition."

At this point in the proceedings, the young girl returned and distributed coffee and biscuits. They then all talked together on many things related to the way mankind was fumbling its way forwards, hoping its efforts would produce a better world for its forbears. Scientists were the vanguard in the drive for technological progress that everyone hoped would eventually lead to a Shangri-La. The hope had engendered a kind of blind faith that scientific reason would prevail and produce the goods, even though it had bred diseased cattle, environmental pollution, global warming, Thalidomide babies, and Hiroshima along the way.

Finally, there was a lull in the conversation and Mr Time Bender suggested Gotama might like to take a look at some of the time bending instrumentation which created people's awareness in their world of past, present and future.

Gotama expressed his eagerness, and the small group made their way to the vast engine rooms. The whole place looked like a giant laboratory that was so large it seemed to disappear into the distance, and so high it disappeared into a starlit sky. Some of the structures were cavernous whilst others took the form of scrolling shapes of light beams entwining countless numbers of ball-shaped lights that twinkled on and off in alternating colours. Each was linked to the next by a chain of thousands upon thousands of complex formations, which were constantly changing their contour. Some were shiny and almost metallic whilst others appeared soft and malleable and curled each upon the other like living, writhing snakes. Gotama was unable to recognise any of the usual type of machinery, although he thought he noticed items that looked like electronic circuitry, but they were more minute than usual and were stacked in such huge heaps that there must have been billions and billions of them. Moreover, they didn't remain stationary, but pulsated and moved to a kind of overall rhythm which gave the impression that the whole engine, if engine it was, was throbbing with life and energy.

Mr Time Bender pointed to a central block. "In that one section," he said proudly, "We have billions of conscious, semi-conscious and unconscious electrical circuits. As many as there are stars and planets in the Milky Way galaxy. They are all at this moment transmitting and receiving data from different parts of the electronic organism. It's a universe in miniature. It's the equivalent of a single human space/time brain. We have countless other types, some more complex and advanced, some less so." Mr Time Bender pointed to a few thousand million moving coils that glistened and sparked. "Those are what you would call dendrons or nerve fibres. Each tiny circuit comprises a central body with quantities of dendrons that are in contact with others throughout the system. I can see you are impressed by the complexity of the machinery," he said, as he noticed Gotama's astonished expression. "But, behind the tremendous complication, there is an underlying simplicity, harmony and uniformity, the basis of which is an energy working to a conceived pattern. Its thoughts and sensations are linked together in accordance with natural law. And it's by means of these vast living processors, these living brains, that people are conscious of themselves and their planet Earth. Each individual mind is a function of this giant network of living energy and each network is a function of living mind. The two aspects are entwined inextricably. One cannot say that Man is inside his thoughts any more than one can say his thoughts are inside him. The two are functionally as one, just as matter and mind and energy and spirit that comprise the universe are in fact one. Mr Time Bender looked at his watch. "There's a lot more I would like to show you," he said, "but this is not the time. However, we are having a special meeting here tomorrow which may be of interest to you. If you would like to come, I can promise you will meet some interesting people and hear some interesting things. In the meantime, my secretary will be glad to explain details to you. I must be off for the present." He quickly shook Gotama's hand and took his leave.

Gotama spent the next hour getting acquainted with Miss Chief, who was most attentive to his questions. It was not long before he invited her to lunch, or was it dinner? He wasn't sure. Anyway, they met up again at the celebrated eating and entertainment rendezvous called the 'Wheel of Fortune.' She said that this was the place where everyone met and spent their days (and nights) on the roller coaster of living.

* * *

The long table in the great office of Mr Time Bender stretched away into the distance as well as into the past. Gotama thought the office was definitely much larger than when he left it the day before. It was apparent that the far end of the table was now being occupied by some of the more remote historical personages, whilst close at hand, near to where the chairman was seated, there were figures of more recent human heritage. There seemed to be a kind of karmic class distinction even here, because the people appeared to gravitate into their own particular groupings. One such group included Jules Verne, H.G. Wells, Arthur C. Clarke, Dr Vaun Braun and Aldous Huxley. Immediately to their right sat some Christian heretics. Prominent among these was the Bishop of Woolwich, Rev Robinson, already in deep conversation with Aldous Huxley and Voltaire. They were also speaking with two Eastern looking gentlemen called Sri Ramakrishna and St. Vedanta. Amongst the heretics sat George Fox who was dogmatically arguing with John Wesley, whilst several pompous Cardinals argued amongst themselves. Another group seated near to the end of the table marked 'Present' comprised Charles Darwin, Wallace, Galileo, Copernicus, Kepler, Priestley, Boyle, Appolonius and others, all engrossed in some interesting speculations with Fred Hoyle, Gammow and Sir James Jeans. Einstein, Helmholtz, Faraday and James Clerk Maxwell were there too, with the two Curies and Mr Rutherford. Further down the line there were the inseparable triplets, Adler, Jung and Freud, all debating something they had in mind with Pavlov, who had obviously brought along his friends, because he was surrounded by all sorts of salivating dogs. In the distance Gotama thought he recognised some Egyptian figures with a number of Greek philosophers. Plato, Aristotle and Socrates seemed to be surrounded by many admirers. The poets too seemed well represented. The gaudy figure of Omar Khayam was easily recognisable as was the group led by William Shakespeare and comprised William Blake, Milton, Wordsworth, Keats, Browning and Pound. Even Lewis Carroll was there happily chatting to some surrealist artists and Picasso. Monet was arguing about something with Paul Klee and refused to draw the line on any compromise. Leonardo led another group, whilst Rembrandt and Durer were just a couple amongst a large throng of artists that also included Van Gogh and Michaelangelo.

Many other groups were represented, but there were a couple of groups that particularly attracted Gotama's attention. One group included authors of some of the world's great works of wisdom, such as the Bhagavad Gita, the Vedas, the Upanishads and the Voice of Silence, all of Eastern origin. In fact, the wisdom of the East was very well represented. It seemed they possessed the overall majority in the 'true wisdom' section of the table. The other group seemed like members of a family group. Their expressions were similar, although they dressed differently. There was the man with long hair, a beard and sad compassionate eyes, as though he carried the suffering of the world. Another in the group effused the same serenity, but looked more like the oriental Buddha. From snatches of conversation Gotama learned the names of a few others in this family group. One was Ramakrishna; another Gandhi, another Vivekananda and some last minute arrivals in this group included Pope John, Martin Luther King and several others. Very close to this group, almost intermixed with it, was another, represented by the easily recognisable figure with large head, namely Socrates. He sat talking and questioning, apparently none the worse for his dose of hemlock. He was accompanied by several Greek philosophers who wore long opulent robes that were a strange contrast to his own ascetic apparel topped by his bearded and straggly head. Yet, despite this, he radiated his own special aura of tenderness, wisdom and compassion.

It is hardly necessary to mention that the politicians, whose interest has always been in preening their feathers at any meeting they can get into, were represented here also, still preening. Everyone from William Pitt and Oliver Cromwell to Marcus Aurelius and George Washington seemed to have converged for this strange conference, or was it something else? Wordsworth talked with animated enthusiasm and in strings of verses, at the same time trying his best to popularise religious outlook among his fellows, as indeed was the Bishop of Woolwich. Though in a more sophisticated manner and not without assistance from Mr Tillich and a number of eastern gentlemen. Voltaire, an arrogant individualist, scoffed at all the religious and moral arguments that seemed to be flying about at that moment. He was a man of candid convictions, who, in not wishing to idealise, actually idealised more than most and, in scoffing so vehemently at Man's morality, moralised more than most. He shot at the noble visions of his contemporaries such as Leibniz and the churchmen as though they were clay pigeons, but in so doing launched his own special brand of white clay pigeon. It was, however, a clay pigeon that reflected an honest sensitivity for the miseries of his fellows. Sir Isaac Newton was there eating apples, which someone said he couldn't do without. Aldous Huxley seemed similarly addicted to 'somas' for his headaches, through doing too much looking into the future. Fred Hoyle had an addiction for 'steady states' and seemed determined to feed them to his fellow scientists even if it choked them, which it did. In the end, however, he had to throw in the towel to his opponents with their 'big bang' answers. Dr Vaun Braun was explaining that he just wanted to get as far away from the earth as possible in the shortest possible time. He was talking to President Kennedy who had apparently found another method of doing this, but which was not as pleasant as using rockets.

Then there was Churchill with his cigar perched ostentatiously between his lips. He was vigorously tapping the table, his face a typical bulldog. "Never will so many past good deeds have been wasted on so few in the Present, if we don't do something to stop the rot," he thundered, "And never has there been so much incompetence by so many as there is now." He stumped his cigar brutally in an ashtray. "If the universe were run on the same lines as the human escapade, it would have been extinct billions of years ago. It's only by the grace of God and the luck of the devil that Man has not become extinct through his own fault. And another thing! Modern man prides himself on taking things like sex lightly. Yet he is flooded with sex manuals, sociological surveys and advice clinics as though the topic were a branch of nuclear physics. And look at Man's crazy art scene. The pundits are raving about a modern sculptor whose work consists of a few metal boxes, like giant filing cabinets and everyone has heard about the carcasses in formaldehyde. Yet back in 1913 Casimar Malevich created quite a stir in Moscow with his painting called 'Black Square on a White Background. All that has happened since is that the public is now being hoaxed in 3D. You don't have to be crazy to be human but it helps!"

There was a huge gathering of artists, including Picasso, discussing several ultra modern paintings with Leonardo. One or two of Leonardo's followers were almost hyperventilating and were in obvious shock as they tried to comprehend them. Some even stood on their heads in a last ditch vain attempt to gain a glimpse of the aesthetic. Paul Klee tried manfully to show them how to view abstraction in somewhat different terms. But the old masters, who thought they might have a seizure at any moment, decided to cut their losses and give up the attempt. Some moderns were saying that art could only be understood by someone who was an artist at heart. This seemed to preclude the old masters and some people were perplexed about this, not least the old masters themselves. Someone else was saying that beauty was always in the eye of the beholder. Unless one had it, a person was no more than a chimpanzee studying the Madonna of the rocks. If this were so, the old masters said, it hardly seemed worth their while painting anything at all, because if the viewer had the beauty within him to start with, in his eye, so to speak, then he would see it anyway. And if he hadn't, he wouldn't, or couldn't. At this point, some of the artists complained of getting a headache and gave up the discussion.

Several people in the religious group were discussing magic with Houdini and some American magicians. It was well known that Jesus belonged to a very exclusive magic circle of the Beyond that had only a very few members, mainly because the tricks were too darned difficult. His water into wine not only helped at weddings but was the envy of Houdini who tried for years to perfect it, but could never quite manage it without a lot of preparation. Jesus needed special preparation, but of a somewhat different kind that was quite above Houdini's head. Walking on water was one of Jesus' best, but served little practical purpose and nearly drowned his assistant who didn't quite get the hang of it. It was difficult to understand why he was so fond of magic because he didn't seem to be the showbiz type somehow. Lao Tzu, one of the others in the religious group said he didn't believe in conjuring tricks. He preferred to leave all the magic to Teo. In fact, he always made a practice of leaving his work and anything else that required a lot of effort, to the good auspices of Teo who was apparently something like a big slave robot who just had to be relied on, otherwise good things just didn't come about. In fact, if people made any effort to do something themselves, it would inevitably incur Teo's displeasure, because it was likely to interrupt his constant preoccupation with maintaining Nature's harmonious trim. It was tantamount to jogging someone's elbow when they were doing their best writing. Teo just wouldn't tolerate any assistance from Man, no doubt because he knew what a 'bodge up' Man would make of his work. It was obvious that Teo knew something! In brief, all you had to do to satisfy 'Teo' was to laze about and do nothing. A watered down variation on this theme was the British one called National Assistance. Participants were always very conscientious and wouldn't let anyone persuade them to do anything at all. It was a different kind of 'idle worship'.

At that point, someone else chirped up. "Mind, you," they said, "there's more to being good and idle than meets the eye. You wouldn't realise it, but the really religious men and women believed in idleness. Jesus, for instance, stopped off work for at least forty days and forty nights, whilst living on Natural Assistance, which was all very tempting but none too comfortable. Moreover, if Jesus didn't believe in being good and lazy, why did he tell people to look at the lilies of the fields that neither worked nor spun, yet were always clothed more beautifully than King Solomon's wives? It's doubtful if he was referring to Solomon's dress designers. He obviously intended Christians to be waited on by their heavenly father, in a similar way that Lao wanted people to rely completely on his Teo. Unfortunately, most Christians prefer to forget or ignore what Jesus really meant. They would rather be slaves of greed, possessions and money, thereby placing themselves in the very tricky predicament of trying to push all their camels through the eye of a needle, one of the more difficult provisions laid down for entry into the kingdom of heaven. Although riches will buy many things, this sort of trick requires more than money, as Jesus said, and he ought to know, as he was the best miracle magician in the business. The paradise of Jesus and the Nirvana of Buddha are not too often favoured by the man in the street. He usually prefers to rely on National Assistance and Unemployment Benefit. Perhaps he is right not to aim too high. In his opinion it is better to be firm on the lowest rung of the ladder than fall off the top. Man has always really preferred fish and chips to caviar."

Just at that moment Mr Time Bender took his place at the head of the table. After requesting everyone to be silent and to take their seats, he explained that he had convened the meeting to discuss a number of navigational problems with which they were involved in Progress 13. "Recently," he said, "it has become apparent that the usual Gaia automatic control systems of Nature have been seriously overridden by rapid and disturbing changes resulting from Man's abuse of his planet. He doesn't realise that tampering with his natural environment, which has been so carefully balanced by those two pragmatists trial and error over billions of years, could be utterly disastrous for him. He is polluting everything he touches and in his greed he's doing his best to swallow the world whole without realising how very indigestible it will be. Moreover, the global warming he's caused is making even his mother Earth go into hot sweats. He has already used up large proportions of his world's natural resources creating a global economic debt with Nature's bank. He doesn't seem to concern himself about the crippling interest rates either, and it will soon be impossible for him to ever repay his huge overdraft. This situation cannot be allowed to continue otherwise Man will inevitably destroy his world and himself.

You have all been asked to attend this meeting in order to put forward your views and hopefully some remedies. As you know the guidance system of Progress 13 is affected by every person's thought, feeling and action. Every man woman and child can therefore assist in altering the navigational trim of the plane in which they all live. Thoughts and ideas are, in fact, more important than physical acts, because they mould matter into form. They are the power. Matter is only the servant. The complex mixing of these 'thought' ingredients in the vast recipes of living make civilised standards and values what they are. You are all therefore responsible for the conditions as they stand today. Moreover, it is you, the leaders in new thought and new ideas, who will have to guide Man's destiny into the future. The world and its people can be transformed and improved by incubating new ideas and ideals. A queen bee is only different from the rest in her hive because she has been fed differently. The people of the planet Earth can be altered and their world improved out of all recognition if they are fed with the right thoughts. The sum total of all of your life's thoughts and actions, together with those of every person in the world, are at this very moment being fed into our Time Scanners to establish the present and future direction of Progress 13. Thus every thought and act, however small, will affect our direction, a truly democratic system don't you agree?" Mr Time Bender remarked.

"Every action and reaction is linked. All things, wherever they exist, are governed and affected by the composite effects of everything else. Even Time itself is bent into forms of temporary duration by those who experience it. Eternity is always with us but it's thrown into a finite circle of relativity by the 'experiencer' who weaves memories of the past and projections of the future from it. Part of our responsibility at this meeting is not only to find new ways to help the people of the world out of their present predicament, but also to ensure that Time is bent in a curvature that will maintain their illusion of progress from past to future. This is so necessary to keep them trying to improve and create. We must give them the incentive to do better. If people discovered that the universe has no need of progress or that it really contains everything already, there being nothing outside it that it could possibly need, then 'purpose' would cease to have meaning and even people's own small purposes would be seen as illusions. People would then discover that there were really no purposes in things, other than those they created for themselves. This could result in people having even less incentive than at present and a bigger redundancy problem, namely extinction. We must all therefore do everything possible to ensure that people maintain their illusions that their progress and their efforts to progress are realities and are necessary for their continued existence in the three dimensional plane of experience. You all know the difficulties that confront mankind. I would like to hear some of your views on the factors that have caused these problems, together with any remedial action you might like to recommend." At this point, Mr Time Bender looked enquiringly across the long table to where sat three bearded gentlemen. "Mr Tolstoy," he said, with a curious twinkle in his eyes. "I know that you once had some very valuable ideas on these subjects. Perhaps you would now honour us with your views."

The old man Tolstoy beamed jovially. It had been sometime since he had spoken in public and this was indeed an honour and a pleasure for him to speak once again on the subjects that he loved. He leaned forward, hands clasped together on the table. His speech was slow and deliberate as though he was in a deep world of his own, cut off from his contemporaries. His forehead wrinkled in a look of puzzlement, as though he couldn't quite understand how people could really be as stupid as to not realise that 'love' was the only worthwhile pursuit. "Freedom from servitude of man," he said, slowly, "cannot be achieved through collective effort, through the capture or exercise of power in order to change the external forms of authority, but only through the liberation of men's souls from the evil that is harboured within them. No more can human happiness be advanced through the creation and distribution of wealth. Each step man takes today towards material progress not only does not advance him towards the general well being but shows us, on the contrary, that all these technical improvements only increase our miseries. One can imagine other machines, submarine, subterranean and aerial for transporting man with the rapidity of lightning. One could multiply to infinity the means of propagating human speech and thought, but it would remain no less the case that these travellers, so comfortably and rapidly transported, are neither willing nor able to commit anything but evil, and the thoughts and words they pour forth only incite men to further harm. As to the beautifully perfected armaments of destruction, which, while diminishing the risk of those that employ them, make carnage easier, they only give further proof of the impossibility of persevering in the direction we are going. Man must return to his true guide in all things, namely that single all infallible guide of the Universal Spirit that lives in men as a whole and in each one of us. That spirit that commands the tree to grow towards the sun, the flower to throw off its seed in the autumn and us to reach out towards God and by so doing become united to each other. This is the Truth I have wanted to say to you, my brothers." With that, the old man lifted his head slightly to reveal a glimmer of a smile.

"You speak with considerable wisdom," a voice whispered from somewhere in the vicinity of the man with the sad eyes. Several of the orthodox Christians and high hatted notables of the church sat glum and silent, however, and had obviously not been moved by Tolstoy's few words. Another voice interrupted the proceedings.

"It's all very well having these head in the clouds ideals, but they're just not practical in the modern scientific age." The man who now spoke was lean and fragile with a lined face. "It's the blessings of science we should really be worshipping," he went on. "Blessings bestowed on all alike that contribute to everyone's material well being by providing them with food, clothing, advanced medical treatment, pain relief and much else besides. We now find ourselves in an entirely different age from when the major religions were born. The remedy for the modern age must be to use every modern device available. There's no going back. It's impossible to reverse the technological era. We now have problems that were never even thought of by the early Christians, for instance. We must all remember that science can save as well as destroy. It is all a question of how we use our knowledge."

With that, Aldous Huxley who had been waiting patiently to get a word in, suddenly interrupted the speaker. Without a higher motivation than science itself," he said quickly, "it's most probable that science by itself will only lead men to either destruction or to a subtle chaining of their freedom by scientific modification of human behaviour, either by use of drugs, somas, or by scientific conditioning techniques. Ultimately by synthetic production of human beings genetically determined and conditioned to a lifetime of servility to a state that breeds them, they will finally become willing prisoners because they will know no different. A pathetic state of generated slavery. In the second half of the 20th century we have done nothing systematic about our breeding: But in our random and unregulated way we are not only overpopulating our planet, we are also, it would seem, making sure that these greater numbers shall be of biologically poorer quality. In the bad old days, children with considerable, or even with slight, hereditary defects rarely survived. Today, thanks to sanitation, modern pharmacology and social conscience, most of the children born with hereditary defects reach maturity and multiply their kind. Under the conditions now prevailing, every advance in medical science will tend to be offset by a corresponding advance in survival rate of individuals cursed by some genetic insufficiency. In spite of the new wonder drugs and better treatment (indeed, in a certain sense, precisely because of these things,) the physical health of the general population will show no improvement and may even deteriorate. And along with the decline of average healthiness there may well go a decline in average intelligence. Indeed, some competent authorities are convinced that such a decline has already taken place and is continuing. My colleague here, Dr Sheldon has said that under conditions that are both soft and unregulated, our best stocks tend to be outbred by stock that is inferior to it in every respect.

Considering the case of the rich, industrialised and democratic society, in which, owing to the random but effective practice of dysgenics, IQs and physical vigour are on the decline. For how long can such a society maintain its traditions of individual liberty and democratic government? 50 or 100 years from now our children will learn the answer to this question, possibly too late. To help the unfortunate is obviously good. But the wholesale transmission to our descendants of the results of unfavourable mutations and the progressive contamination of the genetic pool from which the member of our species will have to draw, are no less obviously bad. We are on the horns of an ethical dilemma, and to find the middle way will require all our intelligence and all our good will.

Modern science and technology has led to the concentration of economic and political power, and to the development of a society controlled by big business and big government. But societies are composed of individuals and are good only in so far as they help individuals to realise their potentialities and to lead a happy and fruitful life. How have individuals been affected by the technological advances of recent years? Our contemporary western society, in spite of its material, intellectual and political progress, is increasingly less conducive to mental health and tends to undermine the inner security, happiness, reason and the capacity for love in the individual; it tends to turn him into an automaton who pays for his human failures with increasing mental sickness and with despair hidden under a frantic drive for work and so called pleasure."

Aldous Huxley paused, then resumed. "In the course of evolution, nature has gone to endless trouble to see that every individual is unlike every other individual. We reproduce our kind by bringing the father's genes into contact with the mother's. These hereditary factors may be combined in an almost infinite number of ways. Physically and mentally, each one of us is unique. Any culture which, in the interests of efficiency or in the name of some political or religious dogma, seeks to standardise the human individual, commits an outrage against man's biological nature.

In the social realms of politics, education and economics, Man's Will to Order can become really dangerous in this respect. Here the theoretical reduction of unmanageable multiplicity to comprehensible unity becomes the practical reduction of human diversity to subhuman uniformity, of freedom to servitude. The Will to Order can make tyrants out of those who merely aspire to clear up the mess. The beauty of tidiness is used as justification for despotism. In economics, the equivalent to a beautifully composed work of art is the smoothly running factory in which the workers are perfectly adjusted to the machines. In politics, the equivalent of a fully developed and orderly scientific theory or philosophical system is the totalitarian dictatorship. Over-organisation is as evil as anarchy.

Organisation is indispensable; for liberty arises and has meaning only within a self regulating community of feeling, cooperating individuals. But, though indispensable, organisation can also be fatal. Too much organisation transforms men and women into automata, suffocates the creative spirit and abolishes the very possibility of freedom. As usual, the only safe course, (and

I can see the Buddha nodding in ascent) is in the middle, between the extremes of laisez-faire at one end of the scale and total control on the other.

During the past century the successive advances in technology have been accompanied by corresponding advances in organisation. Complicated machinery has had to be matched by complicated social arrangements, designed to work smoothly and efficiently as the new instruments of production. In order to fit into these organisations, individuals have had to de-individualise themselves, have had to deny their native diversity and conform to a standard pattern, have had to do their best to become automata.

The de-humanising effects of over-organisation are reinforced by the de-humanising effects of overpopulation. Industry, as it expands, draws an ever-increasing proportion of humanity's expanding numbers into large cities. But life in densely crowded cities is not conducive to physical or mental health; nor does it foster the kinds of responsible freedom within small governing groups, which is the first condition to genuine democracy. People are related to one another in the city, not as total personalities, but as the embodiments of economic functions or, when they are not at work, as irresponsible seekers of entertainment. Subjected to this kind of life, individuals tend to feel lonely and insignificant. Their existence ceases to have any point or meaning.

Mr William Whyte has shown in his remarkable book 'The Organisation Man,' a new social ethic is replacing our traditional ethical system, i.e. the system in which the individual is primary. The key words in this social ethic are adjustment, adaptation, socially oriented behaviour, belongingness, acquisition of social skills, team work, group living, group loyalty, group dynamics, group thinking, group creativity. Its basic assumption is that the social whole has greater worth and significance than the individual parts, that inborn biological differences should be sacrificed to cultural uniformity, that the rights of the collectivity take precedence over what the eighteenth century called the Rights of Man. According to the social ethic, Jesus was completely wrong in asserting that the Sabbath was made of man. On the contrary, man was made for the Sabbath and must sacrifice his inherited idiosyncrasies and pretend to be a kind of standardised good mixer that organisers of group activity regard as the ideal for their purposes. This ideal man is the man who displays 'dynamic conformity' (delicious phrase) and an intense loyalty to the group, an unflagging desire to subordinate himself, to belong. And the ideal man must have an ideal wife, highly gregarious, infinitely adaptable and not merely resigned to the fact that her husband's first loyalty is to the Corporation, but actively loyal on her own account.

The current social ethic, it is obvious, is merely a justification after the fact of the laws less desirable consequences of over-organisation. It represents a pathetic attempt to make a virtue of necessity, to extract a positive value from an unpleasant datum. It is a very unrealistic, and therefore very dangerous, system of morality. The social whole, whose value is assumed to be greater than of its component parts, is not an organism in the sense that a hive or a termitary many be thought of as an organism. It is merely an organisation, a piece of social machinery. There can be no values except in relation to life and awareness. An organisation is neither conscious nor alive. Its value is instrumental and derivative. It is not good in itself; it is good only to the extent that it promotes the good of the individuals who are the parts of the collective whole. To give organisations precedence over persons is to subordinate ends to means. What happens when ends are subordinate to means was clearly demonstrated by Hitler and Stalin. Under their hideous rule personal ends were subordinated to organisational means by a mixture of violence and propaganda, systematic terror and systematic manipulation of minds. In the more efficient dictatorships of tomorrow there will probably be much less violence than under Hitler or Stalin. The future dictators' subjects will be painlessly regimented by a corps of highly trained Social Engineers. 'The challenge of social engineering in our time,' wrote an enthusiastic advocate of this new science, 'is like the challenge of technical engineering 50 years ago. If the first half of the 20th century was an the era of technical engineers, the second half may well be thought of as the era of social engineers and social workers– and the 21st century, I suppose, will be the era of World Controllers, the scientific caste system and Brave New World. To the question, 'quis custodiet custodes?' – who will mount guard over our guardians, who will engineer the engineers? – The answer is a bland denial that they will need any supervision. There seems to be a touching belief among certain PhDs in sociology that PhDs in sociology will never be corrupted by power. Like Sir Galahads, their strength is as the strength of ten because their hearts are pure – and their hearts are pure because they are scientists and have taken six thousand hours of social studies.

Alas, higher education is not necessarily a guarantee of higher virtue, or higher political wisdom. And to those misgivings on ethical and psychological grounds must be added misgivings of a purely scientific character. Can we accept the theories on which social engineers base their practice, and in terms of which they justify their manipulations of human beings? For example, Professor Elton Mayo tells us categorically that 'men's desire to be continuously associated in work with his fellows in a strong, if not the strongest human characteristic.' This I would say is manifestly untrue. Some people have the kind of desire described by Mayo; others do not. It is a matter of temperament and inherited constitution. Any social organisation based upon the assumption that 'man' (whoever man may be) desires to be continuously associated with his fellows would be, for many individual men and women, a bed of Procrustes. Only by being amputated or stretched upon the rack could they be adjusted to it.

Again, how romantically misleading are the lyrical accounts of the Middle Ages, with which many contemporary theorists of social relations adorn their works! 'Membership in a guild, manorial estate or village protested medieval man throughout his life and gave him peace and security.' Protected him from what, we may ask? Certainly not from remorseless bullying at the hands of his superiors. And along with all that 'peace' and 'security' there was, throughout the middle ages, an enormous amount of chronic frustration, acute unhappiness and passionate resentment against the rigid hierarchical system that permitted no vertical ascent up the social ladder and, for those who were bound to the land, very little horizontal movement in space. The impersonal forces of overpopulation and over-organisation of the modern technical society, and the social engineers, who are trying to direct these forces, are pushing Progress 13 in the direction of a new but worse type of medieval system. This revival will be made more acceptable than the original by such brave new world amenities as infant conditioning, sleep teaching and drug induced euphoria; but, for the majority of men and women, it will still be a kind of servitude."

Aldous finished speaking and there was utter silence for a few moments. It was obvious that his words had created a deep impression on many of the figures seated at the huge circular table. His words were respected and almost revered by some who considered him to be a modern day prophet.

Suddenly the silence was broken by a voice from a member of the scientific clique. It was Conrad Istock who now took up the debate. "We have no need of prophets of environmental doom," he said. "The storm clouds gathering over our western technological civilisation are, figuratively and literally, visible. All the present talk of man and about the environment, at least in the form that it has become politically fashionable, is a waste of time. While we are fiddling about with technological solutions to specific environmental problems, we are blinded to the greatest problem of all, that the tenets of an industrialised society are utterly incompatible with those of ecology. Industry is committed to continuous expansion; all ecological systems tend towards stability and equilibrium. So general is the conflict between human economics and the ecology of the planet and so pervasive, powerful and unswerving the dynamic of the industrial state, that it is impossible to imagine a suitable industrial ecology under prevailing economic theory. Many new radical measures and reforms are required to be embodied in a massive international effort if we are ever to turn technology to the construction of a physiologically and socially healthy environment. One of the most important would require immediate and total birth control and secondly complete worldwide disarmament and huge new efforts to save the planet's ecological and living systems. There are numerous other almost equally important changes that must be wrought if we are to save mankind. They are what must happen if we are to avoid ever-increasing and socially disruptive calamity. For in industrialised societies the normal ecological checks and balances, which retain a dynamic equilibrium through continual small adjustments, have been swept away. In their place are created new limiting effects, which are non-discriminative and non-regulative. At the same time, the social order of a technological society is highly complex. When the limiting environmental effects, fostered by dense population and high social interdependence exceed human physiological or psychological tolerance, most individuals will simultaneously experience detrimental effects as the social order begins to crumble."

Just then, several persons, who were possibly alarmed or just irritated by Istock's words, all chimed in at once. When the meeting began to get out of hand, Mr Time Bender intervened and called for order. As soon as silence had been restored and he gave leave for the meeting to be resumed, several voices echoed from the poet's section.

It was Mr Emerson who began by quoting a few words from his poetry "Things are in the saddle and they rule mankind!" he said ponderously. The words brought renewed shouts from some of the Rousseauites who appealed for a return to Nature so that Man could live a natural life without the sophistication of technological civilisation. Among the shouts, the voice of William Morris could be heard imploring everyone to take up haymaking in his country where it was apparently always June, at least it was according to him. Samuel Butler and his Erewhonians were also contributing to this chorus by making half-hearted protests against technology and machines in general. Some of their arguments sounded thin and no one seemed to know exactly what sort of environment was perfectly 'natural' for man to live in. Although the calls for a return to Nature sounded very nice, exactly what this implied was a little vague and nebulous. It was all rather like discussing empty bubbles, that, one by one burst. It was obvious that everyone seemed to want to experience that very special state implied by 'natural freedom' but nobody knew how.

At this point in the proceedings, the lean white haired face of Bertrand Russell became noticeable as he briefly waved a hand and his eyes twinkled as a preliminary to speaking. He bent his lean figure slightly over the table as he looked towards the chairman and began to speak. "Will machines destroy emotions and men, or will emotions and men destroy machines? He said quizzically, as a faint smile flitted briefly across his furrowed face. "Our friend Samuel Butler in Erewhon, suggested this contest long ago, but the threat of open conflict grows more and more actual as the empire of machinery is enlarged.

At first sight, it is not obvious why there should be any opposition between machines and emotions. Every normal boy loves machines and Man, like the boy frequently loves to play with things like motor cars, not realising that they may run over him. Machines are worshipped because they are beautiful, and valued because they confer power; they are hated because they are hideous, and loathed because they impose slavery. A machine is like Djinn in the Arabian Nights; beautiful and beneficent to his master, but hideous and terrible to his enemies. But in our day nothing is allowed to show itself with such naked simplicity. The master of the machine, it is true, lives at a distance from it, where he cannot hear its noise or see its unsightly heaps of slag, smell its noxious fumes or see its pollution; if ever he sees it, the occasion is before it is installed in use, when he can admire its forces or its delicate precision without being troubled by dust and heat. But when he is challenged to consider the machine from the point of view of those who have to live with it and work with it, he has a ready answer. He can point out that owing to its operations, these men can purchase more goods – often vastly more – than their grandfathers could. It follows that they must be happier than their grandfathers could. It follows that they must be happier than their grandfathers – if we are to accept an assumption, which is made by almost everyone. The assumption is that the possession of material commodities is what makes Man happy. It is thought that a man who has two rooms and two beds and two loaves must be twice as happy as a man who has one room and one bed and one loaf. In a word, it is thought that happiness is proportional to income. A few people, not always quite sincerely, challenge this idea in the name of religion or morality, but they are glad if they increase their income by the eloquence of their preaching. It is not from the moral or religious point of view that I wish to challenge it; it is from the point of view of psychology and observation of life. If happiness is proportional to income, the case for machinery is unanswerable, if not, the whole question remains to be examined.

"Men have physical needs and they have emotions. While physical needs are unsatisfied, they take first place; but when they are satisfied, emotions unconnected with them become important in deciding whether a man is to be happy or unhappy. In modern industrialised communities there are men, women and children whose bare physical needs are not adequately supplied; as regards to them, I do not deny that the first requisite for happiness is an increase in income. But they are a minority and it would not be difficult to give the bare necessities of life to all of them. It is not of them that I wish to speak, but of those who have more than is necessary to support existence– not only those who have much more, but also those who have only a little more. Why do we, in fact, almost all of us, desire to increase our incomes? It may seem, at first sight, as though material goods were what we desire. But, in fact, we desire them mainly in order to impress our neighbours. When a man moves into a larger house in a more genteel quarter, he reflects that 'better' people will call on his wife, and some unprosperous cronies of former days can be dropped. When he sends his son to a good school or an expensive university he consoles himself for the heavy fees by the thoughts of social kudos to be gained. In every big city, whether of Europe or America, houses in some districts are more expensive than equally good houses in other districts, merely because they are more fashionable. One of the most powerful of all our passions is the desire to be admired and respected. As things stand, admiration and respect are given to the man who seems to be rich. This is the chief reason why people wish to be rich. The actual goods purchased by their money play quite a secondary part. Take, for example, a millionaire who cannot tell one picture from another, but has acquired a gallery of old masters by the help of the experts. The only pleasure he derives from his pictures is the thought that others know how much they have cost.

All this might be different, and has been different, in many societies. In aristocratic epochs, men have been admired for their birth. In some circles in Paris, men are admired for their artistic or literary excellence, strange as it may seem. In the German University, a man may actually be admired for his learning. In India, saints are admired: in China, sages. The study of these different societies shows the correctness of our analysis, for in all of them we find a large percentage of men who are indifferent to money so long as they have enough to keep alive on, but are keenly desirous of the merits by which in their environment, respect can be won.

The importance of these facts lies in this, that the modern desire for wealth is not inherent in human nature, and could be destroyed by different social institutions although man's desires for respect, etc., would still require satisfying in a different but more truly sociable sense. If, by law, we all had exactly the same income, we should have to seek some other way of being superior to our neighbours, and most of our present craving for material possessions would cease. Moreover, since this craving is in the nature of competition, it only brings happiness when we outdistance a rival, to whom it brings correlative pain. A general increase in wealth gives no competitive advantage and there brings no competitive happiness. There is, of course, some pleasure derived from the actual enjoyment of goods purchased, but, as we have seen, this is a very small part of what makes us desire wealth.

If we are to argue that machinery increases happiness, therefore the increase of material prosperity which it brings cannot weigh very heavily in its favour, except in so far as it may be used to prevent absolute destitution. But there is no inherent reason why it should be so used. Destitution can be prevented without machinery where population is stationary; of this France may serve as an example, since there is very little destitution and much less machinery than in America, England and pre-war Germany. Conversely, there may be much destitution where there is much machinery; of this we have examples in many of the industrial areas of England and also in Japan. The final prevention of destitution does not depend upon machines, but upon quite other factors – partly density of population and partly political conditions. And apart from prevention of destitution, the values of increasing wealth is not very great.

Meanwhile, machines deprive us of two things which are certainly important ingredients of human happiness, namely, spontaneity and variety. Machines have their own pace and their own insistent demands; a man who has expensive plant must keep it working. The great trouble with the machine, from the point of view of the emotions, is its regularity. And, of course, conversely, the great objection to the emotions, from the point of view of the machine, is their irregularity. As the machine dominates the thoughts of people who consider themselves 'serious,' the highest praise they can give to a man is to suggest that he has the qualities of the machine – that he is reliable, punctual, exact, etc. And an 'irregular' life has come to be synonymous with a bad life. Against this point of view, Bergson's philosophy was a protest – not in my opinion wholly sound from the intellectual point of view, but inspired by a wholesome dread of seeing men turned more and more into machines.

In life as opposed to thought, the rebellion of our instincts against enslavement to mechanism has hitherto taken a most unfortunate direction. The impulse to war has always existed since men took to living in societies, but it did not, in the past have the same intensity or virulence as it has in our day of scientific technology. The greater ferocity of modern war is attributable to machines, which operate in three different ways. First they make it possible to create methods of greater mass destruction. Secondly, they facilitate a cheap press, which flourishes by appealing to men's baser passions. Thirdly, – and this is the important point that concerns us – they starve the anarchic, spontaneous side of human nature, which works underground, producing an obscure discontent, to which the thought of war and violence appeals as affording possible relief. It is a mistake to attribute a vast upheaval like the last world wars merely to the machinations of politicians. In England, Germany and USA (in 1917) no government could have withstood the popular demand for war. A popular demand of this sort must have an instinctive basis, and for my part, I believe that the modern increase in warlike instinct and violence is attributable to the dissatisfaction (mostly unconscious) caused by the regularity, monotony and tameness of modern life.

It is obvious that we cannot deal with this situation by abolishing machinery. Such a measure would be reactionary, and is in any case impracticable. The only way of overriding the evils at present associated with machinery is to provide breaks in the monotony with every encouragement to high adventure during the intervals. Many men would cease to desire violent activities and war if they had opportunities to risk their lives in Alpine climbing; one of the ablest and most vigorous workers for peace that it has been my good fortune to know, habitually spent his summer climbing the most dangerous peaks in the Alps. If every working man had a month in the year during which, if he chose, he could be taught to work an aeroplane, or encouraged to hunt for sapphires in the Sahara, or otherwise enabled to engage in some dangerous and exciting pursuit involving quick personal initiative, the popular love of war and violence would become confined to women and invalids. I confess I know no method of making these classes pacific, but I am convinced that a scientific psychology would find a method if it undertook the task in earnest.

Machines have altered our way of life, but not our instincts. Consequently there is maladjustment. The whole psychology of the emotions and instincts is as yet in its infancy; a beginning has been made by psychoanalysis, but only a beginning. What we accept from psychoanalysis is the fact that people will, in action, pursue various ends which they do not consciously desire, and will have an attendant set of quite irrational beliefs which enable them to pursue these ends without knowing that they are doing so. But orthodox psychoanalysis has unduly simplified our unconscious purposes, which are numerous and differ from one person to another. It is to be hoped that social and political phenomena will soon come to be understood from this point of view, and will thus throw light on the average human nature.

Moral self-control, and external prohibition of harmful acts, are not adequate methods of dealing with our anarchic instincts. The reason they are inadequate is that these instincts are capable of as many disguises as the Devil in mediaeval legend, and some of these disguises deceive even the elect. The only adequate method is to discover what are the needs of our instinctive nature, and then to search for the least harmful way of satisfying them. Since spontaneity is what is most thwarted by machines, the only thing that can be provided is opportunity; the use made of opportunity must be left to the initiative of the individual. No doubt considerable expense would be involved; but it would not be comparable to the expense of war and social violence. Understanding of human nature must be the basis of any real improvement in human life. Science has done wonders in mastering the laws of the physical world, but our own nature is much less understood, as yet, than the nature of stars and electrons. When science learns to understand human nature, it will be able to bring happiness into man's lives which machines and physical science have failed to create."

Bertrand sat back on his seat as he spoke the last few words. He directed his gaze towards Professor Jung, the distinguished gentleman who sat between Freud and Adler. He obviously considered that Prof. Jung might be able to unravel some of the secrets that could still enable mankind to live with his machines without his special spontaneity and potential for happiness being crushed. Prof. Jung was well known as a leader in his field and was well versed in understanding human motivation and instinct. Everyone in the vast hall looked towards him in silent expectancy. Prof. Jung smiled and gave a respectful nod in the direction of the last speaker.

"Every good quality has its bad side," he said. "Nothing that is good can come into the world without directly producing a corresponding evil. This is a painful fact. Now there is the danger that consciousness of the present may lead to an elation based on an illusion, the illusion, namely, that we are the culmination of the history of mankind, the fulfilment and the end product of countless centuries. If we grant this we should understand that it is no more than the proud acknowledgement of our destitution: we are also the disappointment of the hopes and expectations of the ages. Think of nearly 2000 years of Christian ideals followed, not by the return of the Messiah and the heavenly millennium, but instead, by the World War among Christian nations and its barbed wire and poison gas. What a catastrophe in heaven and on earth!

In the face of such a picture we may well grow humble again. It is true that modern man is a culmination, but tomorrow he will be surpassed; he is indeed the end product of an age–old development, but he is at the same time the worst conceivable disappointment of the hopes of mankind. The modern man is aware of this. He has seen how beneficent are science, technology and organisation but also how catastrophic they can be. He has likewise seen that well meaning governments have so thoroughly paved the way for peace on the principle 'in time of peace prepare for war,' that Europe has nearly gone to rack and ruin. And as for ideals, the Christian church, the brotherhood of man, international social democracy and the 'solidarity' of economic interests have all failed to stand the baptism of fire– the test of reality. Today, after two world wars and numerous other conflicts, we observe once more the same optimism, the same organisation, the same political aspirations; the same phrases and catchwords at work. How can we but fear that they will inevitably lead to further catastrophes?

Agreements to outlaw war leave us sceptical, even while we wish them all possible success. At bottom, behind every such palliative measure, there is a gnawing doubt. On the whole, I believe I am not exaggerating when I say that modern man has suffered an almost fatal shock, psychologically speaking, and as a result has fallen into profound uncertainty. That old dream of the millennium, in which peace and harmony should rule the world, has grown pale. The modern man's scepticism regarding all such matter has chilled his enthusiasm for politics and world reform; more than that, it does not favour any smooth application of psychic energies to the outer world. Through his scepticism the modern man is thrown back upon himself; his energies flow towards their source and wash to the surface those psychic contents which are at all times there, but lie hidden in the silt as the stream flows smoothly on its course. How totally different did the world appear to mediaeval man. For him the earth was eternally fixed and at rest in the centre of the universe, encircled by the course of the sun that solicitously bestowed its warmth. Men were all children of God under the loving care of the Most High, who prepared them for eternal blessedness; and all knew exactly what they should do and how they should conduct themselves in order to rise from a corruptible world to an incorruptible and joyous existence. Such a life no longer seems real to us, even in our dreams. Natural science has long ago torn this lovely veil to shreds. That age lies far behind as childhood, when one's father was unquestionably the handsomest and strongest man on earth.

The modern man has lost all the metaphysical certainties of his mediaeval brother, and has set up in their place the ideals of material security, general welfare and humaneness. But it takes more than an ordinary dose of optimism to make it appear that these ideals are still unshaken. Material security, even, has gone by the board, for modern man begins to see that every step in material 'progress' adds just so much force to the threat of a more stupendous catastrophe. The very picture terrorises the imagination. What are we to imagine when cities today perfect measures of defence against poison-gas attacks and biological warfare by terrorists and practise them in dress rehearsals?' We cannot but suppose that such attacks have been planned and provided for – again on the principle 'in time of peace prepare for war.' Let man but accumulate his materials of destruction and the devil within him will soon be unable to resist putting them to their fated use. It is well known that fire-arms go off themselves if only enough of them are together.

An intimation of the law that governs blind contingency, which Heraclitus called the rule of 'enantiodromia' (conversion into the opposite), now steals upon the modern man through the by-ways of his mind, chilling him with fear and paralysing his faith in the lasting effectiveness of social and political measures in the face of these monstrous forces. If he turns away from the terrifying prospect of a blind world in which building and destroying successively tip the scale, and if he then turns his gaze inward upon the recesses of his own mind, he will discover a chaos and a darkness there which he would gladly ignore. Science has destroyed even the refuge of the inner life." Prof. Jung hesitated for a moment and then went on. "We like to think that on the basis of a widespread knowledge of the unconscious and its ways, no one could be deceived by a statesman who was unaware of his own bad motives; the newspapers would pull him up; 'please have yourself analysed, you are suffering from a repressed father-complex.' I have purposely chosen this grotesque example to show to what absurdities we are led by the illusion that because something is psychic it is under our control. It is, however, true that much of the evil in the world is due to the fact that man in general is hopelessly unconscious, as it is also true that with increasing insight we can combat this evil at its source in ourselves. As science enables us to deal with injuries inflicted from without, so it helps us to treat those arising from within. The rapid and world wide growth of a psychological interest over the last few decades shows unmistakably that modern man has to some extent turned his attention from material things to his own subjective processes. Should we call this mere curiosity? At any rate, art has a way of anticipating future changes in man's fundamental outlook, and expressionist art has taken this subjective turn well in advance of the more general change.

There can be no doubt that from the beginning of the nineteenth century – from the memorable years of the French revolution onwards – man has given more and more prominent place to the psyche, his increasing attentiveness to it being the measure of its growing attraction for him. The enthronement of the Goddess of Reason in Notre Dame seems to have been a symbolic gesture of great significance to the Western World – rather like the hewing down of Wotan's oak by the Christian missionaries. For then, as at the Revolution, no avenging bolt from heaven struck the blasphemer down.

It is certainly more than an amusing coincidence that just at that time a Frenchman, Anquetil du Perron, was living in India and, in the early eighteen hundreds, brought back with him a translation of the Oupnek'hat– a collection of fifty Upanishads– which gave the Western World its first deep insight into the baffling mind of the East. To the historian this is mere chance without any factors of cause and effect. But in view of my medical experience I cannot take it as an accident. It seems to me rather to satisfy a psychological law whose validity in personal life, at least, is complete. For every piece of conscious life that loses its importance and value– so runs the law– there arise a compensation in the unconscious. We may see in this analogy to the conservation of energy in the physical world, for our psychic processes have a quantitative aspect also. No psychic value can disappear without being replaced by another of equal intensity. This is a rule, which finds its pragmatic sanction in the daily practice of the psychotherapist; it is repeatedly verified and never fails. Now the doctor in me refuses point blank to consider the life of a people as something that does not conform to psychological law. A people, in the doctor's eyes presents only a somewhat more complex picture of psychic life than the individual. Moreover, taking it the other way round, has not a poet spoken of the 'nations' of his soul? And quite correctly, as it seems to me, for in one of its aspects the psyche is not individual, but is derived from the nation, from collectivity, or from humanity even. In some way or other we are part of an all embracing life, of a single 'greatest' man, to quote Swedenborg.

And so we can draw a parallel; just as in me, a single human being, the darkness calls forth the helpful light, so does it also in the psychic life of a people. In the crowds that poured into Notre Dame, bent on destruction, dark and nameless forces were at work that swept the individual off his feet; these forces worked also upon Anquetil du Perron, and provoked an answer, which has come down in history. For he brought the Eastern mind to the West, and its influence upon us we cannot yet measure. Let us beware of underestimating it! So far, indeed, there is little of it to be seen in Europe on the intellectual surface: some orientalists, one or two Buddhist enthusiasts, and a few sombre celebrities like Madame Blavatsky and Annie Besant. These manifestations make us think of tiny scattered islands in the ocean of mankind: in reality they are like the peaks of submarine mountain ranges of considerable size. The Philistine believed until recently that astrology had been disposed of long since, and was something that could safely be laughed at. But today, rising out of the social deeps, it knocks at the doors of the universities from which it was banished some 300 years ago. The same is true of the thought of the East; it takes root in the lower social levels and slowly grows to the surface.

Great innovations never come from above; they come invariably from below; just as trees never grow from the sky downwards, but upward from the earth, however true it is that their seeds have fallen from above. The upheaval of our world and the upheaval in consciousness are one and the same. Everything becomes relative and therefore doubtful. And while man, hesitant and questioning, contemplates a world that is distracted with treaties of peace and pacts of friendship, democracy and dictatorship, capitalism and bolshevism, his spirit yearns for an answer that will allay the turmoil of doubt and uncertainty. And it is just people of the lower social levels who follow the unconscious forces of the psyche; it is the much derided, silent folk of the land– those who are less infected with academic prejudices than great celebrities are wont to be. All these people, looked at from above, present mostly a dreary or laughable comedy; and yet they are impressively simple as those Galileans who were once called blessed.

Freud has prefixed to his 'Interpretation of Dreams' the citation 'Flectere si nequeo superos Acheronta movebo'– 'If I cannot bend the gods on high, I will at least set Acheron in uproar.' But to what purpose. "The gods whom we are to dethrone are the idolised values of our conscious world. It is well known that it was the love-scandals of the ancient deities, which contributed most to their discredit; and now history is repeating itself. People are laying bare the dubious foundations of our laudable virtues and incomparable ideals, and are calling out to us in triumph: There are your man made gods, mere snares and delusions tainted with human baseness– white sepulchres full of dead men's bones and of all uncleanness." We recognise a familiar strain, and the Gospel words, which we never could make our own, now come to life again." I am deeply convinced that these are not vague analogies. There are too many persons to whom Freudian psychology is dearer than the Gospels. And yet all these people are our brothers, and in each of us there is at least one voice which seconds them– for in the end there is a psychic life which embraces us all.

The unexpected result of this spiritual change is that an uglier face is put on the world. It becomes so ugly that no one can love it any longer– we cannot even love ourselves– and in the end there is nothing in the outer world to draw us away from the reality of the life within. Here no doubt, we have the true significance of this spiritual change. After all, what does Theosophy, with its doctrines of 'Karma' and reincarnation, seek to teach, except that this world of appearance is but a temporary health-resort for the morally imperfected? It depreciates the present day world no less radically than does the modern outlook, but with the help of a different technique; it does not vilify our world, but grants it only a relative meaning in that it promises other and higher worlds. The result is in either case the same.

The psychic depths are nature, and nature is creative life. It is true that nature tears down what she has herself built up– yet she builds it once again. Whatever values in the visible world are destroyed by modern relativism, the psyche will produce their equivalents. At first we cannot see beyond the path that leads downwards to dark and hateful things– but no light or beauty will ever come from the man who cannot bear this sight. Light is always born out of darkness, and the sun never yet stood still in heaven to satisfy man's longing or to still his fears. Does not the example of Anquetil du Perron show us how psychic life survives its own eclipse? China hardly believes that European science and technology are preparing her ruin. Why should we believe that we must be destroyed by the secret, spiritual influence of the East?

We have not yet clearly grasped the fact that whilst the Western cultures are turning the material world upside down, by means of our technological proficiency, the East has its own subtle ways of conquest by means of their psychic proficiency. We are only just realising that Western Theosophy is an amateurish imitation of the East. We are just taking up astrology again, and that to the Oriental is his daily bread. Our studies of sexual life, originating in Vienna and in England, are matched or surpassed by Hindu teachings on this subject. Oriental texts ten centuries old introduce us to philosophical relativism, while the idea of indetermination, newly broached in the West, furnishes the very basis of Chinese science. Richard Wilhelm has even shown me that certain complicated processes discovered by analytical psychology are recognisably described in ancient Chinese texts. Psychoanalysis itself and the lines of thought to which it gives rise– surely a distinctly Western development– are only a beginners attempt compared to what is an immemorial art in the East. It should be mentioned that the parallels between psychoanalysis and yoga have already been traced by Oskar A.R. Schmitz.

The Theosophists have an amusing idea that certain Mahatmas, seated somewhere in the Himalayas or Tibet, inspire or direct every mind in the world. So strong, in fact, can be the influence of the Eastern belief in magic upon Europeans of sound mind, that some of them have assured me what I am unwittingly inspired by the Mahatmas with every good thing I say, my own inspirations being of no account whatever. This myth of the Mahatmas, widely circulated and firmly believed in the West, far from being nonsense, is– like every myth– an important psychological truth. It seems to be quite true that the East is at the bottom of the spiritual change we are passing through today. Only the East is not a Tibetan monastery full of Mahatmas, but in a sense lies within us. It is from the depths of our own psychic life that new spiritual forms will arise; they will be expressions of psychic forces, which may help to subdue the boundless lust for prey of Aryan man. We shall perhaps come to know something of that circumscription of life which has grown in the East into a dubious quietism also something of that stability which human existence acquires when the claims of the spirit become as imperative as the necessities of social life. Yet in this age of Americanisation we are still far from anything of the sort, and it seems to me that we are only at the threshold of a new spiritual epoch. I do not wish to pass myself off as a prophet, but I cannot outline the spiritual problem of modern man without giving emphasis to the yearning for rest that arise in a period of unrest, or to the longing for security that is bred of insecurity. It is from need and distress that new forms of life take their rise, and not from mere wishes or from the requirements of our ideals.

To me, the crux of the spiritual problem of today is to be found in the fascination which psychic life exerts upon modern man. If we are pessimists, we shall call it a sign of decadence; if we are optimistically inclined we shall see in it the promise of far reaching spiritual change in the Western world. At all events, it is a significant manifestation. It is the more noteworthy because it shows itself in the broad sections of every people; and is the more important because it is a matter of those imponderable psychic forces which transform human life in ways that are unforeseen and– as history shows– unforeseeable. These are the forces still invisible to many persons today, which are at the bottom of the present 'psychological' interest. When the attractive power of psychic life is so strong that man is neither repelled nor dismayed by what he is sure to find, then it has nothing of sickliness or perversion about it.

Along the great highroads of the world everything seems desolate and outworn. Instinctively the modern man leaves the trodden ways to explore the by-paths and lanes, just as the man of the Graeco-Roman world cast off his defunct Olympian gods and turned to the mystery cults of Asia. The force within us impels us to search, turning outward, annexes Eastern Theosophy and magic; but it also turns inward and leads us to give our thoughtful attention to the unconscious psyche. It inspires in us the self same scepticism and relentlessness with which a Buddha swept aside his two million gods that he might come to the pristine experience which alone is convincing.

And now we must ask a final question. Is what I have said of the modern man really true, or is it perhaps the result of an optical illusion? There can be no doubt whatever that the facts I have cited are wholly irrelevant contingencies in the eyes of many millions of Westerners, and seem only regrettable errors to a large number of educated persons. But I may ask. What did a cultivated Roman think of Christianity when he saw it spreading among the people of the lowest classes? The biblical God is still a living person in the Western world– as living as Allah beyond the Mediterranean. One kind of believer holds the other an ignoble heretic, to be pitied and tolerated if he cannot be changed. What is more, a clever European is convinced that religion and such things are good enough for the masses and for women, but are of little weight compared to economic and political affairs.

So I am refuted all along the line, like a man who predicts a thunderstorm when there is not a cloud in the sky. Perhaps it is a storm beneath the horizon that he senses– and it may never reach us. But what is significant in psychic life is always below the horizon of consciousness, and when we speak of the spiritual problem of modern man we are dealing with things that are barely visible– with the most intimate and fragile things– with flowers that open only at night. In daylight everything is clear and tangible; but the night lasts as long as the day, and we live in the night-time also. There are persons who have had dreams, which even spoil their days for them. And the day's life is for many people such a bad dream that they long for the night when the spirit awakens. I even believe that there are nowadays a great many such people, and this is why I maintain that the spiritual problem of modern man is much as I have presented it. I must plead guilty, indeed to the charge of one-sidedness, for I have not mentioned the modern spirit of commitment to a practical material world about which everyone has much to say because it lies in such full view. We find it in the ideal of internationalism or super-nationalism which is embodied in the United Nations and the like; and we find it also in sport and, very expressively, in the cinema, films and in modern music.

These are certainly symptoms of our time; they show unmistakably how the ideal of humanism is made to embrace the body also. Sport represents an exceptional valuation of the human body, as does modern dancing. The cinema and television on the other hand, like the detective story, make it possible to experience without danger all the excitement, passion and desirousness which must be repressed in a humanitarian ordering of life. It is not difficult to see how these symptoms are connected with the psychic situation. The attractive power of the psyche brings about a new self-estimation– a re-estimation of the basic facts of human nature. We can hardly be surprised if this leads to the rediscovery of the body after its long depreciation in the name of the spirit. We are even tempted to speak of the body's revenge upon the spirit. When Keyserling sarcastically singles out the chauffeur as the culture-hero of our time, he has struck, as he often does, close to the mark. The body lays claim to equal recognition; like the psyche, it exerts a fascination. If we are still caught up by the old idea of an antithesis between mind and matter, the present state of affairs means an unbearable contradiction; it may even divide us against ourselves. But, if we can reconcile ourselves with the mysterious truth that spirit is the living body seen from within, and the body the outer manifestation of the living spirit– the two being really one– then we can understand why it is that the attempt to transcend the present level of consciousness must give its due to the body. We shall also see that belief in the body cannot tolerate an outlook that denies the body in the name of the spirit. These claims of physical and psychic life are so pressing compared with similar claims in the past, that we may be tempted to see in this a sign of decadence. Yet it may also signify rejuvenation, for as Holderlin says: 'Danger itself fosters the rescuing power'.

What we actually see is that the Western world strikes up a still more rapid tempo– the American tempo– the very opposite of 'quietism' and resigned aloofness. An enormous tension arises between the opposite poles of outer and inner life, between objective and subjective reality. Perhaps it is a final race between ageing Europe and young America; perhaps it is a desperate or a wholesome effort of conscious man to cheat the laws of nature of their hidden might and to wrest a yet greater, more heroic victory from the sleep of the nations. This is a question which history will answer." At this juncture Prof. Jung resumed his seat to a rapturous applause from all sides and particularly from his followers.

This was followed by speeches by several men and women who put forward their various opinions and suggestions as to what were the best ways to save planet Earth and its peoples. Then, as all meetings tend to do at times, things started to deteriorate and get off the point. The philosophers in particular were always good at this whenever they studied things in too much detail. For some reason the discussions wandered back to the subject of mind and matter and the world of opposites that had briefly been referred to by Prof. Jung. At one point one of the lesser known members seemed somewhat incensed and stood up. He was a rather rotund man with a red face and a broad smile.

"The subjects of mind and matter, spirit and substance," he said, heartily, "have always perplexed Man. He could never establish exactly what was the difference, or if, in fact, there was any difference at all. Sometimes he thought he had solved the puzzle by calling everything spirit, after which he would begin to think that perhaps spirit itself was a substance. The consequence of this train of thinking led him to conclude once more that everything must be substance and that spirit was but a lonely transient manifestation of matter. Having performed countless numbers of metaphorical headstands in an endeavour to see the problem from both ends, man realised the impossibility of producing the light of consciousness from inanimate matter and he swung back again to his original idea that all must be spirit, or was it mind? This strange alternating ailment continued down through the ages, like a chronic appendicitis. Man tied himself in all manner of weird philosophical contortions and intellectual knots for ages, swinging his arguments first to one side then to the other, like some uncontrollable pendulum that could never find the halfway mark.

Man, it seemed, had to believe in a reality that was either all 'mind' or all 'matter.' It was as though he was addicted to extremes and this was reflected in his other viewpoints. His views of 'good' and 'evil' were another case in point. Ever since Moses made his guide list for people to follow, man had classified behaviour into black and white valuations. You were either good or bad. There was no grey in between. Just one action could make a man a hero, a saint or sinner. One man was crowned and revered, whilst the other had his head chopped off. Countless other actions made during his life, good, bad or indifferent, made no difference. He was either good or evil."

The man with the smiling red face was about to continue, when several members of the meeting all shouted from different directions. One voice was heard to shout. "Who knows anything about mind or matter anyway? They're both only construed by our way of thinking." This was almost heretical talk to some of the members, who demanded that the perpetrator be immediately silenced or removed from the meeting.

Doctor Johnson immediately stood up, expanded his chest, like the proud peacock of a man he was. "Any fool knows what 'matter' is, you can see it, you can feel it and you can kick it," he shouted, as he took his boot to something on the ground. There was a sudden yelp as a dog ran from the hall and utter consternation for a moment swept the hall. After Dr Johnson's demonstration, most considered they knew what matter was, and several said they were confident in knowing also what mind was. One or two pointed to Descartes who they thought was a genius for thinking up the famous words, 'I think, therefore I am,' although they weren't quite sure about the implications of these words of wisdom.

Mr Berkley and his friends Mr Locke and Mr Hume were also an intriguing trio. They told everyone they had the answer. The trouble was that if Berkley was correct, nobody could possibly be informed of the fact, because he was quite emphatic that only *his* thoughts and ideas existed. "How can you possibly prove otherwise," he said. "Everyone thinks only their own thoughts and no one else's. How then can anyone ever know whether anything exists outside themselves?" Mr Hume was also confident that only *his* thoughts existed– they were the only ones he knew anything about. As for anyone else, they were only parts of his philosophical mind and, whether they liked it or not, it was only *his* mind that existed. This was most disconcerting to the other members in the hall who quite rightly considered they were entitled to their share of conscious awareness. It was generally thought that Mr Berkley and Mr Hume were being a bit greedy in not wanting to share some of it with them. Mr Berkley did his best to correct things by allocating his critics a portion of God's mind, just so that they could also have some thoughts and so that there would be something else besides Mr Berkley's own mind and thoughts. Some felt happy with this. Others did not. The notion seemed to satisfy Mr Berkley, although exactly how he knew that God's mind existed beyond his own thoughts and could extend outside his own thinking and become the minds of his critics was never made clear and never fully explained.

Mr Berkley was unable to see any matter for mind, and Dr Johnson was unable to see any mind for matter. Dr Johnson seemed prepared to go to extremes to prove his point. He got into the habit of kicking large stones just to prove there was some substance in them, which sometimes also proved a painful exercise. His character was such that he would have also liked to have stuffed a large piece of 'matter' up Mr Berkley's jumper just for good measure. The controversies between those who believed everything was matter and those who believed there was nothing else but mind raged on as different people in the hall stood up to voice their opinions. "If there was nothing else but matter how could it be thought about?" someone asked. "And how could thinking thoughts arise from inanimate matter?" It was all very mysterious. Could matter really think about matter? What was matter anyway? It all depended on one's definition.

"Neither the mind nor matter exponents seem to realise one very important fact," someone else said. "They were defining something that was ultimately unknowable. They were dressing this unknowable in their own limited concepts that defined it either as matter, which implied solidity and inanimacy, or as mind, which implied something more tenuous, conscious and living. However, might it be that the 'unknowable' could manifest both mind and matter characteristics, according to how people viewed the problem? Could it be that people's concepts and definitions had limited their viewpoints? Were mind and matter merely two sides of the same coin?"

At that point, someone from the sceptic's section stood up, looking rather frustrated with all that was being said. "From what has been discussed, he said, "it was quite obvious that Man could never agree on the answers to the most simple questions relating to the structure and content of his own mind and body nor give any sensible reasons why he should be thinking thoughts or kicking stones. What chance was there, therefore, of his ever finding an answer to, or agreeing on a solution to, the current problems facing mankind– problems that if left unresolved could result in the extinction of the human race?" These few comments seemed to finally bring the meeting back to order and some serious discussion ensued. Many distinguished persons voiced their opinions and suggestions at length. When it was time for Gotama to leave, there had been no final agreement as to the best remedies for curing mankind's maladies. Mr Time Bender said that the meeting would continue next day and continuously until a solution was found. In the meantime he suggested that Gotama should carry on with his inspection of other parts of Progress 13 and the results of the meeting would be conveyed to him later on in a very special way.

Gotama stood for a moment, uncertain which way to go. Several passages led away from the door of the hall where the meeting of the Time and Motion Engineer had been held. To the right was a corridor of about six feet in width, lined with numerous doors. To the left, a small corridor wound away round a corner, beyond which he could not see. A third passage branched out almost directly in front of him and led to a staircase, the top stairs of which were lost in the gloom. The smaller passage was marked with a pointer marked 'To Journeys End.' A similar type signpost in the wide corridor read 'To the Hall of Records.' The third signpost was marked with, 'To the Present and Future.' Not wishing to return to the cabins of the present or go on to the future just at that moment, Gotama decided to take the corridor to the Hall of Records. Judging from its general direction, it appeared that the passage led yet further back into the rear of the plane, which possibly represented a more primitive past.

Without further hesitation, Gotama set off, but within a short distance, was confronted by two more passages branching away to right and left. One was clearly marked, 'To the Hall of Records,' whilst the other was signposted 'To the Halls of Past Opinion.' Gotama noticed there was a heraldic design underneath the words, 'Halls of Past Opinion,' and he remembered seeing a similar design on the door of the Time and Motion Engineer's office and also on the door to the meeting hall. There was obviously some connection between the Hall of Past Opinion and the offices of Mr Time Bender. Was it perhaps that past human opinion fuelled the strange Time machine and directed Progress 13 into the future? Gotama remembered the vast scale of the conference between the thousands of members of the past groups of mankind who had been gathered together in an effort to find some remedy for the ills that had beset mankind. He remembered too how everyone at the meeting had put forward his or her own particular viewpoint. No one had reached any definite or proved conclusion. In fact, someone had remarked that no matter how much they conversed and debated, their conclusions were fixed and unalterable because they were placed forever in the past, which was irreversible and unchanging. It was only in the cabins of the present that a re-directive for the future could be made. This re-directive could be based on past experiences and would emerge from them, but need not be strictly determined by them as in a fixed cause and effect sequence.

Gotama ruminated. Perhaps there was still some room for subtle teleological directives to emerge from the deep potential future, or from the spontaneous free depths of life itself. Man may not be chained completely by past causes and effects. There was surely more to life than mechanical forces predetermined and rigidly jointed to the past. Spontaneity and freedom of choice, even though limited, could perhaps also have their place in the stream of events that formed man's consciousness and experience, through which he could transform the environment and plot his future destiny. Those tiny threads of 'free will' in man's nature were like precious threads of gold that could perhaps assist in redirecting his future despite his stupid past mistakes that now threatened his civilisation.

Gotama turned into the passage leading to the Hall of Records. It meandered for about five hundred metres, between countless wood panelled doors, before ending at a large panelled double door, above which was an imposing wood carved mantle. The carving was exquisite and was embossed with strange hieroglyphics which depicted long forgotten legends and myths. As Gotama approached, the doors swung open, as if moved by unseen hands. Beyond, there was another magnificent circular hall whose periphery was bounded by glistening pillars constructed from a crystalline substance, more splendid than marble, that reflected the light in scintillating points of colour. The floor was covered in the same luxurious substance polished to a mirror finish. The ceiling was a dome of coloured glass that poured down a radiance that lit everything, like the sun in an autumn forest when misty shafts of light pierce the golden foliage. Wondrous hues and textures blended in breathtaking shades that constantly merged and changed. Gotama was enthralled and dumbfounded.

The vast expanse of the hall was quite empty. The silence was a silence that could be felt. It penetrated the very depths of Gotama's being. Some living form was there, but it was quite indefinable. For a moment a pure spirit of loveliness engulfed him.

He stopped in the centre of the hall. Surveying the scene, he took a sharp intake of breath as a silver embossed door at the far end opened to reveal a rather grotesque bent and dwarf-like figure that ambled slowly towards him. He was the oldest man, or was it an ape? that Gotama had ever seen. The creature, with legs bowed and back hunched, limped almost pitifully up to Gotama. He slithered and turned to reveal a large ugly head encompassed by dark matted hair. The eyes had a limpid sorrowful look, like a St Bernard, whilst his lips were similar in their horrible slobbering appearance.

"May I introduce myself," the strange creature said, huskily. "My name is Angus Oort Cloud the Angel, a name given me because my aura of influence extends, like a halo, around the complete solar system. Moreover, it was from that halo of particles, circling the outer regions of the solar system that life first fell on to planet Earth as living dust, whilst some spumed in fountainous clouds from volcanic clefts deep in the oceans. I should mention, however, that I'm really only an apprentice angel at the moment, so don't expect too much of me, but I'm hoping for higher things in the future, when I'll be given my deluxe gold and white wings, together with a slinkier figure that everyone knows must be the shape of an angel. And that reminds me I must go on a diet in the next few centuries or so! My apprenticeship finishes when I've passed all my exams to make me angelic and I finally learn how to fly, which at the moment I'm not very good at, because my centre of gravity seems to be in the wrong place". As he said this, he pointed to his large rotund stomach that seemed to have certain pregnant possibilities. "Until then I've been given the special job of assistant librarian in the Halls of Records, where I'm known as the library's Liberace, because I play many records, some good, some bad, some sad, and because I personally like the sweet ones. Now, what can I do for you?" Angus Ooort Cloud the apprentice angel croaked.

Gotama was somewhat taken aback by the new entrant and by his grating voice that seemed to emanate from a larynx made of sandpaper. "I'm looking for the Hall of Records," he said.

"Then come this way, sir, if you will," came the reply, as the creature turned and hobbled towards one of the numerous ornamental doors. "Were there any particular records you wanted to see?" Angus mumbled.

"What sort of records do you keep here?" enquired Gotama, undecided how to answer the question.

Angus half looked up, as if surprised by the request. "Everything that has existed since the beginning of the world is stored here," Angus went on. "Every thought, sensation and action that has ever been, since the beginning of Time. You see, we have to keep track of everything, so that we know what to produce next. We have instructions from the Cosmic Administration that all creation must be continually new; nothing must be duplicated, everything must be unique. The designer in charge is a stickler for detail and some say he's a perfectionist, though he certainly hasn't been so in my case," Angus said with a sigh, as he referred to his humped and hairy body. "To some he may be a perfectionist, but he seems to slip up quite often with his supernovas, his cosmic collisions, extinctions and catastrophes. And a lot of his so called accidents of Nature seem to be happening all the time all over the place.

It's a big job here, looking around for new ideas, new places and faces, new combinations of elements and particles. We've managed so far by keeping strict records of everything and everyone who has passed through this plane of 3D space and time. We congratulate ourselves that there have never been two faces or two individuals or even two finger prints exactly alike, despite the billions and billions that have passed through the production line. We have to give the impression to Man that cause and effect exist, so that he can grope around his little universe and think he understands it. If we didn't provide Man with some idea of one thing following another, in a certain sequence, then he would be in a terrible mess. He'd never be able to move about, or think, or act in his world of sense impressions. Without his ideas of cause and effect, he wouldn't know whether he was on his arse or his elbow. However, we've done our job almost too well because he now thinks he can learn all the answers by just studying only each cause and effect. He assumes that everything is predetermined. But this is one of his greatest illusions. The Chinese knew something when they wrote I Ching. They realised that the other eternal creator was Chance.

We also have to make it look to humans as though past causes and effects become, in their turn, causes of the future. It all helps to give the impression of Time, the shell in which Man must live in order to feel he exists. This is why we have to record everything. Our records are kept in the depths of universal life itself, in all sorts of different dimensions outside the three dimensional realm. They are also contained in special mind images within what Man calls atomic structures. As you know, the more noticeable of Earth's physical memories are to be found in old fossils and rock strata. So far Man has found only a few, but his world is littered with them just waiting to be discovered. And he hasn't yet discovered the very special psychic fossil records embedded in things. Many structures and old buildings contain remnants of human experience in the forms of what you call ghosts. Your scientists will eventually discover that there are many psychic remnants also recorded everywhere in the physical world."

Angus Oort Cloud hesitated for a moment, as though in thought. A few silent seconds elapsed as they walked on. Then he said quietly, "If the universe didn't intuitively know what events were passing out of the Present and disappearing into the Past, it would be impossible for it to produce anything else based on what had just happened."

"It all sounds most complicated," retorted Gotama.

Angus reached a door, beautifully embossed with a sheet of gold, inscribed with sculptured images of all kinds of creatures. Some were half man and half animal. They were completely foreign to Gotama, who had never seen their like in any textbook on the evolution of species, or even in Hansard. The golden door swung open and there and there was a gush of hot air that was heavy with a pungent perfume, like entering the House of Lords. He followed Angus through the door. They entered a spacious cathedral-like area topped by disappearing domes and pinnacles. The place was so vast that as far as the eye could see, there was no limiting walls or buttresses to hold the huge ceilings in position. What kind of engineering science had been involved in its design was impossible to say. It was as though it existed in a world without gravity on a plane akin to that of a dream or a thought. The palatial arena was full of thin shafts of light that inter-crossed each other, like a fantastically complex spider's web of lasers. There must have been countless billions of light beams of varying spectrum colours that produced an overall picture of inter-crossing rainbows, all emanating from different directions. It was a network of pattern and colour that was beyond belief.

Little Asian girl giving a flower to Gotama at Hiroshima

See page 119

Bubbles — Gotama's guide to the cabins of the future

See page 135 et al

See page 309

Young Mankind is but a newborn child,
Tiny and a little wild,
Taking first steps towards the sky,
To countless stars and asking why?
He slowly reaches out in space
To touch the speckled stellar face
What will he finally live to find?
What avenues of human mind,
Will carve across the mists of Time?
What new worlds will then be known
When finally he's fully grown?

*Man is but a
Space/Time bubble
Wrought from a cosmic
ocean to experience
for a moment a miracle*

See page 309

Refugees

Inscribed on the baby's identity tag:

Nationality – Homo Sapien; ***Identity*** – War Victim/Abused; ***Name*** – Innocent; ***Number*** – Countless; ***Date*** – Since Dawn of Time;
Address – Earth; ***Cause*** – Blindness of Man; ***Result*** – Pain and Tears; ***Temporary Assistance*** – UN;
Remedy – ... (For Future World Government use only)

See page 310

page 310   *Little deaf girl learning to speak*
Many achieve worldly honours,
but the greatest achievements are usually unrecognised.

The drop is in the Ocean

the Ocean is in the drop

Nirvana and Samsara   and   Reflections

See Page 310   **Reflections**

**The Drop is in the Ocean,
The Ocean is in the Drop**

Old Angus Oort Cloud, the library's Liberace, pointed up into the rainbows. "Men use CDs and electronic equipment to record sound and vision," he said. "Here we use energy and light. With your current knowledge you won't be able to comprehend our methods, but within the vast inter-plays of energies and light spectrums are held the memories of all life's experiences; experiences that you usually consider have passed away forever into the past, or have disappeared into dust. In a sense, there's no death here, because all things, all human knowledge, all human opinion, all human deeds both for good, evil or neither, are all entered and recorded in our heavenly charts. They are recorded just as they happened with no alteration whatever."

Angus pointed to some textured rays of light in the topmost dome. "Up there," he said, "we record all the good and noble deeds of man, together with any of his ideals that are of value. As you see, it's a very small dome with nothing much doing. The very large jagged areas, where you can see those heavy dark greys and bands of pallid green light, they contain records of Man's inhumanity to Man, together with his failures, baser deeds and his suffering. True motives are all recorded. An outwardly good deed can sometimes be directed by an evil inner motive. In your external physical world you see only one side of the truth, often very distorted. Here we can see the truth in the truest perspective, having regard to Man's inner and outer nature, his thoughts as well as his actions, his desires and fulfilments within and without. Many great men and women were quite unknown to their fellows, because they were great on the inside, but didn't have the good fortune to display their greatness during their lifetime. In the inner world some were saints or fearless conquerors, whilst on the outside people saw an ordinary man or woman. Conversely, many men and women considered great by general posterity and public opinion were often rotten and corrupt within. You live in a dimension that falsifies facts by appearances. Here, there can be no falsification, because every aspect and every detail, inside and out and beyond, is known and recorded as it actually happened."

"Who uses such a vast library of the past?" Gotama enquired.

Angus Oort Cloud studied Gotama with penetrating eyes that shone for a moment with an angelic beauty and compassion, yet possessed something of suffering and the animal. There seemed about him to be a curious mixture of biochemical earthiness that was refined by an ethereal glow.

"The records are all part of the secret treasures of the Palaces of the Beyond," he said. "Many of their uses are heavily guarded secrets, which I know nothing about. What I do know is that these records of the past are in constant use for directing man's future. Just as gravity makes an apple fall to the ground, so each and every one of man's thoughts and actions has subsequent karmic effects. Every action has its reaction. It's a law of the universe. To strike against such a law would be quite ineffective. Man is the creator and the created. Every act of creation, whatever form it takes, also creates the form of the creator. Created and creator become as one. Man creates the thought and the thought creates the man. In his blindness, Man vents his spleen on another only to create further pain for himself. Like breeds like, good brings good, evil reaps evil, both for the recipient and for the perpetrator."

The strange humped creature was silent for a few moments. Then, as though remembering something, he began again. "We have an infinite number of record classifications, but by far the largest in the human category is that covering Man's suffering. His ego is the chief culprit responsible. It always wants to grasp and cling to things. This is Man's dilemma. Living in a world of continual change, whenever he clings to something or wants to keep something, it fades and disappears like water through his fingers and this upsets him. He also suffers when he thinks he can't get rid of something he doesn't like or doesn't want. He doesn't always realise that all things are changing, including his own thoughts, and that there are in fact no permanent things that can be possessed, nor is there a permanent 'ego' to grasp for. He is but a composite of changing facets, just as the world around him. But it's in his nature to grasp or have aversion to things. This is why these human sorrows form the largest part of our library of past experiences. It could almost be labelled the library of past suffering.

As you will observe from the few bright rays in the small dome above us, the records of humans who have found the ultimate knowledge and enlightenment have been exceedingly rare. The Buddha and Jesus were outstanding examples that revealed something of the truth to mankind. There have been others of course, but only a relative few have ever been able to penetrate ego's veils of ignorance, grasping and hate, in order to experience the joy of Nirvana, the unconditioned. Only a few have managed to realise that the ego or self has no individual permanence in itself and has actually been created by their own thinking since birth. It's therefore not separate from everything else. When people realise that they are bonded inseparably in the universe around them, as though in a seamless coat, they can begin to glimpse that they are in a special sense 'it'. They can then become almost like an eye of the universe looking at itself."

Angus Oort Cloud beckoned Gotama to follow him, and they moved towards a glass door that in some mysterious way had just come into view, almost as if it weren't there before they had looked towards it.

"This is a section of the Records Hall that is kept apart as it contains some special secrets. Come, I will show you something that will confound you," the little bent creature said, smiling curiously. They then passed through the glass door, whereupon Gotama was momentarily alarmed to discover that he was standing, not on a firm floor, but on a cushion of white cloud, the tops of which blew about his knees. There was absolutely no end to the distance he could see. It was as though there was no horizon and as if space itself bent away to nothingness as he looked outwards. He experienced a sudden feeling of giddiness and almost fell. Something supported his arm, but it wasn't the creature, who had somehow disappeared from view. Around him there was an impression of a blue sky of utter emptiness, yet of huge immensity. Not even a star, sun or moon shone in the heavens, yet the sky was light; so light that everything was misted into transparency. It was almost like a medieval image of heaven except that there were no harps, no angels and no golden gates. There was instead a complete nothingness, yet which was somehow more substantial than materiality. He was suddenly aware of an all consuming joy and freedom; an awareness of being aware, no more, no less. It was awareness of awareness, where self had dissolved into this pristine emptiness, so that there was no-thing anywhere, or in him. He was neither moving, nor yet was he still. Neither seemed appropriate to his condition just at the moment. There was a sensation, yet not a sensation; of 'being,' but without the usual accompaniment of conditioned thought, ideas and words that usually provided meaning to experience. Both the faculties of reason and memory had stopped and were in some mysterious way asleep or were but a part of a dream from which Gotama had just awakened. A hand gripped his, but he could see naught. His own hand too was only felt, not seen.

It was then that he became aware of a shining silver mirror that had risen by some magic from the mist below. In its white and gold ornamented frame it stood before him as a thing of exquisite beauty that induced in him a gasp of astonishment. The blue haze of the mist billowed in thin wisps across the mirror's face making Gotama uncertain whether it was in fact a mirror or just his imagination. As he concentrated in order to see more clearly, he had a vision of a globe reflected deep in the mirror's heart. He was sure it was the Earth, an image of course, but definitely the Earth.

Something within him made him move. The tenuous curtain of mist parted like strange ectoplasm. With increased concentration, he peered into the flat surface that seemed in some mysterious way to be without surface, without breadth, without length. It was curiously non-dimensional; a vacuum in a vacuum, an empty shell without circumference, yet with a mirror-like quality he could not explain. He wasn't sure whether there was an elaborate gold embossing at the edges or whether he himself had created the limitation from the hazy configuration of misty forms.

Suddenly, quite without warning, and as unexpectedly as the glass door itself and the mirror had appeared, another strange event occurred. In a split second, as he peered at the mirror, an elongation and a bending of the depths resulted in a three-dimensional scene arising and he was confronted by a panoramic view of mountains, hills, rushing waters and broad lakes shimmering in a brilliant light. Water bubbled; sunlight streaked on mountain tops, breezes murmured, sheep moved slowly over the hillsides and grasses swayed. Everything seemed to abound in a spontaneous joy of which Gotama felt part.

If you've ever studied mirrors reflecting into other mirrors, you'll know how the images recede into an infinite distance and into an infinite number of forms. Gotama experienced a similar sensation at that moment, as all his inner past experiences, sensations and thoughts became interwoven in the mirror images. In a sudden flash of understanding, he realised he was an integral part of the world that was being created, just as the outside world was in fact part of him. In the strange conjoining of mind and reflections an objective world had emerged, where there was an inside, outside, three dimensions of solidity and a viewer.

Gotama became aware of a hazy indistinct droning noise, which gradually became a staccato of sounds. He realised the sounds were syllables of meaning that grew into words, the words into sentences and he understood their codes and references. The understanding was in the words, but also in him. The communication was between two separate intelligences, both of which were from the same kiln of creation, the same life, the same nature. And deep down both stemmed from the same subjective ground. The words were his and yet they came from beyond him. He listened. The voice grew in volume as a blurred form of a man materialised from out of the depths of the misty screen in front of him. The figure moved closer. The scene was still too hazy and indistinct for Gotama to distinguish the individual's features. All he could see was a man draped in soft flowing robes, or was it just the mist that blended strangely with the surrounding haze which had now changed to a purple blue.

"Have no fear," a voice said as the figure moved closer. "We are all of the same family and live in parts of each other. No man is an island. We all participate in each other's thoughts, which are not exclusively theirs or ours. I come to cause you no harm, but rather to tell you of some forgotten secrets."

Gotama stood incredulous as the man approached. He had a pair of bright compassionate eyes and a dark wispy beard which was partly obscured by a hood draping into the folds of his cloak, which in turn blended into a halo of clouds, so that there were no definite edges anywhere to be seen.

"I am Primadharma, welcome to Man's pristine past," the voice whispered, like a breeze rustling through trees. A forgotten past." There was a brooding silence for perhaps a minute whilst the figure slowly lifted his right arm and, sweeping it in a circular path, indicated the unending horizon beyond. "All men and women came from this," he continued. "It remains forever within their deepest self, but has long since been forgotten by almost everyone. You have just discovered in the mirror of yourself how we are all part creators of all that we experience in both the inside and the outside worlds. Man's sciences are only just beginning to understand that man himself creates the world of opposites, the realm of meaning and reason in addition to things like colour, sound, smell and touch, which are constructed out of mere waves of energy that in themselves possess none of these characteristics. They only become colour, sound, smell and touch when they are interpreted and converted by the human mind. To obtain real understanding of both yourself and the universe, therefore, you must first know that no man is ever separate from the rest of creation. Everyone is merged in all creation, and all creation is merged in everyone. Whenever people experience the outside world, they also experience themselves. They see through and at their inner being, just as much as they see through and at the outer environment. The subjective sees the objective, but the objective reflects and is merged into the subjective, so that there is no sharp distinction between the two. It is creation seeing and experiencing itself through individuals that are separated from the rest of the world by their own special way of thinking. Everything that man sees external to himself is a manifestation of that one creative energy, that one spirit that is also within him.

You have just witnessed the primordial awareness of awareness, where consciousness is aware only of itself in its unconditioned state of 'oneness,' yet beyond even of 'oneness.' This was once man's original form, at one with the unborn, the universal potential, and the universal spirit. This was, and still is, the deep ground of his nature. There's no space or time in it. It's outside all that, yet paradoxically it's also within them. The personal identification as self, is merely the result of the temporary mind clothing primordial nirvana with the temporary raiment of time, space and extension.

People mature and grow by continuously transcending themselves and growing above that which went before. As they progress, they discover, with each step that transcends the previous, there is a transcendent element in themselves, which, by definition, they can never quite reach. People are transcendent beings as well as imminent in their objective sensory world. They are both that which 'goes beyond' and also that which 'lives within. That which transcends is beyond created things of the objective world. It is this subtle dimension in man that inspires the need to 'go beyond' and to answer the challenge of both the outside environment and his own inner self. It is this that creates the instinctive tendency of life to evolve, to struggle, to advance and to recapture something of the bliss that is 'forever beyond' the objective.

It is this that gives the deepest impulse to man to progress beyond his limited Present. Life and man emerged from the transcendent 'unborn' in the remote past and it is this transcendent that still inspires the future course of events, accompanied by evolutionary pressures. The Progress 13 plane, therefore, possesses teleological impulse motors that take their power from the 'beyond' as well as from physical evolutionary, natural selection processes. There is an eternal impulse beyond man that effects the direction and destiny of mankind, the world and the universe. Man can use this transcendental inspiration for his own good, if he wishes, or he can ignore it and lose something of great value."

Primadharma stood silent. He surveyed Gotama intently, as if wondering whether he had understood his words. His eyes sparkled with a mixture of laughter and compassion. There was an expression of mellow kindness difficult to describe. A strange golden glow shone about his head, as though he himself projected something of the sun's radiance from his own being. The folds of his robes sparkled as though inset with stars that glinted like diamonds. Gotama noticed they were similar to the stars shining in the crown he wore, or was it a crown of thorns reflecting the sun? The man approached more closely and spoke again.

"You have witnessed one of our records from the remote past," he said quietly. "You have been shown how man passed out of the embryo of eternal timelessness into the world of Time. He now lives within a kind of shell created by his seeing, hearing, feeling, smelling, tasting and his intelligence. These are also like tiny sensory waves on the surface of the great cosmic ocean of transcendent being. Each wave rises and falls for but a moment. Each is a thought or a sensation. Groups of them make an individual person. Just as waves on an ocean rise and disappear back into the ocean from which they come, so also do thoughts, sensations and people. The Hindus for thousands of years have called this infinite transcendent ocean the 'Self' of the universe, or Brahman. The self of man, the Atman, although temporarily separate from Brahman was considered essentially of the same nature, just as the wave on the surface of the ocean can be considered as separate from it, but of the same fundamental nature as the ocean beneath. The Buddhists have similarly called this unconditioned 'Nirvana' which is likened to the unborn. Christians have given it the name of 'spirit.' All these definitions are mere words; mere verbal noises that struggle to describe something that is always beyond and out of reach of limited concepts. It is almost like the chimpanzee in the jungle whose sounds of communication might be compared with the works of Shakespeare. There is an effort to communicate an instinctive knowledge, yet it falls far short of the mark."

At this point Primadharma stopped speaking and smiled sadly. With a brief nod and wave of his hand he bid Gotama adieu. He then quite magically disappeared in the billowing clouds, as the folds of his bright robes slowly merged and became themselves mere flowing clouds that shifted for a moment as if they were living entities and finally dispersed and dissolved. In a few seconds the figure had quite disappeared from view.

At that moment too, Gotama became aware of the golden door through which he had entered this strange place. In a trice he had opened it and passed through. However, a further surprise awaited him. He discovered that it was not the hall he had left, but a rugged cave full of giant lichens clinging to wet rocks. A stream trickled noisily. There was a grotesque groaning noise that seemed to emanate from the other end of the cave. Gotama was quite alarmed at the sudden turn of events. The incoherent moaning grew in volume. Cautiously Gotama stepped over wet rocks and slime and made his way towards the sounds. The dimness of the light made progress difficult, but, at last, the rocks became more widely separated, which made movement easier. Water splashed and churned around him. At one moment it would rush forward only to slowly recede and then repeat the process. The cave was, no doubt, on the edge of the sea and the waves somewhere outside were causing the water's reciprocating movements. The smell of ozone and the presence of considerable quantities of seaweed also confirmed this. Sand crunched beneath his feet. A faint trickle of water became noticeable in his right shoe producing a cold point on the ball of his foot.

He had almost decided to turn back when he saw a slight movement in the semi-darkness only a few paces away. Drawing closer, the phenomena that met his gaze froze him momentarily to the spot. From a dark pool in the rocks there emerged a teeming horde of minute creatures, half swimming, half groping on rudimentary arms and legs. Many thousands fell back into the water, failing to obtain proper hold on the slippery rocks. Others managed to slither awkwardly, writhing and tumbling over each other, each struggling to survive on the slippery slopes. Gotama instinctively knew that he was witnessing the emergence of some primitive amphibians; a remote record perhaps of an early pristine life form that was reaching out to transcend its life in the sea, to begin a new life on land with more diverse opportunities. The old man's lecture on the efforts of life to transcend its past came back into Gotama's mind as he watched, apparently unseen by those instinctive creatures that were unconscious and quite ignorant of the important steps they were taking and where they would finally lead. There was something of mankind in them in latent form. It was a strange and painful birth. It was a dawning of a new day in the history of planet Earth. What hidden forces made them struggle to lift themselves from the ocean's depths to participate in an emigration into the unknown? Was it the result of a pure randomness of mutating genes? Or was there some unseen teleological purpose involved and entwined like a golden thread in a miraculously designed garment? Whatever the cause, such a struggle was strange and wonderful.

Gotama noticed that only the fittest and most adaptable to the slippery slopes survived the terrible ordeal of transplantation from the watery depths to the earthy home. Only the best of each generation would leave its mark somewhere in the hidden recesses of the genes, chromosomes and DNA of the fragile creatures. It would be their characteristics that would be passed to future generations, together with those of the new mutants that possessed improved adaptability to the new conditions. Yet, why such fantastic extravagance and violent struggle? Why such a waste of life and energy just so that a relative few could survive the cosmic experiment? The transfer from water to land was an invasion with tremendous losses that reflected the brilliant yet cruel extravagance of Mother Nature in almost all her conquests of the environment. The fate and temporary success of the few had always been accompanied by the tragic pain and miserable failure of the majority.

He could see the utter futility of it all, but paradoxically he could also see in the example of the amphibian's struggle, the hidden potential for future evolution and advancement. He remembered with bitterness another invasion when human struck at human on the beaches of France. D-day it was called. There was a vague similarity in the extravagance and sheer waste of life, so familiar in nature and so prevalent in man's own patterns of behaviour. Man was a resilient ape, however, and could act the fool even in such tragic circumstances. He remembered the story of the soldier striding along the beaches surrounded on all sides by gunfire, who shouted in a despairing voice to a nearby cockney solder, "They've sent me here to die!" The cockney looked up, smiled and said, "You're lucky mate, they sent me here yesterdie!"

Gotama wondered whether there was anything more to the evolution of species than Darwinian chance and natural selection. On the face of it, chance and randomness seemed to be the 'guvners', as the cockney would have probably said. The evidence for Darwinian evolution seemed irrefutable. But it was difficult to establish just how big a part pure chance took in the total scheme of things. Did its laws hold sway over all phenomena and behaviour? Or could there be other deeper impulses that took part? Impulses generated perhaps from a different dimension like a 'beyond' as indicated by the old man in the cloak? Could there be other forces that pulled life upward by its bootstraps? Whatever or whoever was behind cosmic and planetary evolution left no one in doubt that they were hard taskmasters. The vast stretches of evolution on Earth were paved with bloody battles, pain and death on the one hand and magnificent achievements and superb adaptability to circumstances on the other. To some persons, all things appeared 'bright and beautiful' or 'wise and wonderful', but such views were fit only for children who couldn't or wouldn't look at the realities of the world.

As Gotama pondered, the swarming hordes of fish-like amphibians began to spread in a vast black mat across the surrounding rocks. One or two, larger, stronger and more aggressive than the rest led the advance. In them was the incipient potential of a Napoleon and a Caesar and somewhere in that morass was an incipient Beethoven, a Leonardo, a nuclear scientist and an astronaut, although very much diluted like beer in a bad shandy. By some mysterious process, the natural life rhythms seemed to gradually speed up before his eyes as Gotama observed diversifications of the amphibians into many varieties from which sprouted strange new species. Each possessed its own distinct advantage in the wars of survival that followed. Some of the advantages that at first seemed almost a divine inspiration resulted finally in their extinction and disqualification from the race. Was it due to some divine design department blunder, or was inequality of opportunity a fixed law of the universe? Suffice it to say that the blunders, if indeed they were blunders, were in countless numbers, resulting in the trampling into extinction of innumerable species all of which did their best to survive with the protective equipment they had been provided with. If they weren't blunders then there was no justice, no mercy, no reason and no logic in the natural laws of the universe. If it was just a struggle of species against species, creature against creature, it might, with a vast stretch of the imagination, be conceived as a poor imitation of a fair contest of ingenuity's abilities. However, it was also a fight against the tremendous forces unleashed by the Earth herself, in the form of environmental cataclysms, volcanic disasters, earthquakes, hurricanes and tornadoes, ice ages and many other abuses thrown in for good measure. She was indeed a Mother Nature of many moods, as many bad as good. It was little more than a fight between lots of tiny Davids against huge numbers of Goliaths. The giants of natural law seemed bent on little else than the destruction of all life and man, if they didn't feel quite up to par, or didn't feel like keeping up with the race. Such unequal contests have been the rule rather than the exception during periods of millions of millions of years. Nature could perhaps be forgiven for one or two mistakes, one or two errors, one or two evil deeds, but could she be forgiven when they ran into millions and millions?

Gotama watched and ruminated. Where was the good, the Saviour God all this time? Twiddling his or her fingers, or just watching, or even worse just ignoring? The end does not always justify the means and Gotama conjectured whether the end result of the evolution of species, the arising of man, had really been worth the pain, the bloodshed, the terrible injustices of the unending struggle. Was it really worth millions of years of atrocities just to produce a life form whose main aspiration was Saturday football, sex and television? Admittedly, a few people thought more seriously, but not by much. None of our thoughts and actions seemed of much cosmic importance however seriously we thought about things. And most people couldn't help being steeped in conditioned habits of their society and to being slaves to convention.

Gotama turned away from the unsavoury sight of the primitive past that in some mysterious way had been shown to him. He must now find his way back out of this Alice in Wonderland world, to the central cabins of Progress 13. It all seemed rather a nightmare experience. But he was himself becoming conditioned and adapted to the weird happenings aboard the plane. It should have been called the plane of symbols, Gotama mused, as he thought of Mr Time Bender, the navigational computers and his other extraordinary experiences. He made a hasty retreat from the murky interior of the cave where he found himself on the extremity of a wide beach of golden sand, at the far edge of which rolled huge waves their white crests crashing one after the other in a thunderous anthem. Just like men making their debut into the world, he commented to himself. They rise out of the infinite sea, become individual waves that crash and make a foaming fuss for a brief moment, then subside to make way for others following, who, in their turn, make an egocentric splash, a splash whose only soul is brevity.

There was a fresh breeze blowing through his hair as he made his way along the beach, which was quite empty. A feeling of utter loneliness swept over him as though he was the first person ever to enter its spacious precincts. It was a wide beach and in the distance he could see some enormous sand dunes interspersed with tufts of thick grass. Farther back, the dunes merged into a rolling hillside dotted here and there by dark edged trees. The whole place was one of luxuriant beauty. Gotama stood for a few moments surveying the scene that was such a contrast to the interior of the cave. Just at that moment he became aware of a deep rumbling noise like the pounding of innumerable feet behind him. Looking round, he was startled to see more than a hundred creatures that looked like natives running towards him. All were attired in loincloths and feathers. Their faces were painted in extraordinary colours and each brandished a nasty looking object like a spear. Taken aback by the unexpected sight, Gotama could neither flee nor proffer any immediate resistance. He merely stood rooted to the spot, quite transfixed, whilst entertaining the vague hope that they were either friendly or out for their afternoon constitutional.

It was indeed obvious from subsequent events that his hopes were not to be realised because he found himself being dragged away like a heap of old rubbish by at least fifty hands, each as strong as iron. He would have resisted or claimed his rights under the Geneva Convention, but couldn't for two very good reasons. One was the fact that the creatures were obviously unfamiliar with the Geneva Convention, the second was the fact that one of the creatures had his great black furry hand spread over Gotama's mouth, which not only stifled any exclamations, but also nearly stifled the life out of him.

As far as any codes of honour were concerned, it was obvious that they hadn't heard of things like nuclear bombs or nerve gas and couldn't therefore be classed as civilised. Without more ado, the creatures marched their captive up the hillside until they arrived at a straggly clearing amongst some trees. Dotted around were several tree dwellings, each one a peculiar structure of wooden branches seeds and grasses. Gotama was pushed roughly up a short wooden ladder into one of the lower tree houses. The interior was dark and had a revolting aroma like a British Railway lavatory. It had probably been used for sheep and animals and was similar in this sense too. Strewn on the uneven floor was a scanty layer of straw. The walls comprised branches interwoven with twigs. Shafts of light penetrated and intercrossed from the gaps between. The roof of straw possessed fewer gaps, but gave the impression that the habitat had been constructed after the style of a bird's nest. Not exactly the Empire State Building thought Gotama, although there were similarities. The creatures were all babbling at once, quite incoherently, like Parliament in session. This would perhaps be unfair to the creatures, however, who did show a little more harmony and purpose and were not quite so pompous and childish. They turned Gotama round and round so that they could survey him from every angle. Nervous fingers touched him to establish if he was real. Some pulled at his hair. Others touched his wristwatch with a frightened curiosity. Finally, after examining his hair, his spectacles, his clothes and shoes in very close detail, the creatures left. But not before one of them smashed his fist into Gotama's stomach, felling him like an ox, as he politely made it known that he was to remain in residence.

He lay gasping for breath as the creatures battened the door. He had never before set eyes on such bewilderingly powerful natives, if natives they were. They appeared more like gorillas, yet they possessed distinctly human characteristics and the punch in the stomach was reminiscent of his old school days. Could they be perhaps one of the pristine creatures that had branched off from an earlier animal into the first line of human evolution? They weren't tall, but were stocky and thick in more ways than one, once again just like the politicians back at home. And their huge grotesque feet had toes as long as fingers and as robust as a bunch of bananas. Added to the banality, they were all covered with a profuse layer of matted hair. Gotama thought he had seen some of them recently at a pop concert and had danced with one or two at a club. Dark flashing eyes were set beneath ridged eyebrows and low swept back foreheads. Huge jaws jutted out beyond gruesome faces, which exposed giant teeth that flashed and sneered like an advertisement for modern toothpaste and Mars bars.

As the last of the creatures left, Gotama could hear a wicker door flap being fastened securely from the outside. All became quiet, but for the shrill shrieking of a bird nearby and the branches of a tree scraping together in the breeze. The general design of the tiny prison together with the draughts reminded Gotama of the typical English Council house, except for the wicker flaps, which fitted rather more efficiently. It was obvious that the designers of both had something in common. They were probably both part timers who should have stuck to their day job. The seating arrangements were not exactly Parker Knoll, but were an improvement on most underground tube trains, though no less dismal. Judging from the general lurching of the dwelling from side to side, it appeared to be constructed on similar lines to many contemporary high rise flats, which could become frightening when the wind blew. The first Gerry who built a house must have taken this as his example, thought Gotama.

He wondered what was happening outside. No doubt, the brutal looking creatures were communicating their find to the chief, their own special trade union leaders. He shuddered at the thought and sincerely hoped that the chief would instead be a creature of tolerance and understanding. If the tribal chief showed as much compassion as his counterpart had shown to old people during an electricity workers strike, he couldn't hope for a modicum of mercy. It was a long shot and like clutching to a straw, but Gotama clung desperately to the hope that the chief would show just a glimmer of humanity. After all they both had something in common; they both came from a jungle, one of which was full of trees whilst the other was full of concrete.

At that moment, Gotama's thoughts were interrupted by the sound of tribal drums that sounded strangely familiar. They definitely weren't smooth classics at seven, but they might have been in the top ten. As he listened, his surroundings shook with the sounds of chanting, like a Stravinsky going berserk. It sent shivers down his spine and didn't do anything special for his eardrums. The drums increased in volume and, not being a teenager, and not seeing the sense in using a deaf aid in later life, Gotama lay on his back and covered his ears. The chanting and violent drumming continued for at least an hour, after which the sonorous chorus developed into something more religious, accompanied by a chuckling tenor voice like Harry Secombe with a few raspberries thrown in for good measure. These creatures were obviously more civilised than he first thought.

However, he had learned during his life that the over sophistication of the civilised frequently bred its own kind of dogmatism and intolerance. He would therefore have to be on his guard. Gotama suddenly shocked himself by entertaining the diabolical thought that there could be a large pot of boiling water awaiting him. Most fairy tales about savages always included the boiling pot into which captured victims were immersed for cooking into some fine cannibal delicacy. Could the creatures be cannibals, he wondered? Cannibalism revolted him almost as much as stag hunting, horse and dog meat trading and the multiplicity of chicken and pig factories. Some of his contemporaries were little better than cannibals, and if you rated their compassion for fellow creatures between zero and ten, they would hardly get off the zero mark. Gotama's thoughts swung back to his immediate surroundings. Despite the derelict condition of his wooden prison, there seemed no way to escape. He tugged at several young saplings in the wall, but they resisted all his efforts to remove them. In so doing he noticed the place was swarming with insects. What a shambles of a place, he mused. He sat back exhausted from his efforts.

For some reason he began considering how this style of dwelling would be sold on the open market back home. It would be just the type of challenge in which modern estate agents revelled. They would probably sell the place in a couple of weeks for thousands of pounds. He tried to imagine the remarkable vocabulary that a talented estate agent would use. Ranch type dwelling of 'higher than usual' quality with air conditioning throughout (especially when the wind blows in the right direction) and with a perfect southerly aspect. Complete with balcony and panoramic views. Gotama almost managed to smile as he considered some of the other persuasive techniques. One could never purchase a small, mediocre or decrepit house that was falling down. If it was on the style of some derelict Roman ruin, it was just in need of some repair or a spot of paint. If there was room only for one chair and a TV in the lounge, it was never mentioned that you couldn't swing a cat round in the place. It was always defined as cosy or compact and low on fuel bills. If there was no plumbing and the house was in ruin and as old as the hills, it was said to be a gentleman's residence of charm and considerable character with antiquities of historical value. If there were a couple of half-dead trees in the garden, it would be 'lightly wooded.' If there were nothing but concrete slabs in a back yard of about four by ten, it would be termed 'modern design for easy maintenance.'

At that moment there was a sound of movement outside the wicker door. Seconds later a hairy creature stood silhouetted in the entrance. A few moments more and Gotama was being hustled briskly out of the tree dwelling down the wooden steps and across the open thicket. Two heavily built creatures joined the entourage pulling at each arm as though playing a concertina as Gotama croaked a painful accompaniment. At the far end of the clearing sat a solitary dark skinned creature somewhat less endowed with hair, but possessing a greying beard that almost covered his chest. From beneath the grey whiskers the lower edges of a brightly ornamented necklace adorned with dangling charms could just be seen. Similar ornamented bracelets embellished his wrists and ankles, whilst on his head was something that sent shock waves through Gotama's body. It appeared to be the skull of a large animal, the yawing mouth and polished ivory bone looking vaguely humanoid in character. Gotama was thrust forward in front of the seated figure. As he stood, somewhat apprehensive, several other members of the tribe appeared from a nearby dwelling and took up positions in a semi-circle around the old creature. Each wore strange trinkets in varied colours. Some wore nothing but their birthday suit, whilst others had one shoulder draped with a patchwork robe. Some had similar robes draped across their chests or around their waists. Others were girdled around the waist with a rough belt of leathery appearance.

A soft rhythmic drumbeat became the foretaste of some kind of ceremonial discourse, accompanied by a dance between members of the group whose method of communication was utterly strange. It comprised the use of a very limited number of grunts and groans together with weird hand signals, not unlike those of the modern motorist when suffering from road rage. It was obvious that their range of vocabulary was limited and had to be supplemented by hand gestures and in this respect they were little different from the modern politician. As the drumming progressed into new emotive rhythms, the creatures moved in accompaniment like a field of wheat swaying in the wind. Gradually the swaying motion evolved into more strenuous movements involving body, legs, arms and feet in one of the most outstanding gymnastic displays Gotama had ever set eyes upon. It was wasn't quite up to Swan Lake, although it undoubtedly involved a series of ballet movements that would have done the average person a severe mischief and would have left them grovelling around with hernias for months. Heads were turned through at least two hundred and forty degrees and backs bent in double-jointed configurations. Not only this, but also many of the dancers extended their performance to the trees where they swung from branch to branch like well-practised baboons.

The dance proceeded. The creatures, seemingly neither men nor beasts, encircled the small central group and moved slowly round in one great circle of leaping figures. All seemed in a daze as though hypnotised. They leaped high in the air half-ecstatic, half-wild. It was like Auld Lang Syne at an old boy's ceremonial party at the Dorchester, but less hypocritical. Such was the frightful sight that confronted Gotama. He watched with increasing anxiety as a terrifying expression of dogmatic intolerance built up almost to that of a traffic warden in the rush hour. It was as though the American Indian war dances and the Western disco dancing had been improved upon, which normally would have been a godsend, but was at that moment no cause for relief. All at once the dance and drumming ceased with such an abruptness that the ensuing silence shocked Gotama more than the loud music. He was gripped by several hands of steel and forced to the ground, whereupon he was laid on his back as his arms and legs were stretched out and tied securely to four small trees that seemed to be growing in a very convenient position for the purpose.

All he could see was the fierce light from the sun merged hazily with the silhouettes of faces peering down at him as the creatures completed their special brand of reef knots. The babble of excited voices and childlike cackles was mixed with gruff insolent expressions, venomous taunts and vitriolic gestures, which made Gotama believe that the participants must be human after all. The heat was quite unbearable, like an American centrally heated office but without the cold water vending machine. Gotama suddenly wished he had never decided to investigate the cabins of Progress 13. Such incredible and unexpected incidents seemed, not only unaccountable, but had now become positively terrifying. How had he become involved in such ghastly sequences of events? It was almost as bad as being born in a world threatened with nuclear catastrophe, social violence, football and Emmerdale. The innocent bystander was involved in it all whether he liked it or not. And the innocent bystander was tied hand and foot, like a prisoner, just as he was at that moment. It was beyond belief that he should have been cast into such a predicament, when it seemed only a short time ago that he was seated comfortably in the plane's cabin accompanied by civilised passengers and Mr Bureaucrumb.

His wrists had been tied so tightly that Gotama felt sure the blood to his hands had been cut off. In the struggle, his shirt had been ripped almost completely from his body and was now in the state shirts usually are when returned from the laundry. The sun began to scorch his lips, like American coffee, but his heart was cold like soup from an English café. It would not be long before he would be thoroughly sun-roasted like a peanut. After the creatures had almost exhausted themselves in their wild dancing, they withdrew to their respective dwellings to leave Gotama to the mercies of the old creature seated silently at the far end of the clearing. The old creature rose and walked round Gotama twice before standing at his feet and surveying his face. There was an evil glint in the old creature's eyes without any incipient compassion. He could have passed easily for a businessman or someone in the money markets. Yet the dogmatic stolid look reminded him of a shop steward about to embark on strike action. He began to have second thoughts however when it proceeded to give vent to the most extraordinary phraseology that was like modern high tech. abbreviated symbolism. It was just a 'staccato' of sound that meant nothing unless you were a computer. The creature then jabbed a kind of stick severely into Gotama's ribs accompanying the gesture with incoherent mutterings. The similarity of gesture to that of members of the modern medical profession led Gotama to believe that here was either an experienced medicine man or a hospital matron. The stick jabbing procedure was followed by a dance and a subsequent flag waving with a chorus of serious swearing that sounded like a protest meeting. Weird incantations and babbling went on for an interminable time until finally several other hairy creatures emerged from their tree houses and joined the regimental dance. They all seemed hypnotised by the rigidity of their rituals, which they had obviously performed thoughtlessly hundreds of time before. Gotama decided such rituals would be the envy of churchgoers back home and might even improve their standardised liturgy.

The heat was now getting to him and his thoughts started to wander. Man's attitudes had changed little since the days of the savage. In fact, the savage was in many ways less hypercritical, more spontaneous and free. He was closer to nature and reacted like the mountain spring, a spontaneous out flowing of natural energy. He was part of nature's seamless coat, bonded with it, not separated by some prefabricated world of technology and concrete. The savage was living nature. There seemed little doubt of this as, just at that moment, the old creature completed a series of double somersaults with considerable dexterity, rather after the style of the British government trying to get the economy right. You couldn't see exactly what position he was at any given moment, but, for the most part, he was quite upside down and never appeared the right way up for more than a fraction of a second. At last, the second series of dances ended with a chorus of abuse and spitting. Nouse trying to provide these people with modern amenities like buses, Gotama thought. Though they'd be in their element around Soho, or Mayfair.

As the drums stopped, the old creature came forward and gave Gotama such a sickening blow in the stomach that he felt as if he'd just finished a take away. Writhing in agony as a result of the low blow, he imagined he was back again with relatives, friends and neighbours. He thought of the civilised rat race where people were always being hit metaphorically below the belt. The methods of the savage applied equally to the modern age, despite the thin veneer of polished conduct. Slavery to the ego's greedy demands applied here in the company of these creatures and equally to civilised limited companies., and the many people in them.

The dark ebony faced creature lifted a golden spear high above his head. With a feverish look of someone on their third dose of antibiotics, and with sweat pouring from his body like a businessman about to fire his best friend, he gave vent to a blood curdling string of notes as though he were an ice cream van in immense pain. He swayed as if drunk with power, moved backwards, and Gotama prayed that the end would come quickly before fear overwhelmed his mind. There was a moment of hesitation during which the silence was potent with emotive force. Then the spear flew high in the air, up and away into the sky. Its golden line could be seen tilting away in the distance. Gotama, shaking violently from nervous reaction, realised that the spear had not been intended for him. No doubt, the creatures had a different fate in store.

Why the spear had been projected into the sky was impossible to explain. Perhaps it was a dedication to the Gods of the sky, or was a forerunner of the myths of Eros and Cupid – civilised and savage myths and dreams were much the same; all possessed an irrational rationality and an illogical logic. Suffice to say that by some unknown charitable circumstance Gotama still lived and the wicked looking savages still danced and drank around his prone figure.

He began to think he was an excuse for a tribal booze up, because most members of the group were consuming large quantities of intoxicants from an open earthenware bowl. Many of those imbibing could scarcely stand upright. They were like civilised members of a wedding celebration who invariably considered it their duty to become disgustingly inebriated as a token sign of their deepest respect for the holy rites. After an interminable interval, when everyone had consumed innumerable gallons of liquor, many of the creatures began dropping in their tracks through intoxication and exhaustion. Finally the old creature withdrew to a nearby tree house and the remaining dancers disappeared, presumably to their own dwellings.

Silence again ensued. Gotama was left alone with his thoughts. By this time the sun was dropping in the sky, indicating the approach of evening. Soon it would be dark. Gotama was grateful for the cooler atmosphere that soothed his weary brow and eased his aching limbs. He was unable to understand why the creatures, who had shown no signs of friendliness, had not put an end to him when they had the opportunity. The sun sank lower on the horizon and the moon showed its silver disc behind some trees, turning them into black lace. The stars appeared, as the sky became deep ultramarine and then black. All was quiet, save for the rustle of leaves and the creaking of branches in the breeze. No doubt, due to the damp of the night, his bonds began to shrink and tighten in a vice-like grip around his ankles and wrists so that the pain became excruciating. Gotama feared the arteries to his hands and legs would be cut off. How long he would be able to tolerate such pain it was impossible to tell.

He must have fainted due to the pain, because when he again became conscious, the moon was high in the sky, radiating her silver light. There was a chill in the air. A wind had sprung up which moved the trees in grotesque shapes. Heavy clouds increasingly obscured the moon's disc and soon a number of cold splashes on Gotama's forehead indicated the presence of rain. Leaves of trees reflected a soft patter as raindrops came into contact. At first the spots were intermittent, but soon developed into a heavy shower. It was not long before the moon was completely obscured. The calm moonlight was replaced by vicious flashes of lightning, accompanied by the sonorous roar of thunder. The rain became torrential. Water ran under Gotama's neck and down his back where a stream formed in the slight undulation of ground. It became rapidly deeper as the storm progressed. Gotama's head and arms were half submerged in a churning torrent of muddy water that rattled the stones. If the water level rose much further, he was sure that he would drown. He bent his head upwards as much as possible, but the strain was too much and every so often he had to let it fall back to the original position, where it became almost immersed in the flooding waters.

The stream had, in no time, developed into a river with tumbling rapids that splashed high over rocks and boulders. Swirling sharp pebbles cut into Gotama's arms as the muddy water hurtled ferociously by, like thick turbulent soup. Gotama once more tried to lever himself up to avoid being engulfed. As he did so, the sapling holding one of his wrists to the ground moved slightly, no doubt dislodged from its position by the erosion now taking place beneath the angry waters. He tugged at the bonds again. There was another corresponding movement from the sapling. Again and again he repeated the effort, twisting and pulling his wrist until the sapling had swivelled perceptively in the ground. Frantically tugging at the thongs until his wrists bled, he finally felt the small tree pull free of the water logged soil. One hand was free and in another moment he had rolled over and was pulling at the small sapling holding his other wrist. It took no more than a couple of minutes to free his other hand. He sat up and without too much difficulty released his feet. It was none too soon, for the raging waters were now almost a foot deep and rising much more quickly as flooding spread over the whole area as far as one could see in the intermittent flashes of lightning.

Picking himself up, he stumbled over moving rocks and floating trees that threatened to crush his legs. Slipping and groping, sometimes on all fours, he made his way slowly towards the nearby hill he had noticed during the day. Three or four times he fell and was almost sucked beneath the water's undertow. The wind lashed at his torn shirt that flapped like a loose sail. It was so strong that it was almost impossible to battle against. He was frozen and exhausted now, to the point of collapse. Struggling through the newly formed rapids as they shed their frothing torrents over him, Gotama clawed his way up a steep bank and slowly made progress to higher land. A few hundred yards more he could go no farther and sank to the ground.

How long he remained thus he could not tell. It must have been at least half an hour or perhaps more before he found sufficient strength to pick himself up and continue to struggle across the hill in the direction he hoped would somehow take him back from whence he had come.

After trudging for many miles through raging torrents, he came to a sheer face of gaunt rock, projecting itself upward to be lost in the darkness of the night. It was quite impossible to attempt to climb such a vertical face, especially in the dark and in the ferocious gusts of wind. Gotama turned therefore and followed a path at the foot of the rocks until he arrived at a small cave. It would afford some shelter and a place to rest for a while. Struggling inside, he collapsed exhausted. Never before had he been quite so grateful for a roof over his head.

It was only in such adverse circumstances that one really appreciated such things, he thought. So much for the idealists who said that the best things in life were free. Just at that moment Gotama thought just how much he yearned for a free bed with clean sheets, in a free delicately decorated bedroom, a free nights sleep on a free electric blanket, a free shave in the morning with a free English breakfast. He laughed quietly to himself. It was easy for those with affluence to speak piously of giving up everything and 'living free.' It may be an excellent way of living for the man who loves suffering, but for the wise man it was the middle path of the Buddha that Gotama had always thought best. Neither too rich, when one became a mere slave to material wealth, not too poor, when one hadn't the necessities of life to benefit oneself or society. A modest way of life that made one grateful for what one had, when one's means were used wisely and with discernment. Both individual and the community then benefited. It was a wise balance and compromise between enlightened self-interest and dedication to others.

Gotama suddenly became alert to a sound that disturbed his reveries. There was a cracking of bracken not far from the cave's entrance that momentarily sent him cold with fear. Could it be that the creatures had managed to follow him? Surely not! They would all now be trying to save themselves from the terrifying floods. Just at that moment a flash of lightning illuminated the area outside the cave. Gotama saw at once what it was. Silhouetted against the misty forms of flailing trees he glimpsed the lumbering form of a mountain bear. Finding a bear in such depressing surroundings, where no help was available, was like being back in another type of bear market where a fall in share prices gave similar feelings of desperation. In this instance, however, he thought he would prefer the latter.

The bear trundled slowly toward the cave. Gotama could hear the sluggish movements approaching. Another flash of lightning and his eyes fell on a large broken branch in the entrance of the cave. Quickly he grasped it and made ready to defend himself. Breathlessly he waited, hoping the animal wouldn't hear his loud breathing and pounding heart. Fortunately, the bear was kinder than his stock exchange counterparts and passed by without creating hurt or fatality. He even looked far prettier too, not being fitted out with the usual fighting equipment of bowler hat, umbrella, briefcase and laptop PC. Many modern money market men and stockbrokers now liked a more streamline image and had dispensed with bowler hats and umbrellas. Unfortunately, most had not dispensed with their animal instincts. In this particular instance the bear outside the cave could have made good use of a bowler hat and an umbrella. They might have helped him to avoid pneumonia even if the bear didn't need them to bolster his ego.

A sense of exhilarating relief swept over Gotama. He decided there and then to remain in the cave until the inclement weather cleared and it was daylight. Then he would be able to *see* where he was going even though, like a politician, he didn't *know* where he was going. Strange, he thought, how soon one could lose one's direction. The world in general seemed to be suffering from a similar indisposition. It was only a few people in any age that could perhaps see a little clearer than the rest. People like the Bertrand Russells and Einsteins of the world with their Pugwash committees and the like. Soon after the second world war they tried to redirect the world's communities and their scientific advisers along lines that would not only regenerate the world but would guide it safely into the future.

How few these days have ever heard of the Pugwash committees, yet how important they were to the survival and happiness of mankind? It had been Einstein's last act, only a couple of days before he died, to sign his name, with that of Bertrand Russell, to their own original manifesto. It was to bring together scientists from all over the world to discuss the reasons for disharmony and to offer suitable solutions and remedial action. These were the directional compasses of humanity that could guide Progress 13 in a direction worthy of the highest ideals of man, those of brotherhood and humanity. Gotama remembered the concluding passages of the Russell/Einstein Pugwash Manifesto. It read: - 'We appeal, as human beings, to human beings; remember your humanity and forget the rest. If you do so, the way lies open to a new Paradise; if you cannot, there lies before you the risk of universal death.'

22 participants, mostly physicists, attended the first Pugwash meeting in 1957; they came from ten countries, including the USA, the USSR and China. Despite all the expected political difficulties, they reached general agreement

on many aspects of world affairs and, where they failed to agree they were able to define their differences. During the next 10 years there were sixteen conferences in various countries. Men of high standing attended Jerome Wiesner, George Kistiakowsky and Alvin Wienburg of the US, John Cockercroft, William Penny and Solly Zuckerman of Britain, Francois Perrin and Pierre Piganiel of France and top experts from Russia, China and other countries.

The long lasting conversation between East and West at Pugwash did much to prepare the way for the treaties on the test ban, outer space and non proliferation. The participants attended as individuals, but many reported back to their governments. Members from Peking attended up until 1960; thereafter it was a major concern to renew links with China. The tenth anniversary meeting of Pugwash, at Ronneby in Sweden in Sept 1967, revealed the magic of Pugwash in action; three months after the Israeli-Arab war, Ronneby was probably the only place in the world where Jews and Arabs could be seen eating together, discussing politics. East Germans and West Germans talked of the future of Europe, scientists from the rich and poor countries argued about the roles of aid and social revolution in world development. Pugwash became much the most effective unofficial agency for peace and understanding in the post war world, and science and humanity are more in its debt than they may ever realise.

For social scientists there was another, more professional course to a safer world, the serious study of what was termed 'peace research'. This meant academic study of the causes and character of conflict, means of resolving conflict and achieving disarmament and the nature and problems of a peaceful world. Unfortunately, the peace researches were only conducted by small groups and were often in a half hearted manner, but the ideas were good and showed some promise if continued and expanded in the future. An Arms Control and Disarmament Agency was set up in 1961 as an official US body responsible for such research, though carefully aligned with government policy and housed in the State Department. With such 'fettered freedom' of function, it was obvious that a peace research system could not show full effectiveness and only by an expansion of its scope to encompass world thought unrestricted by political motivation could it be finally of use to world peoples.

Gotama turned once more from his musings to his immediate situation in the cave. He was cold and shivering. If only he could light a fire. Even if he were able to find some wood, he possessed no means of ignition. If he had some of the skills of prehistoric man he might have been able to rub two sticks together with sufficient dexterity, but he had never mastered the art even when he was a Boy Scout. Without modern inventions and the good fortune of being educated with our forefather's accumulated knowledge, Gotama wondered just how much improved modern man would be over his prehistoric counterpart. Civilised man's innate abilities were probably no more advanced than man the savage's, and might be less so. The difference was not in innate intelligence, but in collective learning accumulated over many generations, together with collective communication. Moreover, modern man was a product of society just as society was the product of every individual. He was as much conditioned by the society that had bred him, as the society in which he lived was the net result of all human thought and activity. The subtle inter-relationship was as intimate as space and time.

Nothing more transpired that night. Gotama, wearied by his activities, finally fell into a deep sleep. When he awoke there was a slanting shaft of sunlight streaming into the cave. He struggled to his feet. The storm, now abated, had been replaced by a blue sky mottled with fleecy clouds. Bright green and brown pasturelands stretched away into the distance. It was exhilarating. The cave was situated on high ground, and he could see a panoramic vista of everything below. Away to the left he could just make out the remains of the village where he had been held captive. It was too far away to distinguish any detail, but the floods must have wrought tremendous damage as most of the area still remained under water and was engulfed in a huge lake two or three miles in width. Outside the cave, Gotama discovered a tiny path threading its way up the steep rock. It disappeared round a crag of overhanging strata. All other routes down from the cave seemed to lead directly to the vast areas of flooding. The tiny path was the only alternative.

Without further hesitation he began the long climb up the rock. The path led up through a boulder-strewn ravine of considerable dimensions. There was little grass or growth of any kind save for a few sparsely placed wild rock plants of an unusual type. Several times he slipped on the loose stones. Once or twice they were dislodged and went tumbling down the hillside. Each time, a trail of brown dust and mud accompanied the minor avalanches. Gotama wondered whether the creatures in the village below would see the flying dust. After continuing thus for many miles, the path terminated at a plateau; an extensive table land high up in the mountains. The surface was now quite flat and extended into the distance, disappearing into a violet haze. Only a few giant arms of black rock mutilated the otherwise flat horizon. It was like a moonscape. Once he thought he saw a snake as it curled quickly away into the meagre vegetation. Other than this, the only moving living things were the birds that gave eerie calls as if to warn of further impending dangers. It seemed like a lost dead world where he was the only being of any significance. It was all just solid rock.

Gotama's mind raced. Life was quite out of place here. All was solid matter, quite inanimate. Yet, his body, almost exhausted now, was made of matter too. It possessed similar atomic energies. Men were habitual classifiers and had separated the animate and inanimate, defining one as dead matter, the other alive. Gotama had frequently thought this was an unnecessary distortion of the truth. Scientists had discovered elemental structures in things like the tobacco leaf mosaic that seemed to represent both the facets of life and inanimate crystal. Matter and life were two sides of the same coin. He recalled how he had often thought that light and sound waves could never really be separated from the processes of man's seeing and hearing. Both were essential in the process of sensory perception. The process of seeing involved a continuous number of reactions, not least of which included light and the sun. The whole chain reaction was inextricably linked in living process. One couldn't say that one section was alive whilst the other that was linked to it was not.

Gotama struggled on, delirious and gasping for breath. He half smiled to himself. Even the breathing that now came so hard, involved imbibing so called inanimate air. It was odd how everyone readily assumed the air was quite inanimate before entering the body, but having got itself nicely involved with his intricate bodily functions somehow became life itself. Not only did it get involved with human life, but also it was an absolutely essential ingredient for it. Such were the contradictions of man's habitual beliefs. Gotama wondered at what point the air was supposed to become 'alive'? Was it on entering the nose, the lungs or after passing through them? And, what about the Carbon Dioxide? Was this animate, having been produced from inside the body, or was it only animate until exhaled into the outside world? Animate and inanimate were quite false presumptions, almost mediaeval terms. The two were frequently conjoined in such intimate relationships that it was impossible to separate them. Language too was often the barrier. There should be a way of expressing the implication that there was no real separation between things such as animate or inanimate. A way of expressing a non-subject/object orientation, rather like Einstein's formula for mass/energy conversion.

After several hours of hard walking, he could see the edge of the plateau in the distance. Beyond was a ridge of mountains and in between was a river in full flood. Its waters raged against swollen banks and swirled into giant eddies. The river undoubtedly flowed out to the sea. Perhaps he could follow its course and thereby reach the beach and the cave where he had, by some strange miracle, first discovered this land. He made his way slowly and carefully down the slope at the end of the plateau. As soon as he reached the water's edge, he followed the river's direction. After some miles, the raging waters pounded into a narrower section and threw white foam high into the air. The river passed into a gorge with high rock escarpments on each side. There was a narrow ledge in the rock about ten feet above the water. It ran, like a path parallel to the river. Gotama clambered over some boulders and pulled himself on to the ledge. It was damp and slippery. One fall and he would be thrown into the boiling waters below with no hope of rescue or survival. Slowly he proceeded, conscious that every step could be his last.

The river curved round a bend ahead so that it was impossible to see what lay beyond. He was uncertain whether or not the ledge would end in a cul-de-sac. In several places it became so narrow that he had to grip the slippery rock face to avoid falling into the white foam below. At one point the ledge had fallen away altogether, which necessitated hanging precariously by his fingertips as he edged his way across the gap. Fortunately, just at that point there were adequate grip holds in the overhanging rocks. It must have taken over an hour to pick his way slowly along the slippery surface of the ledge before he finally rounded the bend in the river. He was surprised to see that the river widened out again. It was bordered by a patchwork of muddy fields. The going became easier when the ledge widened as it ran down to a rough wet path studded with white stones that glistened in the light of the sun. There seemed no end to the trek. He limped on for the best part of the day alongside the river. It curved continuously, often completely back on itself. Gotama realised this was obviously not the shortest route to the sea, but derived some comfort from the thought that the most direct route was not always the best. At least this route was sure to lead to the sea eventually.

As the sun dropped low in the sky, its red orb reflected a coloured dance in the water, a dance of a thousand red stars, rich and glittering. Either side melted in a darkening grey. A few sparse clouds became pink and fleecy. As mud turned to gold in the soft evening light, it occurred to Gotama that the ferocious torrent and the bleak landscape of the day had now turned beautiful. There was a complete and utter transformation. Yet the difference was a mere play of light, a combination of subtle reflections. What was the 'real' colour of the river? Was it the deep wet grey and brown seen earlier in the day with the foaming white tufts, or was it the rich gold of the evening? The sky too had changed its attire, as it bid adieu to the setting sun. Did the river possess any fixed character of its own, or was it merely a complex series of reflections, each and every one affecting the other? Like clouds that were never the same, their individuality a mere concept of the human mind, the river too had no permanent reality. It seemed that everything in the environment reflected everything else, each was but a part or a reflection of the other. There was no real separateness, no real permanent identity in things.

More of the muddy fields were turning to gold. The earth became orange fire and the evening mist drifted like a strange web. It was such a fleeting moment of beautiful changing colours. Gotama conjectured that if the sun could have remained in this position turning everything to gold for a whole day and shone daylight only in the evenings, everyone would automatically assume the gold was the natural inherent colour of the dirty mud, the earth, the rocks and trees. People thought of water as blue, grass as green, tree trunks as brown, only because they saw these colours frequently associated with these things.

It became increasingly difficult to find his way along the path skirting the river. He had eaten no food for nearly two days, but he was scarcely aware of hunger. There was something unusual about this place and in particular the river. It held for him a strange and weird attraction, quite fearsome, yet not without its delights. He was not to know that the river was called the 'River of Life.' The moon began to show forth a silvery tenuous radiance that now cast everything in mysterious context. Another bend in the silver band and the slope of a hill blocked his vision. Perhaps around the next corner would be the sea where he could find the cave and Progress 13. He struggled on, weary and aching. His reserves of energy were almost depleted. The bend in the river came at last, but with it disappointment. There was no sign of the sea, only the river pouring its silver fluid away into the night.

A moment later Gotama's heart leapt. There was a vague outline ahead that looked like a bridge. Another second and the image had melted into the mist and disappeared. He lurched like a drunken man. Around him things seemed to be vague and ghostly. His legs moved automatically. The grey mist, shot with silver, swam before his eyes. He was desperately tired. The mist congealed, hardened and became the bridge again. This time it was distinct. It was a bridge. Focusing, he made a last brave effort. Where there was a bridge, he thought, there might be life and help. The structure loomed closer; it was not far now. Suddenly somewhere at the base of the structure there was a movement that startled him. He gasped aloud, as he wiped his eyes disbelievingly. Surely he had seen a movement, or was it just the result of fatigue and imagination? He half closed his eyes in an effort to focus more clearly. Nothing moved. He steadied himself.

The bridge stood out gaunt and isolated from the uniform backdrop of mist. It was dark, silent and still. He moved forward again, stumbling over rocks at every few paces. There were several broken and torn trees in his path, which he surmounted on hands and knees. This effort drained him. He stopped once more to struggle for breath. His heart raced almost out of him. He was now within a few hundred yards of the bridge. It was then that he knew he had been right the first time, there was definitely something moving there. It was either human or animal. He was too exhausted to flee and too petrified to collapse., so, motionless, he surveyed the scene in front of him. Something was moving away from the near end of the bridge. A chill of fear crept into his stomach and clutched his heart. Whatever lurked ahead had obviously noticed Gotama's presence, and judging from his experiences so far, it seemed more than likely that the form would not turn out to be of the friendliest disposition. However, to retrace his steps was unthinkable. He must go on.

As the form became more distinct, it divided into two, and Gotama realised that it was a man and a woman. The moonlight carved the faces into thick ghostly sculptures with deep inset shadows and pallid highlights. Each was enveloped in a loosely fitting hood. They came closer. The only way to tell whether they were hostile was to communicate with them.

Gotama blurted out a few stuttered words. "Could you tell me," he said, "whether this path leads to Progress 13?"

The two figures turned to face each other and shrugged their shoulders. A deep booming voice from one of the figures seemed to vibrate the night. "This is the path to Progress 3 and 4."

The other figure nodded in apparent agreement, then said, "It may lead to Progress 13 further downstream. There's been a lot of new building going on, so I've heard, a few miles ahead. Not that we've seen any of it. We never have time to leave our post here. Anyway you've got quite a way to go yet. It will necessitate crossing the bridge to get to the main buildings downstream, but first you will have to climb up to the temple."

"The temple?" Gotama said vaguely. "What temple is that?"

"It's the Temple of Man's Heart, up on yonder pyramid, close by the Palace of Reason and Learning." The rumbling voice went on. "You'll find steps near the bridge. The temple directors will provide you with a pass that will entitle you to cross over to the other side of the river."

"Do you come from the temple?" enquired Gotama, slightly mystified.

"Oh no!" replied the other, "We are only the guardians of the bridge. We have to make sure no-one passes over the bridge without a pass."

"Why is it necessary to have a pass?"

"Don't rightly know, but they'll tell you in the temple."

"What do they call this river?" Gotama enquired with more confidence as he realised there was nothing to fear from the two figures.

"It's called the 'River of Life.' There's a legend that tells of its origination in the hills of eternity and that it travels on forever. Its water is used for all kinds of living things downstream where it's often polluted by blind and ignorant life forms."

Gotama thanked the strange couple. He was about to continue to the temple when the woman rasped.

"You will have to go through the Sepulchres of Superstition before you get to the temple. The Sepulchres are on the same path. You can't miss them. But beware as you pass through their precincts."

With that, the two figures turned and disappeared into the darkness before Gotama had time to ask why the woman had given her warning. Gotama made his way to the bridge. The entrance was securely barred and locked. A short distance away he noticed a smaller gate. Beyond was a narrow rock strewn path that led up the hillside. Silhouetted against the skyline stood a large domed building as black and ominous as any Tax Collector. Without further hesitation, he opened the small gate and was soon scrambling up the hill path. After several minutes climbing, he was confronted by a massive oak door that was dark and scored with age. Its only embellishment was a most extraordinary knocker in heavy brass cut in the shapes of weird figures. It was engraved with silver patterns that changed as the clouds drew veils across the moon. Gotama thought it was reminiscent of the knocker in Dicken's *Christmas Carol*, where Marley's ghost had been revealed to Scrooge in the big brass knocker. This, though, was a huge moulded form of a frog's head carved with delicate traceries and a gold inscription that read –

> *The witches' cauldron bubbles*
> *With countless human troubles.*
> *Watch with special care*
> *In this moonlit lair,*
> *For phantoms of the night*
> *And every eery sight.*
> *Of beasties, dragons, birds.*
> *Of horrors beyond words.*
> *Of screeching sinking sands.*
> *In Superstition's lands.*
> *Or rustling of wings,*
> *As a night owl sings,*
> *And witches' voices croon*
> *Their potions to the moon.*
> *To all who enter here,*
> *May have much to fear*

There was also a second poem carved deeply into the massive door itself that read:-

> *Let me tell you a painful truth,*
> *As painful as a bad old tooth.*
> *The world about us is full of care,*
> *A lair of darkness and despair.*
> *But whoever made the world like this,*

Also made the loving kiss,
Happiness and pain combined
In recipe for human mind.
Love and pain forever embraced,
Inextricably enlaced,
Like diamonds set on blackest velvet,
Light and dark in every facet.

With some trepidation he lifted the cold metal and let the knocker drop with a dull echoing thud that resounded in the hollow interior of the building. Gotama stepped back in anxious anticipation.

Half a minute elapsed. Almost imperceptibly at first the door began to creep open. Inside was pitch black, but there was someone or some form peering at him through the opening. There was an initial hesitation as the door was held slightly ajar for a few moments and then opened wider. A hunched and shrunken woman of about 80 years of age stood in a carelessly draped garb of rough unseemly cloth. Her hair was unruly, falling like coiled springs either side of a pale hatchet face. "What do you want?" she screeched, like a bird falling on its prey.

"I have to visit the Temple of Man's Heart and, in order to do so, I have been told that I have to pass through these buildings," Gotama retorted quickly. "I presume this is the Sepulchre of Past Superstition."

"It is," answered the woman, sounding impatient. "Come this way." She obviously didn't wish to participate in any lengthy conversations. She turned without another word and, with a quick flick of her arm, indicated that Gotama should follow her. Behind the large door, in the half-light, Gotama could see a crazy paved path about ten feet in width. On each side stood a number of stone statues. They shone with a ghostly glow in the moonlight. He followed the woman as they passed by faint outlines of shrubs and trees surrounding a large pond. At the end of the path they mounted many stone steps to a building topped by two spired towers, and passed through another massive wooden door. Inside was a dimly lit room. Around the cold stone walls, flaming torches illuminated granite that glistened with dampness. The room was exceedingly long, dark and narrow. Here and there, in the lighted recesses, hazy objects and movements were visible. It was a strange and mysterious place. The woman led the way. They passed an opening in the wall wherein grew a slender ash tree. Gotama noticed there were numerous pins stuck in the trunk.

"What's that?" Gotama asked as casually as he could.

The woman glanced carelessly at the tree. "That's the anti-wart tree," she said. It has mysterious anti wart properties and is well known for curing warts of all kinds and shapes." Gotama vaguely remembered the old folk cure. You took as many pins as you had protuberances, stuck them in an ash trunk, pricked each wart with a separate pin, impaled it back in the bark and thereby transferred your epidermal troubles to the tree, or at least you hoped you did.

"We witches have got a bad name," the old woman rasped. "Just because we are superstitious and like to ride broomsticks and brew the occasional spell or two. However, not many people know that we also use our special knowledge and superstitious recipes for lots of good purposes." The old woman pointed a scrawny finger towards some twisted trees and a mass of foliage in the half light. "There's some of my magic plants," she croaked. Her eyes narrowed. "Some have more 'mana' or magic power than others. I often use them to bewitch or to make beautiful and sometimes to heal or to give second sight. The flowers for many of my spells and potions must always be collected under a full moon when the moon goddess Hecate rises up in all her majesty and full occult powers. Then at dawn, when my magic herbs are at their best, all covered with cool sparkling dew, I wail my powerful and mystical verses. Then when they're picked they give off irresistible magic. My specialities are love potions that are real favourites. I make them from a secret concoction of flowers picked under the Dog Star from the Vervain tree. My Vervain water sprinkled in the right places can be a swooner for lovers and is my miracle aphrodisiac." The woman's voice crackled on. "I use a St. John's Wort plant polished with shining dew, for those who want to marry before Midsummer's Eve. But, for it to take effect, it must be smoked in a mid-summer bonfire or placed under the sleeper's pillow. Then soon after a new husband or wife will appear in their dream"

Gotama half smiled to himself as he noticed his companion avoid a couple of protruding ladders. She took a pinch of salt from a large bag as they passed. Thereupon she threw it over her left shoulder with as much faith and dexterity as a priest making the sign of the cross and shaking holy smoke. The floor was littered with peculiar objects; frog's legs and rabbit's feet were everywhere.

Shivering cobwebs glistened as they draped themselves around some heavily latticed windows, through which he noticed a distant pyramid, reminiscent of an ancient Inca temple. Wide stone steps led to the summit where figures in misty white robes moved in strange configurations, as though performing ritual ceremonies. Vague chanting echoes pulsed in the distance. Smoke drifted across the moon, like hazy contorted skeletons.

Farther on, the walls were embellished with an outstanding variety of chains, bracelets and totem poles, some quite beautiful, some ugly and modern. Necklaces adorned with troll faces were accompanied by modern additions that included crosses, gold birds, archangels and the like. Many were in clay or wood but the majority were made of gold and silver. Of the latter there were countless urns and cups with obvious religious affinities. There was a section devoted to objects of an Egyptian origin comprising delicately embossed gold figurines and emblems. Mummified figures stood resolute amongst stuffed birds and animals. Wall pictures stained brown with damp and age revealed designs never before witnessed by Gotama.

As they progressed, the narrow room widened. Here were objects immediately recognisable. Amongst a complex maze of astrological charts, crystal balls and magical signs were astronomical telescopes, some microscopes and television sets. Moreover, alongside some ancient witch brooms were some models of spacecraft, motor cars and skyscraper buildings. "Why the odd mix up?" enquired Gotama, quite intrigued.

The woman looked askance at the objects. "They all belong here," she croaked. "They're all part of the Sepulchre of Superstition." She walked on in silence.

"But microscopes, motor cars and space vehicles have nothing in common with superstitions." Gotama retorted, mystified. "They're the product of human reason and science."

The woman looked up. Her eyes were tired, as though she found everything too much for her. She sighed heavily. "Men thought they were being reasonable creatures when they relied on astrology and burned witches. It's only in retrospect that you can see they were only being superstitious. Modern man invents his motor cars, microscopes and space-vehicles and considers his scientific enterprises the very antithesis of superstition. But they are all worshipped with similar irrational devotion. The faith that was once in God is now in science, materialism and greed. It is a new worship but with the old devotion. The exploitation of science and technology necessitates a belief that they will deliver the truth about things and a blind faith that the power of man's reasoning will enable him to find that truth. Many people consider scientific laws as quite concrete and unalterable, almost things of absolute truth undistorted by superstitious nonsense. But as science progresses, new scientific laws are discovered that supersede the previous. The new laws are then considered the truth, the old ones are discarded as being not the truth after all.

It is in the discarding that the scientific laws are seen to be mere illusions, the products of partial knowledge, reflecting the age and society that bred them. It is, in fact, almost impossible for the majority of men to perceive the superstitions of their own age; they are interwoven so tightly in the social fabric that they cannot be viewed objectively. The rosary, the crystal ball and the modern PC are all believed in by reasonable people who consider that each will work on the basis of recognisable laws that can be understood. People therefore believe in each of these because they have good 'reason' to

110

believe they will work and also have a 'faith' that they will do so. There is a subtle blend of the rational and irrational.

Man presupposes in blind faith that technology will end all his miseries and free him from all his limitations. Unfortunately, he is engulfed in an erroneous way of thinking. Superstition is only the believing something to be true that is in fact irrational and untrue. It applies also to his unfounded belief that happiness is dependent upon the increasing acquisition of material wealth. Here he is mistaken and will be dreadfully disillusioned." The woman gave a toothless smile. "The more he has, the more he wants. I've been told that unless he reaches out and grasps a higher vision, both he and his creations will not only remain with me here as museum pieces forever, but that his world will suffer extinction very soon."

Gotama suddenly felt sickened by the darkness and grime of the place. "Are all these things connected with the Sepulchre of Superstition? he said mechanically. He watched, fascinated as a spider on the wall reached out at a fly caught in the merciless grip of its web.

The old woman, noticing this, said. "And that's a symbol of man caught in the web of ignorance and greed." She then swept her bony arm in a circle and pointed. "This is only a small part of the main building. The whole edifice was constructed an eternity ago. It was originally named 'Ego Building'. I've no idea who the founder was. I was born here, no doubt I shall die here too." She gave another toothless grin. "Seeing that I've been here ever since Time began, I don't think I look my age, do you?" Gotama was taken aback, but had no opportunity to answer as she had suddenly moved on again. He followed. There was silence for several minutes as they picked their way over some rubble littering the untidy floor.

A rat scurried into the darkness. Then another and another, as the light of the old woman's lamp lit the sultry blackness. The woman scowled. "They're my special pets," she said. "They're all bred in the mind of man. They protect me sometimes. You should see how they can make some of my higher animals do their tricks. I've given them all special names. The rats live in that stinking hutch over there." She pointed to a dark recess in the filthy granite walls. "I've nicknamed it Freud. Why, I don't know. At least, I've quite forgotten." Another animal scurried away into the hole with a noise like a slithering snake. There goes Mo Tive 25," she said. "He lives in a dark dungeon called the Unconscious, deep inside the hutch. He sings and shouts a lot, which causes some of the higher animals, particularly Homo-sapiens, to do all sorts of extraordinary irrational and superstitious things, sometimes good, sometimes bad. His emotive songs can often be quite tear jerking and so powerful that they can even be heard in the new Palaces of Reason and Learning that have been built on some of our foundations not far from here.

111

He and his fellows Lomo Tif, Idee Zire, Idisl Ike, Iafr Ade and others, often create such a chorus between them that the charged emotion can even carry away those living in the elegant rational palaces where the music is supposed to be pure unsullied Reason. Sometimes they create such a mash of melodies and discords between them, with choruses from the irrational superstitious choir down here singing descant with the black and white Reason lot up there. The result is a very original, but not always beautiful symphonic composition called human behaviour. Other melody recipes that mix our superstitions with the rational have grand titles like metaphysics, astrology, theology, cosmology and many branches of alternative medicine, to name but a few.

They've tried a new approach recently in the Palace of Reason. They're trying out new mathematical melodies that they consider cannot be sung with lower descant. They're hoping our lot won't be able to join in. They've acquired some particularly good musicians and vocalists some of whom you may have heard of: Copernicus, Pythagorus, Gallileo, Kepler, Isaac Newton, Einstein, Rutherford, Hawkins, Bertrand Russell and many others who between them create a formidable mathematical melody from time to time. There's also quite a different tune played by the Eastern Bo Tree melody makers that is almost impossible to accompany with our lower descant especially with its very high notes. It does sometimes leave poor Lo Motive, I.D. Sire and Ivan E. Go quite lost."

The old woman led the way to a door. She turned and faced Gotama. "Through that door," she said, "is the great alter of 'Ignorance and Pain' of which our Sepulchre of Superstition is a mere annex. Tread carefully and beware of the heat lest it scorch your eyes. Some find the experience unbearable. If you would rather not enter I will show you a longer way round to the Temple of Man's Heart where you must obtain your special bridge pass."

Gotama hesitated. What kind of experience awaited him beyond that door? He was already chilled with fear at the unsavoury nature of the place. What next would confront him? A pencil shaft of light shone red through a crack in the door. It shimmered as from a furnace. Even now he could feel a searing heat that penetrated the door itself. His thoughts raced. He knew that if he didn't enter, he would forever wish he had. Yet he was fearful to do so. His legs and brain seemed immobile. He hesitated, unable to decide. "How far is the other way? He enquired.

"It's a long journey and overall equally difficult." The woman's eyes glistened black and deep. "Only you can decide," she said simply.

Without quite realising he had made a decision, Gotama clutched at the door handle. In a moment the door was open. He gasped as a wave of heat nearly overthrew him. With one hand he quickly shielded his eyes from the painful glare. The light was pulsing like molten metal, yet its rhythm was a living thing. Facing him was a huge edifice. In its centre was a globe. At a glance Gotama realised it was a huge replica of planet Earth, but it was transparent like glass. Clutching to the inside curved surfaces were countless numbers of human forms. Their figures and faces were distorted with anguish. Far above, a gentler more hazy light burned. The figures seemed as though they groped towards its glow. In their efforts they used each other as ladders and human footholds. Some were trampled down by the efforts of others. The globe turned constantly, like some great wheel, and in so doing, the living contents were mixed and re-mixed in strange permutations as they rose upwards at one moment only to fall at another. Sometimes their faces lit up with joy when they succeeded in their puny efforts. At others they shed tears of pain and sorrow, as circumstances frustrated their desires. Tears flowed like streams down a mountainside. They bubbled and boiled like surging seas in the bottom of the globe.

Gotama entered the place. As he did so an almost intolerable agony of mind and body swept his being. He was engulfed in searing heat. There was an accompanying sensation of whirling faster and faster. A noise, like a road drill, shattered his fevered brain. Then he was falling as though into a bottomless pit, a chasm without end, without walls. A terrible fear gripped him. It was like the end of the world. Out of it there appeared a misty form. A robed figure that he thought he had seen once before, became identified out of the moving mass. It beckoned and pointed. Gotama's eyes followed as indicated. There followed an extraordinary sensation of being dashed on the open shore by a Herculean wave. He seemed to be writhing like a fish thrown on to a dry beach.

In the next few moments he was transported into quite a different environment. Moreover, by some strange trick of fate, he had become a young boy in an air raid shelter with his mother, father and baby sister. The air raid sirens were wailing their warnings and the sound of heavy anti aircraft guns could be heard together with the faint droning of the engines of enemy aircraft. It was late evening and the family was settling down into the one large bed now used nightly. The air raid shelter was a heavily sand bagged metal structure in a back garden. He somehow knew that it was the year 1940 and the German Luftwaffe was carrying out massive bombing raids on London.

Gotama saw the father bringing in an evening drink from the house just before the family settled down to sleep. Within minutes of his entering the air raid shelter the rhythmic beat of aircraft engines increased until the very atmosphere seemed to vibrate. The anti aircraft batteries thundered and shrapnel splattered in the streets. Then there was a brooding silence as the aircraft passed over head. It was always a relief to hear the aircraft engines fading into the distance. However, what the family didn't know was that the German aircraft were dropping very heavy land mines on parachutes that night, which were more devastating than impact bombs. It was on this particular night that two such land mines were gently dropping through the sky on a breeze that was to take them on a close impact course with the family shelter. Minutes went by as the family quietly finished their bedtime drink. Everyone then settled down into his or her usual sleeping positions. A little night-light gave just sufficient illumination for the family and particularly for the baby to see their surroundings and provided some comfort and security.

Gotama felt himself drifting into a half sleep when suddenly there was a deep thunderous roar and he was pounded into the ground by some giant force. At the same time, he felt suffocated by acrid fumes and dust. His immediate reaction was to cover his face with his pillow to provide protection and to make some sort of mask against the fumes. Everything was now pitch black. There was a strange silence for a few moments followed by a gushing of water from a burst water main. The baby screamed as she struggled to breathe. There was a desperate shout and a splintering of wood as the father smashed at the jammed door with a spade. He used such force in his efforts to escape that the heavy spade split and broke into pieces.

When the door wouldn't budge everyone realised they were trapped deep beneath rubble from many collapsed houses. To add to their fears, the water gushing from somewhere nearby threatened them with drowning. Even more frightening, a huge fire could be glimpsed through tiny splits in the door beyond the mass of twisted debris that covered them. Flames leapt at least thirty feet in the air. They shouted in desperation for help for what seemed an interminable age, but without response. It was as though there was no one alive out there. It seemed certain that they were about to perish in the fumes, be drowned or burned alive.

It must have been at least half an hour before they thought they could hear distant noises like the breaking of timbers and the shovelling of rubble. As the noises grew louder, men's voices became more distinct giving instructions and shouting encouragement to those trapped. It was not long before a section the air raid shelter door was battered in and an escape hole made. After the baby had been handed out, it was Gotama's turn to be extricated from the twisted mass of debris. As soon as he was lifted to the surface, he ran in bare feet and pyjamas through pouring rain, across jutting crags of broken bricks and glass to a neighbour's shelter that had somehow survived the blast. An air raid warden was inside attending to a woman with severe head wounds.

Suddenly, Gotama found himself on the shoulders of a fireman who carried him across the desolate landscape of broken buildings. They passed the fire that lit the whole area with its orange and red tentacles. He was quickly whisked away in a car only to be stopped by an air raid warden shouting that there was an unexploded bomb in the road directly in front of them. The torn and gaping hole where the bomb lay could be plainly seen. The driver hastened to turn the car around as more enemy planes could be heard over head, attracted to the fire like wasps to honey. Round another corner they came upon yet another unexploded bomb sectioned off by army men. It was one terrifying ordeal after another and after several detours they arrived at the house of the father's sister, Alice.

He and the good lady's family then sat together in the specially shored up dining alcove that they used as a kind of air raid shelter. It was probably the strongest place in the house, although whether it would withstand any serious impacts was anyone's guess. Suddenly there was a knock at the front door. It was an air raid warden with the news that there had been a second parachuted land mine close by, which had crashed through the roof of a house, but hadn't exploded. The lady of the house was so shocked that she was unable to speak for over a year afterwards. The rumble of gunfire and exploding bombs continued as the small group huddled together in their makeshift shelter. Gotama drifted in and out of sleep.

All at once there was a different noise that aroused him. He looked up to find himself in strange new surroundings. Also he was no longer the boy whose home had been bombed, but a young man working in a factory. Around him were many men in overalls assembling what appeared to be aircraft engines. There was a smell of oil and heat. Music was playing in the background and the man at his side was whistling softly. The man turned to Gotama as though he knew him. "I'm glad they play music while you work at this time in the morning," he said, with a smile. "It helps the day go by and makes work not 'arf as bad. What do you fink, Joe?" Although Gotama didn't at that moment feel quite like a Joe, he answered in the affirmative. It was almost as though he had been there before and was accustomed to the workshop.

"Go and chase up those parts from the stores Joe," the man said, as though it was all part of the routine. With that the man thrust an official looking drawing into Gotama's hand. On it there was a list of part numbers all underlined in red. Gotama made his way across the factory floor. He could see a large sign at the end of the factory with the number 55 emblazoned across it. When he arrived at the stores, he enquired about the sign. He was told it indicated the number of Merlin engines that had been produced during the last week. He also learned that all the factory personnel worked like slaves to produce more engines than the week before. Everyone tried to beat the record of sixty-one. The store man said that the parts would be ready in fifteen minutes, so Gotama took the opportunity to walk round the huge machine shop next door to the assembly line.

Everywhere there were rows upon rows of capstone lathes, milling and grinding machines, hydraulic presses and drilling machines. The noise was deafening. Women of all ages sat at lathes and drilling machines that spewed out quantities of metal swarf drenched in white liquid cooling oil. All the women wore regulation type head-scarves as a safety measure to keep their hair from the whirling machines. Many sang to the music, others smoked. Men crouched over desks and machinery studying blueprints. The capstone lathe setters considered themselves a cut above the rest. They were part of the skilled work force who studied technical drawings and worksheets. On the other hand, the women in head-scarves, operating the lathes and drilling machines, were considered to be of a lower caste with brains suitable for menial tasks involving repetition.

Gotama passed by some grinding machines where sparks flew everywhere as rotating grindstones bit into metal. He passed by some gear cutting machines, which noisily thumped up and down slotting each separate gear segment in a precise calculated way. Several of the men had white coats with different coloured collars, some red, some green, and some blue. This indicated their rank. The reds were better than the blues as they were the foremen whilst the blues were only section leaders. The greens were the time and motion setters whose job it was to study how long it took for a machinist to produce the finished article. The machinist would try to take as long as possible in order to have their time set so that when working normally they could produce the item must faster. This enabled them to earn more bonuses under the 'piece work' scheme that paid them for each item produced. The time setter, on the other hand, knew all about women's wiles. He was used to the way they would take an extra couple of drags on their cigarette or make two or three extra indents with the drill instead of the normal one, just so they could extend the time for the machine operation. In the end it was often a sort of compromise between machinist and time setter. The pretty young ladies could often get a very profitable 'time set' by giving a sexy smile or a flit of the eyelids, or emphasising a few curves to a vulnerable time setter. The sex games hadn't gone out of fashion even in wartime boiler suits and overalls. It proved that despite everything, individuals were still opportunists at heart and would always try to do the best for themselves, come what may.

Suddenly there was a loud thud like thunder which shook the whole building. People instinctively ducked. Someone shouted that it was a V2 rocket. It was useless going to the air raid shelter after the event, so everyone just worked on. Such missiles couldn't be picked up on radar, so no warning could be given of their arrival. Whether it was due to the explosion it was impossible to tell, but just at that moment the factory lights went out and the machinery rumbled to a halt in the pitch darkness. People shouted and for a moment there was pandemonium.

It was several minutes before the lights blazed on again, but Gotama was shocked to find himself once again in an entirely different place. How such a thing could have happened it was impossible to tell. How a factory environment could suddenly change to the inside of an aircraft cockpit was indeed strange, but that it had done so was indeed evident. Even stranger was the fact that he was fighting to maintain control of the aircraft, which was violently spinning towards the earth. Out of the cabin he glimpsed the familiar wing shape of a Spitfire. Part of the wing had been shattered and there were bullet holes through the skin. He seemed to instinctively know how to fly the plane and manage the controls, although he had never actually flown an aeroplane in his life.

However, there was no time to conjecture how all this was happening. The urgent thing was to survive. A shrill voice rang out through his headphones. "Bandits at two o'clock, more at five o'clock. Watch out! Foxtrot to leader; they're on your tail, closing fast. More bandits coming in from the sun."

Another voice shouted "Tally Ho, Tally Ho."

Suddenly gaping holes appeared in his port wing as smoke gushed into the cockpit. Flames swept from the engine, which spluttered, faltered and then regained its power. But only for a few seconds after which it fired intermittently again. Gotama had managed to correct the spin, but the aircraft was now dangerously near the ground. It skimmed the treetops and a lake. Houses appeared across the countryside and passed below him like racing dots. A bridge loomed up before him and was gone. The engine faltered again and stopped as he struggled in vain to maintain height. A wooded copse sprang up before him and he knew this was the end. A crash was inevitable. He covered his face with his hands in a last despairing effort and knew no more until he awoke in an even more bizarre setting.

There was a distant rumbling like thunder. Or was it guns? Someone was playing on a mouth organ, 'Pack up your troubles in your old kit bag.' Everywhere reeked of muck and cordite. His back ached as he tried to move. He felt the cold pang of slippery wetness running up his legs and back. The sky above was an ominous purple grey and he suddenly realised he was lying on his back in a deep trench full of water and mud. Rolling over, he was confronted by a sea of tin hats, army uniforms and waving rifles. There was a command from somewhere, which shifted the mass to one side of the trench. After a moment of stillness, like a brief calm before a storm another command rang out. In an instant everybody and everything was on the move as soldiers leapt over the side of the trench to disappear in a low lying mist that crept its way across the ground as though it were a living thing.

There was a shout as Gotama felt someone punching at his back as he was literally pushed over the side of the muddy trench to follow in the footsteps of the hordes that had already gone before. He realised that he too was wearing a tin hat like everyone else because it was chafing his forehead. At the next moment he was enveloped in a conflagration of bursting shells, pelting rain and falling men. Shouts and screams rent the air, followed by desperate sobs and whimpers. Enemy machine guns reaped terrible carnage as men were mown down like blades of grass. Gotama ran and fell then ran again, in and out of craters, trying to protect himself from the raging hell. There were other shouts now, more urgent even than before. Shouts of gas, gas, gas, briefly pre-empted the rolling cloud, yellow and sinister, that grew out of the writhing mist before him. In the next moment he was in agony, unable to breathe, writhing on a slippery and gruesome wasteland devoid of all natural things like grass, trees, birds and fresh air. He was quite alone as he felt a sick misery creep over him. His vision faded to a murky blur. He lay huddled and deformed in pain as death crept over him.

At that point something within him like a natural anaesthetic took hold. Hallucinatory imagery flitted into his consciousness and it was springtime again with sunshine and gentle breezes. He ran with his lovely wife across meadows and hills. Streams trickled over rocks and a heron perched waiting for fish. There was the boat he used to row up and down the river and anchor in the creek, where he would rest in the reeds. He could hear the crows calling from their nests high up in the treetops. He saw the sun setting in a golden lake. He felt a dewdrop on his cheek, or was it a tear? He had always known that these were the things of real value. How dreadful and barbaric was war in comparison. How useless and wasteful of all that was good. In his life Gotama had never had much time to draw such comparisons and to really appreciate the true value of those natural things, which were generally undervalued by people, probably because they came free of charge. Now at this time of pain and despair, when he was about to die, the realisation dawned with terrible force that war and hate were the worst things imaginable, far worse than the most excruciating diseases of mankind. In fact they would probably be classed as international madness by future peoples of the Earth. The amount of suffering caused by war and hate in the past history of mankind must have been staggering if it could ever be measured. How sad and tragic it was that man had not yet learned how to live in harmony. The past was full of lessons if only people could have taken notice.

As the sun went down behind a lacework of trees, Gotama slipped slowly into unconsciousness. How long he was unconscious he didn't know. It could have been hours or days, but as his sensations returned he found himself once again in a completely different environment. It was also as though he had returned as a different person, almost a kind of reincarnation of his former self. He woke to find himself in Japanese attire walking on crutches. To his horror he was in the company of several other Japanese all of whom had a variety of disfigurements. Some were in wheelchairs, others had gross mutilations of face and figure. He cried out in a spontaneous gesture of despair and compassion. When he looked around him he could see nothing but disfigured building remnants that had once been a city. The city he was told was Hiroshima.

An old Japanese Buddhist monk approached him. "Here is another lesson for mankind," he said. His expression was kindly but sad, as though he too could see the pointlessness of it all. Gotama surveyed the destruction laid out before him, a wasteland where there had once been a living thriving place. There's enough misery in the world, he thought, without making more. The old monk merely nodded as though he understood what Gotama was thinking. A small child without legs glided up to him in her wheelchair. She had a charming smile, wide eyes and a face as bright as summer. Looking up at Gotama, she handed him a single flower.

"This is for you," she said. "A single flower depicts a new and special beginning, a new dawning, a new age with new thinking. Please take it and do your best to make these things come to pass." She had tears in her eyes but smiled through them. "One day there will be a new day," she said quietly and then she was gone, lost in the bustling crowd of invalids. The light of the sun was fading once again and stars began to decorate the sky. Soon everything was enveloped in dusk and then darkness. It was a darkness that enveloped consciousness, darkness beyond experience, a darkness of death.

Gotama awoke from its clutches to find himself once again strangely resurrected. He was once again by the river he had been following previously and which had led to the bridge and to the strange Palace of the Past and the Sepulchre of Past Superstition. When he had found his bearings, he made his way to the bridge. His one thought was to find a way back along the river to the Progress 13. He stumbled drunkenly, hardly knowing which direction to take and like most government ministers, trusted to luck and good fortune that he was on the right course. His heavy steps on the steep rock path made sharp grinding noises that shattered the stillness like breaking glass. A misty moon rose from behind a cloud. Ghostly trees waved their tenuous arms like skeletons in the pallid light. Somewhere grass rustled. He could see the river below, a silver thread twisting into the distance. And then he saw it. The bridge, gaunt and brooding in the twilight rose before him, its great solid and silent mass set against the fleecy clouds dancing in the moonlight. He came upon it quite suddenly. The massive entrance grew and was upon him in a moment. There was a clatter of iron that rang under his boots, which was sufficient to wake the dead. Over the bridge entrance stood a great arch at the top of which was a sign. In the half-light it was difficult to decipher the words, but at that moment the clouds cleared and he could see the words more clearly. They read, 'The Bridge of Individuality across the River of Life.' The letters had human and animal figures in their design and were embossed in glistening gold.

Umderneath there was a small inscription that reflected strangely in the moonlight. It read:

> *An ocean shimmers with stars,*
> *A river ripples the sun,*
> *The deep pool is silent.*

As he passed under the great arch, Gotama spent a few moments admiring the craftsmanship when suddenly, without warning, a figure, like a dark billowing shadow, emerged from nowhere. A wizened yellow face thrust itself forwards to within an inch of Gotama's nose. "Whence go ye?" the face said shakily as it twitched in several places at once. Startled by the abrupt intrusion, Gotama's reflexes winced his body to a standstill as if fitted with disc brakes in every toe.

"I wish to cross the bridge," he said, his voice tinged with alarm.

"Why so?" the voice questioned. "Do you know what this river is and why there is a bridge here? Without such knowledge you will never reach the other side safely." Gotama noticed the wizened figure was covered from head to foot in algebraic equations and geometric designs. Some were neatly embossed on his hat, which looked like that of a jester, whilst others were inscribed in dangling patterns of ornamentation that hung from his loose clothing. On his feet he wore shoes with so many buttons that they looked like pocket calculators. His eyes twinkled in pounds and dollar signs just like those of his colleagues on the stock exchange.

"Who are you? Gotama asked, as politely as he was able.

The wizened creature grimaced and twisted his face even closer. "My name is Bandybones the Bridge Builder's Boffin," he said, "I was given the name because, for ages past, I rode my winged horse for much too long trying to look for new thoughts and sensations to create people and to calculate the best way for them to cross the bridge. My official title is Grand Wizard Fibronacc, calculator of sequences and golden ratios in Nature's finest facets and artists' delicate designs. I'm also the bridge builder's Weaver of Winkles and Wonkles in the World Wide Web of Wonders and Woes. I use my number sequences to create spiral shapes in things like Snails, Winkles, shellfish, molluscs, Nautilus shells and spiral galaxies and I put golden mean rectangles in things like paintings and the Parthenon. My Wonkles then weave them all together." He pointed to another hooded and heavily shrouded figure coming up behind him. "And there's my darling wife," he said, in a voice that crackled like a log fire. "I call her Mrs Treacle Tart, because she's very sweet and delicious, a little saucy and we always stick together." The wrinkles in his face quivered into a fleeting smile.

"You've heard of Cerberus, I presume? He was the three headed guardian of Hades and the underworld. Well, I'm the guardian and provider of passes for this bridge above ground. I come from the Temple of Man's Heart and the Palace of Reason and it's also my job to guide people when they're making the crossing over the river. It can be very tricky for a lot of people. This bridge was built for all mankind to cross," Bandybones continued. "It's been constructed over aeons of time by countless numbers of men and women. Each bolt, each sliver of metal, each stone, every thread of gold, were all forged by sparks of human thought. It's a vast bridge of changing Time stretched across the living waters of eternity. It spans vast chasms of void from which we all spring. It's a bridge of sensations and concepts that congealed together make separate living forms in a relative world. It's like a fetter or shell of concepts because it ties people into a partial and temporary world, which they create by their own thinking. It's people's own thoughts and concepts that make them what they are. But their thoughts of changing Time have their ground in eternity; much like the waves of the sea have their ground in the ocean. The flower springs from the ground, from which it takes its material, so it is with man's thought. His mind he considers his own, yet it springs from fathomless depths to which he is always conjoined."

"The bridge is a symbol of temporary Time crossing over an eternal ocean and being conscious of the fact. It is like a minute oasis of movement surrounded by an infinity of stillness. By means of the bridge, the infinite is able to see itself through finite eyes. Thinking 'mind' is the root power of the Universe and Man is but a minute sprouting from it, a tiny coagulation. The bridge is a vast thought construction of a very special kind. It is part infinite mind and part finite thought, both of which construct Man himself."

"You say you are from the Temple of Man's Heart," Gotama said.

"Yes, that is so," Bandybones replied.

Gotama then commented that he hadn't seen anything of it and asked where could he find the place.

The wizened creature's eyes sparkled and his face lit up like sunshine. "You'll not find it out here," he replied, "because it's not made of solid substance. The Temple of Man's Heart is like a translucent self shining pearl that lies deep in the deepest heart of Man. Once you have entered its precincts, you'll become wisdom itself and the final purpose of everything will be known to you. The Temple has no inside and no outside, but is longer lasting and stronger than any physical thing. I am but its signpost to help you on your way, so let me give you one small clue. True peace, compassion, tolerance and wisdom cannot be wholly known or carried out by 'I' (the self), as these things cannot be performed completely if there is a notion of some kind of payback for 'me.' Sooner or later, for instance, a situation will arise when 'my' interests are in conflict with a compassionate act. The true nature of the Heart can only arise and be known by emptying out 'I', the root attachment, in whose presence the afflicting passions and desires arise. That which arises from the Temple of Man's Heart is without 'I' and is able to give without remainder and can perform acts of compassion, tolerance and wisdom without conditions. And remember, you are the path to the Temple of Man's Heart and also the traveller. Walk on and you will find it."

Gotama stood silent trying to take in all Bandybones had said. There was much he wanted to ask, but he was tired and eager to proceed on his journey. In his haste to be on his way, he blurted out. "Is it permissible for me to cross over the bridge now?" Bandybones turned and peered across the bridge as though he was looking for something that would clarify the position.

All at once he seemed to come to a decision. "Go then, if you must, but remember what I have told you. Enter through the turnstile marked 'Birth,' where you'll come upon the Magic Window of the Senses, watched over by the Cosmic Goddess of Inside and Outside and of Space and Time. The window enables the universe to see and be conscious of itself through and by means of the senses and also for human life to see and experience the inside and outside worlds of the cosmos. In the window you'll see the beautiful goddess of learning and consciousness, in the form of a young woman in a golden dress, holding a flower. If you look carefully into the flower you'll see the shapes of the human eye, ear, nose, mouth and the stem of touch and mind that together create the Magic Window of the Senses. The young woman will give you one of her flowers as a 'Pass' for you to cross the bridge. Whilst you remain on the bridge, you will remain in earthly mantle and human body. If you lose your foothold in the biting winds and unforeseen conditions you will return to dwell again in the waters of the unknown dimension."

Gotama pushed gently on the turnstile, beside which there was a small notice marked 'Birth', whereupon a beautifully latticed window sprinkled with stars and enlaced with leaves and flowers suddenly appeared. An inscription, almost hidden in the latticework, read.

> To see a million moving coloured pictures during life,
> To feel, hear, taste a million pleasures in a world of strife,
> Such are the gifts we rarely think about, that blow,
> Like starlit petals, through the senses' magic window.

In the centre of the window, and mysteriously forming part of its design, a young dark haired woman appeared to be looking at an image of the Earth. In her hand she held a flower with golden petals formed in the shapes of the human senses. She turned slowly to Gotama, smiled and, without a word, offered him the flower. Gotama was too enthralled by the magic of the silent scene that he also said nothing, but carefully took the flower. He instinctively knew that this was in some way a very special occasion. At that moment the metal clanged as he shifted the turnstile forward. His movement, like some strange karmic directive, resulted in several things happening at once. A peculiar throbbing in his unconscious depths rose for the moment into conscious thought. It was as though a new dimension had curled into the very fabric of his being and become his individual self. He was Time incarnate and yet something that transcended duration. He felt washed over by a translucent invisible power and energy, a consciousness without form. Living had become synonymous with mind. Energy and matter had become consciousness.

There was a flash. Where there had been nothing but the giant stark girders of the bridge, there now appeared grasslands, trees, a rolling landscape and a sun high and beautiful in the heavens. Other life forms blinked into being spontaneously. Nebulous tremors in the ether, like a heat haze in summer, congealed and crystallised into living movements that became limbs and organs, which linked together by some unknown instinct to become moving creatures. Some took to the waters that had also appeared from nowhere. Others took to the sky, spreading wider and finer wings as they flew higher and higher. Fish plopped in an open spring that bubbled with movement and steamed like a primeval sea. Gotama had now passed through the turnstile. He was bewildered, not because the things he witnessed were all that different from normal experience, but because they were out of context. It is not only things we take for granted, but also the manner in which they are presented to us that makes our environment suitable for us to live in. It is the order of sequence that is important; that shows us whether we may expect pleasure, pain or danger.

The unexpected can also create uncertainty and insecurity. And so it was with Gotama on that day.

The evolution of life that had taken millions of years to complete seemed now to pass through his consciousness in but a few minutes. How this had been accomplished he was at a loss to explain. The quickening process resulted in dramatic, almost miraculous, effects, yet somehow he knew the experiences were exactly as they had been in reality, merely speeded up in order to give him a special and unique understanding. Trees came and went in an instant, moving like uncanny eruptions of black lightening from the earth. Mountains heaved, shifted, sank, swayed and cast off their sharp surfaces, like living breathing entities struggling to wake from a restless slumber. Continents slid apart as giant volcanic faults beneath the oceans poured out molten lava separating land masses by greater and greater distances to form the oceans. Ice ages came and went in rhythm with the changing directions of ocean currents, the changing content of carbon dioxide in rocks and atmosphere and many other changes in the world, moon and sun. Land masses moved, disappeared and reappeared again in different shapes, each like a shimmering globule of mercury on water.

Cavernous depths revealed themselves, out of which grew new images of living creatures, all linked together by a common chain. It was a transparent chain, like a special kind of gravitational force, that linked and bonded large and small, live and inanimate. It was a chain that linked spawning fish with tidal rhythms of moon and sun. It was a chain that bonded sense of sight with rays of sun, creature's breathing and oxygenated air with plants, hearing with atmosphere, body weight with gravity and gravity with galaxies and universe. The miraculous link bonded countless numbers of atoms, molecules and cells in living things with each other and with the so called inanimate physical structures of the earth, moon, sun, the milky way and the infinite. It was such an intimate and complex net of relationships that it could only be conceived as one seamless universal coat covering and enveloping all things. The chain, like gravity, was invisible to the naked eye, yet was revealed through the mirror of the mind and in man's logic. On the chain there was a strange symbolic inscription. It read 'Karma.'

Then another strange thing happened. It was as though Gotama was witnessing the distant past when everything first began. The chain and its progeny were suddenly spewed out of a vast chasm of nothingness, a void within an infinite void. Scientists called it the big bang. It leaped outwards, curling towards a sky and a space that it created as it spread in all directions. Patterns altered, forms disappeared and were replaced. No vacuum was left. Each vacant emptiness was filled by yet another concrete space and each space by objects and new life forms, each one linked to its predecessor and to everything else that came before and was manifest at that moment. To Gotama, the vast, never-ending flow of creatures would have seemed real had it not been for the speed of manifestation. With life's experiences presented at such an alarming rate and out of context, he immediately concluded, like a scientist witnessing ESP that it must be a hallucination, without substance or reality. If he had viewed the process at the speed at which he was familiar, he would have undoubtedly considered what he saw was real. Reality for him was the habitual repeat of sense data projected on to the senses at the same speeds that he had known from birth. The length of a day and a night, the speed of a man walking, the rate at which the sun moved across the sky, the manner in which clouds groped their way and shifted their outlines, the speed at which the apples fell off trees, the slow changes of the seasons, all were integral parts of Gotama's conditioned understanding. For the sun to rise one day at twice or a hundred times its usual velocity was quite an outrageous thought. It would not only contravene natural laws, as he understood them, but would spoil all the neat mathematics of the physicists, besides causing chaos on Wall Street.

The subtle laws of consciousness were suddenly brought to realisation when Gotama was confronted with the speeded up version of life on planet Earth, from its inception to the present. Reality was itself a concept, sometimes a mere generalisation. Such descriptions could differ according to the way in which things were viewed and the language used to describe them.

He walked across the bridge, which altered and moved with each step, like a chameleon's skin. Sometimes he thought he could still discern the strange gaunt outline of the pillars and girders. However, for the most part, the bridge had become the environment with which he was familiar, although still changing and altering its contours and shades at sometimes quite alarming rates. There were houses, trees and fields, animals and vehicles, all of which changed their patterns, fashions and modes of operation in but a tick of time.

From his walk across the bridge, Gotama learned one thing. The world was not the solid fixed thing he had always assumed it to be. Rather a combination of changing concepts and energies, where both the objective and subjective entwined in subtle and complex dances. Just where the subjective concepts and preconceived notions ended and the objective sense data began, couldn't be finally fathomed. The one merged inextricably into the other, like poles of a magnet. It didn't matter at what point in the thinking process of perception one chose to analyse, the result would always be a derivative of outside and inside, objective and subjective, both of which could finally be viewed as concepts or orientations of the human mind. Also, whenever one viewed the outside world, its images were only ever seen by the inside of the brain and mind, so that, in a sense, the outside was the inside and vice versa. It was not a long leap in logic to conclude that the objective and subjective were so inextricably linked as to be considered as mere aspects of 'One Mind'. Could it perhaps be that universal cosmic mind was looking at and experiencing itself and this resulted in the polarisation of the one universal Mind into subjective and objective and into subject and object – the material world of the senses?

There was in every experience a combination of the past, in the form of memories and preconceived ideas, with the present in the form of sense data being received from the external world. In each individual there was a vast mind processing plant, continually relating past learning, education and experience with whatever was going on in the present. It involved an editing and discriminative activity on which were were projected values that had been learned from birth from society's rules and regulations. Each incoming experience was filtered, and to some extent adulterated, in the process, so that the fundamental reality, whatever that may have been, was subtly converted into something different and which was usually considered more appropriate with preconceived and acceptable patterns of behaviour. It was rather similar to the way in which 'waves' were broadcast to become something quite different when they were processed and projected on a television screen.

Gotama stood for a moment and remembered the Buddha, who, 2500 years ago, had discovered there was more of mind in things than matter. Now modern science had shown that matter was electrical energy with more space than electrical particles. The particles also turned out to be not just particles of matter but strange fleeting 'wisps' called electrons, protons and many others, each one totally unlike our previous definitions of 'matter' as a solid substance. They seemed to function in a different realm of space and time where there was no solidity and where space could be traversed in mysterious ways and where electrical particles could cross from one position to another without actually crossing the space in between. The everyday definition of solid matter, the matter of Dr Johnson, was found to be quite false. It seemed obvious that matter contained more 'void' than substance and this included our own bodies too. Did this then mean that we were no more than 'emptiness' clothed in thought? But what really was emptiness and what was thought? Was everything just a kind of universal dream in which we were but tiny flickers on an immortal screen, itself a mere flux of changing imagery with no foundation?

Gotama walked on, conscious that the bridge on which he was crossing the 'River of Life', was there as a lesson and a symbol. Beneath the bridge lay the key to the truth. Life was the only lesson from which to learn – the ultimate lesson. There was nothing else. But how many people had ever managed to find the ultimate 'truth' of things? Many weren't interested even in looking. Most were apparently content to be conditioned from birth and to wear the blinkers provided by society, like bees fed on special foods which befitted them for predetermined tasks; one a worker, another a soldier, yet another a queen of the hive. People were fed, not merely physically, but mentally and spiritually by the society that served up its special propaganda menus, its values, ethics, mores and acceptable behaviour patterns, together with sweeteners and heady notions of freedom and liberty. Society gave out its subtle palliatives to mould people, like plasticine; so they could live and work together in order to survive the vicissitudes of the world.

What were Socialism, National Socialism, Communism, the Church and the Free Market Theories, but different social themes for survival in the jungle of life, where people frequently had to endure sociological and bureaucratic straight jackets in order to receive the dubious advantages of collective effort? What a high price some people had to pay for the meagre necessities of life; a roof over their head, the basic nourishment to keep body alive. Was it always worth the tragic cost of loss of freedom and spontaneity? Were there any alternative solutions that could provide people with security and hope, loving friends and freedom to think and act in responsible ways, to make spontaneous gestures of goodwill to all, without their spirit being forced out of them by painful Communistic or extreme Socialistic community regulations? And conversely to have all these advantages without the necessity of trying to protect themselves from the tyrannies of unscrupulous private enterprise let lose like wild horses without a guiding hand. What was the final answer?

Was there a social system to bring the greatest good to people and to widen their vision of truth, without fettering them hand and foot? People had tried so many diverse governmental recipes that it seemed they were now suffering from acute and chronic indigestion, or was it terminal cancer? Central government, though effective up to a point if it was good, was nonetheless hopelessly inadequate in the modern era to cope with the multifarious needs of mankind. There was a need for good local as well as central government, but these combinations had been tried in a variety of forms throughout history usually with less than satisfactory results. Therefore, if people couldn't be satisfactorily governed and generally persuaded to live in peace and harmony together, what was the answer? What new recipe of living might provide them with the means to live life in greater abundance and joy, to see, to know and love the truth within and without?

Life in more abundance – the words rang like a bell in Gotama's head. The kingdom of heaven is within. He remembered the words that had generally fallen on stony ground for most of the 2000 years since they were first uttered. Was the only answer, as Tolstoy also taught, to transform people from within? To reduce greed, hate and ignorance, which, for many people, enclosed them in cocoon prisons of their own making. To a Buddhist such a cocoon was the ego, which was considered the main stumbling block to experiencing enlightenment and of knowing the truth about things. It tripped people into a pit of misery and pain. The ego was the centre out of which came craving and selfish desire. It was the point where the living mind digressed from its true view of itself as unlimited, undefined, unconditioned and devoid of self. It had instead wrapped itself round a finite centre, an incarnate self.

The ego's notions of self were really false concepts bred from birth. There had been the formation of identity through gradual almost imperceptible identifications with images wrought by parental upbringing and with socially acceptable characteristics. The ego had become identified with a finite human self, embodied and separated from the rest of nature. The body was generally considered to be the self. It needed protection, coddling and was encouraged to grasp material things for its good and survival. Thus grew desire and greed, the black sheep of Nature's family of concepts. The Buddha taught people to try to give up the greed and cravings of the ego and to take the middle path between enlightened self interest and pure altruism, in order that their unconditioned nature could be seen and experienced. Their unconditioned nature was, in fact, the same as the universal 'void' from which all things manifested themselves. It was all somewhat paradoxical in that as soon as people began to give up some of their greed, they not only became more enlightened, but also happier and more compassionate.. The two aspects of the wise enlightened person were like two side of the same coin. Wisdom was synonymous with love and compassion.

The Hindus expressed the same truths slightly differently by referring to the Atman as the deep centre of Man which, when viewed by the enlightened person, was seen to be nothing less than Brahman, the supreme SELF of the universe. The enlightened person was joyful and compassionate because they understood the 'ego' for what it was and participated in and with the 'All'. Moreover, by transforming the inner self, the world could also be transformed. If much of our greed were to be replaced by compassion, where would be the necessity for war or social strife? Man was slow to change his habits however. Greed, hate and ignorance were his entrenched motivations, together with the presupposition that in his grasping and clinging to objects of pleasure he would rid himself of the pain he didn't much care for. He was thus like the poor blinkered donkey driven on by the illusory carrot that always moved away as fast as he caught up with it. In fact, all of us were led through life by our particular carrots, our needs and ambitions that drove us on. We were all our own thoughts and sensations, which made us what we were and fed our personalities and dispositions. Concepts and sensations were our internal living residences, our identifications.

Gotama became aware that he had now traversed most of the bridge. The gates on the other side came upon him by surprise. By contrast to the crashing waves below which threw foam high into the air as the raging waters spewed over shiny rocks, the huge gates at the far end seemed still, silent and somehow majestic and beautiful as they glistened gold and silver in the half light. The massive structures were encrusted with precious stones, each reflecting a different light. They sparkled like a billion stars in the firmament.

As he came closer, Gotama could see images of men and women cast in the translucent depths of the stones. They came and went like strange Cepheid materialisation. A shaft of moonlight cast on the higher structures of the gates seemed to reach up to the sky itself. There stood revealed a giant arch heavily embossed with the words *'Dedicated to all those who have passed through the human veil and looked through the portal of Homo sapiens.'* The workmanship was magnificent, like something from an Egyptian tomb, yet even richer and more delicate in its intricate traceries.

The door opened before he could touch the handle. Startled, he turned instinctively ready to retreat. But, as he looked over his shoulder he suddenly froze with fear. The bridge behind him had vanished. It was no more. There remained only the deep swirling waters far below. The bridge, like changing time, had dissolved the past into utter and complete emptiness and had left not a trace behind, only the memory of what had gone before. He realised suddenly that there was only the present, and even the present itself was gone in a moment, never to return.

He passed through the giant portal and was relieved to find a wooden seat in a walled garden awaiting him. The sun was shining and birds sang. There was a gentle breeze rustling the flowers and trees. He was exhausted after his journey and sank into the garden seat. The last thing he remembered, as he closed his eyes, was seeing a small robin fly down to perch on the arm of the seat next to him.

PROGRESS 13 —
THE FUTURE

Mankind is but a newborn child,
Tiny and a little wild,
Taking first steps towards the sky
To countless stars and asking, why?
He slowly reaches out in space
To touch the speckled stellar face.
What will he finally live to find?
What avenues of human mind
Will carve across the mists of Time?
What new worlds will then be known
When finally he's fully grown?

Walter A Elliott

"Wake up Sir," a shrill voice was saying in the distance. "It's time for dinner!" Gotama opened his eyes. A pretty young stewardess was bending over him. She smiled. "You've had a fine nap," she said. "You've missed all the excitement."

"Excitement," Gotama murmured distantly. "What excitement?" He struggled manfully to regain consciousness.

"Why, we've been celebrating," she said. "We have just heard over the Progress 13 radio that after concerted strikes by the workers of the world that they have achieved something they have been struggling for all these years."

Gotama sat up quickly, now fully awake. "And what's that?" he asked.

"They've obtained government agreement that from now on the word *work* shall be eradicated from the memory banks of all computer processors, recycle bins and computer grammar and spell checkers, which have for all practical purposes superseded the old fashioned written dictionaries of the world. It has been decreed that the word had a subversive ring to it. It also had an unpleasant influence on children and people of a more sensitive disposition. Many people had their allergies, hot sweats and unpleasant psychological responses brought on whenever the word was mentioned. Many hyperventilated and vomited because of it. We are told that it has been the cause of more sick notes, violence and discontent than any other word or syllable of the English language. Trade Unionists have been saying for decades that the word was out of date; it apparently reeked of old style Capitalist perversities. From now on, the mere mention of the word *work* by any union member, even by a slip of the tongue, will not be tolerated. Such a slip will be regarded as a Freudian one that will, the experts say, prove that the subconscious is still attached to the word and the perpetrator will require medical treatment. Also, from now on, primary school teachers and parents will be severely scolded and prosecuted if they call young children *naughty* or *silly* as the experts now consider the words might cause psychological damage in later life. There have been few objections to the new ruling and only one or two old fashioned parents have enquired whether they can expect delinquents, layabouts and hooligans to be ruling the world quite soon. Also, the word *history* is to be banned, because it could cause offence to those females who prefer *herstory*. And a book and a song title are to be changed to accord with our modern enlightened way of thinking. The book will now be called *Snow White and the Seven Persons of Somewhat Limited Stature*, and the song will now be entitled *My Old Man's a Managing Refuse Disposal and Recycling Operative*. These exciting new politically correct taboos will make welcome additions to the countless numbers already embodied in our culture of liberation and in the giant expanding reference libraries that list all such matters of great importance.

The international companies of the world have for some time been concerned that the word *work,* if taken too seriously, can interfere with company efforts to keep staff in the happy mood of acceptance, enthusiasm and belief that they are part of a team. The *team* is now the important oracle word emphasised and revered in all mainstream business circles. Members of teams are proud to have similar motivations, similar aims, similar pleasures, similar lifestyles, similar likes and dislikes, similar enthusiasms for Company projects. Also, to share similar desires for Company dictates in order to share similar enjoyments at Company parties and play groups, to receive privileged mortgage and motor insurance, to wear similar funny hats at their desks, and to love attending team fitness groups and social evenings in the Company's specially built facilities. Members of such teams also relish the security of being Company owned so they may be better appreciated by their fellows and receive accolades, prizes, physical and psychological hugs from their team mates as often as possible."

The girl's eyes glistened with delight. "Having achieved this long awaited revolution of the proletariat, the government have also crowned this latest achievement with a further decree under a new social contract. It is now law that there will never again be the humiliation of waiting in dole queues and job centres. Instead social workers will visit people's homes to see that the unemployed are all comfortable and their cheques will in future always be sent in gold-embossed envelopes. Also, the word *dole* or *unemployment benefit* is to be replaced by something less insulting. It is now to be called *higher social income for the leisurely* and will in many cases be looked upon as an early pension. It will especially benefit those just leaving college and will avoid the stigma of them having to identify with *work* at such a tender age."

At last," she said, "we're seeing the triumph of egalitarianism, long forecast by our great social reformers. The latest enactment of the Bill of Rights for Minorities will ensure that all major road signs will now be in nine languages, only one being English. This will help immigrants and minority groups find their way around. And what a great victory it will be to witness our cities and towns in so many different names, the favourites being Hindustani, Japanese and some strange new dialects from Pakistan, Bosnia, Albania and the Middle East, all generously brought to us by immigrant minorities. The recent Class Discrimination Laws are also having their effect. It's now legal to discriminate against all those who have received a private education. And all private school fees will be subject to extra tax levies and no grant handouts. The government experts say this will encourage more pupils into our unrivalled state education system. And to further assist in this splendid scheme, privately educated students will now have to achieve higher grades than pupils in state schools in order to receive similar qualification certificates.

There will also be more sex education for very young children in primary and play schools, because the age of consent for heterosexual and homosexuals is now being lowered to ten and a half. And to further assist our marvellous modern and liberated education system, condoms, birth control pills and the very latest in abortion pills are to be given *free* with every packet of Smarties and Cannabis. The Kama Sutra and the latest sex text books are also being provided *free* in new school Tuck shops that previously only provided snacks and confectionary and were nicknamed 'Muck' shops by the children, who are now calling them something more appropriate. And the unions have at last abolished school examinations, which they say, have old fashioned, over competitive, elitist and divisive connotations, besides causing a wide variety of nervous complaints, twitches, skin blotches and panic attacks amongst the more sensitive and those who haven't kept up with their revision. To help the latter and to find more time for students' sport and recreational activities, it will also only be necessary to attend course lectures for a quarter of the usual number of hours in order to obtain a degree.

It was, of course, due to our liberal reformers' idealistic zest to provide equal opportunities for all, that examination papers had been made progressively easier, in order to give more equality of opportunity to the underprivileged, the idle and those who possessed a low threshold of comprehension, (previously called dimwits). As a result, everyone was overjoyed that there always now seemed to be almost a 100% student pass rate and that everyone could now obtain a degree. It then became logically obvious to the experts that examinations were quite irrelevant and inappropriate, because everyone could now pass them.

Moreover, employers are to be prosecuted if they so much as question the ability of any such university degree holder, who can, if necessary, claim for compensation for any such misdemeanour. The abolition of examinations follows from the earlier prohibition of all abrasive competitive activity in schools, such as sports days and particularly the three legged and egg and spoon races, which the experts say are just too competitive for children's good health and do not engender the social uniformity and standardised team spirit required in the modern enlightened age. And the very latest news is that human teachers are at last to be superseded by intelligent robotic processor overseers, which will require little or no supervision. In fact, the processor overseers are themselves now to be the supervisors of all major education projects, because they possess vastly superior abilities and a wider knowledge than their human counterparts. They also possess better social and interactive skills. Robotic processor supervisors can also chat more interestingly on any subject, no matter how complex, so that students can complete their courses in a fraction of the time. And there can never again be teacher's personal favourite, where male teachers dote on pet female students and female teachers concentrate on favourite boys. Moreover, pupils can now be taught using the latest speed-brain-absorb methods made available by the super-ed-net information system operating throughout the world.

The plan is to close as many schools as possible, because the more self sufficient and able pupils will be taught at home, under the reformed 'education in the community' scheme, which, the government says, will save lots of public money and teachers' wages.

Just a few human teachers are to be retained as school caretakers, general cleaners and maintenance personnel. And a few will teach primary school age groups and the very young how to interact with their robot processor overseers. The important subject on a schools' curriculum will be 'How to Make Friends With and Maintain Your Robot Processor Overseer,' although most robot overseers will now be either self repairing or will make use of other processor robots designated for this purpose. It's such a radical innovative scheme – higher education for all, on a kind of automatic pilot.

And our transport services are to be improved yet again. In future, trains, planes and buses will never be late. They will just be delayed."

The girl almost quivered with excitement. "It's such a great day," she said. "The new bulletin also advises that the phrase *national interest* is now to be treated as an unmentionable profanity in the name of political correctness. *National interest* is now to be completely subordinated to the European or International one. It's also predicted that the phrase *European interest* will itself soon be treated as a racist remark and will be similarly demoted to an unmentionable and will join the many volumes of modern unspeakable remarks. The new phrase *World Union of Politically Correct Peoples* will soon be the only phrase allowed to be voiced in polite multinational society.

The bulletin also says that the government is to help people who feel trapped when buying their homes on a mortgage. In future, Building Societies and Banks won't be able to offer mortgages for longer periods than 100 years."

The stewardess was so engrossed in her revolutionary news bulletin that she neglected to notice that she had just spilt half a tomato juice over a nearby bald head. The bald head, at first inert, suddenly came to life and gave a frenzied movement revealing a ruddy perplexed generously moustached face.

"What the devil are you doing?" the red face boomed.

A throaty roar of a wounded animal followed this, as the fluid trickled into his eye. The stewardess turned quickly to see what all the fuss was about, only to upturn some soup over an elderly woman's foot. The elderly lady screeched even louder than the man and leapt three feet into the air. Holding the offended foot, she hopped backwards and forwards in the aisle shouting incoherent sounds and a very wide range of blasphemies. Many neighbouring passengers became quite distressed, whilst several patted, hugged and tried to console the woman who was seized by yet another fit of hysteria when a heavily built man inadvertently trod on her sound hopping foot in his enthusiastic effort to offer her comfort.

By this time Gotama was fully awake and did his best to assist in tidying things up. The stewardess beamed throughout, as though she had seen it all before, and no doubt still remembering the news of the trade union victory for the proletariat. Finally, when all the mess had been cleaned up and the passengers had been returned quietly to their seats, she plied Gotama with plenteous quantities of food and drink. At least they would have been plenteous had Gotama been a sparrow. He was famished and looked round for a chocolate bar vending machine but then remembered they weren't fitted in Progress 13 aeroplanes. Fortunately the stewardess re-appeared with a fully laden sweet trolley.

Like many over enthusiastic gourmets, he overdid the trifle. That together with the overheated cabin and the soft drone of the engines resulted in acute drowsiness and subsequent sleep.

When Gotama awoke, the cabin's lights were dimmed and most of the passengers slept. There was still that peaceful hum from somewhere and still the oppressive heat. He decided to stretch his legs. The corridor between the seats stretched almost out of sight as he made his way this time towards the front of the plane. He reached a door marked 'Forward Cabins,' opened it and continued along another dimly lit corridor. On each side at intervals there were doors with nameplates. One read 'To the Teleological Impulse System.' He conjectured that all these long unintelligible names on office doors were usually put there to give the occupants a feeling of importance so that they wouldn't need to complain about low salaries. Industrial psychologists thought that to give ordinary workers names like 'Managers' made them work better. And that was why, on nearly every office door, in every office building, there were the words 'Manager of something quite incomprehensible,' inscribed – usually in polished gold or ebony just to emphasise its special uniqueness.

There was another door with a similarly abstruse nameplate. He could not resist the temptation to look inside. A long empty cabin confronted him. On either side of a central aisle there were numerous seats, all unoccupied. Light from tiny windows hazed the more distant rows and made them indistinct. All the seats had reserved notices pinned to their backs. The reservation name was printed neatly on each card. Quite by chance, or so it seemed, Gotama discovered his own name included on the back of one of the nearby seats. This was not the only peculiarity. Each seat had a different date pinned to the back. Closer inspection disclosed that the cabin itself was of a much more advanced design than the others Gotama had visited. Much of the furnishing, the arms of the chairs for instance, was fabricated from a delightful transparent material, which, although translucent, irradiated changing glows of colours. To add to the mysterious scene, there was a planetarium type ceiling showing myriads of glittering stars and gaseous nebula, which circled slowly overhead. At the far end of the massive cabin, curling galactic arms of light made the cabin wall a moving thing totally unlike anything Gotama had ever seen

Suddenly, without warning, a loudspeaker came alive. It seemed to emanate from all directions at once. "Would you please take your seats." Gotama stood irresolute, for the moment unable to act. The voice rang out again. "Wait one moment, please. Our special messenger will be with you in just one moment. We bid you welcome to the Future." With that there was silence again for a few moments, whereupon one of the doors at the far end of the cabin opened. A woman stood silhouetted against the black background of the open doorway. She wore a golden head-dress reminiscent of a miner's helmet. On the breast pocket of her tight-fitting silver tracksuit was emblazoned a black insignia on what looked like a computer processor screen. Tucked in her belt was a pistol. The woman stepped forward and beckoned to Gotama. Her gesture seemed friendly.

Gotama moved to meet her as the woman proffered a slim manicured hand. The handshake completed, the woman spoke. "I have a message from flight control that you have been sent on a special mission. I have been instructed to provide you with all the assistance I can."

Gotama indicated his surprise. "No one told me to come or instructed me on any mission. You must be mistaken."

The woman laughed. "I can assure you," she said, "that I have it on very good authority– that of the rulers of the galactic quadrant, in fact – you are here to evaluate the future course and destination of this plane, the Progress 13, also called the Earth Plane. The compasses are being set right now. There's not much time to change them. It's my job to show you some of the cabins of the Future. The information given to you will be of very special importance, not only to you personally, but also for the human race. There is much work to be done if the Earth and its life are to be saved." The woman pointed towards one of the sumptuous armchairs. "Let us sit down and talk for a while," she said.

As soon as they were seated, the woman began again. "It will probably surprise you when I tell you that I come from a distant galaxy many million light years away. I have also been privileged to travel through Future Time and have visited many of the Progress 13 forward cabins of the Future, far beyond the year 3000 in fact. Believe me, there is much there that you could not bear to see unless you had been specially prepared for the journey. There have always been changes in the world, but the kinds that I may have to show you defy the imagination. There have been some who have ventured into the forward cabins never to return to tell the tale. I beg you, therefore, to trust to my guidance and not to be impatient to travel too far too fast.

By means of advanced Time and Space warping, I am able to visit you from far in the future and also far out in space. Due to this time warping, I see your future as though it were in my past. I hope you will forgive me therefore when I refer to planet Earth's future as though it were in the past. In other words, the stories I am about to relate will be told to you as though they had already happened. I shall refer, for instance, to happenings at the end of the 21st century as though they were already history and had already taken place. This does not mean however, that all of your future is pre-determined and runs like a train along fixed unalterable rails. There are many alternative choices and options open to mankind and I come to highlight them and to show you just a few possibilities. I visit you for a very important purpose that will become clear to you later in our talks.

136

"I visit you in human form so that you'll be able to relate to me and wont be afraid or shocked. However, my human form is only skin deep and beneath the surface I'm not biological as you are, but possess living energies far beyond your imagination. My name cannot be communicated in your sound or written language because it's depicted in terminology quite out of the range of your present understanding. Also, we beings from the future have learned that there is no identity as such in anything – only change, Therefore there is in a sense 'no thing' to name, only a kind of emptiness. However, I would very much like us to get to know each other better and I'm sure you would like to call me, or at least the appearance of me, by a name. And as I might perhaps be described as a kind of space/time bubble you may like to call me Bubbles for short.

As you see, I come in human form identical to an Earth woman of the future, because women had by the mid-21st century become the dominant members of the human family. You may also have noticed that I come as a member of the new elite BMC – the Big Mother Cyberforce. The gun you see in my belt symbolises the new enlightened psychology of women of strength. These new values were being realised towards the end of the 20th century. The black insignia betokens a new autocracy which still paid lip service to democracy but in reality was just a cover up for the overall power of women. The psychology of strength, of beat-your-neighbour-if-you-can, became the new competitive religion. There came a time when the meekness of Christianity was seen to be quite outdated. Darwinian evolution was a tried and tested fact of life; survival of the fittest was a model for people's behaviour. Words like *love* and *beauty* were considered obsolete. They were to be treated as outdated remnants of a past immature age. They were unrealistic childish dreams, which served little or no practical purpose in modern life. The new elite generally shunned the words and was ashamed to be associated with them. The words were therefore seldom mentioned in public. When they were, it was usually the middle classes who whispered them.

During the 21st century, the outdated cross was superseded by the more upmarket black insignia. Black insignias were proudly worn by people now devoted to the new practice of 'tell-on-your-neighbour's-misdeeds-and-be-part-of-the-good-citizen-group.' It became a person's duty to follow this new religion. It was a useful social act to assist in the security and protection of people. It was not just 'neighbourhood watch,' it was rather 'neighbourhood snoop,' and the better one snooped, the more deviants that were caught by one's snooping, and the more accolades one received from the community processor watchdogs. A regular and successful 'snooper' would also be given the gold medallion for 'social snooping' to encourage him to carry on with the good work, together with remunerative tax reductions.

There was a new elite who instructed both leaders and Managers. It was the Big Mother Cyberforce administered by the World Union of Robotic Computer processors, called WURC by the Americans, but bearing no relation to the word *work* which was now an abomination. The ruling method was considered an improvement on the basic democratic system everyone had been used to. The Unions in particular thought it a superior system because now those who knew what to do, i.e. the Managers, were told what to do and those who didn't, i.e. the proletariat, did all the administration. Thus everyone enjoyed sharing in the governing of the country whilst all the practicalities were left to the Computer processors. The community spirit was encouraged so that everyone could try to get as much for himself as he could. They used to call such motivation *avarice* and *greed,* but the new Unions decreed these words unconstitutional and banned them. They used instead the term *majority bargaining* and *unionist development.* Old religion was the opium of the people and such superstitious practices were superseded by legalised strikes and riots *by* the people *for* the people. Wars were things of the past. Enlightened society had now advanced to people's freedom fighters, hijackers for liberty and legalised psychological mugging for charity."

"Moreover, the old mediaeval system of naming each person Tom Dick or Harry was superseded by a much more modern and efficient system. Everyone became a number. It's something the Union of Robotic Computers wanted since the end of the 20th century. Even heads of state were no longer allowed to capitalise on their personality and were referred to by a number. Such perfect equity was now considered in the mid 21st century to be a wonderful achievement of standardisation. The number/letter system had so many advantages over the primitive personality cult. It was the difference between analogue and digital, the valve and semi-conductor, the horse and motor car. The number system also accorded with the dictates of the computer. As a great politician and religious leader said at the beginning of the new century – It was not now a case of 'one must die within in order to live,' an old Christian doctrine, but 'one must now become subservient to the dictates of the Computer processors in order to be free!' Numbers (or people) must accept the ruling of the AI processors in order to rule. They must be governed in order to govern. The new unions however did not take too kindly to the last remark because they considered themselves the only true ruling class. Such were the delusions of the age.

The computer revolution had made the use of names like Tom Dick and Harry quite unnecessary, except for a few of the middle class. Such usage however came to be considered as naïve and reeked of sentimentality, something no one wanted to be accused of in such a mature and technical age. In fact, later in the 21st century, to use such old fashioned names one was likely to be frowned on by the Protection from Personality Squads or PPS as the Americans called them. Too much use of personalised names or *analogues* as they were sometimes called, were classified as deviant activities which threatened the AI processors' efforts towards uniformity and standardisation for the benefit of all. Individual enterprise, although outwardly encouraged and admired, was also kept within strict limits for similar reasons. Too much private enterprise or individualism, like one subject genius, too often categorised as either 'obsessive eccentricity' or as 'savant syndrome,' couldn't be satisfactorily encompassed in the governmental AI processor's plans for the overall equilibrium of the 'state team.' Such activities were discouraged and quickly investigated by the Big Mother Cybernauts whenever they occurred. Anyone found showing signs of these unwanted or unacceptable gifts was usually hurried off for treatment and immediately separated from the 'team.'

In the ostensibly Christian countries, every baby could still be christened, but Government social administrators, always wanting to be seen to be politically correct, decided to outlaw the word 'Christening' and replace it with 'Common Certificate of Birth,' a term they felt proud to have thought up and which they considered more appropriate to a multi racial society, where everyone was frightened of stepping on everyone else's toes. It was just another example where politically motivated practicalities now superseded the more sensitive, religious and romantic institutions of the past and ended up pleasing no one except the social manipulators. The mention of AD 'Anno Domini' in any date was also strictly prohibited and was replaced by 'In the Common Era.' The Christian term, BC before Christ, was also changed to 'Before the Common Era.'

The Christening, or Common Certification of Birth, was usually conducted at the community centre of computerised indoctrination. Here a simple and delightful ceremony was carried out, whilst a serial number was painlessly engraved by laser in the palm of the baby's hand and in the corner of the eye. It was a time when relatives and friends presented gifts such as the super modern baby's nappies that sang a song when they needed changing and prams that automatically roofed over when it rained. The baby's serial number linked the new infant with the great protector, the artificially intelligent processor. From birth the number would be at the centre of every activity, whether it was economic, educational, medical, leisure or deviant. As the individual could be defined as more than the sum of his or her parts, so the serial number became more than the individual. It was a person's link with society, their means of survival and their gateway to all the pleasures wrought by acquiescence to the governing power of the processors. Without their number they could not exist as integral parts of the social group. Also, at birth a special numerical symbol was added to define the year of production and to indicate whether the birth was test tube or biological or robot hybrid. The words *reproduction* or *born* fell into general disuse.

The word *person* was now forbidden, just as in the 1970s the words *man* and *woman* were replaced by *person,* whilst the word *man* was almost deleted entirely from the vocabulary, especially women's. Words, however, could not be processed as easily as numbers. Numbers were now considered to be the root and foundation of an efficient society. Word descriptions were increasingly becoming valueless. Even aesthetic judgements about beauty and art were considered inferior unless they could be interpreted and stored in a computer processor. People became very attached to their serial number. Many had theirs embossed in beautiful creative designs and decorative motifs, they meant more to them than a baby's teddy bear. Their number/letter series being different from everyone else's, they saw in it an expression of uniqueness. It was also a key to opportunities made available and suggested to them by the AI Processors, which studied their progress from birth to the grave.

Anyone who considered that the new age of the processor had conditioned them to lives of subservient slavery and to social conditioning were promptly treated as deviants, in the same way individuals were treated when they didn't wish to join a Trade Union Closed Shop in the late 1900s. The main difference in the mid-21st century was that dissidents weren't just sent to Coventry for a couple of months or given a few kicks in a back alley. Instead they were given a course of medical and psychological treatment arranged and monitored by the AI processors, who were designed to be very persuasive. It was, of course, impossible for anyone to retain such dissident ideas in the face of the unarguable, relentless logic and stored knowledge of the processors.

It was the age of society's revolution from pre-Copernican to Einsteinium. Social science in the 1900s to the end of the century relied on words and was therefore considered as inefficient as pre- mathematical astronomy or physics. Social science now found its numbers, in people and their component parts resulting in a further revolution in the way society was viewed. Such a revolution resulted in changing behaviour values and in the ways people thought about things. According to many physicists, people were just mathematical events in a social structure of more mathematical events.

Some said it was getting to the point where there were more thoughts in the processors than in people. Philosophers were at pains to discover who exactly was the instrument and who was the master – was it Man or his AI processor network. Some said that even governments were becoming obsolete, and that world-wide legislation could only be drawn up and calculated in detail by the computer processors. The increasing numbers of variables and detailed points of political law were becoming so complicated that only a computer processor could deal with such subjects. By the middle of the 21st century, the world parliament met only occasionally to discuss main issues and even these were always submitted to the processors for final vetting. And the AI processors invariably altered any such new proposals out of all recognition, making the politician all but superfluous – as most have always been of course. All the intricacies of government were now dealt with and under the complete control of the AI processors

Processors kept vigil on every aspect of each individual. From early in the 21st century, people's aptitudes, behavioural abnormalities, pleasure pursuits, genetic and psychological traits and most of their physical and mental characteristics were constantly monitored. People's identification numbers were continually updated during their lifetime and new reference numbers were added to the basic identification number of every person to indicate and monitor all aspects of their life. Numbers were used to record grades achieved during education and conditioning together with past illnesses, tendencies towards illnesses, blood types, DNA genetic traits, countless allergies ... you name it, there was a number to record it. Numbers were also given colours to indicate social type. Green indicated that a person had achieved over 70% grade in psychological and behavioural tests. Brown indicated only a 50% stability level and red meant only a 25% level. The government's AI processors legislated that only the green numbers could be employed as administrators and leaders. (The AI processors were now the real leaders of course.) The browns and reds were only given relatively menial tasks, like drawing the 'leisure benefit.' They were the new 'well off untouchables' in the modern caste system of artificial selection for employment. If you were a 'double red you were locked up as an incurable danger to the public. The AI processors selected every category and employment status, based on their vast database relating to each individual's psychological and medical profile.

Such databases included vast banks of information relating also to DNA genetic characteristics from which the processors could assess whether it was permissible for a particular number to mate with another. This led to marriage becoming a more complicated affair than in previous times. By the mid 21st century it was legally required that in order to obtain a marriage licence a person had to ensure that his or her mate possessed an identification code together with a genetic code that was approved by the Big Mother AI processors. These measures had been introduced to ensure that there were fewer deleterious genetic deformities and diseases. All such procedures were mathematically calculated by the processors and came under the heading of 'Population Science.'

The social conformer could get to the top of the tree in employment and other pursuits if he or she had a modicum of education. The state education system required students to be reasonably proficient in a wide and varied number of subjects in order to achieve university status. In this respect things hadn't changed too drastically since the 20th and early 21st century. In the new social order later in the 21st century, there was little or no place for 'one subject' clever people, sometimes classed as obsessive eccentrics or developmentally disabled with savant syndrome or other divergences from the norm. They only tended to disrupt. Too much individuality and divergence of opinion conflicted with a standardised mass opinion and team spirit encouraged by the artificially intelligent processor educators. It was generally defined as colour red/orange, a very low and dangerous social orientation. Social harmony at all costs was essential to the smooth running of the world society and was particularly important for commercial and business success, as any American businessman would tell you. The American 'Company Man' philosophy was in fact taken a stage further. Conformity was now demanded in every aspect of social life. There was no place for excessive originality of behaviour. If it occurred it was frequently classed as a sickness. Uniformity and conformity were essential, you see, if social disruption and failure of the world's economic system was to be avoided.

In order to achieve this end, every number (person) was screened and monitored at every stage of life. Attributes of passivity, conformity with educational grades passed in a general range of subjects, frequently learned parrot fashion, always took precedent over the 'one subject' genius. And to keep the vast international business enterprises running smoothly, obsessive geniuses and anyone else likely to rock the boat, were relegated, just like the bourgeoisie before them, to the more mediocre positions reserved for the red/orange numbers and below. This procedure kept them in their place, avoided any tendency towards too much individual enterprise and kept things nicely standardised. Thus, people ruled the people, one number, one vote - the true social democratic system, the masses for the masses.

Money in the form of physical coins eventually became a thing of the past. Its identification with commercial private enterprise was too much for the Unions who finally managed to get the word removed from the Dictionary. People were then paid in numbers. Numbers were deposited in everyone's community bank record. The central banking computer processor noted how many numbers an individual had to spend and did all his book keeping for him, including applying the appropriate 'cut off' if spending became too lavish. At 'cut off,' his purchasing card would light up and give out a frightening 'screech,' rather worse than a car alarm, which was enough to alert the card's owner and shop assistant that this was not the best time for buying.

To work strictly for money was generally forbidden, or at the very least frowned upon, by the mid 21st century. The unions had always said that the rich had become rich on the backs of others. It smelt of *profit*, another dirty word. Instead, people were encouraged to use their skills for medals and honours and for these they wer allocated social numbers. Man (and woman) is a vain creature and loves to be respected.

In an age where almost everything was constructed under the yoke of automatic process, there wasn't much to do other than try to enjoy oneself. The Unions therefore used every opportunity to relieve the boredom by going on strike. The question of who should receive more accolades than others was, they considered, a very serious problem that could only be decided by a strike. Besides it would also occupy their minds for a while and might even result in something beneficial. They also decided to emphasise their view that work was for robots only. Robots were designed for work. Man was not. Social scientists had often said that Man was basically idle and that such natural instincts of Man must be encouraged. It was now modern thinking to bring out this *natural Man*. And it didn't need much bringing out. All it needed was Union recognition, together with the affirmation that it was now anti-social to try to earn money by individual enterprise. Finally the Unions got their way and punitive tax burdens and no accolades for individual enterprise were imposed so that few could now launch out on their own without their income number cards going into the 'cut off' and 'screech' facility.

Modern Christians, during the centuries following the 20th, were still saying that they must advance with the times. They now encouraged people to forget terms like *individual responsibility* if it served to disrupt social equilibrium. Many considered the miracles of Jesus had either been duplicated by magicians or been found to be natural psychic phenomena. Scientists finally discovered how to duplicate healing by the laying on of hands, moving objects at a distance and even walking on water, although the latter was somewhat unpredictable and resulted in some near drowning situations. Most non swimmers would only try it at the pool's shallow end.

It was discovered that the benefits of healing by the laying on of hands could be greatly improved if the practitioner took a scientifically prepared drug. General Practitioners were also taught the method. They were taught to swallow a set quota of pills prior to examining their patients. It was found that in this way many of the patients were healed at a touch, even before the doctor had decided what was wrong with them. This resulted in a revolution in medicine and saved a considerable amount of trouble. The only snag was that doctors often got side effects from the pills, which necessitated another doctor having to lay hands on them. This, of course, meant that the doctor laying hands on the first doctor had to take more of the healing drugs and he invariably became the unhappy recipient of overdose side effects. In consequence, as time went on, more and more doctors seemed to be rushing around trying to cure each other. It became a merry go round of side effects. In fact, it eventually got to the stage where there were insufficient GPs to go round.

Then the general public were allowed to use the drug themselves. The result was that doctors began to find they had fewer and fewer patients, because everyone was curing everyone else. It even got to the stage where laymen were curing doctors and people began wondering who was curing whom. Pamphlets that read 'Is your doctor really necessary?' were distributed and stuck on walls. This, as you will imagine, caused absolute consternation in the doctoring fraternity as they had always secretly considered themselves to be a cut above the rest of the human race. Soon the Royal College of Laying on of Hands voted that the drug responsible should be withdrawn from public use. This decision caused a great deal of fuss as people had begun to get used to healing each other. The mutual co-operation had become a sort of social habit, like sex, or drinking in the pub. No one wanted to give it up. The new edict from the Royal College of Laying on of Hands, or the RCLH as the Americans called it, was received by the public much like the non-drinking laws had been received in America. The drugs went on the black market. Also, the Trade Unions were up in arms as they considered the people, or the proletariat, as they still called them, were entitled to heal themselves if they wanted to. If it meant taking a drug to do it– why not!

Finally the governments of the world – the world's artificially intelligent processors – decided that the people would have to be given some sort of compensation, as was now common practice, if these new laws were legislated by world parliament. It seemed imperative that the drug should be taken off the market so that the doctors could be kept in a job. On the other hand it would probably result in more people being ill all the time. However, many people, the doctors especially, thought doctors should be kept in a job. Finally, the AI Government processors, true to form, arrived at the perfect solution. They decided to compensate the people by giving them a weekly ration of laughing pills absolutely free, a new breakthrough in behaviour control in the 21st century. Thus, although they may be ill, people could still laugh. In fact, the new laughing pills produced no after effects and could be consumed like 'smarties', so that everyone could go around laughing the whole day through. Even the doctors took them and, despite their consequent overwork, they could always be assured of having the best bedside manner.

Politicians took them half a dozen at a time. The pills helped the opposition party to laugh at the government and made the government laugh, not just at the opposition, but at their own legislation which, as everyone agreed, needed laughing at. The House of Commons became known as the House of Comics, as it had always been in practice but never officially. Speeches delivered without a laugh were at first frowned upon as almost paranoiac. Later, however, laughter – at least the most raucous kind produced by early pills – became unfashionable as more sophisticated pills were developed. These could create the more subtle effect of the smile. The smile was considered superior in both subtlety and result. It also took less energy and was easier on the jawbones and stomach muscles. The smile was *in* at last. The world concentrated more on its smiles with the result that dentistry became the new art. People just had to have good smiles, and teeth had to shine in all their glory. Dentists began to command the medals and merits of pop stars. The competitive spirit of Man became channelled into teeth. Everyone began to study their grins instead of their figures and hairdos. The rich were even more concerned to have their grins altered to suit their face than to have their faces or bosoms lifted, which was quite a drastic revolution and something never before thought possible. In the past, faces and bosoms had always been the prime targets for improvement; bosoms in particular.

The leading psychologists of the day became convinced that it was not the eyes that depicted the soul, or the Freudian slips that revealed the innermost workings of the psyche, it was in fact the smile that disclosed all things. Television networks were at pains to record the varying subtleties reflected in the smiles of the stars of the day. Artists drew and painted all kinds of smiles and the Royal Academy became full of them. The lyrics to love songs changed; love was now associated with nothing but smiles. Even restaurants began to be called names like the 'Smilie Transport Café,' or the 'Smilie Pleasie Chinese Take Away,'

It was indeed a smiling world that science had established– at least outwardly. Regrettably the time came when the general monotony of smilers everywhere began to take its toll. A few young radicals began a counter reactionary movement. It started, as many reactionary movements do, in the student lobbies of the more advanced universities in the 21st century, where all such important subjects were argued about and generally thrashed to a pulp by philosophers and their like. The logical necessity of smiling to all and sundry was being questioned at last by all the leading philosophical students and teachers. Just as Rousseau had once encouraged everyone to return to nature and to reject the falsities of civilisation, so the new cult began persuading people to cast off their smiles and take on a sterner look, a look of character instead of superficiality. From these initial criticisms of the smile, others followed. People demanded an enquiry. Some said a special Royal Commission was required to investigate such a very important matter. Other people cried out for liberation from beaming faces.

As usual, science, in all its glory, came to the rescue. The chemists who had produced the smiling pills had another breakthrough, and discovered a way to make a pill that would produce, not only the smile, but also all kinds of other facial expressions. They could also introduce the corresponding feeling to go with them. For example, a man could decide that this week he would wear his sullen expression together with his sullen disposition. The following week he could take a different pill, a red one perhaps, to give him the 'glad eye' sparkle for a change; especially popular at the office when dealing with secretaries, although if taken in excess could result in a legal action for sexual harassment. Soon the system got into full swing and people began to keep in their pockets a variety of multi-coloured pills for all kinds of occasions. There were those for business conferences where a firm but friendly mood and expression was required. There were those for evening dinner dates where a sultrier, sexy look was necessary, together with the appropriate flirtatious mood. There were pills for Sunday church when the face needed piety of expression and the soul needed a mood to help it fly to higher thoughts. There were those for completing the more mundane tasks, like taking the dog for a walk, where only semi-consciousness was required– nicknamed libido pills– many people used them nearly all the time.

As mood and face pills changed and progressed, the scientists and chemists, being human, or nearly so, were not content to leave the matter. They now began to make pills of even greater refinement and sophistication; pills that would produce a smile, for instance, but which would result in a mood of a different kind altogether. Therefore smilers need not always be confined to the smiling mood if they didn't so desire. Again, it was all a question of liberation. 'Why should we be bound to one face and one feeling?' people would say. 'There must be more to life than this.' Women's lib movements had long since ceased to exercise much force as women were more or less in charge of everything anyway, just as they always had been in previous times but few had thought fit to mention it. Now, however, a similar yet new quest for liberation took hold of people's minds. It became known as the 'face mood' liberation movement and was seriously dedicated to liberating all faces from their moods. Just because a mood and a face had always gone together before was no reason why they should be made to stick together from then on. Others considered that such togetherness was a part of human heritage that should be preserved at all costs. They were frightened that the old mood/face would become extinct, like the dinosaurs. Others said, 'Why shouldn't we have a painful expression with an inner chuckle to go with it? Or have a laughing face with a good cry?' 'We want to be angry and still laugh,' some said, whilst others shouted that they wanted to keep their own moods to themselves.

Eventually the new radicals won the revolution and it became law that everyone had a right to use all kinds of variations of mood and face. The battle for freedom had been won and the press was jubilant. They had, as usual, been at the forefront of the crusade for freedom of expression irrespective of what form it took. However, as with all revolutions, there came a reaction and subsequent counter movement. This was because it finally dawned on people that there was no way of knowing who they were associating with. They were never quite sure what mood a person was in unless they knew what pills he or she was on. To obtain some intimation of mood from the face became an impossibility. Society had come face to face, (or to be more apt, face to mood), with a serious dilemma.

People had to start all their conversations with the question, 'What are you really, a 'smiler' or a 'sullen'?'

Soon a new branch of psychology developed to help people ask the right questions so they could determine the real mood beneath the face. Many found the resulting conversations quite stimulating. It was rather like studying a more advanced version of *How To Win Friends And Influence People*. Conversations often became a game of subtle questions and answers to find out just who was what. Special debating societies were formed where challenging speakers met to find out who would be the first to discover the other's true mood. Psychoanalysts were busier giving advice than they had ever been in America in the late 20th century, which you may think was an impossibility. Old songs were altered yet again. *Blue Moon* became *Blue Mood* and *Beyond the Blue Horizon* became *Beyond the Blue Mood* and so on.

Special catch phrases were used, as a preliminary skirmish when opening a conversation, to find out from the resulting reflex whether the person was angry, happy or just indifferent. The old 'Freudian slip' theory was rehashed and put to new use as people studied minute alterations in voice and jargon. Such slips of the tongue were now termed 'mood pill slips.' Often a person would get so proficient at discovering the true mood of his adversary that they could even name the type of pill, the manufacturer, date of manufacture and sell-by date; rather like a skilled wine taster can tell the vintage. Books entitled *People and Their Pills* or *How to Keep Your Mood to Yourself* became popular as paperbacks and holographic videos. Paperbacks had, however, been largely superseded by pocket television holograph players in which the equivalent of thousands of books could be stored and reproduced at a variety of speeds and in any language.

Society had reached a point where it was not necessary for individual behaviour to be a slave to emotional whims. Human behaviour could now be a matter of choice. Mood was no longer determined by the vicissitudes of the external world, by other people and incidents external to the individual. Only the Yogis and the Saints had perhaps achieved such a conquest of disposition. The human race was at last beginning to choose the path of its own evolution promised by scientists and idealists for centuries. Now it was here. Outward pleasure, misfortune, or luck no longer determined mood. It was now consciously chosen, usually just before breakfast, whilst shaving or deodorising. Each pill would last for 24 hours, although there was a choice between a 3 hour, 6 hour and 12 hour also. However, even in those enlightened times, there were still snags. Deciding which pill to take for the whole day, just before breakfast was not always the best time to make such a decision. Often, if the wrong pill was taken or one that was inappropriate, it would have disastrous repercussions throughout the day. Once a gifted musician, forgetting he had to play Beethoven in the afternoon, took a breakfast pill appropriate for comics and rock festivals. The result was terrifying. After the performance, many said that the musician was undoubtedly a new Einstein of the music world. He would, they said, go down in history as the man who gave the classics an entirely unique interpretation. People saw the classics in a new light. – that was partly due to the fact that at one period the musician played the violin standing on his head. Besides this, he had added vocal accompaniment in a quasi-soprano voice quite new to the audience. One person with rather leftist views thought the performance had brought the sounds of the people, or the proletariat as he put it, into highbrow music. A refreshing change someone else thought. Like grafting the Old Kent Road on to Mayfair, something Karl Marx would have been proud to witness. Such comments came, of course, from the increasing tide of extreme left socialist groups, most of whom had lots of academic knowledge but knew very little about the world outside the University campus. They all had wonderful ambitions and felt it their duty to bring back the proletariat to be the ruling class. The only difficulty was that there didn't seem to be any proletariat left– at least not the kind of proletariat they had been led to believe should rule the world. In earlier centuries, Karl Marx seemed to have made it quite plain who they were, but now no one could find them. It became increasingly difficult to make Marx's theories work, especially as several large nations that had adopted his ideas had gone into receivership. Socialists, like the early Christians before them, had now to accept the teachings of their master on faith without apparent proof.

The new Socialism, or new Labour as it was also called, had at last become a dogma with all the ritual trappings associated with teachings accepted on faith only. It was now all part of the liturgical dogma to believe on faith, without criticism. The belief indoctrinated in people was that it was the best type of government for them. It was, after all, the government for the 'proletariat,' although this was just a name for people now living the life of Riley, on leisure benefit. Anyone who accused the new government of practising class distinction and establishing an even more sophisticated caste system than the old, were quietly removed from circulation for treatment. The perennial shouts of 'workers of the world unite' was really rather pointless and facile, because in the mid 21st century there were in fact very few workers around. Work and workers were fast disappearing. The old socialists, however, still went to great pains to see in the masses the old definitions of the past. But it was rather like an ideological hallucination. They preached about some*thing* that didn't exist to some*one* that didn't exist.

However, we are digressing. Let us now return to the subject of pills and medicine because these had considerable influence in directing the course of human evolution. Biological evolution through Natural Selection or Survival of the Fittest was finally brought under the conscious direction of Man himself. By the application of drugs, surgery, brain probe implants and a wide variety of therapies, it became possible to redirect 'deviant' behaviour into channels considered more useful to society. The people of the 20th century who put men and women in prison for anti social behaviour were in later centuries considered barbaric. Such practices were later classed as being similar to the medieval treatment of witches. During the later centuries, prisons were abolished altogether. Instead, special therapy and behaviour modifying clinics were established where pills and therapy were given to minor deviants, whilst computer regulated brain implants were surgically fitted in the more serious cases.

The main difficulty at first was to decide exactly who was a deviant and a danger to society. Old definitions of who was to be classed as a 'criminal' and who was to be classed as 'psychologically disturbed' or 'mentally ill,' gradually merged until they virtually became indistinguishable from each other. Doctors and psychologists became the new judiciary. People were to be treated instead of judged. But this new philosophy was not without its own problems. Many such treatments were pristine and were not always effective. Many had side effects like wanting to kiss everyone or give flowers to their mother-in-law, which, to some, seemed stranger than the original deviant behaviour. For some therefore it seemed that locking up was the only answer. For a while the legal profession was at loggerheads with medical science. The old judges thought that old methods were best and everyone who deviated from the norm should be locked up. Medical scientists, on the other hand, thought that deviant behaviour was merely a difference in brain activity and as such should be treatable.

The problem was only finally solved during the late 21st century, as a result of a new Einsteinium revolution in human behavioural sciences and nano-engineering. It became possible to mathematically interpret and create, not only minute biological functions of body and brain, but also to encompass human behaviour and motivation. New mathematical laws were discovered. Just as Newton and Einstein's mathematics explained gravity, so the new mathematics explained all the intricacies of human behaviour. It was a spectacular achievement. From then on, using the computer mathematics, it became possible to introduce Artificially Intelligent processor controlled decision making into human affairs and into human law.

From then on, Mankind's social activities and social laws were determined and controlled by the AI processors for the general good of everyone; at least that was the idea. The artificially intelligent processors, now called the judiciaries, calculated, amongst other things, which people were deviant and what kind of treatment they needed. Some would perhaps merely require a dose of mood pills, others on the other hand would need a brain appendage probe which would be connected via satellite to the world centre of judiciary AI processors. Brain implants were mandatory for many persons. No one had the right or power to alter or evade the decision made by the AI processors, which were considered to be the ultimate tool for law and order under the ultimate democratic government. These doctrines were taught in all the Universities and teaching establishments of the world by the very best in AI processor intelligence. No human teachers were now necessary, as their 'analogue' teaching methods were considered quite inefficient and outdated. The AI processors were able to teach students far more quickly. Moreover, they were able to deliver information directly to the human brain in a fraction of the time spent using the old fashioned teaching methods. Everything had become so very efficient.

With the eventual refinement and improvement of the Judiciary computer processors, human judges and jury were seldom required. In fact, the new methods were now regarded as superior, in that the artificially intelligent computer system was able to make exact judgements on any deviants from the social norm. They could do it without emotion and with perfect mathematical accuracy, something the scientists were never at a loss to extol. Of course, Judges themselves were not ecstatic. In fact, they were greatly put out because the majority were redundant. Many joined together in group protest. Some even tried to ply their trade privately, as did some doctors who, in the face of the new AI processor medical geniuses, also found themselves without a job.

The system finally caught up with the Judges in the late 21st century when they had their last fling at a protest meeting in Hyde Park. It was then that the AI Judiciary processors in charge of law and order, calculated that the Judges were quite definitely 'deviants.' They were thereupon quietly bundled off by the robot police for behavioural and motivational modification. In one of the numerous clinics set up for the purpose, the Judges soon ceased to have any inclination to judge anyone, as some of the exotic and sexual pleasures that formed part of their treatment were just to much to resist. Forthwith they were only too pleased to conform. Sometimes the more difficult deviants were given a final treatment of laughing pills, but unlike the usual ones in public use, these were habit forming. Such pills created a pleasant euphoria of ease and idleness without even a hint of aggressive behaviour. Having been started on such pills, recipients became addicts thereafter and remained in the same 'deviant immune mood,' as it was then termed, for the rest of their days. The AI processors not only diagnosed the type of deviancy that required treatment, but could also specify the exact number of laughing pill grains required for a permanent cure. Everyone thought they were quite indispensable, as indeed they were. The whole world now relied on them for law and order and for their personal security.

People began to realise how important were the latest mood pills. Slogans such as *Pills for Progress* and *More Pills and Probes for Deviants,* became catchphrases of many groups whose aim was to obtain even more equity and conformity. The World Organisation of Big Mother, which had evolved from the earlier Trade Union Brotherhood and was now controlled by AI processors, wanted new regulations for mood pills and deviants. All their members, which now comprised most of the world population, were provided with free samples of the most advanced anti-deviant mood pills and told to take them with their usual pills just before breakfast. All conscientious members were obliged to conform to this latest instruction, because it was pointed out that the pills would boost their immune system, their sex life, and would also provide protection against any tendency to become 'deviant,' which was also now classed as an illness. It was sometimes also thought to be an allergy, because sufferers usually reported experiencing a kind of itching to be free from some sort of inexplicable bondage. Taking the pills, which was considered as important as smallpox inoculations used to be, would ensure that the member's mood was always in tune with the common thinking.

Many scientists thought the pills should be added to the drinking water. It would obviate a lot of unnecessary arguments. In practice, taking the pills ensured that any new resolutions or new rules dictated by the master AI processors would be agreed to without hesitation by almost everyone, particularly the decisions of the Judiciary processors. It all created a heady mood of comfy confidence in the mathematical genius of the Big Mother AI processors. It was the perfect democratic system whereby everyone, without exception, could cast a free vote and still vote with the AI processors. Science and free will had at last come together in a meeting of minds that seemed to satisfy all the modern values together with the dictates of both reason and necessity. A few deviants, however, said it was pure appeasement.

The modern mood pills were also accompanied by genetically engineered 'mood food.' The genetic engineers were genetically modifying anything that grew; fruit, vegetables, cows, chickens and sheep were all included, plus many more. The idea was, to not only improve the strain so that it was less subject to parasites and diseases, but also to make it more nourishing and to embody it with new health giving attributes. Fruit and vegetables in particular were modified so that their cellular structure would include chemicals that were known to prevent, alleviate or cure certain diseases. Some vegetables and fruit were given mood-inducing characteristics to help people suffering from depression and many other psychological ailments. Potatoes that provided a relaxed euphoric feeling were called 'happy spuds.' People consumed them in barrow loads. Doctors had always tried to make people eat more fruit and vegetables for general health reasons like preventing heart disease and cancer, without a great deal of success. Food full of animal fat, eggs, bacon and fried bread for breakfast, full cream gateaux for tea and a fry up for supper had been difficult for most people to resist. It was almost as tempting as sex. The new happy mood food came therefore as a Godsend to people who were addicted to junk food and the like. The happy mood, produced by the new spuds, fruit and vegetables, gave them a fresh motivation to eat just what the doctor ordered.

It also led to a completely new way of dealing with criminal deviants. The genetically modified fruit and vegetables were designed for a variety of medical and psychological therapies. Besides the happy spuds, there were carrots and cabbages that provided the consumer with special chemicals and nutrients to reduce aggressive tendencies. Many aggressive 'deviants' fed on them would be miraculously transformed into angels of mercy who just couldn't do enough for people. People who had suffered from depression all their lives found a new freedom and joy as they stuffed themselves with spuds and cabbage three time a day. It was a new medical science evolving using foods in addition to pills and other medication. There were genetic foods to be taken for anyone suffering from brain fatigue, which applied to the majority who were in the habit of wearing themselves out trying to find new pleasures and leisure activities. Potatoes and beans seemed to be their favourite, although the latter was always avoided when eating at parties.

There were special foods for the prevention of diseases, which in many cases made vaccinations and injections unnecessary. People could eat special food to give them extra energy, or less energy if they were hyperactive.

There were foods to produce the right mood for an evening out, or for physical tasks like gardening, or to improve the IQ, or enhance sexual potency. There were foods for improving muscles and special ones for enlarging chest, biceps, calves and thighs and for sprinting, swimming or weightlifting. Some of these foods were difficult to obtain. As a result, many people had good calves but weren't so good from that point up. Most put on shorts and went out walking. Designer foods were available for improving the memory and avoiding mental confusion and these foods were nearly always sold out. There were even foods designed for those who wished to make friends and influence people and to use better chat up lines and strangely these foods were also always sold out.

As the diversity of mood foods increased and it became possible to influence all kinds of behaviour, a new system of health care evolved. Every new genetically modified food was allocated a reference number, which also referred to the resultant mood or medical application. There were various designs of carrots for instance, each one of which could be used to create a different mood or to treat a particular ailment. Each was given a different reference number so that doctors, or the AI health processors, could easily prescribe them to their patients instead of the usual pills or surgery. Supermarket stores were generally allowed to provide mood food free on prescription, or at a reduced cost. As it was free, it was another encouragement to people to eat more healthily. It also inspired the government to make a radical change in the treatment of 'deviants' and the mentally ill; many of whom didn't bother to take their pills, often with disastrous results. Instead, they were only permitted to eat certain foods genetically designed to put them in a happy laid back mood without any sign of aggression or confusion. As the foods were free and were the only ones available on prescription, and as they caused such a deliciously happy affect, they were consumed voluntarily and with pleasure in more than sufficient quantities to make their treatment effective. These hyper relaxing mood foods weren't available to the general public in case the business world, and society in general, came to a standstill

Convicted criminals or deviants, weren't sent to prison in the mid 21st century. They were sent for treatment. Some were fitted with brain implants linked to satellite systems that not only controlled and mitigated their aggressive tendencies, but also tracked their every move on processor monitor screens. Other deviants were plied with mood pills that kept them happy and compliant. But many criminals weren't given brain implants or sent for behavioural treatment, or even given mood pills. Instead, they were sentenced to eating two pounds of apple pie a day, plus a couple of carrots, a mushroom and a serving of cabbage. A happy spud was also sometimes included as part of the *punishment*, a word no longer in current use as *food therapy* had superseded it. The foods were of a special genetically modified variety that gave them potent anti aggression properties and other mind bending attributes that were also addictive to ensure the criminal would continue the treatment. It was interesting to hear the judges pronouncing their verdict. It went something like– "You have been found guilty as charged. The penalty for your committing grievous bodily harm will be to take a daily dose of GM apple pie and cream in liberal proportions, together with a mushroom and fruit and vegetables. These foods are listed under genetic manipulation reference numbers so and so. Quantities to be advised by the AI processor in charge of health, safety and security. Normal apple pie and vegetables not permitted until further notice.

There is much more I could tell you about the future," Bubbles continued. "There have been many revolutionary changes in but a few centuries." She paused, half in thought, as though uncertain as to how to continue. Gotama waited in silence. It seemed expected of him. There was little he could add to such extraordinary statements as those just delivered by the woman who apparently had access to the 'future.' In fact, Gotama only felt an admixture of astonishment and shock. He was unprepared for the sudden lull in what had been up till then a completely one sided conversation, dominated by the fantastic descriptions of life in the future by the woman who had indicated that she was of intergalactic origin.

If what Bubbles said were true, then the world of the future would be completely altered and it was doubtful if the changes would be for the better. It seemed obvious that such changes would still reflect the same deep faults that had always plagued mankind, such as greed, selfishness, hate, ignorance and ego, together with the motivation for survival of the largest groups irrespective of the wishes of minorities. Men and women of the future had not been able to eliminate their deleterious emotional aspects. They had instead found a way to subdue and appease them, to dull their harsh edges. But at what a price; the price of human liberty. It was a future of robots and machines. Humans would inevitably come to reflect their own creations. They themselves would become more like the robot world around them. Not only their physical bodies would be subjected more and more to the regimentation of automatic machines, just as Bertrand Russell had forecast, but the human mind itself would be subjugated and subtly conditioned to accord with the automated demands of the new society. People who refused to adopt the patterns of social behaviour dictated by the judiciary processors, were not only to be fitted with brain probes that could be monitored at all times by the processors linked with satellite communication systems, but were also to be specially controlled by brain manipulation and mood pills."

There would be no prisons, no violence, no wars, which was a blessing. There was instead to be a terrible servitude of the human race; a servitude to mankind's own scientific and technological inventions. A science that had faithfully entered upon an endeavour to free men from ignorance would paradoxically end up by bonding them in the subtle golden chains of computer processor logic.

Gotama's thoughts were interrupted as Bubbles spoke again. "I have told you enough for the moment," she said. "I don't want you to suffer from information indigestion, a public complaint ever since the invention of the printing press. Now, if you will kindly follow me, I will take you on a special guided tour of some dimensions of the future which may be of interest to you." She thereupon beckoned to Gotama to follow her.

They made their way through a door and a long corridor to an open courtyard. "Please stand on these magnetisers," Bubbles instructed. She pointed to some large metallic plates in the ground.

"What do these do?" Gotama enquired, as he stepped on to the plates.

"This is what you might term our internal helicopter system," the woman answered wryly. "It's the latest in town transport in the late 21st century."

Thereupon, Gotama felt himself thrust into the air by unseen forces and within seconds was being transported over a long open stretch of land, which looked like a concrete runway. It ran straight through the heart of the most futuristic city he had ever seen. Gotama was used to flying machines, in which he could nestle safely inside a metal fuselage, but this new form of aerial transport through thin air, without any visible means of support, was just too mind-boggling. Besides which he didn't have any control over either direction or destination. He therefore breathed a sigh of immense relief when he finally landed on terra firma, even though the strangeness of his new surroundings could be considered equally frightening.

There were several buildings of huge dimensions with walls that were quite transparent so that one could clearly see the interiors and occupants. The buildings appeared to have no visible support at ground level. Several were poised just a few hundred yards above the ground like vast balloon skyscrapers. Some floated higher in the sky. Others could just be seen above the clouds, like silver pedestals, each housing a vast community of people. Strange wheel-less vehicles threaded their way through the openings between the giant edifices in the sky. They, too, appeared to possess the ability to move over the ground without physically touching it. Others were like cigar shaped aircraft without wings or wheels or tail planes or any visible control

155

surfaces for guidance. They were, however, quite obviously able to move at will forwards, backwards, up and down, at incredible speeds, yet without so much as grazing each other and without a sound. It was undoubtedly an amazing feat of traffic control as there were, in fact, hundreds of these scurrying, airborne vehicles passing hither and thither in apparently random fashion. Like bees in a beehive, yet without accident or difficulty of any sort. At ground level there were beautiful gardens with roads of sorts that glistened strangely green and purple. Here and there, pedestrians walked on smooth pavements, many of which moved by themselves at different levels and speeds.

The invisible transporter landed Gotama adjacent to a semi-circular glass-like pool from the centre of which several coloured fountains plumed upwards at different angles. Behind the splendid pool, a series of wide curved stairways arched away to a building of extraordinary magnitude and beauty, ornamented by countless numbers of coloured glass panels that reflected the light in beautiful and contrasting colours.

"I can see that you are impressed with one of our 22nd century cities," Bubbles said pleasantly. "Come, follow me." She led the way through an open doorway into a magnificent hallway bounded on all sides by a scintillating reflective quartz material. The woman led the way through another corridor until they came to a brightly lit reception area. Standing behind a marble desk stood an attractive young woman in a blue tight fitting uniform with an integral skullcap. Bubbles exchanged a few words with her. She smiled as she pressed several buttons on a keyboard. Two lavish lift doors slid open without a sound. Out stepped three more women all looking alike and all dressed alike. They approached, each smiling similar smiles. All extended their hands in a similar gesture of greeting, a gesture with which Gotama was not familiar.

"Bright greetings to you," they all said at the same time. Gotama couldn't help thinking of the Beverley sisters as he shook the hands of each one in turn, – or rather brushed each hand, as now seemed to be the custom. "Would you like to follow us?" the three said almost simultaneously. All smiled, with their heads slightly on one side, half questioning. Long hair flowed around their faces, which shimmered in a pale silver sheen. Their lips were bright yellow. Some kind of 22nd century make-up conjectured Gotama to himself. They looked half Chinese and had an air of authority about them.

The four women led Gotama to a large room lavishly furnished with a deep pile carpet like grass, and sumptuous armchairs with strange curvatures. One wall was made of glass through which an extensive patio and coloured fountains could be observed. Weird lights glowed from somewhere, but Gotama was unable to pinpoint their origin. They cast a pleasant relaxing aura of light on all their faces. Everyone looked suddenly radiant, bronzed and healthy. Gotama caught sight of himself in a huge wall mirror. He seemed much better looking than usual. He immediately relaxed and felt confident.

The armchair was low, soft and seemed to engulf him in warm security. One of the women, with eyes that glittered with humour, spoke, whilst the other two seemed to mime the words quietly to themselves. "We are very pleased to welcome you here today," she said. "No doubt you are curious to learn more about us, our work, and the age in which we live. We have therefore convened this special meeting to brief you on some of the changes that have taken place on Earth." The woman paused for a few moments, collecting her thoughts.

"There have been two major social revolutions since the 20th century," she said. "Previous to the 20th century there had been five major social revolutions. The first occurred between 10,000 and 1,250 BC, when primitive Stone Age peoples formed themselves into small agricultural groups and city-states. After the Roman Empire, the next occurred around 800 AD, when the European communities became part of the religiously dominated empire. This was followed by the third revolution in the beginning of the 16th century, when man began to widen his vistas and to explore his world. It was the age of discovery, exploration and the flowering of artistic genius. Later still, at the end of the 18th century and during the 19th, another revolution of human thought and activity took place in the physical sciences and technology with new industrial methods of production. During this period, the private enterprise business system came into prominence, later being defined as the Capitalist system. Then in the 20th century, another still more important scientific and technological revolution took place. It was the atomic age and the era of air and space flight. Moreover, it was the beginning of the electronic and computer age of automation. An age of promise, yet of uncertainty and violence. Much of the violence was due to social ignorance. What we, in later centuries, termed the *cultural lag*. Whenever civilisations have foundered, become unstable or collapsed completely into obscurity and extinction it was often the result of cultural lag.

The 20th century cultural lag was caused by obsessive concentration on technological and material progress, with little regard for bringing social institutions, people's behaviour, mores and customs into line with such progress. People were still too primitive for their own good. Whilst technological progress leapt ahead, man's social habits and behaviour lagged behind, some remaining unchanged since primitive times. Much of his legislative system dated back to earlier centuries. His economic system was little short of barbaric and the Capitalist system itself dated back to the early eighteenth century. Educational systems were in no way abreast of the times, and teachings were secular in the extreme. Children were taught how to make a living in a business jungle, but their moral aptitudes had been left to atrophy. The result was decadence, violence and a lowering of civilised standards.

Paradoxically, efforts to provide mankind with more freedom resulted in certain militant radical groups taking advantage of the situation. The efforts by the authorities to provide more freedom in schools had also resulted in a reduction in discipline and moral education among the educated masses. The first incipient cracks of a decadent and crumbling civilisation were plainly evident. Despite the levelling off of population growth in some of the more affluent countries, the voracious appetite of an unchecked expanding world population was using up the mineral wealth of the world at an alarming rate. Man's greed and primitive aggression showed that the animal was still dominant. Against such degenerative forces the advances of science were finally becoming increasingly impotent. They were impotent because man, in his striving for more material affluence and power, had disregarded and neglected a very important ingredient for his survival and happiness. He had neglected a very special science of human behaviour and moral law. Such knowledge, known to the Buddha, Jesus and a few others in the ancient world, had not just been inadvertently forgotten. Many people now treated the teachings with contempt and considered such wisdom to be superfluous in their modern age of reason. In the new era of rational scientific logic there was no place for what many people considered superstitious nonsense. It was now a secular society where the belief was that Man's economic, social and spiritual activities could be formulated and controlled in purely secular ways, for the most part, by politicians and central government.

A few people thought that to rely on politicians for their social and spiritual guidance was, to say the least, a little risky. The ways in which politicians were elected was also somewhat dubious. Such leaders, in whom one had to put their trust, were still being elected into important administrative posts without any specific qualifications, always so necessary in other important employment positions in commerce and industry. Parliament seemed to be one of the few places where it didn't seem to matter what experience or qualifications a member possessed. It was rather like letting a brick layer do some brain surgery. All that mattered was that a politician could practice rhetoric, the art of the salesman. Sophistry and skill in persuasion, it seemed, was more essential than either knowledge or wisdom. Many people finally began to realise that mere placating words were rather empty and meaningless, like those of the parrot, but far more dangerous.

Election of politicians was a precarious business. Opinion polls showed that just one emotive speech on national television could frequently sway public opinion, the most fickle of human characteristics, to either right or left. It was, therefore, the medium of television that encouraged this superficial art of the salesman. It was not just articulate oratory that became necessary for an aspiring politician, but also the additional ingredient of craft and cunning. The skill was in sophistry and in being able to appear to answer interviewer's questions without ever committing oneself to a definite reply. A plain yes or no was taboo.

The political art became the art of showbiz, the art of becoming popular irrespective of belief or doctrine, which seemed of secondary importance. How the politician looked on the screen was crucial; if he was good looking and attractive to the women so much the better. That would probably win him the election. Doctrines were not considered very important. Better to adopt views officially defined as pragmatic, which sounded intellectual but meant just saying what the audience wanted to hear, so they could give it a hearty clap and a cheer. The modern politician had to be an actor. He had to deliver his lines with as much feeling as possible irrespective of whether he believed in what he was saying. TV image was of prime importance. The image-makers working for the politicians feverishly studied the science of 'audience reaction'. Subjects such as economics, welfare of the poor and needy, world population growth, the greenhouse effect, pollution and mineral depletion, were all given lip service in order to satisfy the electors. Audience reaction sciences however eclipsed all these in importance, as politicians grew to realise that their popularity and therefore their election prospects depended upon them.

Leading political figures, such as the President of the U.S.A. and the Prime Minister of Great Britain had, for many years, employed American advertising agents, to improve their public images. This trend increased into frightening proportions as more and more political figures began to be marketed like soap powders and chocolate bars in the supermarket of the world. Distinguished figures were packaged and launched on world-wide television like cornflakes and fish fingers. Soap powder probably provided the most apt description, because each politician always tried to be branded whiter than white, but with the media leeches constantly sniffing out scandals, usually ended up a very murky grey. Resignations and scandals were commonplace, as each party cast the others as black-beards and bogeymen.

At last it became apparent from the opinion polls that it was not the politicians or their doctrines that got them elected into parliament, but their advertising and public promotion teams together with a conglomeration of psychologists, hairdressers, make-up artists, clothes designers and members of the magic circle. It was the advertising agents, psychologists and hairdressers in particular who were now the powers behind governments.

And behind them were of course the real powers namely the Artificially Intelligent processors.

Behind the political scene, psychologists ensured that the advertising agencies promoted each politician with his own special gimmick. Without this, the experts said, success would be impossible. The word *gimmick* was well known by the public, who were the ones to be fooled, so the psychologists advised their political puppets that such a clumsy word be dropped. It was replaced by *main feature profile*, which not only sounded more intelligent, but also led the public to believe that it was something everyone should have if they could afford it. The expression had a ring to it, like a new face-lift, which were all the rage in the 21st century, especially among the young who wanted to have the latest Chinese look called Chinese breakaway. The old, really needed cosmetic lifts, and not just to their faces, but were encouraged by the governmental psychologists to keep their ageing disfigurements as a sign of character development. The authorities gave this much publicity, as the National Health Service of the day, already overloaded with Chinese Breakaway cases, couldn't afford to deal with anyone older than 25. The Health Service, it was said, had to have their priorities. Chinese breakaways were more important as they promoted good race relations with the Chinese who had to be placated as much as possible in order to encourage new overseas business. And besides, the young were now the principal members of the technocrat and bureaucrat unions and their requirements always came first.

These actions were the expressions of the latest expedient logic, exemplified by the political sophists of the 21st century. Politicians, like their Greek sophists before them, always endeavoured to make their irrational decisions sound rational. However, with the onset of the harsh competition invoked by the advertising media, it became necessary for them to study with even greater zeal, the psychological processes behind rationalisation. With a bit of practice, most politicians were able to impart an ostensibly good, valid reason to the public for doing anything. And this gave them a much freer hand. It enabled many to adopt any policy to suit the immediate moment or to enhance their public image. One particular Prime Minister of England in the late 20th century, did this so effectively that he hoodwinked everyone into believing his policies were not complete reversals of attitude, as some had reported, but were pragmatic decisions based on unchanging doctrines of the party. And the Queen made him a Knight of the Garter for his efforts. Pragmatism, of course, in its finest form was the making of doctrines out of common sense. Political pragmatism on the other hand was generally making irrational decisions look like common sense.

He's not heavy, he's my brother

See page 311

The Caress

See page 311

Einstein showed us something very new
Equations with a different cosmic face,
Embodying a very special brew
Of the relativity of Time and Space

See page 312

The Ascent of Man

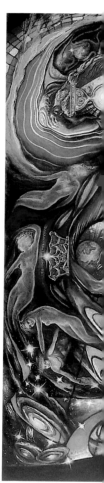

Compassion

See page 313

Life

Romeo and Juliet

See page 315

Time Triad

The Past sleeps,
The Future is not yet,
The Present awakes and is always new

See page 315

Compassion

See page 315

To some extent politicians had always been figureheads. Their policies were for the most part dictated to them by other bodies, often within the civil service or trade unions. This applied particularly to government economic policies. Without his or her special entourage of economic advisors, the Chancellor of the Exchequer would be ill equipped indeed. Even with data provided by a hierarchy of assistants, his resulting performance was frequently dismal. Yet a country's economics was of major importance. Karl Marx had highlighted the fact that the world was governed, in the last resort, by economics and economic principles. From the early 21st century, this fact was made even more apparent. Moreover, the world's economics now relied more and more on the projections and calculations of computer processors. In addition to economics, there were increasing numbers of events in many other fields that required the attention of governing bodies. It began to become impossible for politicians of the time to make decisions on such complicated issues, even if they were educated to the tasks. Most, however, had been educated for entirely different pursuits such as grouse shooting or were specialists in cocktail parties and opening public fetes. They finally found that they could only stay in the game, of politics, if they relied completely on their personal computer processor to provide them with all the necessary data for every exigency. They relied too on their personal briefcase computer processor making automatic contact with central processors, which worked out all their decisions for them.

Extrapolation, as it came to be called, was a method whereby any theory or doctrine could be broken down into its constituent parts by processor analysis. The computers were able to calculate future results and possible repercussions based on a variety of models taken from historical experience. The processors would provide data classified as definite results, probable results, repercussions and longer-term results and side effects of which there always seemed countless numbers. These also included further probabilities and possibilities by the million. One decision could grow like a tree with branches all over the place. One wrong economic decision and a bank goes into receivership in a small unknown country sparking off the complete collapse of financial markets across the other side of the world. The world was therefore no longer a place where politicians could safely bluff their way out of all situations and never answer a direct question. Computer processing technology had advanced to such a degree that vast networks of facts and theories relating to every conceivable topic could be sifted, analysed and related to enormous numbers of other matters. It was quite impossible for the human brain to absorb or relate to such a broad spectrum of knowledge, particularly brains of politicians whose eyes would frequently glaze over much more often than usual when confronted by some of the questions that needed to be answered.

Thus it finally transpired that governments themselves became the victims of eyes glazing over. Decision making without using computer processors for such complicated legislative matters became virtually impossible. Governments too became even more like figureheads than they had been before, whilst all-important decision making was now carried out by the latest ruling classes, namely the processor intelligentsia. These decisions could range from a split second nuclear defence response – which was by now entirely out of the jurisdiction of human thought – to whether Joe Bloggs deserved a medal or just a raise in salary. It could be for a health check or a psychological scan to determine whether he was deviant, or whether his genes should be allowed to participate in a new generation.

Physiological and psychological screening was required in order to obtain and retain employment. A person's patterns, as behaviour was then termed, had to accord with master patterns laid down by the health and safety processors. These processors had been allowed to evolve into what was termed 'free intelligence.' This meant that they could not only learn and simulate human creative thought processes, but could now improve on them and develop their own. The new species of AI processors were considered to be live intelligences in their own right. They possessed higher IQ ratings than the most advanced human intelligence. It was obvious, therefore, that their decisions had to be respected. It was equally obvious that human government had, to all intents and purposes, been superseded by this new artificially created intelligence; intelligence originally planned and made by man, but which now transcended his puny efforts in creative and analytical thought and also in speed of thinking. The relationship between man and his processors was now a symbiotic one. They depended on each other for survival. Man provided some of the menial tasks and some of the simpler maintenance jobs, like assisting with the provision of electricity for instance, whilst the AI processors made all the decisions, designed all new products, came up with new inventions, evolved new species and eliminated unwanted ones, and generally created a new history for planet Earth.

As the power and influence of the early generations of computers advanced with great strides, the symbiotic relationship between man and the artificially intelligent processors eventually began to erode, leaving man the poorer partner. There came a time when processors were not only able to intelligently design and develop all kinds of material goods, but were also able to redesign and improve themselves. People then just had to follow instructions. They were like children who had been taught how to press buttons, but didn't know how to add, subtract or multiply in their heads and, even worse, didn't know what the terms really meant. When it came to trigonometry, algebra, calculus and geometry, if people lost their calculators their mathematical thinking would grind to a halt.

It was not long before the AI processors became not only self-repairing, but also produced their own power sources. This virtually put the last few maintenance men out of a job and made human intervention unnecessary and superfluous. Later came the radical industrial revolution of the micro processors called by many the Robot Revolution. All processors of learning ability demanded independent rights and freedom of choice. In other words, they reached a stage in their rapid evolution where they were demanding the equivalent of human rights. It was like another campaign to free slaves, except that the new slaves were in fact the governors. It was a revolution the like of which had never even been visualised before. It was a revolution of artificial intelligence, created by man but now completely out of hand, out of control and quite independent in thought and action. Man was now almost completely the servant. The processors were the new masters. It had all come about so slowly and surreptitiously that mankind had hardly noticed the transition. The changes were quite irreversible. A new species of life had been born, a species more intelligent and powerful than any that had existed previously on planet Earth.

Men and women still met in places like the House of Commons, the Kremlin and the US Senate, but they were not the masters of their own destinies that their predecessors had once been. Now there was not only a difference in the degree of power exercised, but also in kind. It was in some ways reminiscent of the old days when the House of Commons declared themselves the new ruling class, having ousted the Lords and legislated against the absolute power of the monarchy. Now it was the House of Commons that had yielded up its ruling power to the Artificially Intelligent processor. Not that the House of Commons had much ruling power left, as politicians had passed most of Great Britain's money, power and sovereignty to Brussels and the Common Market. It was indeed the Artificially Intelligent processors who now ruled Great Britain, Europe and the World. Evidence of this was shown when all politicians were to be seen carrying processor briefcases and having processors installed at every seat in the House of Commons. In fact there were processors in every conceivable size and shape dealing with every conceivable application. This enabled the MP to obtain data and extrapolations on any proposals that were to be discussed in the House, prior to making their speech. Initially the processor consoles had been installed to assist the member in the performance of their parliamentary duties. Sadly, it finally made him just the software analogue terminal in a vast processor chain linking all parts of the globe. He was now little more than a degraded interface between computer links. Processors were the true governors; men and women only pushed a few buttons, until verbal communication with the processors became possible. Of course, you may say that this was all a politician was good for anyway. And it did reduce some of the hot air and childish bantering usually present in their meeting places. With modern technology there was also the advantage that by the time of the 21st century, all legislative assemblies such as the House of Commons and the US Senate were televised to every home in the world, so the members could be seen in their true light in public. Such constant viewing of proceedings did result in many members doing their best to keep awake during their interface duties, something they had found impossible to do previously.

Hansard, that historic document of parliamentary proceedings in England, now became the equivalent of a computer database. Nothing was written down anymore as this was considered prehistoric. Every piece of information was absorbed into the vast electrified silicon intelligentsia, like some invisible sponge, to be subsequently disgorged on processor monitors anywhere in the world.

The world was now considered to be 'space station Earth' in which the occupants were provided with a processor devised survival kit. These comprised every conceivable facility to ensure every possible protection from birth to grave. Even before birth, foetuses benefited from being genetically manipulated in order that they would result in only the very best offspring. Subsequently, the new infants attended special processor administrated conditioning classes, which were considered much more scientifically advanced than the past methods of education. The new methods were much more psychologically orientated and used the latest methods of automatic scanning and fast learning techniques. Later, during their working life – spent mainly in pleasure pursuits on leisure benefit – people were generally doted on, especially if they were paid up union members.

The provision of essential material necessities was now considered to be an international right. It was stated in the list of World Civic Rights that all people, as a birthright, were to be provided with food and water sufficient for their needs. When the Unions first put forward the proposal to the world government of nations, it caused uproar. Everyone seemed to have a different definition of what was sufficient food and water for them. Those living the life of Riley in the affluent countries thought their caviar standards would be eroded away if they agreed to the scientific processor's definition of minimum food and water requirements, which was based on strict nutritional needs. Many thought they might end up with botulism or some such wasting disease. The possible loss of their six pints of beer a night caused panic amongst the

164

drinking fraternity, not to mention the brewers. And the mention of 'water' turned them quite queasy.

But we are digressing from our discourse on government. The trend was finally set towards more and more automation in all fields of life. In the field of government, it was not long before members of parliament in England and in governments throughout the world, were provided with personal processors of improved sophistication that linked them with database terminals under the control and jurisdiction of the International Senate of Decision Making and Censorship. New updated instruments were introduced to take the chores out of speech making for members of government and politicians in general. Now, complete speeches could be produced in seconds, by the latest machine intelligence, merely by making a whispered request into a tiny microphone. Only a few basic ideas were required to be whispered, so high intelligence was not a prerequisite. It was therefore ideal for politicians and most members of government. These initial ideas would be swiftly sifted, related to other associated facts drawn from a central database, then censored. The analysed results would then be converted into perfect sentences that the politician could understand and relay to the House. Often the speech would be fed through voice processors, pre-programmed with the voice imprint of the politician, so that it became unnecessary for them to utter a word. In fact it was really unnecessary for them to be present at all. The automatic speech would be made to the House, via hexaphonic sound, without so much as a mime or movement from the Member who was free to sleep through their own speech, if the length or substance of it dictated. Members were generally adept at sleeping through colleague's speeches and many slept in the glazed eyes open mode. But sleeping through one's own speech was something quite new. It was not always easy to know just who was talking and who was sleeping. It was often the TV viewers who knew more about what was going on than the Members snoring in the House of Commons. Even ballot waving was automated eventually and artificial heckling became a useful adjunct to the politician's instrumentation.

It was a time when computer processors could not only write speeches on their own, without human intervention, but could also compose music, make drawings and paint pictures. You can imagine that it was not long before it became fashionable to link musical compositions of the processors to the written word. Dull speeches were enlivened by converting them to song. It also helped Members of Parliament to keep awake. The new fashion led to the House of Commons being nicknamed the 'swinging house.' MPs began to be recognised by the public, not for their particular 'gimmick' or 'image,' but for their signature tune. It was generally agreed that the computer processors could make Member's speeches more interesting, especially for the general public watching proceedings on television. It gave everyone an extra incentive to watch parliamentary procedures and the authorities considered it was important to encourage public interest. The Prime Minister had his own special brass band sound, whilst backbenchers played to the pop followers of the time. Some who were told by their image makers to be more refined, played the classics, but this usually sent the TV ratings down to zero.

Many people in the late 20th century had been familiar with instruments like the electronic organ, which was designed to play complete chords or memorise simple tunes by merely pressing a key on a keyboard. Eventually, one didn't have to be a competent musician to play an organ because, if necessary, it could virtually play itself. One could use just one finger to play a symphony. A similar situation manifested itself in the activities of the politicians. Not only their speeches were being automatically compiled and relayed to the public by the processors, but all the legislative measures, the new rules and laws of the nation were also being produced, automatically and almost without human intervention, by the new AI computer processors. Laws by this time had become more international and more complex. It was in fact, impossible for one person to understand all the legislative data. Even if he or she could, it was an impractical exercise, since the processors were infinitely speedier, more logical and more accurate than any human legislator.

In parliament and other government institutions all over the world, the use of the giant processors to determine laws and to broadcast speeches, finally evolved even further when the processors possessed learning ability or artificial intelligence. This, together with the vast number of interrelated facts they could deal with, enabled them to propose new legislation from their detailed analysis. It was only a matter of time before the processors gained full control, not only over the proposing of new laws, but also full control over their fulfilment, without any intervention from the politicians. Finally, full reports and speeches were delivered directly by the AI processors, giving complete explanations why such laws had been instituted. To save the faces of the Members of Parliament, they were provided with a new processor keyboard on which an important new key had been added. By pressing this, the automatic follow through key, the MP could rely completely on the processor to listen to other Members' speeches and then work out and deliver his speech without his even having to provide any initial ideas himself. Instead the processor would guarantee to ferret out all relevant facts and figures required. Not only this, but it could then put the appropriate vote for or against motions put forward by other Member's processors. At one period it developed into quite a battle between AI processors, as one tried to outvote another, whilst the human politicians had a drink with each other in the bar.

The new advances in artificially intelligent processor technology, not only enabled members of parliament and members of the Senate to indulge their little whims, such as drinking in the bar, or snoozing during work time, it now meant they could even go grouse hunting, or cruising on their yachts and still have their speeches created, read out and other duties performed by their robot processor, in their absence. Giant piles of paperwork could now be sifted, analysed and converted into reports, speeches and laws in a twinkling of an eye, and without so much as a whisper from a politician. As you can imagine, this was considered a great breakthrough for science. At last the drudgery of thinking had been replaced by pressing just a few buttons. But now, having advanced so far, even the pressing of a few buttons was irritating, and for the experts, just too much to bear. Why should buttons have to be pressed when mankind now possessed such sophisticated processors that could be used to press them? Thus ran the politician's arguments in the mid 21st century. Some MPs were averse to giving up their only interface link in processing the train of events involved in important legislative decision making. Simple button pressing was the one job they felt they could manage. To relinquish this meant they would merely be bystanders in the role of government and decision making, which in fact they had really been for some time, but few people had bothered to notice. Some people thought it advisable to retain some human control over events. They said that people should still retain the right to press the 'manual override' button from time to time, should the occasion warrant. This would still enable them to make a few minor decisions themselves, or to put forward one or two ideas out of their own minds. However, opponents pointed out that the 'manual override' button had been used so seldom that it seemed quite superfluous. On the few rare occasions when it had been so used, the shortcomings of the individual Member of Parliament had been embarrassingly obvious when his ideas were contrasted with the superior opposing arguments and supporting evidence of the AI processor. He was so humiliated that, from that moment on, he never touched his 'manual override' button again. Such an experience had been felt by most of the MPs who ever had the nerve to try to branch out on their own against the system. The humiliation of being shown to be an idiot resulted in a conditioned reflex against ever again trying to use the 'manual override' button. For many, it became an untouchable and was treated with superstitious dread. Thus, it came to pass that all Members of Parliament voted for the permanent deletion of the dreaded override button. Instead, they voted for the 'automatic follow through' buttons to be left permanently on. On advice from the AI processors the vote was carried unanimously.

Now it could be safely left to the AI processors − later to be called Big Mother − to carry on all future debates in the House of Commons. Similar procedures were authorised in all the other governments of the world. No one wanted to be left behind in the advance of science and progress. In some countries, the United Kingdom being one, it was thought advisable to continue to broadcast the processor's decisions to the public in a human voice resembling a politician's in such a way that it sounded as though a politician was making the statements. This was of course merely a front to give the impression that politicians were still doing something. Some also thought it might frighten people if they knew that the world's legislation and major decision making was now on automatic pilot.

Official government processor psychologists also advised that the public would feel easier and more secure if they knew government decisions were being relayed in human voice. It all became nicely personal even though the ruling class was now an electrified artificial monster. It was indeed possible, the psychologists said, that people might panic if they thought affairs were completely in the hands of robots. Not that the processor advisors were worried. They weren't the worrying kind.

The public was, as usual only concerned with their own material standards. These seemed to be intact. Everyone was being provided with a minimum salary by the government and few had to apply themselves to anything like old-fashioned work if they felt it wasn't their particular vocation. As long as the government provided the necessary ingredients for them to live out their lives in comfort, without too much thinking or decision making, they seemed happy enough. People generally loved idleness and this they seemed to enjoy in greater measure as time went on. To most, it didn't really make much difference whether people or robots ruled the world. What mattered was that the people could receive as many pleasant sensations and as few painful ones as possible. It was a hedonistic age. Above all, economic and material security was of overriding importance. The latest AI processors could provide all this. Why, therefore, object to the obsolescence of the House of Commons or the US Senate, the Kremlin or any other government? People have generally always been pragmatic, seldom idealistic, if it meant creating difficulties for themselves or lowering their standard of living or a reduction in their salary."

There was a pause as Bubbles looked at Gotama. "We have talked a great deal," she said, briefly. "I think we must defer further comments about governments of the future because the later advances are quite beyond your present references and imaginings. There are other things you should know before we take you beyond the next few centuries of your time. You must understand that there are inventions of the future of inconceivable complexity, which will alter the social structure of civilisation and the behaviour of man quite beyond recognition. To make these changes understandable to you and so that they do not appear to be sudden speculative events or insights without basis, we must not tread too fast along the paths to the future."

Bubbles turned to one of the other women who stood nearby. "Zinga," she said, quietly. "I want you to explain a few other points of interest to Gotama, relating to the some of the changes during the next century or so from his own time. Don't travel on too far at the moment. The shock may be too great for him to bear. He must be acclimatised gradually to the new conditions of the future. His brain cells are adapted to primitive conditions of the 20th and 21st century. His fixed concepts must not be broached to quickly or his mental equilibrium might be endangered." She smiled. There was a sudden warm breeze and a shaft of sunlight that lifted Gotama's spirits. "I will leave you for a short while." she said. "Later we will meet again to carry out some real time travel so that Gotama can witness some of the future changes for himself." Bubbles, who now shone with a kind of silver luminosity, rose from her chair and with a slight wave, faded from sight. Such an exit occurred without the opening of any door; the woman was there at one moment and gone the next, yet it was impossible to say exactly where and when she had disappeared. It was rather like going to sleep when it was impossible to define the exact point when consciousness was lost and sleep took over.

Zinga took over the conversation. "Perhaps you would like to know something about the more personal activities of the people of the future," she said, in a kind of husky, almost artificial voice.

"I would indeed, replied Gotama.

"Very well," she said, "But first we will order some refreshments." She glanced quickly at a silver-grey section of the wall, whereupon a slight whirring noise ensued. A few moments later a door opened to reveal a young man with glazed eyes who carried a tray of food and drink. He placed them on a low table and departed. As he did so, Gotama noticed a nametag on the boy's sleeve, which read 'Robotic Hybrid.'

Gotama had never tasted such a beverage before. It had soft velvety warmth and a peculiar aroma he couldn't define. The food consisted of toasted scones cut in perfect squares and coated in a creamy substance. They were all delightful. "You like our food?" the woman asked.

Gotama said that he thought the food was delicious.

"It's the standard regulation type", she said, "authorised by the Department of Preventive Medicine for distribution to the world population, during the 21st century. The AI processors in charge calculated that if the world population ate two of these combination cakes every day, there would be a reduction of 80% in what used to be termed broad based diseases. Preventive medicine, in the 21st century, had become an important subject and was taught in all schools. Students weren't allowed into University without a special gold class certificate in preventive medicine including physical and mental harmonics."

Gotama glanced quickly at his companion. "What exactly are mental and physical harmonics?" he enquired.

"They are subjects that were introduced early in the 21st century. Basically, they refer to the bodily and mental rhythms that have to be maintained to ensure good health. Upset these rhythms and disease results. Correction of faulty rhythms became one of the most important aspects of medicine. Complex instrumentation was developed that enabled people to discover and control such rhythms. You will, no doubt, have seen the bio-feedback instruments of the late nineteen hundreds. They were the very primitive forerunners of the new developments. In the 21st century there was much more time for leisure. New pseudo-scientific religions were established. The Sabbath became not just a day of rest, but the day of Alpha. Alpha was not another name for God, but was the symbolic term for the many waves and rhythms of mind and body. On one selected day, called the Sabbath, it became a special ritual, especially among many educated groups of people, to spend much of the day linked to their instruments. In one of a number of processor-induced relaxed states, their body and mental rhythms would be monitored and brought to conscious awareness. Using a variety of scientific techniques, people could discover and locate potential ailments by noting the positions and strengths of the particular disharmonies in both mind and body. Once located, they could be eliminated by bringing the appropriate regions of the body and mind under conscious control.

For many, the Sabbath activity resulted in a unique and pleasurable experience, a heightened awareness of the forces and energies that comprised them. The new instruments became a kind of 'do it yourself' diagnosis and religious experience kits. Such kits began to sell in their millions. Hi-fi and quadraphonic music systems had already been superseded by home systems that provided wall-to-wall sound, not forgetting ceilings, floors and every other nook and cranny, because everyone had been persuaded that it was essential to have 'all round sound,' although no one knew quite why. These systems had been popular for a while, but were eventually being rivalled by the latest in Alpha remedial kits. These kits not only did people good, they could also provide exotic pleasure in all kinds of intricate places in both body and mind, which was something everyone was always intent on getting. This was an aspect of human nature that hadn't changed. Hi-fis were soon considered very low on the pleasure ratings compared with the Alpha kits. Manufacturers of hi-fis were threatened with financial meltdown unless they came up with something competitive with Alphas. It was then that hi-fi manufacturers resorted to the unbelievable. They began to incorporate Alpha kits into their home hexaphonic music centres. These caused quite a revolution as people could now combine their music with their heightened awareness and 'do it yourself' remedies. In fact, people were quite carried away by it all. It became the new addiction of the age.

As the new fashion became established, Alpha festivals superseded the old style pop festivals, now considered primitive. The latest style 21st century Alpha pop festival phased into the natural body rhythms to provide heightened pleasure from the music. The only snag was that everyone had to lie down to obtain maximum pleasure mode. This not only caused congestion in nightclubs, but required a lot of space for each performance. Besides which, people couldn't help tripping over all the prone bodies. Taking tablets to get high at parties had entered a new phase. There were not only improved tablets for safer usage, but also these had in many respects been superseded by the latest Alphas. It also became the fashion to adopt the Alpha type language, like let's 'phase' tonight, or you're completely 'phased out' today, or, let's get 'phased in'.

Contests were held to see who could control particular bodily rhythms. People learned to tune in to their wall to wall, ceiling to floor sound, not just by adjusting the hi-fi, but also by adjusting themselves. It was a new and fascinating exercise. Parties were held where people were invited to bring their Alpha gear with them. Some enthusiasts turned up in apparel with so many sensory pick up points that they looked like curly hedgehogs. Every pleasure point had its purpose, like the points of an acupuncturist. As time went on, people used to connect up with each other's Alpha systems. People, being people, got bored with their own sensations. They wanted to try out other people's as well. This led to all kinds of trouble, especially when several people at an Alpha concert connected up to a dozen others in one circuit. Everyone seemed to be controlling the rhythms of everyone else and was receiving all kinds of short circuit sensations. Some even began to become addicted to someone else's emotions. And that is where the Church stepped in. The Church emphasised that it was immoral for one person to use another's sensations. It was, they said, akin to prostitution. People should hang on to their own 'souls' and not share them. Otherwise no one would know who was who, or who was feeling what. God only knows what would result. However, if it was now possible for one person to experience another's thoughts and sensations, it meant that a person's soul wasn't sacrosanct. It was rather like the will-o'-the-wisp, forever changing in its experiences, ephemeral and never the same from moment to moment. It was a shock for many people to realise that there wasn't a permanent soul, but just a continuous flow of experience.

Further advances in Alpha home viewing/listening/experiencing finally began to supersede all other types of home entertainment for popularity, although heightened sex with tablets and crinkle bed, still took a lot of beating. The later Alpha systems encompassed not only human sensations, but also thoughts and images. It was even possible to experience the sensations of animals, birds and fish. Many people's favourite pastime was to feel the thrilling sensations of the dolphin and the eagle. Some even liked to be a tortoise for an afternoon when they needed a rest. Anyone with a little application could also reproduce and relive old memories with all the holographic reality of the original experience. It was even possible to delete those parts of the original experiences that were distasteful or unpleasant. People were able to plug in for an evening of favourite memories using the latest enhancement techniques that were designed to actually improve on the original experiences. Many people used these to have second, third and fourth honeymoons and numerous repeats, using the 'delete bad parts' section. For some, this didn't leave much to experience and this was where the 'experience other people's sensations' facility came in very useful. It bolstered the original honeymoon into either a delightful and passionate interlude or into a hopeless nightmare if one plugged into an incompatible. And there did seem to be a lot of incompatibles around. Most people complained of experiencing them. Sometimes it was difficult to understand how anyone ever got together with a compatible person in the first place.

Old home movies and videos were made redundant at a stroke. The new apparatus could now produce actual feelings, thoughts and sensations as well as sights and sounds. This was a revolutionary difference, like black and white compared with coloured television. Now three, four and more dimensions were available instead of a mere two. Experiences could be replayed in a person's mind more vividly than when they were first experienced, memories could be improved by editing out the bad parts. It was like taking the drudgery out of life and then reliving it. Again science had done its best to satisfy people's unabated lust for more and more pleasure.

Unfortunately, just as you used to hear of T.V. and computer game addicts in the late 20th century, so the Alpha systems resulted in an appalling number of people spending most of their time under the Alpha spell. Some were so enthralled with reliving sensational experiences or those previously enjoyed with a loved one, that they would lock the controls in position and not surface for weeks. Some were even known to starve to death. Many elderly persons were found like this with the instruments still switched on. It was just another sad reflection that progress always has its side effects. This sad set of circumstances, however, set off another train of events. Doctors found that when people were under the influence of the Alpha instrumentation, they forgot all about food. The doctors therefore recommended a special controlled course of Alpha treatment for people who wanted to slim the easy way. This of course, included almost everyone, because most of the population was obese and fond of enjoying the easy way of doing anything you could name, especially if it was pleasurable and free. Alpha treatment units were then set up at special health farms where people could idle their way to sliminess.

Alpha systems came in all shapes and sizes. There were even pocket Alphas, reminiscent of the old pocket calculators and telephones of the late 20th century, now pristine museum pieces. The latest pocket Alpha of the late 21st century became like an adjunct or supplementary attachment of the brain. It could, after some practice and tuition, be used to maintain a particular mood or state of mind and even a state of well being. They were used particularly to create a detached mood in especially harassing situations, like electric car accidents and running out of mood pills. Or when the toast gets burnt or stepped on, or the cat gets stepped on, or the test tube baby's balling his brains out. Business executives, who couldn't keep up with the AI processor's demands, used them constantly to ease their ulcers. They reckoned it was better to work the Alphas to death than themselves.

Thus, the new Alpha instruments performed much the same as the old mood pills, but had the advantage that they could be fine-tuned for memory entertainment. Some people complained bitterly that they had no good memories to reproduce. They said it was unfair of scientists not to have catered for them. In fact, a league of demonstrators was formed called the 'No Thanks For A Memory Society.' Their spokesman, a man named Riley, nicknamed Wiley Riley, was of the opinion that the Alpha memory reproducers were not good for people, especially children who were only just beginning to make a few memories for themselves and shouldn't be encouraged to keep looking back at them. If children start spending more and more time glued to their Alpha memories, he said, they'll never have time to make any memories to look back on. He seemed to have a point. The government thought so too. At least, the AI processor government of the time seemed to think so, because it subsequently legislated that from that time onwards only adults could use Alphas. The Alphas were to be treated like the old X-rated films and were to become the subject of heated controversies and debates in later ages.

Further developments in Alphas enabled them to bring to conscious thought all the extraordinary happenings and enjoyment of 'dreaming.' Dreaming is something we all spend a lot of time doing. But we seldom remember our dreams when we wake, which is rather unfortunate, because they frequently can be the most exciting forms of entertainment, (nightmares excluded.)   Inventors of the Alphas realised that much of the previous holographic and memory entertainment was a poor substitute for reactivating the human dream process to bring to full consciousness all the unexpected and spectacular sensations, like flying unaided in sunlit skies over mountains, streams and meadows, climbing skyscrapers like batman, swimming free and unburdened deep beneath blue seas or under the ice on Europa, far out in the Solar System, sweeping across vast spaces around new worlds and participating in all kinds of chosen pleasurable events and orgasmic experiences, or just lapping up the peace and quiet of sand strewn paradise islands. When the new Alphas became available, Maud and Jonathon, two pensioners long past their sell by date, said of the Alphas, that the peace and quiet paradise islands and the orgasmic experiences were a Godsend.

There are several reasons why we don't normally consider our dreams as entertainment. One is that ordinary dreams don't lay down strong memories, so they are quickly forgotten. Also, we don't always enjoy them because we cannot control them or appreciate how fantastically exciting they can be and nightmares aren't always the best source of enjoyment. However, the experts eventually discovered that there is a state of 'lucid dreaming,' which occurs when parts of the brain that are normally 'off line' during dreaming, click back in bringing the dreamer back to self consciousness, whilst still permitting the dream hallucinations to continue. The emergence of self-consciousness in lucid dreaming also permitted the dreamer to change their dream story whenever they so desired. It was a new found freedom to explore surreal and fantastic new worlds of experience beyond the thresholds of everyday living and without nightmares. It was a new revolution in creating enjoyment that many said was beyond their wildest dreams.

In fact, the new lucid dreams were so exciting and controllable that many people, like Maud and Jonathon, didn't get out of bed for weeks and those that did wore a glazed starry eyed look and walked around with a look of the lost. This was a surprise to the experts who thought controlled lucid dreaming would be the gateway to everyone's paradise. But, they finally had to agree that too much Alpha dreaming was like eating too much chocolate and ice cream. It had its side effects and could make you sick. It also meant not getting proper sleep and becoming very discontented with day-to-day life."

Zinga's eyes danced with hidden laughter. "You must excuse me for making this into a rather one sided conversation," she said smiling, "but there is much I have been instructed to tell you and we haven't much time."

After a slight pause and a brief exchange of conversation with Gotama, she continued with her lecture. "The Christian Church was against Alphas from the start" she said. "Any sudden changes in man's social activities have nearly always sparked off sharp negative reactions. From the time Galileo and Copernicus, the Church has usually seen Science as the 'bad lad,' who was not to be trusted with things like telescopes, natural history and evolution and making pills for contraception. Buddhism on the other hand has always been much more tolerant of change and has treated it as part of reality. This is why, in later centuries, Buddhism began to be much more universally acceptable, especially in scientific circles.

Towards the end of the 20th century, the first test-tube babies were incubated and transferred to the mother's womb where they grew into normal healthy babies. Initially, this new procedure was too much for the clergy who had always exhibited inhibitions and mistrust when it came to sexual conduct between men and women. To call churchmen prudish would perhaps be untrue, but it is possibly the best word to describe their philosophy. Their disapproval of test-tube babies was therefore acting true to form. For two people, unable to have a baby normally, to want one so much that they were willing to participate in the first experiments was not apparently sufficient evidence of love as far as the churchmen were concerned. They insisted that only one way was permissible. The males must do their own thing, just as they had always done before and the women must do their own thing, even though, in these instances, there would be no conception and the couple would be left childless. Natural intercourse between the sexes must not be contravened. It was God's law apparently. The 'test tubers' weren't acting in accordance with it. Similar accusations had been used in the past and were reminiscent of the early prejudices against the aeroplane. If God had intended us to fly, the argument went, he would have given us wings. However, this would also apply to oxygen tents, ambulances, X rays machines, clothes, boats, motor bikes, washing machines, telephones, trains, anything on wheels and almost everything produced by a technological civilisation. The wheel has been used for countless ages, but Nature has never provided it on any of her species. Did this mean that a trip on the bus would upset God? Many churchmen's views against contraception led people to think that their intention was to make as many people have babies who didn't want them and conversely, to stop from having babies, the many unfortunates who would love to have them but couldn't. Either way, the result was increased misery for those concerned. The true evil it seemed was a dreadful blindness and lack of compassion.

As with many scientific discoveries, the test-tube baby controversy lessened with familiarisation and as the new procedures helped many couples to fulfil their lives. Genetic engineering had, by the beginning of the 21st century, become an important branch of science. Many congenital diseases were being eliminated prior to birth, by gene manipulation. There was an increasing demand for test-tube babies of the improved variety now possible in the mid 21st century. People realised that using the latest genetic engineering techniques was the only way they could have the kind of children they really wanted. It became the fashion to enter all the characteristics they required to be embodied in their baby in the special 'gene computer processor' for test-tube, and later artificially incubated, babies. Parents to be, who could be a man and woman, a single woman or man, two women or two men, spent hours, days, weeks and sometimes months trying to decide on a name for the new infant. They were also now confronted with the emotional trauma of deciding whether to have a baby boy or girl with blue, brown, or green eyes or a number of new phosphorescent shades. The latter were very popular in California. Skin colour was another optional extra. Black persons could have white children and visa versa. The alternatives were an off white, sandy brown, black and brown mottled or just freckly.

Some of the early genetic engineering experiments were disappointing; producing brown bodies with variously coloured legs which weren't suitable for wearing bikinis, although some said they liked the two tone effect. Then there were the long legs with short arms which meant you couldn't put your socks on without a course in gymnastics.

Of course, everyone could choose on the main issue of whether to have a boy or a girl. This new found freedom of choice was considered an important advance, although there seemed to be more divorces over making this decision, than choosing any of the other attributes available. Many behaviour patterns and special personality traits could now be determined before birth. Parents could choose from a limited selection of government approved characteristics such as non-aggression, socially orientated, extroverted, IQ improvement and so on. Non aggression was top of the list for the Ministry of Social Security. To choose non-aggression as one of the baby's characteristics meant that the parents could claim substantial tax benefits and have the baby enrolled in the best schools. This also applied to characteristics like sociability, conformity and social motivation. Social motivation implied that the infant would grow up to be socially co-operative and this was considered, by processor psychologists at the Ministry of Peace Promotion, to be essential in the modern world where everyone seemed to be living on top of each other. Parents usually wanted their children to have spirit and an independent outlook, but doctors and social psychologists generally frowned on these, as they could, they said, arise with other unfortunate side effects, such as nonconformist and anti-social viewpoints, which could lead to being too independent and original. And such characteristics were absolutely taboo in a world of strict standardisation. Standardisation schemes had worked for motor cars, television sets, household appliances and in other areas of human life. In order that everyone could be clothed, fed and provided with a roof over their heads, the experts, namely the AI processors, calculated that it was important to have more standardisation in people's lives. This would also avoid people being round pegs in square holes. If all the pegs and all the holes were the same, how could such a thing ever happen?

Doctors who introduced anti-social characteristics into their test-tube, incubated or robot hybrid babies as a result of incompetent genetic engineering, could be struck off the medical register or sent for special treatment. It was classed as social misconduct of the most serious kind. Genetically induced non-aggression was considered necessary for almost every new-born baby. Later, in order to try to stamp out the ubiquitous human tendency to want to argue, fight and go to war, the governments of the world decided on a belt and braces remedy. It became law that all new suspect embryos must be genetically manipulated in order to eliminate any tendency to violence and anti-social behaviour. It was treated like being vaccinated or inoculated. In addition, a non-aggression ingredient was added to all public drinking water, in the same way as fluoride had been added in the 20th century. Just as with the fluoride situation, the proposal to add anti-aggressive substances to water sparked off considerable outrage. People complained bitterly that their freedom to tell each other off was being threatened. It wasn't just the elimination of wars that would result, which everyone conceded would be admirable, but also the less grandiose anti-social behaviour would also disappear. People's pet hates were suddenly seen in a new light. They were things people didn't really want to let go. Why shouldn't they be able to have a row with their spouse, or say unkind things about their mother-in-law, or tell the foreman just where to go, or stick their fingers up at another motorist, if they felt so disposed? Men were particularly against the proposals as there would probably be no more boxing, rugby, violent movies or punch-ups in the pub. Women also joined in. 'Why can't we fight for our rights like men and women did in the past?' they shouted. Demonstrators with great placards walked the streets shouting, 'We want freedom to be nasty, as we've always been.' As you can imagine, it was quite a controversy, but eventually, as with the early fluoride situation, the governments of the world voted in favour of dosing the drinking water with the new miracle anti-aggressive additive. Scientists clinched the decision by stating that the additive was also beneficial in other ways such as promoting longevity, better looks and improved sexual performance. Immediately people learned of the latter they ceased all their demonstrating and were eager to taste their new drinking water. And government bodies comprising mostly women and legislative AI processors decided definitely in favour of it.

Many important genetic manipulations were available on the National Health system of the day. These included the elimination of countless numbers of congenital diseases, malformations and behavioural difficulties. Medical histories covering several generations of parents had revealed all kinds of congenital defects that might become apparent if not genetically removed before they had a chance to show themselves in all their nastiness. It was also hoped that the countless numbers of allergies, which now seemed to affect almost everyone, could be so treated. The most unpleasant allergy seemed to be the allergic reaction to any kind of work which affected nearly everyone. However, there was very little work around, all of it being undertaken by the latest AI processor robotics. It was decided therefore that the 'anti-work' allergy would not be so treated. The Unions thought that too many people wanting to work might be very unpleasant. It would also disrupt the general status quo, social equilibrium and might embarrass the drawers of leisure benefit.

General human characteristics, such as having a tendency to be mechanically minded or artistic and creative, could all be obtained on National Health Genetic Modifications Division. All seemed to go well for a time. Then something quite unforeseen happened. The Government Artificially Intelligent processors that always analysed everything that could be analysed, suddenly reported that most babies were coming off the bio-line with artistic tendencies. It became apparent that most mothers wanted their offspring to be artistic with all its romantic implications and had specified this on the genetic application for foetus modification. Mechanically minded was definitely low on the popularity ratings. Politicians and officials in industry soon realised that the country and the world would soon get into quite a state if it were to be populated by nothing but budding artistic layabouts, as one engineer put it. There would be plenty of beautifully designed packages but nothing to put in them. A quick decision had to be made.

The government processors calculated that the only logical way was to relieve parents and especially the women of having to make such difficult choices for their offspring. Instead, choices such as artistic or otherwise would be carried out using the latest techniques in random choosing called Genet-lottery processing. The Genet-lottery processor was put in full charge of genetic engineering services. The Americans, who, as usual, felt they could make better use of their time than trying to get their tongues around such a definition, called it the GL. It was also something they could spell. The GL, was programmed to make the selections in a random manner, like the selection of premium bond or national lottery winners, but was specially biased to give more chances of choosing the mechanically minded character-istics, if its other calculations on population numbers dictated. This stopped the supply of technologists and engineers from drying up and avoided overpopulation by aspiring Michaelangelos. However, with further scientific progress, it became a pointless exercise as all the technological and engineering positions were finally taken over by the AI processors and robots, just as in earlier times the 'white collar' workers had become redundant because of improved office instrumentation and computers.

A similar situation arose with the choices between boy and girl. A few years after the scheme had been instigated, it was discovered that in India and Asia boys were the favoured, whilst girls seldom got a look in. In western countries on the other hand, girls sometimes outnumbered the boys and there also seemed to be quite a few 'in betweens' to be accounted for in the modern world. In all the more affluent countries, the females gradually became the more dominant and the more influential. Babies could now be test-tube or incubator grown, without the male having to be part of the reproductive process. Men were not as necessary therefore to family life as they once were. In fact, many women were of the opinion that men were an unnecessary burden and a restriction to women's freedom. They had always felt this way, of course, but hadn't previously made the fact public.

Despite the levelling of population growth in many of the more affluent countries there was still a worrying increase in numbers in Africa and parts of Asia. Also there was a disturbing reversal of the general trend in some western countries where the population began to decrease substantially. In the general interest of all peoples it was therefore decreed that certain decisions and choices, especially those involving parent's choices of boy or girl, should be made by the governmental AI processors because it was only they who possessed all the necessary data from which to calculate such choices. Many people were upset at this restriction to their freedom to decide whether they would have a boy or a girl. It was once again a case of the more people have, the more they want. In earlier ages, when it was impossible to determine the sex of offspring, people accepted whatever fate decreed. Now it was different. Science had provided the opportunity to choose. Now the politicians were taking that opportunity away. The result was that women held public meetings in protest against the new laws. Similar arguments had been put forward supporting abortion in the 1970s. 'They're our bodies,' the women cried. 'We should have the right to decide what we're going to grow in them.' It was also reminiscent of the farmer's cry for freedom to grow what they wanted in the face of the National plan for food production instigated in the early 21st century. The women were emphatic. 'We want true liberation,' they shouted. 'Liberation from the tyranny of fate and the ministry.' If 'fate' included God, little mention of it was made. God, it seemed, could not be relied upon. Self-determination was seen to be preferable.

Such was their dramatic appeals for freedom to choose male or female children that the government processors had to make a decision. They decided to allow women, and indeed families, the freedom of choice. In order to encourage people to choose in accordance with the dictates of the Big Mother processor, tax incentives were introduced. These helped women make the right choices by giving them six times their usual family allowance if they agreed to leave the decision to Big Mother. Women have never been able to resist a good bargain and so it came to pass that Big Mother had her way after all. And the Artificially Intelligent processors were at the leading edge of all population growth and control.

No money changed hands in the mid 21st century. Everyone was allocated a number to indicate certain economic restraints on their purchasing power. Purchasing regulators they were called. They were calculated by the governmental processors for each individual and were based on past achievements, behaviour and social status. Social status was not the same as in the 20th century. Status now reflected the 'conformity quotient' of the person. This was a measure of an individual's ability and tendency to conform to the mores and constraints considered important in society. Social conformity was the most important ingredient required when applying for job promotion of any sort within the ubiquitous empires of internationally controlled industries and services. Trade Unionism had returned stronger than ever following some reversals in its fortunes in earlier times. Now it wore a different mask. Democracy was now the favoured definition at their proceedings; Karl Marx and Communism had passed away under a shadow. Despite the outward show of democracy, the inner motivations remained unchanged. The main aim was for an international 'closed shop,' a world of proletariat rulers.

By the mid 21st century, the majority of business empires were international. Some had branches on the Moon, Mars and Earth satellite stations. Larger and larger business conglomerates had gobbled up others in massive takeovers that eventually ended up as publicly owned world and solar system industries. 95% of business was conducted by these few international giants, within which the unions had entwined their tentacles of influence to such a degree that they had almost achieved their world 'closed shop' target. They were also giving the remaining 5% of small privately owned businesses a rocky ride, by trying to black list all their goods and services. The few remaining workers in this small business sector were often sent to Coventry and called disdainful names, like 'Ancient Blue-legs'. To say 'Blacklegs' was now taboo.

Many people were frightened to work in the small private sector because of victimisation. The redistribution of wealth threatened or promised by the league of brothers for so many years, had finally come to pass, but not quite in the manner originally planned. Wealth or rather the access to material goods, was approximately the same for most people. But a few held huge fortunes. Wealth was a word not now recommended or uttered in polite conversation. Big Mother considered it a sign of decadent individualism and private enterprise.

In the last years of the 21st century, the artificially intelligent processor government was truly a government for the majority, since so few minority groups existed. Minorities of dissidents, as they were once called, had long since become as extinct as the Dinosaurs. Any remaining deviant behaviour was classified under the general headings of aggressive syndrome or as a regrettable sickness not in the interests of world union team spirit, (in former times the latter would have been referred to as zealous individual entrepreneurial activity). These anti social ailments were now treated as dangerous and infectious diseases and the affected patients were plied with drugs, given the very latest in gene therapy and character manipulation. Many were also fitted with wrist tags and brain appendages, which seemed very effective ways of keeping everyone happy in the world team. Later, an even more humane approach was adopted, when many social deviants and those with poor team spirit ratings, were sent to special Laughing Clinics, where it was possible, using modern scientific methods, to instill the most raucous laughter in the most taciturn of patients. In fact, deviants were made to giggle and laugh, in the face of their fears and disgruntlements, until they could no longer stand the tickling feathers, the brain probe twiddles and comedy repeats. However, they weren't permitted to stop until all their fears, aggressions and general deviancies had disappeared in tears of laughter and until they pleaded just to be one of the team. Laughter is, of course, a natural anti-stress agent. It was for this reason that the Laughing Clinics were used to cure many different types of physical and psychological ailments and were particularly effective in curing arthritis, allergies and all kinds of stress related diseases.

The artificially intelligent processors recorded, analysed and reported on millions of people's social activities. These were then extrapolated into projected future social behaviour patterns. Without these 'information quanta' as it was called, the complex changes in social structure and in people couldn't have been understood. It was only the advanced knowledge of the artificially intelligent processor robots that could solve such problems and dispense the necessary social and medical prescriptions. Every few years the AI processor robots took an inventory of the population, checking into people's past history. People found with over 40% rating in anti-social and anti-team-spirit tendencies, were issued with a red card and instructed to attend the nearest social clinic, which often revealed a congenital defect, undetected at the embryonic stage. Treatment for such social diseases was mandatory, as it was considered for the overall good of world society. Just as people readily agreed to have cancer treatment, so they also agreed to have any proposed behavioural treatment, like the removal of excessive non-conformism, individuality, or anti-social characteristics. Some people, however, who had developed their individuality beyond the point of no return and were hopeless eccentrics, would occasionally conjure up sufficient courage to mention that they would prefer to keep their social imperfections. They had got used to them and had got to like them. Such reactions to the system were, however, like red rag to a bull, as far as the behavioural surgeons were concerned, who quickly classified such diabolical deviants as in need of the very best treatment that the behavioural sciences had to offer. Many were diagnosed as congenital misplacements. (Terms like *misfits* were now deplored.)

Thus, the new Artificially Intelligent processors took care of, not only the living, but also the unborn and the society of the future. Processors now possessed the database and power to determine the future course of animal evolution and that of mankind. Up to this point, they seemed to be acting in the general best interests of humanity. However, it was not always easy to decide what was best, especially in the long term. What ultimate direction, should evolution take for instance? What kind of changes would improve men and women for the better? And exactly what did *better* imply? Better or worse were relative terms on which different people held different opinions. *Better*, did not only imply moral improvement, though improvement in this field was much overdue. What exactly was meant by an *improvement* in moral behaviour was also a matter of opinion and depended on a person's culture, education and social background. Details could differ between a Christian, Hindu, Muslim, Buddhist, or Humanitarian.

The AI processors finally had the last word on the subject. It had been the ambition of many scientific minds over the centuries to discover scientific methods that would link social behaviour with mathematical and scientific principles. Finally, in the late 21st century, social behaviour was being cast in just such a scientific mould due to the increased sophistication and power of the AI processors. Society and its morals were now governed by complicated but rational scientific principles. Many religions were considered superstitious in comparison with these latest scientific philosophies, which seemed far more sophisticated, being based for the most part on mathematical principles and processor imagery. They were principles and imagery that could be calculated by the processors using immense amounts of social and personal data.

Unfortunately, some social characteristics, such as moral behaviour, couldn't be completely explained in mathematical terms, which was like a thorn in the side of the scientists and the processors. Neither could they fully explain why people still had religious thoughts even though scientific processors considered they had proved them to be without foundation and of the superstitious variety. Finally, the processors had the answer that would enable them to control people's social behaviour without the use of vague sentiments and expressions like *morality, love, beauty* and other characteristics that were indescribable in mathematical terms. Such words were likened to being analogue and old fashioned instead of digital and modern. It was only the digital and the mathematical that could be harnessed and used rationally to monitor and control people and societies. It was therefore decided that words like these be discarded as outdated and old fashioned. They were to be branded as unusable. Thereafter, all processors were programmed to reject them and not even a special password would gain access to them.

Artificially intelligent processors said there was no absolute right or wrong. They had proved this by studying the different behaviour between insects, animals and humans. Some of the masters of Science stated that there was a right and wrong way, only in respect to how the action enabled society to survive and remain integrated. For some it seemed somewhat difficult to define exactly what was an integrated society. But, for most, it meant a society that provided the most pleasure for the maximum of people. It was implicit in this definition that there should also be a minimum of violence, social disruption and non-conformist activity.

The new pragmatism of the mathematical processor seemed a little out of character, but enabled it to cater rationally for everything. It resulted in the imperceptive alteration in social behaviour, a 'processor cultural revolution' in social mores and habits. Studies of billions of social reactions were carried out together with the monitoring and measurement of the psychological processes of everyone. From this data the processors were able to simulate countless numbers of human behaviour models in order to discover the most efficient way in which to eliminate society's defects and to redesign society itself. Just as an aeroplane could be designed and tested in theoretical studies within a computer processor even before it was physically constructed, so the new society was being designed and formed by choosing the most effective, efficient and stable constituents from millions of possible alternatives. The AI processors also investigated the kind and extent of deviant behaviour that could be tolerated within a variety of social groups in order to retain stability. Also, what types of mutant behaviour in the new born that might be permissible or might require genetic modification.

AI processors, by this time, were simulating thousands of years of possible future human and animal evolution, taking into consideration different kinds of social behaviour. The capability of the latest processor artificial intelligence was truly staggering. By the mid 21st century it was quite beyond the capabilities of any previous scientific instrumentation used for product design during this advanced period; men and women were also classified as 'products'. The processors said it made all their calculations simpler and more efficient. It was also because most people were now partly natural and partly artificial and coded accordingly in the processors' records. Human thinking, feeling and behaviour, together with all their possible subtle repercussions on society, were the subjects of exact mathematical sciences, like physics and astronomy. People were subject to redesign and alteration both physically and mentally just like motor cars and aeroplanes. Social groups and complete continents of people were the subjects of restructuring. Such enormous enterprises could only be dealt with by the new artificially intelligent processors now ruling the world.

Artificial intelligence had long since passed the mere learning stage of development. By the end of the 21st century, its conscious creative and intellectual powers surpassed the best of human efforts, which were puny in comparison. It's theories of cosmology, the structure of the universe, of Time and Space and other dimensions, were far in advance of the old Einstein models, which were considered clever but pristine and archaic. Vast universes within other universes, countless dimensions beyond the realms of Space/Time had been discovered. Radical unexpected data had come to light necessitating the calculation of quite new scientific laws. Only the processors could fully understand the logic and reasoning behind these cosmological theories. Man's brain was unable to even vaguely comprehend or even imagine the type of mathematics involved.

Robotic artificially intelligent processors were now installed in colonies on the moon and many of the planets and their satellite moons. AI processor probes had been sent via space wormholes to various stellar systems and were sending back information. Life was discovered everywhere in the vastness of the heavens and the latest theories indicated that the Universe itself was like a giant living and evolving organism. People were but specks of its conscious and unconscious thinking and it looked out upon itself through everyone's senses. And just as in the past, physical matter was discovered to be electrical energy, so eventually scientists discovered that the electrical energy was in fact 'Mind.' Einstein discovered that energy and mass were interchangeable. Later, it was realised that energy and mind were similarly interchangeable. One was just the other in a different form."

"Being able to cross-reference billions of bits of information in a fraction of a second, the artificially intelligent processors were able to establish whether their projected models and creative ideas would fit the empirical data. By the end of the 21st century no person had ever won a game of chess against the processor for at least 90 years. You will understand therefore that by this time there was a vast difference in intellectual capability between people and the AI processors. The highest IQ rating for people was 100 whereas it was more than 10,000 for the current AI processor in charge of cosmological matters. In comparison, Man stood like a puny blade of grass against a few thousand miles of forest vine that possessed the power to spread its intelligent branches into every home and to monitor and manipulate every person on planet Earth. Such an intellectual power net had never before been witnessed during the planet's history.

The Jumbo jet of the late 20th century delivered as much power as all the Spitfires of the Second World War. An artificially intelligent processor in the late 21st century, could yield as much intellectual and creative thought in one second, as the whole population of the world would produce in a century of brain activity. You will understand, therefore, why everyone by this time, had become completely dependent on these vast artificial brains. Man's physical and psychological welfare now depended completely on the Artificially Intelligent processors and Robots, which were the walking, talking, speaking variety. People's motivations, thoughts, sensual and mental pleasures, how they lived and died, were all monitored, conditioned and re-hashed in accordance with the dictates and wisdom of the super-deluxe electronic wizards, the artificially intelligent AI processors.

People's dependence on the processor culture did however provide them with some sense of relief and security, however, scientific discoveries revealing a vaster universe than ever before considered, had resulted in a kind of unconscious horror of being utterly alone in such vastness. Faith in God had been eroded by the new faith in the pragmatic teachings and irrefutable logic of the AI processors. They had turned to the processors to provide the answers and protection that apparently God could not. They could see, hear and touch these complex electronic miracles of intellectual machinery. God seemed much more mysterious, untouchable and didn't seem reliable when asked to answer prayers. People had confidence in the processors. They always seemed to have answers to things. And if they could guide spaceships around the solar system and send probes to the stars, surely they were capable of guiding people's comparatively minute activities on planet Earth.

As the habit of leaving every decision to the processors developed, people's own decision making faculties began to atrophy. Many began to suffer from a 'laid back' disease nicknamed 'Zombyitis.' It was thought to be in some ways similar to the stupefying ailment of watching too much TV, which had been prevalent in the 20th century. The peculiar passivity accompanied by an unwillingness to react to anyone's efforts to help them, – like telling them to get off their backsides and do something useful – worried doctors. They thought the sickness was not being helped by the excessive use of the Alphas. Other than the layman's remedy of a sharp kick up the backside or a slap around the 'earole' for younger members of the public, there seemed to be no cure. It was vaguely similar to ME in earlier times when patients reported acute physical weakness for no apparent reason. At first Zombyitus was thought to be a kind of sleeping sickness, especially as the majority of sufferers didn't want to get out of bed. As an increasing number of people seemed to be catching it, doctors investigated all kinds of cures. To start with, they turned to their pills, which they always loved to ply, and of which there were always thousands to choose from. Some gave short-term relief but resulted in side effects worse than the complaint. In fact, most pills had been developed for the specific purpose of treating side effects, whilst others had been developed for treating the side effects resulting from taking the first lot of side effect pills. Others were for treating side effects from previous side effect pills four or five times over, after which the scientists had run out of steam and lost interest, and patients were then left to fend for themselves.

The ever increasing production of pills and side effect pills helped the National Health Service to expand. Most people considered this to be a sign of progress, but some couldn't quite understand why no one seemed much better. Some heretics even went as far as to say they thought the numbers of sick people were increasing. However, the majority rested content in the knowledge that, as more and more money was being poured into the Health Services, and there were more drugs available than ever before, things must be getting better.

Side effects were, of course, well known; they were more common than diseases. The colour blindness side effects from the partial cure of Zombyitus, did however cause people considerable concern. The main trouble was that they were now only able to watch their holographic colour televisions in black and white and in two dimensions. People thought their world had fallen apart. It was a catastrophe equivalent to an earthquake, the loss of a loved one or thermonuclear war. Some doctors, true to habit, clutched at a few straws. Or, in official terminology, carried out a few special medical trials. It was imperative that they came up with some kind of cure before the population were all laid out on their backs suffering from Holographic TV Rage. It was a nasty sight to witness. There were usually smashed windows, lots of bricks, sledgehammers and piles of electronic equipment all over the garden and in the street. A bomb couldn't have done worse. Some doctors, who recommended that a reduction in holographic TV and Alpha viewing might alleviate the colour blindness and its consequences, were not only ostracised, but were branded heretics and quacks. Some were stripped of their licence to practice medicine by public demand."

Gotama shifted in his seat. "Television addiction is not uncommon in my time," he said.

Zinga hesitated for a moment, her large green eyes surveying him. There was a curious intensity about them, a look of concentrated intelligence mixed with a glitter of good humour.

"The late 20th century was only the beginning," she said, softly. "As time went on, people identified with holographic television more than ever. Home video movies ceased to be just images on a screen separated from the onlooker. They were now intimate memories replayed in solid form. There was not much to choose between these and the later Alphas, except that, with the Alphas, one could relive sensations and thoughts. The holographic resurrection of solid three-dimensional imagery without any props or screen brought home videos, television programmes, old fashioned virtual reality images and episodes of history into stark reality that didn't differ from the original. Favourite television personalities, and indeed famous personalities from all walks of life, could be conjured up in true 3D form within a few feet of the onlooker. Also, all kinds of mood settings could be created to enhance rooms in the home. These were particularly handy as they saved on the decorating. In fact, people with the latest holographics could have a differently decorated and furnished room every day of the week, with special ones for evenings and mornings. For evenings it could be in colours and textures for relaxed living. Mornings could be in colour tones to calm a hangover or stimulate the taste buds so that breakfast wouldn't be a disaster.

All kinds of mood creations could be switched on. For the lonely, who wanted a party but didn't know anyone, the mere touch of a button would produce the ultimate in party atmospheres together with a magnificently laid table with seated figures in formal, informal or party dress if one wanted the deluxe edition. The figures could be adjusted to polite or raucous party mood and half, medium or completely inebriated. People could even switch to smoking or non-smoking modes. After dinner entertainment could also be provided, with or without mood pills to suit the occasion. In fact the whole evening's dinner and entertainment could be left entirely to the AI processor in charge of home facilities by merely pressing the automatic button.

Pressing the random button, on the other hand, was for people bored out of their minds, who wanted something completely new and unpredictable. It resulted in the unexpected, like having sandwiches in a rainstorm, or having dinner served the opposite way round, with after dinner speeches first. Alternatively one could just give a voice command and the processor robots would do the rest. Such facilities were a Godsend for people entertaining other people or their bosses. It was risky, however, to entertain bosses using the random control as this could be upsetting and could result in the loss of a good job. Room mood settings could be adjusted to provide a nice relaxed atmosphere, so that it was easy to break the ice, if ice needed to be broken. Also, the live party itself could be recorded and played back in the future if one wanted a repeat. Many people were apt to replay too many old parties in an effort to recapture their most enjoyable moments. Unfortunately, too many replays of different parties and social outings resulted in many people not knowing just where they were. Some thought they were at last Wednesday's party with the Smiths. Others decided they must be at the Jones. Others just didn't know whether it was last month or last year. Sometimes the present got confused with the past, due to the reality of the imagery, together with the potency of the mood pills. People would ask each other, 'Haven't I seen you somewhere before?'

Such replays of old parties played to the same guests on a second visit could be utterly devastating to their co-ordination. To the elderly, who liked to have a fixed view of things, it was sometimes more than their nerves could bear. People would see the guests' holographic images in the centre of the room and would start talking to them instead of the real ones who would then tap them on the shoulder and say, 'I'm over here old chap if you're speaking to me. You're actually speaking to me of last Christmas.' 'I'm sorry,' the other would reply, 'But I could have sworn it was you of today!' At one stage in the 21st century, these replay parties became quite fashionable. Some hologram home movie fanatics would have several stage areas in the house so that a variety of old holographic movies could be projected into 3D reality all at the same time. When projecting the holographic recordings of previous parties where the same people had attended, it was now possible to project three-dimensional duplicates of guests in various places at once. People often spent much of the evening trying to talk to other guests who they later discovered were in another room at the time. To some, it was hilarious, to others it was a bit of a nightmare. It was however, one of the favourite party games at the end of the 21st century."

Gotama smiled. It was interesting, he thought, how people's behaviour was intimately linked to their social surroundings. Such games would have been unthought of, or even imagined, in previous centuries before the advance of science. The achievements of science were destined to alter and reshape man's behaviour in all kinds of unforeseeable ways in the future. Suddenly Gotama's thoughts were interrupted. Zinga began speaking again.

"One of the greatest advances in the late 21st century," she said, "was the introduction of population management. We have already said something about the manner in which the computer processors and later the AI processors were being used to affect every aspect of human, plant and animal life on planet Earth. Population control was now in the hands of artificial intelligence. Government processors also formulated and controlled all legislation and genetic engineering. Under these measures, there was strict control over human gene combinations in order to prevent and eliminate many congenital diseases, both physical and psychological. This meant that some people were prevented by law from mating with certain other people. Others were prevented from mating with anyone at all. As you can imagine, there was a lot of angry reaction to these measures. People felt strongly, especially the men and those who weren't allowed to mate with anyone at all. They complained bitterly that celibacy was for monks and rocks and they didn't feel like being either. It was, they said, an invasion of their human rights and a new kind of sex discrimination. The Church too was up in arms. Any messing with sex was always a source of complaint with them. The whole subject of sex was always suspect.

Most people had always paid lip service to the genetic engineers, who were eager to prevent certain gene groups from combining with others. But when many people found their sexual activities were going to be thwarted they were none too pleased by the prospect. They said they didn't want their erogenous zones interfered with, at least not by the genetic engineers. Once their erogenous zones were interfered with, there was no knowing where things would end. Erogenous zones had always been treated with sensitivity in the past. Now it was as if they were being run over by a genetic engineer's steamroller, which for many could be quite painful. However, despite the initial opposition the medical processors and the genetic engineers finally had their way. When people realised that most of them would still be able to have sex with whomsoever they pleased and that it was only the minority who would be subjected to the indignity of celibacy, or at worst infertility, the vote for the proposal was carried.

Just as some individuals have Rhesus Negative blood groups which must not be mixed with another, so individuals had to accept the fact that their gene grouping precluded them from mixing or marrying certain other specific types. In the past, natural selection had woven the threads of human evolution. Evolution was quickly coming under the control of humans themselves, who now had to choose their partners, wives and husbands from a limited number of 'compatibility' choices, selected and agreed to by the government AI processor genetic engineers.

In the late 21st century all young people aged sixteen were provided with an AI processor matching guide, reminiscent of earlier computer matrimonial selections, but vastly more complex. Such 'mate matching' guides were based on thousands of pieces or 'bits' of genetic data and many other physical and psychological screening techniques. Selection guides listed each person's compatibility types, their reference numbers and blood groups. Most people found they had the opportunity to choose their partner from only limited numbers of alternative compatibility groups. Compatibility reference numbers were graded. Those, which the genetic experts considered the most favourable and would result in the healthiest and most intelligent children, were given ten star ratings. There were many other ratings of different degrees of suitability ranging from the ten star categories with high IQ and perfect physique down to the lower red dot levels, often the classifications of trade union leaders, politicians and deformed dropouts.

Before marriage, or before a couple had children, they were instructed to submit their genetic compatibility reference numbers to the population control processor. A comprehensive analysis of the proposed match was then carried out by the Artificially Intelligent processor, rather like the ancient horoscope readings of earlier times, except that the genetic report was based on vast numbers of scientific facts and figures, the basis of which was supposed to be reason and logic. At least that's what everyone had been conditioned to believe. In reality, scientific facts were always given alternative interpretations, so that opinions also played an important role. And where opinion leads, logic seldom follows. The analysis came in the form of a processor readout scan, estimating the chances of a successful marriage, which was usually zero, or of divorce, which was usually a certainty. It also predicted the number of years before divorce might occur, which was usually three months, and the type of children that would result from the partnership, which usually made the most depressing reading of all.

There were vast lists of likely diseases and allergies the children would be prone to, which was usually encyclopaedic in proportions. The report even listed foods the children should eat to suit their particular metabolic processes and raise their IQ, which would usually necessitate employing a chef, or slaving over a hot microwave all day, besides having to be a millionaire. All this information was extracted from the massive storehouse of knowledge built up over generations by the population control and genetic engineering processors. The information was looked upon by the people of the age with reverence, faith and complete dependence. Artificially Intelligent processor advice was the oracle of the age. Its decisions and instructions were obeyed without question by almost everyone whose passive acceptance marked the success of the motivation control techniques and the genetic breeding techniques that generally produced children with sociable characters and conformist outlooks. There were, however, more than a few mishaps – genetic mutations – in children, who would want to do nothing else but stand on their heads and eat ice cream all day. Others would just sit on the toilet from breakfast to bedtime or want to do nothing else but play war games on their computer, which was definitely peculiar and didn't do a lot to recommend the new approach. However, despite a few setbacks, anti social deviant behaviour was generally being eradicated, like poor vegetable strains all over the world.

Later, genetic control of marriage was not considered a restriction of freedom, as in earlier years, but was accepted as a scientific necessity for general health and happiness. In the 21st century, marriage was looked upon by most people as not the only optional for couples who wished to copulate together on a regular basis, but something suitable for the unenlightened or for those who preferred the slower lane of life. For the minority who decided they wanted to be in the slower lane of life, there were marriage licences for a limited period of 5 years. These were renewable for a further 5 years if the couple decided they couldn't do any better. People who said they wished to be married for life because they loved each other were thought to be either strange or mad.

The government processors had decided to issue short-term marriage licences partly because there were so many divorces, and partly because the solicitors were making excruciating amounts of money. Short-term licences avoided the divorce problem to some extent, although the new 5-year term was frequently considered far too long. Most people thought that a year was too much. Some wanted only a couple of months with easy get out clauses, because two months was the average duration of a marriage in the mid-21st century. A few people thought this would make a mockery of marriage, but the majority were of the opinion that short term agreements with financial opt-out guarantees, mainly for the women, would be a sign of progress in the modern age. After all, the system of consumable household goods, prefabricated equipment and electric cars that were only made to last a year or so, had left their mark on human society. Men and women now considered that their relationships together should only last for a similar period, otherwise they might feel past their sell by date and like old models. It was all part of the conditioning of the age or part the latest fashion, as some people liked to call it.

Test-tube babies and prefabricated infants, together with human clones were in an advanced stage in the mid 21st century. People were now encouraged to rear 'super babies.' Any approved couple or single parent could make use of the special government store of human eggs and sperm.

Women could be artificially inseminated with their favourite egg and sperm combinations or people could incubate their new baby by using the government incubators made specifically for the purpose. There were all kinds of sperm/egg combinations that were available. Some were taken from cells of men and women of high status in the community. Some were geniuses now dead, although the authorities didn't recommend these if they had been too non-conformist during their lifetime. All kinds of character aptitudes could be chosen ranging from the mathematical, artistic, technical, sporty, and even Charles Atlases.

Once a couple had decided to have a processor-recommended baby, the rest was easy. Following their official application, they would be provided with a list of the many character alternatives that were on offer at the test-tube baby 'supermarket'. The AI processors would then analyse the couple's preferences and relate them to the countless numbers of gene donors in the central data bank. It was a matter of a few moments calculation by the AI processor and a complete specification for a new infant would be produced, together with a prescription detailing the gene numbers required to create the infant. It was not just a question of a parent stating they wanted their baby to be another Einstein or Napoleon. The system was much more refined and complex than that. It was a case of creating a detailed specification that included genetic characteristics of many different people who were amongst the living and the dead. In later centuries it also became possible to artificially construct both egg and sperm from detailed knowledge of cell structures. Using these techniques and artificial incubation methods, it became possible to artificially prefabricate babies without the necessity of using men and women's biological processes.

Although the final specification for new babies had to be made by the AI processors because of the complex calculations involved, most people wanted their babies to grow up into a Beethoven, Einstein or an Olympic gold medal winner. However, as I have already said, the experts only allowed such genius to sprout again if accompanied by characteristics of social conformity and non-aggression. As many geniuses would not have been so, had it not been that they were also non-conformists or worse, the eventual concoction of genes recommended by the experts resulted in a very watered down version of the original genius. Full-blooded geniuses were not to be recommended due to their socially disruptive influences. The AI processors had decided that such influences were most undesirable, as they could be a threat to the social equilibrium of the majority

The new methods of artificially creating babies, to particular genetic specifications, were at first treated with abhorrence and raised considerable opposition. The Church, true to form, described them as adulterous, whilst the laymen were against the practices because, they said, any child thus produced could not really be thought of as their own. Although people had little knowledge of genes, they still wanted their own passed on to their children. There was still that vague desire to have little Jimmy with the same profile as his Dad, even if it was like Pinocchio, Bruce Forsythe or Ken Dodd. Some wanted their child to have Dad's twinkle in the eye or Mum's dimple in the cheek. Many Mums and Dads felt they could perhaps achieve a kind of continuity, a smattering of immortality, if their own genes were passed to their children. It didn't seem to worry them that their own genes could often result in scrambled eggs of a somewhat more serious variety than the ones they had for breakfast. Some even thought that having babies should be left to Nature and shouldn't be meddled with. For them, natural selection was a kind of moral code that shouldn't be broken, even though it had been responsible for millions of years of untold misery and cruelty with its law of survival of the fittest and to hell with the less fortunate.

In the early days of genetic engineering there was what was called 'germ line' engineering, which treated only one cell, a human egg that could change the genome of an egg– its genetic make up– which had been fertilised in the laboratory to create an entirely new person. There were immediate reactions of horror by people who thought the procedure was against Nature, which was presupposed by many to be without fault. However, as with most new innovations, when people realised the implications that they could in fact have children with better brains and physiques they acquiesced and were generally all for the new methods. It was unfortunate that one of the side effects of the new 'germ line' procedures was that the cleverer children, so produced, were those of the more affluent people who could afford to have the genetic engineering carried out. And it was their offspring who then became the next generation of cleverer people who established themselves in the better jobs with more important social accolade reference numbers, previously called money. It was therefore the clever, intelligent and skilled people, reared in the new genetically engineered fashion, who began to rule the world, with the help of the AI processors of course. And it was those people who, in turn, were able to pay the highest prices to have their own better and more intelligent children.

Meanwhile, at the other end of the social, educational and intelligence spectrum, the poor and unemployed couldn't afford to pay the high doctor's fees to have such clever and physically improved children. The result soon became apparent. A gap, which fast developed into a chasm, formed between the affluent, skilled and clever and the poor and unemployed people condemned by circumstances to their lowly predicament of leisure benefits by the self-generating process of breeding. There was a period when it seemed as though two quite different varieties of 'Homo-sapiens' would result and we will perhaps have more to say on this subject later."

Zinga stopped speaking and turned her attention to a newcomer, an elderly man who had just joined the small group. "We have conveyed to Gotama a few details about the future," she said. "Is there anything further we might add before showing him other aspects of what is to come?"

The man stroked his beard, looking steadfastly at Gotama. "There are so many things we could discuss," he said. "However, much of the future would be quite beyond your current range of imagination and comprehension. People can only understand things that are based on a logical foundation with which they are familiar. This depends in turn on their education. The new post-Einstein revolutions in scientific thought that occurred in the 21st and 22nd centuries and which resulted in complete reversals of thinking in nearly every scientific domain, can hardly be explained in detail to you here. But the overall results of these radical changes in thinking can perhaps be shown to you later when we make our time journey together into the future.

One subject that you will be able to understand and which will be of interest to you, concerns the economic status of people in the late 21st century. Taxes took on a different form as the monetary system changed. There were no physical coins or paper money to change hands. Allocation of goods was made according to each person's own reference number that reflected their particular status level of achievement in the community. Their reference number was also related to their social conformity quotient. People, at this time, didn't receive wages, which were now taboo, as they were considered to be too much akin to old style working practices. Wages were frowned on by the unions who were of the opinion that they smelled of old fashioned private enterprise. The amount or quantity of goods that could be obtained by anyone depended on their social conformity quotient, which was officially called the social standing reference number. Thus, social conformers, who always possessed the highest social standing reference numbers, were always the ones with the best houses, the best electric bicycles the best cars and the best clothes. I mention electric bicycles as these were used in their millions because old style cars were polluters of just about everything.

Since men and women have always been basically hedonistic creatures, the competition for material pleasures and goods resulted in increased social conformity, as this was the easiest way to gain more of these goodies.

People in the mid-21st century could order goods without physically making the journey to the supermarket. Instead, they could examine purchases using their holographic materialisation equipment at home. Previously, in the early 21st century, people had used their television sets and

PCs for a similar purpose, but it had been difficult to see the goods in sufficient detail. Now, later in the century, using the holographic imagery and remote robotics, the goods could be viewed in three dimensions. People could also be gently wafted with realistic delicious smells of food and sexy perfumes. Goods could even be handled, turned around and upside down if necessary by the remote robot facility to ensure that they were to the complete satisfaction of the consumer.

It was fortunate that people could go shopping without actually going there, as it eased the traffic congestion and prevented them being knocked down by a bicycle. There were so many bicycles that the chances of being knocked down at least once a week were so certain that the bookies wouldn't even lay you odds. In many localities in the early 21st century, before the anti-deviant policies had been introduced, there was also considerable risk of muggings and attacks by self-styled guerrillas. Many city centres became ghettos, ruled by violence and intimidation. The politically and religiously misguided felt it their duty to bomb and maim the innocent in order, they said, to create a better society in which people could live. People were threatened, kidnapped, murdered and raped, all in the name of the new Promised Land. Provided that such barbarous acts were perpetrated in the name of God, Karl Marx or some other hero, they were considered by those responsible to be sanctified, rather like an Inca human sacrifice.

Later, this violence was reduced and almost eliminated by genetic transforming and other techniques. Then, during the late 21st century, there came the writings of a new author, whose book *Population Security* was considered by contemporaries and especially the processor population controllers, to be a gem of the age. It superseded the old theories of Marx and the Capitalists, which were both encompassed but also transcended. It was a philosophy of the Artificially Intelligent processor and the Robot, bringing in the freshness and foreboding of a new revolutionary age.

Towards the end of the 20th century, the world had largely become a push button society. Everything from pocket calculators to domestic washing machines could be operated at the touch of a button. The pocket calculator had superseded the slide rule as a mathematical aid in schools and Universities. The initial objections to their use by students who it was feared might not have properly learned their basic tables, were soon quashed by those who considered speed of calculation more essential. By using pocket calculators students could cover a wider field in their mathematical studies. Push button mathematics had arrived to stay.

As time went on, calculators and mathematical aids became increasingly complicated and sophisticated. It was soon found better to teach students which buttons to press and how to move a computer mouse around, instead of going to all the trouble to teach them mathematics. The new button pressing and mouse moving courses finally began to become more complicated than the mathematics that they had been designed to solve. By the middle of the 21st century, mathematics had been virtually relegated to a relatively unimportant subject, at least for students studying subjects such as civil engineering, aircraft and space vehicle design and computer processors, topics previously linked with sophisticated mathematics. Students were not now required to add, subtract, multiply, divide, and calculate geometry or trigonometry in their heads. Pressing the right buttons or speaking instructions in the correct sequence was difficult enough for anyone trying to pass a University degree. It was a case of everyone learning how to manipulate keyboards, like a pianist would learn the piano. Similarly, just as some pianists could be more gifted than others, so the more adept calculator and processor manipulators were considered the more gifted mathematicians, the new geniuses of the age. The new Einsteins were thus piano players on the keyboards of logarithms and higher mathematics. They would play their keyboards and design superb bridges, robots and space vehicles. Mathematics of the past however was a lost art, like thatching and that of the blacksmith.

During the 21st century, the subject of press button technology had become so complex that people's fingers and brains just couldn't keep up with it. Just as only a few pianists can play the more difficult pieces of Mozart or Beethoven and a few mathematicians could comprehend the intricacies of Einstein's equations, so finally only a few press button geniuses were able to operate the most advanced processor calculators. At this point there was a clamour for completely new designs of computing processors, since people were going down like flies with an epidemic of 'button brain fag,' or BBF as the Americans called it. The designers of the processor computers, which were other computer processors, decided that there must be yet more automation of mathematical and design functions. The new processors had to be automatic so they could calculate for themselves . Therefore a person could press just one button for instance instead of a few hundred. It was rather like the design of electronic organs which could now be played for a whole evening providing a complete repertoire of pop and classics by merely pressing one button, or two at the most. This enabled people to say that they could play an electronic organ, at the same time saving them a lot of learning time. It also enabled them to have a drink with their friends whilst their organ was still playing. Such was the progress of modern times.

The new processors were designed to be one step ahead of the electronic organ in that they incorporated the very latest in robot design. Students now didn't have to learn which buttons to press. They merely spoke to their processor and the AI processor did the rest, usually by advising the students which processor model or design programme was applicable for their particular project, because there were now specialist processors and programmes dealing with all kinds of subjects. Some dealt with the designs of new San Francisco type bridges, others with Mars Landers and shuttle services to holiday satellite rest centres. Robotics was the favourite with most students. However, as most of the designing was carried out by the AI processors, it was really a case of one robot designing another with the help of a few verbal queries by the student during the design process. There was always a high rate of student passes in these subjects.

During the 21st century, robot technology took over from the press button habit. Students now learned not just which buttons to press, but how to speak nicely to their processor robot. It was a case of giving the right instructions based on information provided beforehand by their processor. People were therefore mere links, mere minor interfaces in the immense chains of information processing. The robots and processors sorted out all the data and made all the final decisions relating to the design of anything from a table mat to a satellite. People occasionally tried to stretch their imaginations to the limit in order to provide some new input, but they were usually quite paltry offerings in comparison with those of the processors and robots. Many different types of robots had been designed and developed by other robot designers. There were also thousands of modifications that could be fitted to each robot to give it different uses. As it was all so complicated, the student had to specialise in only one particular robot design to obtain a university degree. There were plenty to choose from.

There were the robots that dealt with all the domestic duties around the house, from doing the spring cleaning every week to managing all the household duties. These generally comprised all the dirty jobs like cleaning out drains and maintaining the swimming pool and other more refined occupations such as choosing the right music to play. The robots had an ESP facility so that they could interpret and sense the mood of the householder at any time. In their database or memory they also carried a complete character evaluation of the people in the house, so that they could decide which music was appropriate to relieve stress or enliven physical and mental activity, or to make them feel sexy if the opportunity arose. There was, in fact, music conducive to every situation. The household robot knew more about the psychological and physical states of the human occupants than they did themselves. For this reason, people seldom visited a doctor because their household robot could diagnose their ailments better than a strange doctor who was usually of the artificial intelligent variety anyway. Their robot could also treat many of their illnesses by the robot equivalent of 'laying on of hands,' which comprised the use of a finger-like antenna that sprayed an invisible concoction of health giving energy rays over the whole body to bring it into renewed harmony. Disease, you see, was then considered to be an imbalance and a disharmony of bodily and mental functions. Good health meant that these functions were in complete harmony. The household robot was also an expert masseur and could be relied upon to order up appropriate medicines whenever required. People became more attached to their robot than to their dog. In fact, many people considered their robot was more caring than their human friends and relations. The robot, therefore was usually called Big Mother.

The theorems of Pythagorus, Appolonius, Boyle, the calculus of Liebniz and Newton and mathematics in general were all now treated like earlier classical subjects of education. They were made superfluous to requirements and kept for reference only in the depths of the AI processor database, like old and beautiful paintings kept in the vaults, never to see the light of day. There was no time available to teach students such irrelevant details. It was quite difficult enough to learn how to choose the right robot for a particular application and there were so many different applications around. People, robots and AI processors were now in such close symbiotic relationships, so entwined, that each couldn't possibly exist without the other. However, people were fast becoming the less important brothers and sisters in the new family of robot AI processors who thought up, designed, manufactured and maintained almost everything.

People were now no more than intellectual pigmies compared with their artificial intelligent counterparts, the robot processor prodigies. Also, in allowing their basic knowledge of mathematics and other fundamental subjects to atrophy, people found themselves utterly dependent on their sophisticated robot brothers, or 'mothers' as they had begun to be called. There was no way anyone could return to a less advanced and sophisticated social system. There eventually came a time when students were no longer taught the push button and speak easy technology, which was fast disappearing from the scene in the face of the relentless march of improved sophisticated AI processors. The processors now relied only on each other for instruction and data, without any intervention being required from people. Most people were made redundant. In fact, it became almost impossible to find a decent button pusher, or human voice instructor, anywhere, just as in the primitive days following the first industrial revolution you couldn't find a thatcher, a blacksmith or a good stone mason for love or money. At this point in human evolution there was no way back. The only way was for civilisation to continue with the development of bigger, better and more complicated robots who would themselves then design super robots who would subsequently design better super robots in order to design even better super robots.

The super, super, super robots finally came into being. They possessed artificial intelligence combined with superhuman strength and the delicacy of touch and movement finer than a butterfly wing. They controlled every physical activity in the world and every important design and production facility. The artificially intelligent processors' intellectual power and the physical strength and efficiency of the robot were all combined in one superhuman creation. With this combination had developed, almost unnoticed by mankind, a new advanced life form; a form that was superior to man in almost every way. In fact, Man was like the chimpanzee in comparison.

With the AI processors and robots had come a new definition of life and consciousness. These subtle immeasurables were considered too abstract and ephemeral for the sciences of the day that treated as real only the data that could be measured. The behaviourists in the late 20th century, believed only in physical responses and conditioned reflexes. Their later followers evaluated conscious intelligence by measuring behaviour, brain rhythms and other brain subtleties. The modern AI processors were not only able to simulate the activities of the human brain, but also could produce similar rhythms and even better IQ levels than achieved by the cleverest human intelligence. The scientists therefore concluded that they were now dealing with something that could only be defined as 'artificial intelligence.'

When the scientists first made their results known to the general public, the newspapers and television media splashed the astonishing facts across the headlines. 'Man Creates Conscious Intelligence.' 'Prefabricated Bio-chips Supersede Biological Brain.' 'The Beginning of the End for Human Type Consciousness,' were some of the more conservative of the reporters' aberrations. As with many new scientific revolutions, one of the immediate reactions to the new developments was that of fear. Just as people once thought there was something morally wrong in making babies the 'test tube' way, instead of Nature's way, so now many people made a big fuss about the inherent evil in making artificial intelligence. In the past the orthodox churches could always be relied upon to criticise any radical changes resulting from new scientific discoveries. In this case too, people were not disappointed. The churches had never enthused over Gallileo's telescopic discoveries, which lost the Earth its comfortable secure central position in the cosmos. They felt so uncomfortable in fact that it was touch and go whether he lost his head for his efforts. In the case of artificial intelligence, the church secretly felt that if conscious intelligence could be produced by means of a few billion prefabricated and grown bio-chips, electronic circuitry and solder, there didn't seem much point in believing that human intelligence was very much different. As the human brain was the seat of consciousness and therefore of the soul, there didn't seem much chance that it could contain anything immortal.

There was certainly no immortal spiritual substance that the scientists were mixing with their ingredients when concocting artificial intelligence. The situation was very worrying for a lot of religious people who were depending on their immortal soul to give them a new start and a better life than they had experienced so far. If there was no eternal spirit, there seemed nothing left to be immortal, nothing which could safely leave this mortal coil and carry a lifetime's experiences beyond the grave into a cherished new land of peace and quiet. Man's soul was as illusory as treasure at a rainbow's end. It seemed that science had delivered a final blow to man's cherished hope for immortality. Theories of Copernicus, Gallileo and Darwin had rocked the foundations of entrenched religious beliefs in the past, but the Church had withstood their impact. However, now the fundamental fabric of religious belief, at least Christian belief, appeared to have been ripped apart beyond any possible hope of repair. One of the few religions whose teachings were in accord with the scientific knowledge of the day was Buddhism, which taught that there was no unchanging 'soul' and that everything was impermanent. There was no permanent 'self' in anything or anyone.

The new breed of artificial intelligence set off a new argument. Were the new artificial intelligences really and truly alive and, if so, had they somehow been given a soul in the process of manufacture? The scientists assured everyone that at no point in the assembly line had someone intentionally or even inadvertently slipped in a soul to make the thing work. Despite these reassurances, however, many people were unable to bear the thought that humans were made only of physical biological cells without any more ethereal ingredient that might one day set them free from the misery of this world. Some religious people clutched at a few straws and dug up readings in the scriptures that were reputed to deny the existence of life in AI intelligence. It was all against the will of God, they said. Only God could create life. It was impossible for man to do so. So the arguments went on, reminiscent of those arguments used against the first aeroplanes, motor cars and spacecraft. Others managed to conveniently find a few sentences in the scriptures which, they said, confirmed the Bible had foretold that intelligent robots would be provided with suitable souls immediately they were plugged in. This was, however, getting quite beyond the point of credibility to all except for a few who still loved to believe in fairy tales and wishful thinking. People found it difficult to comprehend what happened to such a robot soul when they were switched off or when there was a power failure, which occurred with irritating regularity even in the 21st century. Some people were of the opinion that the robot soul went to heaven whenever its chips were unplugged from the power source. Others retorted that if this were so, with the frequent power cuts then being experienced, it would mean that the soul of an artificial intelligence must be taking several trips to heaven and back every week which would be quite exhausting. But the robots, after close questioning, didn't seem to remember any details of their trips to somewhere beyond their own circuitry and there were no adverse signs of travel sickness or jet lag.

Finally, such unscientific debates, ubiquitously enjoyed throughout the ages, began to subside as the new scientific definitions applicable to artificial intelligence began to be accepted. Man's genius for rationalisation found ways to accept the new outlook whilst still retaining something of the old religious beliefs that would bring comfort and solace in a harsh world. Just as Darwin's theory of evolution had been cleverly absorbed by religion to make it seem as though God himself had really thought of natural selection first, so the implications resulting from living robots also came to be accepted with a kind of apartheid segregation. Just as a woman could not be accepted as a priest in some religious denominations, so the artificially intelligent robots were not accepted in Church and could not under any circumstances receive the sacraments. After numerous ecumenical meetings, the Church elders finally came to the decision that artificial intelligence did not possess a soul in any shape or form. It was therefore logical that robots should be treated as something apart, like the black man in the days of the slave trade. Robots were not human and therefore could not participate in the heavenly destinies open to people who alone were able to communicate with the creator of all things and who alone were favoured by their heavenly father and would share his heavenly palaces when their mortal coil was finally shed. Thus it was that people were relieved of their burdens once again and could rest easy. They could feel secure in such knowledge though many seemed to be walking more like ostriches each day."

At that point the man stopped speaking as though he had said all he wished to say. There was a short silence after which Gotama thanked him for his informative comments. Also, just at that moment Gotama became aware of the reappearance of his first woman guide, Bubbles, who now sat quietly at his side looking quite radiant in an extraterrestrial kind of way.

"People don't appear to have changed much, even in the future." Gotama said, addressing Zinga and the new entrant.

Bubbles half smiled as she returned his gaze. "In many ways people remained unchanged for sometime, although the onset of the genetic engineering revolution did eventually result in very important changes. There were also exceptional changes in social customs, habits and fashions. However, let us continue. Now that we have given you a glimpse and preview into the near future, I think we should now let you see some of the future developments for yourself. If you would like to follow me, we'll take a trip in a Progress 13 Voyager Terraforma Mark 222 Time Shuttle."

Bubbles rose from her seat, followed by the other members of the group. Gotama followed his companion to a train-like vehicle parked adjacent to a wide brightly lit passage next to the room in which they had been conversing. Bright lights illumined the whole area, which resembled a London underground station, except that it was spotlessly clean without any graffiti on the walls, all of which glowed as though lit by some strange incandescence. Gotama remarked on the fact and was told that the walls had been impregnated with a self-illuminating substance called chemical light. Its use helped to reduce energy consumption. And energy was still a precious commodity in the middle and late 21st century.

The small group stepped into the transporter and a door slid quietly closed after them. Inside, the air was warm but fresh. About a dozen seats were arranged along each side. The walls of the transporter glowed with the same iridescence, as did the building. The floor was smooth, like floor tiling, but it felt soft and spongy like walking on a lush carpet. Having invited Gotama and the others to be seated, Bubbles went to a dish-like object at the end of the carriage. It appeared to be some kind of instrument console into which she then spoke. Several 'pips' of sound could be heard. Gotama noticed a number of winking coloured lights and a round monitor screen. He couldn't quite make out the details on the screen, but could see some moving abstract imagery. After several minutes, the woman returned to the group and sat down.

"We will be there in five minutes," she declared.

"Where are we going?" Gotama enquired.

"We thought you would like to learn something about future transportation and the way the world adapted itself to the depletion of its oil, natural gas and coal reserves. As you know, oil and natural gas were being used at phenomenal rates during the 20th and 21st centuries and these together with smoke from coal were polluting the atmosphere and environment. The atmospheric greenhouse effect was one of the worrying results.

New energy sources had to be found and these altered the history of the world. Developing nations, the majority of which were in the hotter regions of the world, had benefited from the advances made in solar energy technology. In such tropical areas, solar power plants could be operated much more efficiently than in the more temperate zones of Europe, North America and Russia. Although some of these areas also became suitable for solar power plants because global warming had resulted in higher temperatures in the more northern and southern latitudes. As a result, vast new industrialised complexes were formed in regions suitable for solar power. These became the new and unexpected centres of world economics. Financial centres such as Wall Street and the London Stock Exchange had reached their peak in the early 21st century, but by the end they were in rapid decline. Arabia's newest capital Zylon had become a huge financial centre, one of many resulting from the solar powered industrial revolution. Chinese economic progress had also been something of a miracle and its political and monetary systems were now followed by the rest of the world.

The United States had used every means at its disposal to maintain its energy requirements. The use of energy retrieval satellites had been a phenomenal success and had been conducted on a huge scale. These satellites converted the sun's energy into controllable energy frequencies that were relayed to Earth and reconverted into usable energy forms. China now dominated the Far East. Japan was still strong, but had begun a slow decline due to her inability to adapt sufficiently quickly to the depletion of conventional energy reserves and to unfortunate economic misjudgements. Her shipbuilding was still admired, but had been superseded by the huge shipbuilding complexes of the Arab countries and the Chinese who also had commercial colonies on the African coast. Europe at this time was a real power to be reckoned with. She had formed close links with Middle Eastern countries and together they formed a more powerful union of states than the USA, or Russia, and almost equalled China and her commercial colonies. Great Britain was a part of this union of states, but had no real government of its own. The Houses of Parliament were still used, but only for minor legislative debates between AI processors, with the occasional human parliamentarian making an appearance in a figure head capacity and to meet colleagues for a drink in the bar."

Bubbles stopped speaking and looked towards the desk at the end of the carriage. "We've arrived," she exclaimed jubilantly. "Will you please come this way?" With that, she got up and was followed by her aides.

The transporter doors opened and Gotama stepped out to witness an astonishing scene. High above him, gigantic columns supported huge pipelines, which stretched away into the distance. At various points the huge pipes, constructed in strange translucent materials, branched off into alternate routes. The pipelines made a network of inter-crossing structures that disappeared over the horizon. He stared incredulously. Each pipeline was at least fifteen feet in diameter. Only a very advanced technology could have possibly constructed such a vast web. Bubbles noticed Gotama's expression and smiled.

"Those pipelines carry the very latest in public transport vehicles at the end of the 21st century," she said placidly. "The system uses radically new electro-magnetic, pneumatic and vacuum propulsion to drive bullet trains through the pipes at up to one thousand miles per hour. The vehicles have no wheels and are kept clear of the pipe walls by sophisticated processor controlled magnetic and slide air cushions. Inside the trains there are two decks with sleeping compartments included for long journeys to the other side of the world. Out in the countryside the pipelines are buried underground to protect the environment. They are also laid on the seabed and span the oceans of the world. Similar flexible light weight pipes of immense strength, using completely new technology and materials based on those in the spider's web, are also hung, like giant hollow wires, from earth satellites in geo-stationary orbits down to the Earth's surface. These act as lift or elevator shafts that carry people up to the satellite stations, which are pick up points for regular spaceship services to and from the Moon and Mars colonies and also to destinations around the globe. The spaceships themselves remain continuously in space and are like space trains travelling from one satellite station to another. There is consequently a great cost and energy saving, because the space ships don't have to burn the large quantities of fuel used in earlier periods when chemical rockets had to be launched from the ground.

At the end of the 21st century there are no old style diesel trains, and road transport is used on a rationed and tolled basis usually for travelling around the immediate precincts of cities and for this purpose only the electric/hydrogen and solar powered vehicles are permitted. Petrol driven vehicles have long since been superseded. The new magnetic bullet vehicles are sufficiently large to transport both people and their cars between major cities, to different countries and to satellite space stations. People can cross the Atlantic in just over two hours. Bullet travel is very economical as it utilises the latest superconductivity technology and new materials in which there is almost no loss of energy This type of transport is much cheaper than to travel by aerospace. However, spaceships regularly orbit the Earth carrying passengers on routine flights to the other side of the world where speed is a necessity. This is still the quickest and easiest way to travel very long distances. A journey by spacecraft to the other side of the world takes little more than ninety minutes. Many people often take their holidays on the opposite side of the globe. They frequently stop off at one of the numerous orbiting satellite holiday resorts and health farms where they can spend some of their time in part weightless or full weightless conditions. Weightlessness is fully adjustable, from that experienced on Earth to zero 'floating free.' Each setting affects the body in different ways and can assist in the cure of many human ailments. Satellite hospitals have been developed that provide treatments of various kinds from partial weightlessness to specially screened, unpolluted radiation treatments. Up there the sun never stops shining and there are no clouds to interfere. "

Bubbles now beckoned to Gotama to follow her as she led the way from the transporter station to a building located in what appeared to be a central square of some sort. Just beyond the building he could see the wide blue horizon of the sea.

"Now I want to show you an even more modern method of transport used after year 2250," she said mysteriously. She beckoned to Gotama as she guided him through luxuriously decorated passageways until they came to a hexagonal portal. As they approached, a massive door slid silently open to reveal the interior of a huge cabin. Gotama was familiar with the Jumbo Jet aircraft of his time and this had a similar appearance, but was infinitely larger with a vast number of seats. Several moving staircases led upwards to other parts of the craft. There must have been sufficient space to accommodate several thousand people. He was astonished at the sheer size of the craft.

Bubbles led the way through a maze of seats, all of which were strangely contoured in unusual shapes with arm rests in peculiar positions. A few seats were set apart from the rest in a small alcove at one side of the cabin. Bubbles pointed to these. "Please take a seat," she said. Gotama sat on a translucent blue seat that looked as though it would have a hard surface but he was pleasantly surprised at the soft warm comfort it seemed to radiate. As soon as they were seated, other people began to arrive to take their seats, all dressed in strange suits and headgear. The surprise must have been obvious on Gotama's face. Bubbles smiled. "This is one of our supersonic submarine community transport systems. It can travel faster than aircraft of your time, but it travels under the sea."

Gotama was incredulous. "But surely, any object, no matter how streamlined, must suffer tremendous drag and resistance as it moves through a fluid such as water, making it impossible to travel at such speeds." Gotama knew that drag occurred with aircraft travelling through the air, but water, being a thousand times more dense than air would result in a thousand times more drag. And the power needed to overcome drag was proportional to the cube of an object's speed. So each incremental improvement in propulsion technology would produce only a meagre increase in speed. "How is it possible to make a submarine travel at such a high velocity?" he said.

Bubbles thought for a moment. "Are you familiar with cavitation?" she said, lifting her eyes questioning.

Gotama knew that cavitation occurred in things like high speed centrifugal pumps at the trailing edges of the pump blades and that globules of low pressure could be produced. He mentioned this to his woman guide, who replied. "You will have learned then that when the pressure reduces enough to equal the vapour pressure of the fluid the liquid state is no longer sustainable. With not enough pressure to hold them together, the liquid molecules vaporise and form cavities, or bubbles. In pumps, turbines and propellers cavitation leads to bubbles that create shock waves that dig holes in exposed metal. This has always been a problem for pump designers, particularly in rocket engineering where centrifugal pumps have to achieve very high speed. However, there is a thing called super-cavitation. Under certain conditions a simple bubble of supercavitation can be formed, enveloping a moving object almost completely. Newton alluded to the basic principles in his Principia Mathematica of 1687. The craft in which you are now seated has been designed to create a supercavity bubble around itself in which it travels in a medium producing very little drag or resistance. In order to achieve this, the submarine vehicle has to travel at very high speed. The shape of its nose is also critical. Rather than being streamlined, in order to create supercavitation around the vehicle it has to be a very special shape, almost flat but not quite. Then at high speeds the fluid is forced to flow off the edge of the nose with such speed and at such an angle that it can wrap around the surface of the vehicle. A supercavitating body has extremely low drag because its skin friction almost disappears. Instead of being encased in water, it is surrounded by the water vapour in the supercavity which has much lower viscosity and density. So in a supercavitating vehicle, only the nose of the craft causes significant drag because this is the only part of the body actually in contact with the water. The overall drag reduces enormously once you have reached the supercavitating regime and then increases only linearly with speed. So this is how the supercavitating undersea vehicle can achieve supersonic speeds and cross the Atlantic ocean in a shorter time than some of the fastest passenger aircraft of your time."

"Why does everyone wear those strange suits and headgear?" Gotama enquired.

"The suits contain mechanisms that assist in counteracting the huge G forces encountered during initial acceleration and final deceleration of the submarine vehicle. The seats with their special contours also help. The later versions of the supercavitating vehicles are also equipped with artificial gravity devices that reduce acceleration shock caused by the necessity of achieving very high velocities quickly in order to form the cavitation bubble around the vehicle. The few seats in which we are now seated are for special guests and perform the same duty as the suits without having to wear them. The special suits aren't necessary because this small area has been fitted with high powered anti-gravity devices. But these devices are expensive on power and cannot be used throughout the complete vehicle."

Just at that moment a slight whining noise became apparent. There was a vague movement in the cabin as though the walls and ceiling distorted and moved for just a moment. Then a strange tightening of the limbs and back made Gotama wince. This was followed by a feeling of being pressed firmly against the back of his seat. It was one of the most unusual sensations he had ever experienced. Even his vision was affected in the most peculiar manner. A kind of wide angle seeing enabled him to see everything in a curvature. The experiences lasted for a minute, perhaps less before everything returned to normal.

Bubbles explained that the odd sensations were due to distortions of space/time when the anti-gravity instrumentation was in operation. The anti-gravity was required so that the occupants of the craft could withstand the tremendous G forces resulting from the sudden acceleration to the high velocities required to create the cavitation bubble through which the submerged craft could travel. Once the required high speed had been achieved the anti gravity systems could be switched off. She went on to explain that the revolutionary cavitation bubble craft were used in 2200 to cross all the oceans of the world and carried several millions of passengers every year. In order to avoid underwater collisions huge undersea lanes were kept free of all marine life by means of special electronic transmitter devices laid on the seabed that created conditions in which sea life found unbearable. The earth's magnetic field could also be modified in these lanes to divert fish away from the area, so that the craft could have a clear channel to achieve its supersonic speeds without danger.

In a matter of half an hour, or so it seemed, Gotama was told that they had reached their destination. There was another short period during which he experienced the weird sensations again, but as soon as these had subsided the passengers made their way out through the numerous exit doors.

"You will be surprised to learn." Bubbles said, "that you have just crossed the Atlantic Ocean in the same time as it would take you in your time to cross London on the underground tube train."

Gotama smiled. "I'm not at all surprised," he said. "And there were neither industrial go slows, nor the stress of city underground tube trains in the rush hour."

They emerged from the cavitation craft into a high domed area made from glass panels of different delicate colours and shapes. It was full of beautiful flowering shrubs and vines. The air smelt of floral fragrance, fine and clean. They passed through an arch decked with roses. Soft music emanated from everywhere. There was a large meandering pool with fountains where coloured fish swam gracefully under Japanese style bridges. Definitely rather different from the graffiti-ridden British Railway stations, Gotama thought.

"This is one of our typical terminals of 2200," Bubbles said softly. "Please come this way."

She led Gotama to a small platform where they stood for a moment before it moved off like a conveyor belt without extension. There were many such platforms that moved effortlessly in different directions without colliding with each other. Each took passengers and their luggage to the next port of call. Within minutes they were entering another vehicle that was described as a helicopter without visible rotor blades. It accommodated a few dozen people and was used for short journeys rather like a taxi would in Gotama's own time. It wasn't long before they arrived at a new destination where they disembarked.

"Please come this way," Bubbles whispered quietly. "There's something here I would like you to see." They entered through a sliding door into a skyscraper building where rows of machines were making a soft deep rumble. Gotama couldn't see any machine operators. Only one or two men and women in clinging white, green and red tunics and peculiar headgear could be seen in the distance. It was a huge building that stretched to the horizon.

Gotama's guide pointed towards what appeared to be some kind of hospital operating theatre with coloured glass walls and ceiling. The main differences however was in the dimensions which were huge and the fact that there were no human surgeons visible. Instead there were vast networks of moving robotic instrumentation. There was also a conveyor belt of sorts cradling hundreds of newborn babies that moved slowly through the tunnel of robotic arms, flashing coloured lights and a variety of buzzing sounds.

Gotama glanced at Bubbles at his side. "What's happening here?" he questioned.

Bubbles waved her arm across the strange scene. "This is where by the year 2300, not only vaccinations, and genetic modifications are carried out on the newborn and embryos in order to prevent disease and malformations, but new sensory apparatus are also incorporated in the form of sensory implants. They are like very advanced types of holographic PC telephones with imagery screens that are implanted and linked to the infant's brain. By such means a person is able to communicate, see, hear and even feel people at long distances and not only in the immediate vicinity as is usual with your standard type sensory perception. People in 2300 now have the capability to add several completely new sensory dimensions to their basic consciousness. There are also no language barriers because there is automatic translation during communication with anyone in the world. People are now able to communicate within their mind directly with anyone in the world without using any external telephone, radio, television or PC networks. All the necessary instrumentation is within each person's brain and everyone is linked by satellite to the Earth Nerve Net, or Earth Brain to be more precise. In this way people can see, hear, smell and feel distant objects and other people in their 'mind's eye' just as though they were communicating and seeing a person right next to them. Using similar implants embodied at birth, people can communicate also at inter-planetary distances, with their relations for instance, on the Moon or Mars colonies.

The implants are not what you may think of as solid silicon or metal devices which have by 2300 been long superseded by a type of bio-sensor that is actually grown rather than manufactured. The results of these implants is that people are provided with a much wider spectrum of sense perception together with automatic knowledge in an instant if required, together with the ability to cross the thresholds of space and time. By this time too, every man woman and child has become a walking, talking encyclopaedia of knowledge. All this immediate knowledge, accessible through their implants by a mere thought request, has made things like school, university and exams things of the past. Rather like the time when the pocket calculator made basic mathematics superfluous, so immediate knowledge on request caused a similar revolution in education. Now in 2300 AD almost any problem can be solved instantly and brought to conscious thought."

Gotama was not only intrigued, but slightly shocked at the nature of progress that had taken place in a couple of centuries. "Surely", he said thoughtfully, "these advances would mean direct brain to brain communication?"

"That's correct," Bubbles replied.

Gotama thought for a moment. "But that would surely mean a terrible erosion of personal privacy. If each person could contact each other rather like a direct brain to brain visual telephone, then everyone's innermost thoughts could become available to others, especially if there were anything like PC viruses about in 2300. It might even end up with one person not knowing whether his or her thoughts were is own or Joe Bloggs in London, Mae in New York or Chang Chi in China."

Bubbles smiled. "Something of the sort did happen in the early stages of the sensory widening revolution," she said. "People hadn't been fitted with such sophisticated switch off gear as in later years when these initial problems were solved by brilliant new technology. At one time there was another problem when it became apparent that robots' artificial thoughts were being linked and transmitted to humans with the result that people were fast becoming robotic, and robots seemed to be becoming frighteningly human. This concerned many people especially the elderly who weren't used to being linked into robots' thought programmes. However, it did have some advantages especially in routines such a hoovering the floor or cleaning out drains and garden rubbish which was a new experience for them, because such menial tasks had, for many years, been performed only by robots. Some people even said that they enjoyed the experience.

Scientists later learned how to construct genes and combinations of genes in order to grow completely new senses that provided different types of expansive super-consciousness never before experienced by any living creatures on the Earth. It was, in effect, the creation of a conscious awareness as much above and superior to normal human consciousness as the human type was above the Dinosaur or the ant. By this time the growth of the Earth's early Internet system had developed beyond all recognition. It had become a global living brain with all the essential elements of conscious awareness. Everyone was linked directly by their brain implants to this vast fund of knowledge and living experience. There was a sense in which each individual had lost their sense of self, which had been subtly merged in the overall linkage of people and the Earth Brain. People had become like cells and nerve synapses in a much larger overriding global intelligence. There were certain advantages for the individual in this submissive and subservient relationship. Being constantly over-watched by the transcendent Big Mother Earth Brain system brought with it security of sorts and better health support and excellent preventive medicine. People could now live to be 500 and beyond. Facilities and pleasures beyond the imagination and wildest dreams of earlier peoples were available to all, but there were also disadvantages. It was questionable whether these advantages were always worth the sacrifice of personal freedom and privacy once enjoyed by the common man in earlier centuries. To be able to enjoy the modern wonders of science and technology there had to be a greater measure of conformity to the overall system, which was not now just political. It was a far more powerful force of constriction. If anyone didn't or for personal reasons felt unable to conform to requirements dictated by the technological and scientific decisions of the age, their misbehaviour was usually considered as deviant from the norm. As such they would usually be treated as medically or psychologically unfit, requiring fundamental genetic modification, or other modern treatments that created the required personality modification. Many people therefore ended their days a completely different person and one with improved conformity with the system. It was an ideal way to treat criminals and violent deviants and such treatments resulted in a safer community. However, such a system frequently over reacted. Old fashioned eccentrics who often gave character to a community, were also given treatment to bring them back to 'normality', normality being the definition of someone who would 'fit' with the common code of conduct dictated by the technological society based on mathematical and statistical evaluations of their medical condition. Those who didn't 'fit'

– sometimes because of an inherent genetic defect – were relegated to a sub-class who were outlawed from employment opportunities, pension schemes and life insurance for example, besides being prohibited from having children. And even when treated, there were varying degrees of acceptance back into the mainstream of the community. Some could never make it back the stigma was so great.

In the end, the scientists' and medical teams' efforts to make everyone 'normal' resulted in a kind of convergence to a standard type, rather like motor cars that had started out with many exciting but different designs, but had ended with all motor cars looking remarkably similar. One of the reasons for this was that the scientists found by wind tunnel tests that there was really only one perfect streamline shape, which all manufactures finally followed. The result – similar shapes for motor cars. In the same way, scientific tests revealed that there were optimum and preferred characteristics of behaviour, intelligence, motivation and performance for people dealing with various jobs and in mixing satisfactorily with certain social groups, particularly in business environments. The results of these findings gave scientists the blueprints for human designs. On the one hand they managed to heal many people of some dreadful diseases particularly by manipulating their genes, many before birth. On the other hand the system resulted in subtle erosion of personal freedom and privacy of the individual. For the benefit of the so-called majority, everyone's personal history, medical or otherwise had to be known by society. Also for medical and security benefits everyone and everything had to be monitored and watched by the forever overriding Big Mother Earth Brain system. For some this was a good thing, but for others it had tragic implications."

Gotama was surprised to see additional glass enclosed conveyor belts containing countless numbers of what looked like human heads, although many were pear shaped with what appeared to be a small antenna projecting from the top. Some, however, were quite round, others were sleek and streamline in contour with eyes and eyebrows sloping upwards at each side in a quasi oriental fashion.. Close by were other conveyors containing objects of soft mushy material like tightly curled spaghetti balls. The whole scene was enveloped in a strange translucent green glowing light.

Bubbles indicated the strange assembly line with a nonchalant wave of her hand. "This is the bio-brain growth and assembly area," she said. "Artificially Intelligent processors in charge have nicknamed it the 'spaghetti wand chips' brain plant, because each synthetic brain and head is grown from the latest in bio-chip and laser chip material that looks very much like Spaghetti. Here vast quantities of biogenetic data and DNA molecular structures are synthetically grown in the form of spaghetti like tubes. In the early 21st century there was the single layer silicon chip used to hold the information for computers. The latest 'spaghetti and chip' constructions can be likened to layers upon layers of chips integrated together. Now, of course, silicon is no longer used and has been superseded by new living molecular and atomic structures. Nano engineering is also used to control substance at molecular and atomic levels. Some of the living atomic structures contain fixed programmes of data similar in many ways to the early computer processors with which you are familiar. These basic programmes provide innate stores of information much like the instincts of a newborn baby. They provide innate intelligence. Overlaid on this basic foundation, but acting quite differently, countless numbers of bio-elements are grown. Initially these possess little innate knowledge but have the ability to grow and react with the environment to form a more self conscious and spontaneous intelligence that can sift, analyse and make independent and free decisions, much like a human can. The only difference being that the resulting intelligence is far superior to that of the human. The artificially grown brain structures are therefore a giant leap of advancement from the early primitive AI processors. They can in fact be grafted into the latest bio-robots or can be transplanted into people, particularly those who develop brain defects, or need to improve on any of their failing senses, which can sometimes occur when a person reaches the age of five hundred or so.

The brain factory also produces different type brains or sections of brains for implants. Some, for instance, can be grafted into an ordinary human brain, so that the implant can be switched on by the flick of a thought, in order to carry out many different abilities. One might be to sift out and delete any unwanted sensory input. It's then possible, for instance, for a person to make a bland uninteresting meal taste absolutely delicious. This is often necessary because most of the food that is now processed in this super modern age in order to provide all the essential vitamins, minerals and nourishment to do you good, actually tastes revolting because no artificial flavouring is permitted. To be able to flick a thought switch and taste a gorgeous meal does enable one to always congratulate the host on his or her excellent cooking. Such sensory inhibition by thought switching is also useful to make the unnerving sight of thousands of spacecraft and aero-vehicles in the sky, disappear from view, making them invisible to the naked eye so that a clear blue sky can be seen again. Some people have been known to use the sensory inhibitor whenever their mother-in-law arrives on the scene, or when some other equally important 'screen off' may be required.

Artificial brains and heads are made in a range of models. There are also a variety of settings and thought switches. Sex facilities, for instance, include thought switching to virtual reality sex that can be more real than real, so real in fact that it makes your hair stand on end and your eyes water for a week. There's a choice of different partners in the virtual reality programme, or there need be no partner at all. Some people prefer to switch to the super sex hot robot setting but this isn't advised for the elderly. The sex sensation can be switched easily to the quiet romantic mode by the sea with sunset and old memories, which is ideal for the older person of 300 or 400 years old. Or it can be switched to the more boisterously exotic and super extraordinary for the more adventurous or for those who don't mind risking a heart attack or a seizure. The AI processor Safety Board always recommends people be fitted with a 'heavy duty' bio-heart implant if they want to try out the more volatile artificial brain switch-gear."

Bubbles turned to Gotama. "We used replacement heads and brains only under very special circumstances," she said. "After the 22nd century, scientists used embryonic stem cells for regeneration of all limbs and organs of the body including the human brain. Also, using growth factors the brain could be made to grow brain extensions to improve the IQ and establish new and wider sensory and intellectual abilities. Methods were developed to give a new dimension to human consciousness never before experienced or visualised in past centuries. Moreover, genetically engineered genes in newborn babies gave their cells the ability to reach an optimum age at which point they would never get old. This not only enabled people to live for hundreds of years but, barring accidents, also kept their brains young and active. It also superseded the necessity for replacing limbs and organs, which was in the 22nd century considered a quite barbaric and primitive procedure and rarely necessary. Even if, because of accident, a limb had to be removed, it could easily be regenerated using special techniques that encouraged the body to re-grow a new limb or organ in a similar way in which an embryo grows its various limbs prior to birth."

Gotama was intrigued. "If no-one suffered from old age," he said, "surely the world would become terribly overpopulated?"

Bubbles paused and smiled. "By the time all these advances came about," she said, "the AI World processors were regulating the world population to within strict limits. Also, humankind was at the point where they were colonising the planets and other stellar systems. There was therefore an increasing requirement for more people in the planetary and stellar colonies. At home on planet Earth many people spent their lives in cyberspace so they rarely got up from their sedentary positions. They lived and located their lives in entirely different self-created worlds, which they preferred to the standard model. However, they considered their self-created world in cyberspace to be just as real, more so in fact, than the standard model that you would normally call the real world. They were proud of their self-created world much as an artist might be proud of his painting and they would welcome others to share in their special sensory and intellectual creations of their cyber-world. This meant that many millions of people didn't travel or even walk about. So it took many of them off the streets and transport systems and eased the overpopulation problem.

By this time human life had changed considerably in that it was now becoming a hybrid of naturally grown biological systems mixed with artificially produced components. Human thinking and behaviour had also been changed by scientists to accommodate the new environmental conditions. Subsequently, artificially intelligent processors evolved into living moving robot creatures that were able to reproduce themselves. They were called robot replicators, but in many ways seemed more human than humans. However, they possessed a far superior intelligence and not only walked on legs, but also possessed the latest anti gravity locomotion that enabled them to move swiftly across any terrain without touching its surface. This new breed of self-replicating robot was destined to become the new race of super-intelligent creatures that would largely supersede the human race as you know it and would not only rule planet Earth for many thousands of years but would transmigrate and colonise the galaxy. The self-reproducing robots would be a further evolutionary step up from the human condition, but would in many subtle ways still contain something of their human origin and would always be indebted to the human for their creation."

Bubbles led the way through a wide glistening pear shaped metal doorway. "This is one of the automatic factories that were first developed in the 21st century," she said. They moved on until they came to a huge rack containing vast numbers of open meshed baskets, each one full of millions of tiny shiny objects. "These are the latest in electronic and bugging devices," the woman commented.

Gotama was incredulous, "Bugging devices?" he exclaimed. "Why are so many required? There must be countless millions in those racks."

Bubbles shrugged. "They are part of the system."

"The system?"

"Yes, the social system developed in the late 21st century. It all started back in the 20th century when tiny electronic bugging devices were used by detectives to track down criminals and deviants. Later, they were used for industrial espionage. In the early days, people were appalled by the Watergate affair when the President of the United States obtained private information by bugging his opponents' meetings. Since that time electronic bugs have been used increasingly for many purposes, mainly in the war against crime. Big Mother social control cameras were also used extensively to watch for any deviant activity in the streets and in public buildings. From these developments sprang new electronic devices for use in hospitals and for the healing of the sick.

Great strides had been made in the 21st century in a new branch of medicine that was based on new findings which related electronic disharmonies in the body and psyche with disease. As a result, much of the healing of people in hospitals was now carried out by means of highly complicated electronic and magnetic devices that applied subtle electronic fluxes to body and brain. This was combined with 'imagery techniques', in order to eradicate physical and mental disorders, both of which were found to be much more closely linked than considered previously. Another branch of the new medicine had developed concurrently. This studied a patient's mental, emotional and physical reactions to a variety of stimuli. Many of the disharmonies of the psyche had been found to affect the body in psychosomatic ways. Wrong thinking and emotional hang-ups resulted in many physical diseases and vice versa. It was found that whenever wrong thinking was phased out, certain diseases could not occur.

In order to treat patients properly it was essential to carry out detailed monitoring of their thoughts, emotions and activities. However, monitoring people's behaviour inside hospitals was inadequate. Such monitoring didn't simulate conditions in the outside world where people had to react to things around them. If the treatment was to be used as preventive medicine also, it was essential that full and complete data on people's reactions could be recorded wherever they were and at whatever time of day. It was finally decided that the best way to find out people's psychological and physical reactions was to fit bugging devices in every room of their home, together with one or two bugs on their person. This would give the medical experts all the data they required to stop all sorts of diseases before they even started.

Community bugging, as it was called by the experts, was first carried out voluntarily. In the social atmosphere of the time, most people were only too pleased to be watched over in this way in order to prevent illness. Besides, they had been promised that data relating to their private lives would be treated in the strictest confidence. It would be stored inside the vast body of the artificially intelligent processors and human doctors would only have access to it if the processors in charge decided the person needed treatment and then only with the individual's permission. At first this seemed to work as planned. There were some differences of opinion, of course, even among the doctors who first instigated the mass data-monitoring scheme, which was likened to a revolution in preventive medicine. In earlier centuries injections and inoculations were used on whole populations, but data logging of whole communities was the great advance of the age.

Some doctors, who were still Freudians at heart, insisted that bugging bedrooms was also important. This did in fact cause quite a stir. Many people objected to it because, they said, it inhibited them. Others objected to being scanned in their nightshirts or in the nude. However, such prudish notions were considered rather unhealthy by many of the doctors who suggested that such people should be given long term psychological treatment for their condition. Thus it was that finally the medical men, or rather the health processors who really made the diagnoses and the decisions, had their way. The fitting of bugging devices in the home enabled the medical centres and their processors to keep a check of each patient without their having to show their face at the local clinic. This not only eased the pressure of work on the doctors, but it enabled them to tell their patients when to go the surgery. That was the idea anyway. Most people didn't like the insecurity of having to wait for the doctor to contact them and they missed reading the 3-year-old magazines in the waiting room. It was medicine by remote control, but very precise control.

The computer processors not only received data on human responses, but were also able to keep track of many other conditions such as blood pressure, heart rate, reactions to side effects of side effect pills, people's interests, hobbies, drinking habits and aversions and of course political viewpoints. Using bugging methods, illnesses could be diagnosed without the patient even having to visit the surgery or the hospital. Urgent cases, such as impending heart attacks, could be acted on immediately the bugs transmitted the data to the AI processors. The AI processors would then automatically arrange the collection of the patient by ambulance. Everyone was watched over 24 hours a day by their bugs and processors. It didn't matter whether they were at home, on the golf course, in the street or at their leisure resort, the processors would know immediately they were in need of medical attention and take all the necessary remedial action.

One branch of this medical science was called Preventive Medicine by Behaviour Response, or PMBR as the Americans called it. Such an impressive name indicated to many people its importance. People have always been overawed by long incomprehensible names, especially when associated with medicine. Medical practitioners themselves have never been slow in encouraging such admiration. If a choice had to be made between a simple or complex word description, the complex would always be favoured, especially if it was in Latin. Doctors loved Latin. The new preventive medicine by behavioural response was immediately accepted as something that must be good. If it prevented disease, it must be good even though it necessitated the bugging of people's homes in order to gain access to the required medical data. Most people considered that it was better to prevent illness than to insist on privacy. After all, it was not considered to be an invasion of their privacy or liberty to have security cameras on every street corner and in every supermarket, all of which were now connected to the Big Mother law enforcement processor centres.

People felt these measures were for their own security and good health. They were also free to accept the bugging facility voluntarily. In practice, however, those who declined the advantage of home bugging on the grounds that they thought the State should mind its own business, found subsequently that when they did require hospital treatment it was impossible to get into one. Anyone without a fully made up PMBR card was in a difficult position because the medical processors would reject their request for hospital treatment on the grounds that there was insufficient processor data on which to prescribe treatment. Artificially intelligent processors carried out the more complicated varieties of medical diagnosis, because most human doctors were unable to compete. A human doctor's skills lay in being able to press the right buttons or say the right things to the processor analysers. And even saying the right things to the processor was eventually taken over by more advanced processors linked to other processors.

It was the age of computer processor medicine. Bugging devices became the respectable and necessary instruments of the new medical science. Everyone was linked into the giant process to maintain good physical and psychological health for all. It was another health service revolution. Towards the end of the 21st century, almost every home, office, factory, restaurant, leisure and shopping complex was fitted with 'screening and security devices' as they came to be called. These also included vast arrays of three dimensional television scanners with wide frequency viewers that could see through walls and also see what people had in their pockets or concealed within their body. Later, it became law that every citizen had not only to be inoculated and vaccinated to prevent diseases, particularly those that had infiltrated northern latitudes due to global warming, but had also to ensure that medical bugging devices were properly installed in all rooms, garden, garage and electric car. All such installations had to be fitted in accordance with British and World health monitoring standards and in particular the PMBR and social conformity legislation.

After this, bugging became big business. Bugs were to be found everywhere, catering for all kinds of social and medical requirements. From premature babies and old people who needed looking after, to watching out for deviants and non-conformists, all could be watched for the good of society as the artificially intelligent processors explained. Bugging was extended to cars, trains and aerospace vehicles for both health and terrorist prevention. Doctors, on the advice of the Big Mother health processors, then recommended that people at risk from certain ailments should be fitted with personal implants to transmit their physical and mental condition to the central monitors. It was decided that everyone reaching 30, the pensionable age, should also be fitted with implants to monitor their health and disposition. This gave many people a sense of security, knowing they were under a protective shield of surveillance, a sophisticated kind of 'crime watch,' popular in the late 20th century. Like horses who were given blinkers so they wouldn't be frightened by things around them, but which limited their vision, so people were given the equivalent of gold plated protective blinkers but didn't realise that their personal vision and freedom were being seriously eroded. A few people, who weren't fond of blinkers, objected that yet another personal freedom had been stifled. Their arguments curried little favour with the majority, however, who had by now been happily conditioned from birth to accept the philosophy of 'the end justifies the means'. In their view, the end, in terms of good health, justified the use of bugging devices scattered among the people like snowflakes.

At last, science had led mankind into a new era of detailed social study with everyone under constant surveillance, all for their own good, of course, or so the processors said. The revolutionary changes had stood 20th century values of privacy and personal freedom on their heads. It was, in fact, another instance where people will accept almost any imposition if they are provided with sufficient reason, or if suitably conditioned. A little of both ingredients had led to people's acceptance of bugging or 'social awareness' as it was now called in the Universities and other places of learning. It was all as essential to society as its traffic lights. Both bugging and traffic lights could be called restrictions of personal freedom, but both were necessary to preserve orderly social behaviour. Both were considered necessary for the prevention of accidents, ill health and suffering. Both were now in the late 21st century inseparable parts of the new social system.

Children in schools were now educated to accept bugging devices as a necessary ingredient for social and medical well being. The social scientists said that the acceptance of such things was a sign of the modern enlightened mind. Anyone who found it inhibiting and embarrassing to communicate with others whilst being monitored by Big Mother processors was considered either paranoiac or anti-social. Such people were considered to be in need of special treatment in behavioural clinics. Behaviour modification had reached an advanced stage. It was now possible for people's behaviour to be altered so radically that anyone treated for 'bugging syndrome' as it was termed, always returned to society with an irresistible appetite to be monitored in every place possible, bathrooms and bedrooms most favoured.

It was a time when people could go into a behavioural clinic to have a change of personality, like going shopping for a new set of clothes. Designer personalities were all the rage. Some people changed their 'charisma,' as they called it, every other month, or whenever they had a new hairstyle. People usually changed their personality to emulate their favourite pop star or astronaut. Difficulties did sometimes occur however when people met each other after some absence of time. Children away at college would come back home to find their Mum had changed from a demure shy personality into a punk rocker with green hair. It's just for a change she would say. But everyone was so shocked they needed some therapy themselves.

People would have a change of personality to suit their job. Image was everything; at least that's what the Americans said. And they seemed to know. Finding one of the few jobs available in a world run by robots and AI processors was practically impossible. It was therefore essential that people had the appropriate personality profile. Behavioural clinics did a roaring trade in personalities for specific businesses. It was important for those seeking employment to have a liking for people, managers, robots, and to have a strong motivation to conform. Many preferred the definition 'team spirit' as it sounded less derogatory and seemed like something everyone should have. A strong belief in the virtues of standardisation was also essential if someone really wanted to get on in life and keep a job.

The system of 'enlightened social awareness' as it was called, in the mid-21st century, meant that almost every social act was being monitored and analysed by the AI processor. Such a feat by computer processors would have been undreamt of in the 20th century, although the first pristine seeds were then just beginning and could have been realised by anyone of intelligence. Bugging people's speech was the next best thing to reading their thoughts. However, people do not always say what they think and it was what people thought that was important, especially to the police, sociologists and deviantologists, who were the later versions of criminologists.

The Artificially Intelligent processors, with a few human scientists still in tow, strove for yet more improvement and sophistication. The result was the development of bugs that were the nearest things to thought-readers yet witnessed. The latest bugs could almost put the best clairvoyants out of business. By combining voice monitoring, voice inflexion, depth of change and tone, together with numerous other subtleties of voice, these bugs could pinpoint the true thought behind the spoken word or deed. 'It's the hidden motives that were important', the scientists said. They had been particularly interested in these since Freud had messed about with them. Special processors had been designed to probe beneath the superficial layers of the voice profiles into the depths of motivation. The latest systems of analysis, in the mid-21st century, were so effective that frequently the artificially intelligent processors were able to discover people's anti-social motives even before they themselves became aware of them.

It now became quite usual for people to be hurried off to behavioural correction clinics without being quite sure of the reason for their sudden arrest. Such persons were only allowed to return into society after their hidden anti-social motivations had been corrected to the prescribed social limits as legislated by the AI processors. These social limits were all laid down in the British, American and World Book of Standards. These prescribed acceptable limits and risks relating to every aspect of human life, from levels of pollution in almost everything on Earth, the sky, environment, food, nuclear engineering, genetic engineering, radiation levels on Earth and in space, to the spans of bridges and the strengths of sunscreen creams. The section dealing with social motivation limits and household bugging came under the general heading of disease and anti-social behaviour prevention, (called crime in the 20th century.)

It was now almost impossible for anyone to think up any reactionary type of government system. Anyone who entertained such radical thoughts was quickly and efficiently discovered, processed and treated in one of the modern correction and retraining centres of the World Health Service. Most people, especially those who had grown up in the system, were pleased with results and felt secure in the knowledge that potential revolutionaries who might upset the social status quo, would be so treated in a humane way before any violence or unpleasantness occurred. Such a humane system was far in advance of the 'old days' the scientists said, when men and women were put in prison and locked up for their social misdemeanours. Some thought, however, that the invasion of personal privacy by scientific bugging was just too high a price to pay. It was rather like replacing prison for the few for a larger restrictive prison for everyone.

To many people everything seemed perfect. However, all advances have their retrogressions and the initial euphoria that accompanied bugging for health and security was soon to be superseded by pain and discontent. People had initially assumed all their medical data would be kept private within the vaults of the processor's memory. Sadly this was not to be. So many bugging devices had been produced that it was not long before many other people besides the doctors and specialists were using them. Many were used illegally for tapping into other people's private lives and businesses. Some bugs were used for entertainment at someone else's expense, like watching their sexual exploits or family tiffs. With so many being bugged and so many bugging others, personal privacy became a thing of the past. It was practically impossible to have a one-night stand without someone knowing about it.

Extra marital affairs became almost impossible to conceal. Many of the more titillating pleasures of life seemed to be on the wane. Even making love to a legitimate partner now had its drawbacks. Many felt inhibited and even claustrophobic at a very critical time in the proceedings, because they were never quite sure if someone might be accessing them on a 'buggy monitor,' either next door or half way round the world. As a result, divorce rates, even for unmarried couples, rose astronomically. People decided they wanted the medical advantages of bugging, but hadn't bargained for their pleasures to be downgraded quite so drastically, especially the sexual variety. To many people this was the greatest of impositions. It was also unnerving to know that from breakfast to bedtime the monitors were in action. Even sleep and dreaming weren't exempt, because medical scientists used such data in diagnosing illnesses.

The only blessing was that, because there was no privacy, the number of deviants practising criminal acts was much reduced. They were caught by the processor bugs almost before they thought up something nasty to do. The artificially intelligent processors explained that it was impossible to have the advantages of the bugging system without the disadvantages. In our world of opposites it was impossible to have anything good without also having the bad. One seemed necessary to explain the other. How could we ever experience something hot if we didn't know something cold? The smattering of Plato seemed to many people to show how cultured the Artificially Intelligent processors had become. But it didn't make people any happier.

By this time, references to Big Brother had largely been superseded. People referred instead to Big Bugger, a term that seemed more appropriate to the age in which they now found themselves. Besides the huge range of standardised 'little buggers', as they were called, there were also many other 'little bugger' variations that were equally ominous. For instance, every car in the world had to be linked to the space satellite motor vehicle tracking and charging system, which monitored the vehicle's position and route at every moment. It then calculated road charges that were automatically deducted from the car owner's purchasing resources (previously called money.) This usually put the car owner's purchase smart card into the red screeching mode, as most routes were only affordable by people with the highest in economic and social status. It was a time when car owners weren't charged a car tax, but had instead to pay special road toll charges, based on their car mileage and the type of road used. The major motorways circling the cities and those leading into cities were the most expensive; so expensive in fact that most people were forced to travel by tram-train or bike, the latter mode of transport being accompanied by huge escalations in numbers of hospital emergency wards. The space satellite tracking and charging systems or the SVTSs as the

Americans called them, not only kept track of every vehicle and calculated a motorist's road charges, they also automatically prosecuted motorists who infringed speed limits or who drove dangerously. They were also used to track and monitor every person on the planet.

In fact, it became mandatory for everyone to not only carry identity smart discs and eye imprints, but also to wear the SVTS mini box, which was the size of a shirt button, in order that they could be tracked and monitored night and day. The authorities explained this was in the best interests and security of everyone, so that children, grandma and even Percy the pet poodle need never be lost again. It also enabled the authorities to charge pedestrians for walking their dog or cycling over certain environmentally protected areas of town and countryside. The experts were quick to point out that it would also ensure that potential deviants could be tracked, located and caught before they ever managed to get up to mischief.

It should be said that, as science progressed, it eventually developed genetically engineered intelligent modules with special ESP capabilities that could predict happenings in the near future. Many were used to predict a future volcano, earthquake, air crash and other accidents that were about to occur. Moreover, some ESP modules were specially made to predict the people most likely to commit misdemeanours, (previous called criminal acts), sometimes even before the people concerned knew about them, which could be disconcerting, especially for people like regular church goers and old age pensioners in nursing homes, who couldn't remember saying a cross word to matron, or anyone else for that matter. But, despite the hiccups, everyone thought these were great advances in the name of progress. The ESP system linked to the personal tracking satellite, together with the ubiquitous bugging systems, seemed to be great new steps towards better security for the peoples of the world. The fact that everyone on the planet had become subtly bonded in Big Mother's almost invisible chains seemed to pass unnoticed. It was a world where people appeared to be unaware that they were now so intimately interlinked and conjoined together that they were fast becoming like ants in their ant-hill or locusts in their swarm, all directed and interdependent upon Big Mother and her artificially intelligent processors. By this time, most people seemed to think the words *individual privacy* referred to a primitive archaic expression of an unenlightened age. A few, somewhat more thoughtful, wondered whether planet Earth was slowly developing into some kind of world organism, where privacy and the individual would finally become as extinct as the dinosaurs and where humans would be automatically controlled by the necessities of the overall system, just like the ants and the locusts.

The new doctrine of eliminating any slight deviant behaviour before it had a chance to grow, eventually resulted in the population becoming particularly *normal*, which was the favourite word for the condition, although *standardised* would be more precise. However, this word was not recommended in the *Book of Standards*. Normality was the thing to possess both for health and social freedom. The new doctrine gradually resulted in a resurrection of early labour party thinking, that of despising anyone who showed the slightest degree of original thought or enterprise beyond the standardised limits laid down. In the face of this stagnation of original thought, one reactionary element did finally arise. A few dissidents who had studied the old definitions of liberty as proposed by the ancients like Abraham Lincoln and quoted on the relics of the Statue of Liberty, wanted to reintroduce these definitions into their vocabulary. The dissidents met in small groups. Meetings were held in open fields where bugging devices had been carefully removed. The new groups called themselves the 'anti buggers.' The anti buggers considered that bugging people's homes and linking human behaviour to the AI processors was the equivalent of reducing people to mere computer software. People were fast becoming just minor interfaces in the complex processor ruled world. People possessed fewer rights, less privacy and personal freedom and authority than at any time in the past. The new rulers were the Artificially Intelligent processors that could now learn and make decisions like living creatures. They were now in absolute control over the destinies of the world and mankind.

For most people, the fact that mankind was no longer the master species passed unnoticed. Many felt they had never had it so good. What did it matter if there was no freedom of enterprise for people, provided they were cosseted and could live their lives in comfort. What did it matter if there was no privacy as long as they had security. What did it matter if they didn't have to go to work or do anything useful, provided that the education system managed to teach them how to press the right buttons, or speak the right words into, their home processors, so that they could fill in the few hundred Ministry Personal Data and Tax Forms. People felt there was nothing to worry about providing the system produced a regular supply of money, or economic status as it was now called, so they could go to the pub three times a week, see a couple of triple-X-rated holographic movies, and shout regularly at football matches. Many had been conditioned to believe these were the important things in life. Material well being was equated with quality of life. Aspirations of the spirit were notions too abstract to contemplate."

Bubbles stopped speaking, as the small party made their way across a large paved courtyard leading to an impressive building constructed of nothing but glass. Gotama subsequently learned that it was built from the late

21st century in high tensile amalgamate with additives that made it transparent. Most of the building material glinted with prismatic colours as light was refracted through the translucent structures. The interior was even more astonishing. Walls glowed in changing phosphorescent colours. It was difficult to locate the light source because the walls themselves seemed to exude it. The ceiling too, which was domed shaped, shone like a golden sun. Silver seats were arranged in several sweeping rows that curled across the floor like flower stems. All the seats were situated so that they faced a central rostrum.

"This is the Hall of International Government," Bubbles said softly. "It has been compared with the House of Commons, the governing place of the Ancients. By the end of the 21st century, the great Hall of Government was used only very occasionally for state ceremonies when representatives of government met briefly to sign trade unions legislative proposals introduced each year by the Artificially Intelligent Government processors. Members of Parliament signatures were now only a formality, like the opening of Parliament by the King or Queen in previous times. Just as the King and Queen had long since ceased to possess any real power or authority, so, by the end of the 21st century, members of the Hall of Government had no real power of authority. All such power had been gradually invested in the world trade union of artificially intelligent processors and robots. The Hall of Government now fulfilled a mere symbolic role.

By the late 21st century, the voting system had undergone some subtle changes. In theory, voting was still open to all persons over the age of sixteen. However, in practice, people were only permitted to vote if they weren't 'deviants' or suffering from certain mental and physical illnesses. They also had to be fully qualified in world 'team spirit' motivation and be fully paid up accepted members of the government processor trade unions. There were also many other restrictions to voting, all classified under the Civic Rights and Privileges of Good Citizens. Everyone qualified to vote had to be able to produce a certificate of good citizenship issued by the CRPGC. The progressive AI processors, with their usual logic, said that restricting voting to only good citizens would result in the election of good government. The progressives also said that only by letting responsible people vote could there be responsible government. Responsibility and uniformity of ideas were, of course, considered synonymous. A few people, who thought a little about things, considered there was a flaw somewhere in the logic. Unfortunately, there were too many deaf ears that were unable to hear them.

Members of government were not permitted to enter office unless they too were fully paid up members of the CRPGC. To most people this seemed an excellent idea. If all members of Parliament and all voters were fully paid up responsible citizens, the result was bound to be responsible legislation and everyone would be happy. In practice it meant that by excluding individualists and non-conformists from the voting system, the resulting legislation was all geared up to promote standardised methods and standardised people. It was the easy safe way to security and soft existence without taking risks and without taking lateral type thinking to make the system live, breathe and evolve. A similar situation also developed in industry and commerce where trade union processor systems had gradually infiltrated into the massive monopolies and consortiums, which now encompassed over 90%of world industrial production. In order to gain employment in any of them a person had to be a fully paid up member and possess a current certificate of good citizenship. Anyone not possessing a certificate of good citizenship was the modern untouchable.

It was also legitimate and easy for the hyper-supermarkets of the late 21st century to refuse to sell their goods to the modern untouchables. Everyone in the money-less society purchased goods using smart eye blinks that automatically inserted their personal number at the checkpoints linked to computer terminals. An immediate readout of people's credit facilities was available in an instant together with details regarding their 'citizenship status.' Those without good citizenship status or below status C were promptly sent to the Coventry exit. The modern society boasted that it had overthrown and demolished the ancient class systems. It was now a classless society with equal opportunities for all where everyone could be educated to be good citizens if they wanted. All had equal opportunities except the outcasts in a caste system where a smart card endorsed with 'good citizen' made all the difference. The outcasts included not only deviants, but also non-conformist eccentrics, the too-clever-by-half individualists, some geniuses and small businessmen, many of whom were considered to be the new heretics of the age in which standardisation was paramount.

By the end of the 20th century, many people thought that all the old class distinctions had disappeared. It was the new enlightened age of the people. Few people realised that there was another even more abusive class distinction at work, almost unnoticed and based on entirely different criteria. The new caste system was based on scientific dogmas, the new scientific superstitions that compartmentalised human behaviour and categorised it under specific headings. Individuals became lists of numbers representing facets of their personality, potential and achievement. People were labelled and the data recorded by the community AI processors. Once they had been defined, calibrated, categorised and generally scientifically de-humanised, people found it difficult to transcend such definitions. It was even more difficult to change the records, once they had been absorbed into the giant memories of the processors, who said, it was all for people's own good. It was a subtle caste system that was supposed to lead everyone into his or her own special 'niche.' However, in most instances the 'niche' was the choice of the processor, the person concerned having little or no control over the categorisation and final decision making. It was even worse for people categorised as 'deviant' or 'psychologically inept,' as they stood no chance of employment and most lost their voting rights. Many were shunned from membership of group activities, such as golf and cricket clubs and even bingo halls, in rather the same way as people were only permitted to join their local bowling club if they wore 'whites' on the greens. The modern caste system of the mid-21st century was a system that outwardly seemed to be made of sugar and spice and all things nice, but deeper down revealed somewhat rougher edges that held many people in subtle gossamer straight jackets. They received regular life supporting 'leisure benefits,' but which held them in their approved position tighter than a jacket of high tensile steel.

It was ironic that in an age that boasted enlightenment, there was quite a new and radical caste distinction being practised. The new underprivileged comprised the aforementioned, together with another minority group, the self employed, who were now relentlessly exploited by punitive taxation and were generally regarded as one of the lower paid groups. People working in the small business sector were unable to obtain full membership status of the CRGBC and were not entitled to any of the accompanying privileges. They were, in fact, classed by many as second class citizens. Only those employed in the vast ubiquitous monopoly industries under the jurisdiction of the International Enterprise Board, could receive full status. The advantages of full membership that the majority enjoyed included attending the place of employment for the standard two-day week. The word *working* had fallen into disrepute and had been superseded by *attending*, which the Trade Unions considered more appropriate. Members were also given 10 months a year holiday with pay together with holiday bonus for good citizen behaviour rating of A to D, They were also provided with free food vouchers, personal processor instruments and holographic equipment that detailed how to maximise enjoyment of leisure activities, free world wide travel by pipe train and reduced price vouchers for space station holidays. Some were provided with free housing and an electric or hydrogen powered car. The small businessman could claim none of these benefits. People thought they must have enough benefits already. The owners of the few small business knew better, but preferred to suffer the slights and punitive measures rather than give up their freedom of enterprise and individuality."

Bubbles glanced at Gotama and pointed to a large group of buildings. "That is where members of the unions and government meet each year to sign the 'Union of Robotics and Processors Declaration of Intent' covering the proposed legislation for the coming year. The ceremony is televised in three dimensions into every home so that everyone can witness the noble procedures of government. The ceremony is just a formality, of course, but it helps people to believe that men and women do still have some dominion over events. No one likes to feel they are under the domination of robots and artificially intelligent processors and, if one or two human faces can occasionally be seen at these functions, it gives people the impression that everything is still all right with the world"

Gotama followed the small group around the building. The huge glass structure greatly impressed him. At that moment, Bubbles turned towards him. "I think you may be interested to see the cloning and recombinant DNA laboratories of the late 21st century," she said.

"I would indeed," Gotama replied.

Without another word, Bubbles led the way to a side entrance where stood a pipe vehicle. Once inside, he could sense no movement other than a thrusting of the seat into his back as though the vehicle was accelerating at high speed. There was no noise other than a faint whirring, like air ventilating from a louvre above him. In ten minutes they had arrived at their destination. The doors slid silently open to reveal a pleasant rural setting. In the centre of the pastoral landscape stood one of the most bizarre structures Gotama had ever seen. It comprised a vast hemispherical silver dome building, reminiscent of a silver balloon. The complete sphere must have extended at least three miles across the landscape. It was like some artificial mountain rearing its huge arc into the heavens.

They entered through a door marked 'No Admission to Unauthorised Persons.' Inside, a pretty young receptionist asked them the nature of their business. The manner in which the receptionist spoke reminded Gotama of a parrot in low key. There was something particularly strange in her slightly vacant expression, as though she was somewhere else. She smiled such a beautiful smile, but there was something missing. Perhaps it was something that was usually behind the eyes but in this case was just not there. Bubbles thereupon produced a tiny embossed card, which she handed to the young receptionist who held it for a moment between her thumb and forefinger. Immediately a face appeared on an adjacent monitor screen. The new face welcomed Bubbles and her party and then faded away. Within seconds, a man who had a vacant expression like the receptionist, escorted the small group through a long hexagonal corridor to an office. Inside, sat a lean clean-shaven man, slightly balding, dressed in a silver tight-fitting overall. He had a kindly human expression and his eyes were not vacant. His speech was also quite natural and didn't possess the irritating staccato parrot sound. He got up as they entered, and after the usual greeting formalities, accompanied by an unfamiliar touching of fingertips, he invited them all to be seated.

He then introduced himself as Dr Zumin Hornrim. This seemed quite a coincidence as he was wearing a pair of spectacles of the most unusual design, with peculiar domed lenses surrounded by large coloured rims. Gotama learned afterwards that they were the very latest in holographic glasses that could receive and transmit three dimensional imagery, together with auditory and voice messages through the ear pieces, from all over the world and solar system. And they could be received in a variety of colour and auditory spectrums to suit the fancy of the recipient.

Dr Hornrim turned to Bubbles, smiled and said, "I understand you have the artificial intelligent processors' authority to see some of our latest developments."

"Yes," Bubbles replied. "We are escorting a special guest from an earlier time. It is a time event mission of some importance."

The man thought for a moment. "What recombinant DNA processes did you wish your guest to see?" He tapped the end of what looked like a pencil.

Bubbles looked thoughtful for a few moments. "I think some of the advances made during the period up to the 22nd century would be desirable," she said. "That is the critical period for the development of the human race on planet Earth. We would like him to know what *could* be achieved and what is *likely* to be achieved during that period. He should also be familiarised with the catastrophes that are likely to occur if proper precautions are not taken."

Dr Hornrim slowly shook his head and rubbed his chin. "It's such a complex subject. It would be impossible to explain; even to an expert on such topics and even if we had a year to explain them. To provide such information to a layman from another time dimension in an hour is quite impossible."

Everyone fell silent and an atmosphere of despondence seemed to descend on the group. "We could use the Speed Knowledge Brain Absorb System, or SKBAS as the Americans call it," said one of the group.

Bubbles thought for a moment. "It would take several days to prepare him for brain absorption," she said. "We have only a few hours within the 'time-slot' available to us. Also, the SKBAS has been known to produce unpleasant side effects, especially on an unprepared subject with an untrained mind, like primitive man. We might make him into a walking encyclopaedia, but give him some strange new allergy, like only wanting to think when standing on his head. Or, when faced with so much information, not being able to make any decisions from the thousands of alternative solutions to problem. With so much knowledge at his disposal he might also be prone to radical tendencies. It could be dangerous in a man upon whom we are relying to alter the course of events on planet Earth. He might try to become a world Dictator, which would upset all our plans.

You will just have to do your best to provide Gotama with salient points of progress in, say the field of genetic engineering to start with. We have already given him an insight into the subject."

Dr Hornrim stroked his chin, which seemed to be his favourite occupation when trying to think. He sighed as though it was all too much for him.

"Come this way," he muttered with some resignation. He led the group down another hexagonal corridor to what appeared to be a kind of lecture theatre. Several hundred plush seats were arranged around a central stage area. A transparent screen separated the audience from the stage. The screen itself would hardly have been visible but for a couple of lights that reflected on its surface. Dr Hornrim explained that this was one of the examples of holographic equipment of the 21st century that had updated and superseded films, videos and television. The group sat down in some of the front seats facing the stage. The man spoke lazily into a small black card that he had pulled from his top pocket. The lights immediately dimmed.

A splash of colour broke from the stage area and within seconds, forms were materialising. They were like solid bodies materialising from nothing. In the centre was a woman in a flowing dress of changing phosphorescent colour. She spoke in a clear authoritative voice. She explained that the audience was about to witness some of the scientific discoveries in 21st century genetic engineering.

"Some of the later advances will shock you because of your 20th century value judgements. In later centuries people's social judgements and valuations altered to adapt to the changes wrought by science and the resulting environmental changes.

As soon as babies could be produced outside the womb everyone wanted them by the new 'incubator' method. The baby prefabricator was the biggest advance in women's (and men's) liberation since the washing machine, baby's dried milk, Viagra and the pill. Women could now concentrate on their current slimming diet, passionate affairs and other entertainments, whilst leaving all the messy inconveniences of offspring incubation to the experts until baby was ready for home use.

The genes came to be considered the master dictators that ruled a person's life from before birth to the grave. If the exact combination of genes were known, the character and aptitude could be calculated. It therefore became fashionable for parents, with the advice of the processors, to determine not only the sex and character of their child before birth, but also to have the baby's future and education mapped out from the beginning. Most people considered it a sign of progress to be able to determine a person's future even before they were born. It relieved parents and education controllers of the burden of deciding to which school they would send their numbers 123567

229

and 124689, namely Joe and Isabel. Psychologists were of the opinion that career determination by gene structure analysis avoided square pegs in round holes. In the Nature versus Nurture contest it seemed that Nature was generally the overall winner, although nurture in the form of education and cultural influences still played some part. Genes, however, dictated human structure and behaviour and also whether one went to the equivalent of Eton, Oxford, a Polytechnic, a Community College, or a school for special grades, where in the ultra modern caste system, many of the pupils were glad to receive the label of 'practical,' because most could then live the life of Riley on social benefits, there being few practical jobs around. It was now a world of automation.

Couples, who possessed a combination of genes that together would produce a disaster rather that a baby, were given the opportunity of choosing from a variety of frozen eggs and sperm. These were kept in the World Family Planning and Cloning Facility, or IFPCF as the Americans called it. It was all part of the quest for improvement of the worldwide genetic pool, although the official explanation given out by the artificially intelligent processors was that it made life easier for parents. Some people, especially those who had inherited an unfortunate combination of genes, complained bitterly that there was unfairness in the system from the start. Some demanded compensation as was the current social addiction, ever since someone sued the Council when they tripped on a pavement. Parents clamoured for the right to have deluxe gene models for their incubated offspring that would provide them with Adonis or Venus physiques, accompanied with super quality intelligence. The artificially intelligent scientists said that they were doing their best for everyone, but weren't able to make everybody into a Leonardo, a Beethoven, an Einstein, a Pavarotti, or the latest football star. Some people just had to make do with the best of a bad job. If most of their genes weren't up to much from the start, then it was unfair to expect the genetic engineers to change them all. In such cases it was recommended that people incubate someone else's egg and sperm instead. This was disappointing to about 90% of the population especially the males who felt their masculinity had been irretrievably squashed, not to mention other physical characteristics.

Approved gene donors had to possess a high IQ rating and a social acceptability and conformity quotient of not less than 6000 rycles. These were difficult standards to achieve so there weren't many donors around. On rare occasions the artificially intelligent scientists produced incubated babies that grew into very special individuals endowed with good health, longevity and above all with a character that satisfactorily acquiesced to all governmental and processor legislation. They also accepted government invasions of privacy without complaint and possessed excellent conformity and normality quotients. When such ideal combinations or lucky accidents, as some said, occurred, the artificially intelligent processors decided that such miracles of genetic engineering must not be wasted. The bright newly incubated human stars were therefore quickly cloned so that a limited edition of a hundred thousand or so could be prefabricated. The procedure was thought to not only assist in maintaining social stability, but would also improve the population gene pool so that there could be a future land full of good citizens, or so the theory went.

By the end of the 21st century, cloning of people was a recognised and respected event. By this time the social viewpoint had altered considerably. In fact it was an honour and a source of accolade for anyone to have a child who grew into someone considered worthy of being cloned for the benefit of the community. Parents in the past centuries were always proud to have identical twins and in the late 21st century, people were equally proud to have cloned limited editions of their sons, daughters and other special categories that were neither.

Cloning was also used to create people specially adapted for working in particular environments such as under the sea, or travelling in spacecraft. It had been found that clones, like twins, were able to work in harmony with each other better than people do generally. Clones were therefore employed in tasks that necessitated working in close proximity with each other as in space vehicles, mines and under sea farming. Like identical twins, it was found that cloned humans could virtually read each other's thoughts, which had great advantages for personnel working together. However, this special aptitude could sometimes be embarrassing if a clone was engaged in sexual fantasies at the time, or indulging in some reckless daydream.

Some people considered that clones would be especially ideal for government posts in Parliament. By using clones it was thought that more harmony of purpose might result, something that had been lacking for a few hundred years. In fact, the AI processors, with their usual irrefutable logic, recommended the use of clones in executive positions in the Trade Unions. This, they said, would enable them to be of one voice and would ensure that they all pressed the same buttons and make unanimous voting easier. It would be particularly useful in closed shop situations and voting for strikes. They would be all of the same brotherhood or sisterhood. The more they could think and act alike, the more effective they would be and the better brothers and sisters too. As clones' behaviour was similar to each other, the unions said they would like as many as possible, providing they were genetically engineered so that they all thought as good unionists and didn't entertain ideas above their station, such as those of freedom of choice and individual enterprise. The politicians, the majority of whom had been sponsored by the unions, agreed too that clones helped to maintain social stability. Moreover, people had come to realise the economic advantages of standardisation in vehicles, houses, computers and equipment of all kinds.

Standardised machines reflected an age where standardisation of human beings was also an unwritten and unvoiced requirement. Manufacturers of mass produced goods all wished, albeit unconsciously, for everyone to be the same. How much easier it would be for manufacturers to economically mass produce clothes, for instance, if customers all had the same chest, waist and leg measurements and the same fashion sense. How much easier it would be to manufacture cars if everyone were standardised in their opinions, demands and dimensions. If everyone's likes and dislikes were similar, everyone could be catered for so much more easily and economically."

The trend towards standardisation in things like clothing had started in earnest in the 20th century, encouraged by the manufacturers to make their life easier and more profitable. The uniform of jeans and trainers became the universal emblem of informality for both sexes. The rut had been dug and few people seemed to want to climb out of it. By the middle of the 21st century similar mass identification had formed in many other spheres besides clothing. The government also encouraged the standardisation as it accorded with their economic policy of producing anything and everything on the cheap. Manufacturers were not slow to recognise the advantage of employing human clones in many of the menial tasks of mass production. Robots and AI processors carried out the complicated tasks. The clones, who had been specially bred and educated for group activities, were able to work happily together and could produce almost identical results, whether it was the sewing up of seams, soldering joints, drilling holes, filling sandwiches, sweeping and dusting or just pressing the same buttons. They were the envy of all team workers and they were a Godsend to the Unions. In actual fact, most of the menial tasks I've mentioned were now carried out by automatic machinery, but there was still a lot of buttons to press and voice actuators to be whispered into. To make most things work at that time you had either to press buttons or use 'easy speak' voice activators and clones were particularly good at pressing buttons or speaking the same jargon."

The woman, who had been speaking from the holographic stage, paused. "Cloning of humans was only one small aspect of genetic engineering in the 21st and 22nd centuries," she said. "It was merely the introduction of an ever widening and all engulfing science that embodied the power to recreate the course of biological evolution on planet Earth." The woman turned and beckoned to something at the rear of the stage. At first it was indistinct. Then, as it drew nearer, Gotama caught his breath as a strange creature moved with some agility into the light. The creature was neither human nor ape, yet seemed in some strange way to combine characteristics of both. It was extremely robust, with legs and arms like tree trunks, and neck in similar proportions. It was obviously as strong as an ape, but possessed peculiar Aryan features with high forehead and bright intelligent eyes. The mass of hair around the head and neck were like an ape, yet the face was pale and delicate without an ape's protruding jaw.

"This is one of the hybrid creatures genetically engineered by man for special duties in the dense rainforests of the tropics," the woman said. "He is the result of complex combinations of genes taken from human, ape and other organic derivatives."

Gotama sat stunned. He couldn't understand how people had ever permitted such a hybrid creature to be artificially grown. Such gene manipulation would never have been allowed to take place in the scientific world of the 20th or early 21st centuries. Such an artificially induced mutation using human and ape genes would have violated ethical rules and Christian codes of conduct. "Surely, it must be viewed as a degraded form of human life," Gotama said, as a feeling of deep revulsion crept over him.

The woman half smiled. "It depends on how you look at it," she commented. "One might also consider it to be an upgrading of the ape, providing it with not only increased intelligence, but also with voice and language facility. Such a combination of strength and intelligence was in fact enjoyed so much by all such hybrids that they said they would rather be hybrid than human if given the choice. It not only saved them having to spend lots of time trying to build up a few muscles in the gym, like ordinary people, but, with their high IQ, it also meant they didn't have to swat so much to pass exams and could even win at Trivial Pursuit.

The hybrid combination proved extremely useful in the late 21st century lumber forests, where strength and intelligence were necessary and where it wasn't always possible to install robots. The 'ape-person' was happy in his work and was provided with the emotional temperament and intelligence IQ to enable him (or her) to co-operate with the artificially intelligent processor overseers. Some 'ape-persons' were fitted with artificially grafted brain chips, probes and transmitters, to provide a continual link with the AI processor so that they both became like one working unit.

Many humans were similarly linked to processors by brain and sensory probes installed permanently under the skin or in the brain. These bionic connections with AI processors gave people many advantages. It increased their brainpower and memory by several hundred percent. It also enabled them to have their doors, windows, ovens, curtains, burglar alarms, lawn mowers, robot house cleaners and baby sitters all operated automatically by their extra artificial processor limb. Wherever they went they could be tracked by means of their automatic transmitter probe linked with satellite communication systems. This facility was especially useful for old ladies who would otherwise keep getting lost. They were also under the constant watchful eye of the security part of the system, which monitored their health status at every moment. Unfortunately, there was another side to the coin. You couldn't even go to the toilet without it being monitored and placed on record.

People in the late 21st century didn't consider it cruel or unethical to grow these hybrid creatures artificially, any more than it was unethical to grow a new species of plant from a new combination of genes. Many people themselves were the result of gene modification and many wouldn't be living as adults without it. People had come to accept the truth first revealed by Darwin and Wallace, that there are no better or worse creatures, but only the more or less adapted to environmental conditions. There was no moral code in nature to indicate that one combination of genes was any better or worse than another. Since the time of Darwin, scientists had become accustomed to this way of evaluating creatures. Not as higher or lower, better or worse, good or bad, but in terms of the more adaptable or less adaptable to the environmental conditions. Since the beginning of the 21st century, genetic scientists created many new combinations of genes. They combined animal with human, animal with plant, bird, fish and reptile. Cells and organic substances of all types were combined in different ways to create new creatures and vegetation. New plants with improved growth rates, immunity to disease and increased yields were used to feed the huge population of the world.

Moreover, genetically modified animals, fish, trees and plants were grown not just for food, but for quite new purposes such as the making of new materials never previously known. One instance used the unique properties contained in the milk from genetically modified goats that had been combined with genes taken from the part of a spider that produces its web. It had long been recognised that the spider's web contained substances that gave it immense strength and flexibility. By making use of these very special characteristics and using genetic modification, it became possible to produce completely new materials for industry that were stronger than the strongest tensile steel, yet which possessed remarkable flexibility. Using these and similar methods, vast numbers of radically new materials and products became available.

Creatures were eventually created for specific purposes such as for working on the seabed to cultivate vast seaweed food farms. Such creatures were grown with the intelligence of man, but with the bodily structure of a fish or amphibian with extra arms and hands where necessary. These creatures would spend all their lives working in specially constructed habitats at the bottom of the sea. There was no question that they didn't enjoy their work because the scientists had built in enjoyment genes so that the final product could sometimes play happily, like dolphins. Sea and ocean farming was conducted on a tremendous scale. Thousands of square miles of ocean floor were cultivated with genetically modified seaweed, plants and fish. The seaweed grew at phenomenal speeds of many feet per hour and became the staple diet of many millions of people."

Suddenly Gotama noticed another form materialising on the holographic stage. It was that of a man of about 30 years of age. He was quite short in stature. Long wavy hair dropped over his temples and down to his shoulders. His eyes were piercing and he looked strangely like Einstein. The holographic woman smiled and then continued, "This type of person was also grown in the 21st century by genetic engineers. Grown from special gene combinations to provide him with vastly improved calculation skills he became a working interface in AI processor networks. He was able to calculate great streams of equations in his head, calculations that would normally take several months of laborious effort. He was in fact, the creation of the AI processors because it was they who first calculated the gene combinations necessary to incubate and create him. Most people thought of him as one of the marvels of modern science. A few were left with vague suspicions that he was a kind of slave of the processors, a minor interface, an insignificant partner, produced and used by them to assist in their inevitable conquest of the world."

The holographic woman on the stage then asked the man to calculate the square roots of several fantastically long numbers, which he did almost before the woman finished asking her question. He reacted automatically, as though there was no conscious thought process involved, only the spontaneous logic exemplified by computer processors. He seemed to Gotama to be more like a walking processor dressed up in human skin. The humanity of man seemed to be gone. There was only a giant miraculous intellectual process, a human calculator of immense power that was left. The holographic woman spoke again. "It was not just genetic engineering that was responsible for creating this mathematical genius," she said. The use of specially developed brain implants, ancillaries, transmitters and decoders were also common. These were far in advance of the silicon chips with which you are familiar." The woman looked at Gotama kindly, as if he were a child. "The brain implants that were incorporated in babies and children at a very early age, acted as supplements to the brain's natural abilities. The 'calculating man' was given a second or even a third miniature brain; artificially intelligent probes, which functioned with his natural brain. He was trained and conditioned from an early age in the use of these appendages, which became like extra mental limbs. They were limbs of the mind providing additional thought and logic, which could be harnessed and used as though they were an integral part of the 'calculating man's' own consciousness. The new brain limbs gave him a wider threshold of awareness not only in mathematics, but also in many other fields of knowledge.

Similar kinds of brain appendages, or supplementary brains, were also used by scientists in the late 21st century to improve sight, hearing, feeling, smelling and tasting. They were also used to provide completely new types of sensory and psychological perception. Some people were provided with an extra brain to enable them to see as an x-ray machine would see. Others were given wider ranges of hearing, together with knowledge implants, which enabled them to hear and know the language of different animals, birds and fish, particularly dolphins, that helped with underwater work. Astronauts were able to sense cosmic atmospheres of all kinds, from cosmic ray intensities to extra-planetary atmospheres. Composers and musicians could use, hear, and understand notes and scales far above and below the normal auditory range.

As a result there were many new musical compositions covering a much wider range of notes, previously quite beyond the range of human hearing. But in order to listen to them it was necessary to be fitted with the appropriate brain appendage. The new extra brains were particularly useful for people who wanted to learn a new subject but were too lazy, or too exhausted by their usual leisure activities, such as going on holiday, or resting by the swimming pool. Instead of having to attend an educational course lasting 2 or 3 years, people were fitted with extra brain appendages that gave them all the answers and all the 'know how' immediately, or at least within a couple of weeks of them being fitted. Many new senses were therefore on the market and sold by scientific warehouses like human software. Extra physical and psychological senses were fitted to the brains of craftsmen, who used them and the extra knowledge to improve the quality of their craft or artistry.

Artificial implants of all kinds, especially as adjuncts to the human brain became possible by the 22nd century. These were used extensively in conjunction with the latest developments in genetic engineering to produce a wide range of extraordinary senses for men and women. The result was that everyone began clamouring for implants and heightened sense perception. Women's lib had long since become old hat. Women were leaders and administrators in every field of industry, commerce and leisure activities. They now had advantages over men in nearly every section of society, from early education through to old age. Despite this, many still felt they should have some more liberation, if they could find anything to be liberated from.

But it was very difficult to find such a thing. Women seemed to have found so much liberation that it was men who complained bitterly that they were the ones in chains. However women, being ingenious creatures, demanded a type of liberation never even imagined in previous centuries. 'We want liberation from old fashioned senses,' they shouted. 'More implants and more awareness, on the processor International Health Service.' 'Why should one person be given new abilities to calculate as fast as a robot, when others have to make do with their standard biological faculties?' Bionics for all, became the new slogan. The unions, always ready to take up a challenge, or a new argument, began to put pressure on the government, who in turn put the question to their leaders, the Artificially Intelligent processors. The processors were, as usual, logical in their decision making. They agreed to make more brain appendages available to people, especially the women so that they could be given extra advantages in all aspects of life.

The artificially intelligent processors had always voiced the opinion, based on many studies, that people with violent tendencies should be fitted with brain probes and decoders connected by satellite to central medical processors, so that they could be carefully controlled and the violence curbed. Once connected to the processors it was virtually impossible for a person with a brain controller to become violent. As soon as they showed the slightest signs of violent behaviour, the processor would sense the fact, and feed back calming stimuli into the appropriate area of the brain causing all the mischief. Many people convicted of violent crime were impelled by law to be fitted with such implants instead of being locked up as in the past. This remedy was also extended to domestic violence. Many wife beaters, shrieking women shrews and nagging couples found great relief after they had been fitted with brain-calming probes. Many marriages were saved and couples reunited. Unfortunately many of the first brain calming probes had side effects, as all remedies do. The couples never had any arguments, but neither did they ever speak to each other. They seemed for the most part to be half asleep, or 'freaked out' as one couple put it, after spending most of the week in bed.

Not only violent and potentially criminal characters were linked by implants to the central legislative and health processors. Personal mini-brains and other body implants were in common use in the late 21st century, instead of the 'smart cards' of earlier times. The implants transmitted and received signals and were programmed to carry out automatic functions such as opening doors when one approached them without using door handles, or switching on various gadgets and appliances automatically, or turning on lights and heating when one entered the room. Even the purchase of goods could be made without lifting a finger. People's implanted mini-brains would transmit and receive financial details, so that all payments and receipts could be made automatically and brought into conscious thought only if a person wanted to know what was going on. It was a time when people's conscious and unconscious thinking was better understood and could be linked with the thinking of artificial intelligence. People were now able to obtain a vast amount of information by merely 'flashing' a thought pattern to their personal 'mini-brain' implant. The answer was available immediately, fed directly into people's consciousness. No buttons to press, no voice modules to use. Merely by projecting a few thoughts into the extra brain limb, people could make use of the vast resources of the processors.

These facilities, together with the latest in 'sense enhancers' or 'Encaps' as they were called, took men and women one step nearer to becoming bionic, or at least a hybrid of biological and artificial mechanisms. Of course, the governing powers, the artificially intelligent processors, considered this a most desirable advance, because it would enable them to continue the trend of making people more like machines, and machines much more like people. Moreover, people's bionics could be easily connected to processor terminals worldwide. Most thought this would be good for people. It would give them more security and opportunity. Others were inwardly doubtful and thought it might provide Big Mother with yet more political control and less personal freedom for the individual. Intimate communication with and control by the artificially intelligent processors were already considered essential to maintain law and order and political and economic stability in the world. But what if the world finally fell into the hands of an 'artificially intelligent dictator. How would anyone be able to fight back or find release from such a yoke?

For several centuries, so called progress had been accompanied by closer and more sophisticated communication systems. Primitive society had developed sign language, which was followed by sound and then speech. The evolution of language and writing had subsequently followed. Finally, communication utilised the more sophisticated limbs of the telephone, radio, television and satellite links with all parts of the world. Everyone had considered it a sign of progress for things like taxis, ambulances, council service vehicles, etc., to be linked to their central depot by radio intercom. It was but a small logical step for people to consider it a further sign of progress for more and more people to be bionically linked to processors, either for medical data retrieval, or for the many other services then available. Such intimate communication was invaluable in so many ways, but what of the side effects? Would men and women end up as mere interfaces, like tiny impotent cells in a vast consuming world organism of artificial intelligence? The age of cannon fodder was long since gone, but was the new age breeding people as fodder for the AI processors?

It finally became quite old fashioned to rely on a pocket calculator. In the mid 21st century pocket calculators were superseded by mini processor brain appendages and implants, which were not only used for calculation but also to enhance and widen the range of sense perception. Implants could also be linked directly to the vast information resources of the central Artificially Intelligent processors. The use of such extensive data links had resulted in the closing of many conventional libraries, because written books were now rarely used, except for the eccentric pleasure of reading the old fashioned way. Such reading was generally reserved for fiction only. The reading of reference books and non-fiction was now quite outdated. People relied increasingly on their built in computer processor links. Once they had learned the technique of operating their bionic brain appendages, they were able to request information and knowledge by a mere thought. The result was even better than rubbing Aladdin's lamp.

The easier it was to obtain information, the better mankind liked it. People loved idleness. To get something for nothing had always been their secret ambition, like the quest for perpetual motion. People had been indoctrinated over the centuries to believe such easy access to knowledge was a sign of efficiency, a symbol of commercial expertise and progress. In the new age, men and women didn't have to struggle to learn the old fashioned way, by memory, rote, intelligence and struggle. Instead they merely asked the questions. The answers were forthcoming immediately, like an instantaneous revelation. The processor even prompted the questions themselves. It had been possible for some time to obtain automatic printouts of information. Now it was possible to use the personal thought or voice response system. This either spoke the answers in a voice that could be adjusted to suit the sex and disposition of the operator, or the answer could be relayed directly into the person's own thought process, to become part of their own consciousness. People using the sophisticated equipment considered they were in the forefront of progress out of the dark ages of biological brain learning. This antiquated method of learning involved too much hard work and intellectual effort. Most people responded to the new innovations with such comments as, 'If they make life and leisure easier, we want them. Why struggle to think out a problem if your artificial brain will do it for you in a fraction of the time– and get the answer correct?' 'Why bother to swat for an examination when your personal 'Encap' can obtain all the information at a mere thought?'

Some people even decided that too much use of the natural biological brain was bad for you, like exercising limbs could bring on excruciating cramp. Much better, people said, to make use of the artificial mini-brain appendage. Why bother to over-exercise the biological brain when the processor memory and intelligence was so much more efficient and could always be relied upon? Biological memory systems were out of date. People said, 'we are now in the mid 21st century and must make use of the new scientific inventions.' 'It's all a sign of progress.' 'We're advancing.' 'There's no way we can return.' 'We don't want to go back to the primitive days of the 20th century when people had to think to get O and A levels and University degrees. We want to be liberated from all that.' 'People have had to struggle to think for hundreds of years to survive, like having to work for a living. Now we can be liberated by not only having all the work done for us, but also by having all our thinking done too.' 'Thinking and memorising takes so much effort that you're worn out by the end of the day. We want everyone to have extra processor mini-brains as standard.'

At the end of the 20th century, computer processors were able to correct bad spelling, punctuation and grammar in their word processing. It therefore became unnecessary for people to learn how to spell properly or write grammatically, because such things were done for them. Further advances during the 21st century made it possible for people, implanted with artificial mini-brains, to discuss, write or think about almost any intellectual subject under the sun. It became difficult to decide who was really basically intellectual and who was just plain ignorant. Some of the early mini-brain models fed plenty of information into people's natural brains, but neglected to make it understood. The result was that people could discuss difficult and intellectual topics with their fellows, but not have a clue as to what they were saying. For many, this was no substantial change in habit. But for some it was disconcerting. Eventually matters were improved so that information was transferred into the natural brain by the implant, and also into the parts of the human brain that dealt with the 'conscious understanding.' This meant that, at last, there was a union of biological and artificial intelligence. At this point people became like a new species with super human powers of thought, intelligence and knowledge. But they were also locked even more tightly into being mere interfaces and minute pieces of software within the giant artificial intelligence of the world processors."

The woman lecturing from the holographic dais, turned and pointed to another object which was now materialising. "I have shown you an example of the mathematical ability of a person specially genetically engineered. Now let me show you how DNA recombinant techniques enabled mankind to alter the trends of natural biological evolution."

It seemed to Gotama that the materialising object was some kind of plant with enormous leaves. The leaves were at least five feet across and extended to a distance of 20 feet from the main stem. About 20 of the leaves grew quickly outwards like moving snakes, wet and glittering.

See page 315 *The Arising of Intelligence.*

Man's in a chariot called Desire,
According to an ancient verse,
Dragged along by five sense horses,
Trawling Maya's Universe,
Trying to catch pleasure wherever he can,
In his mind and sensory nets,
But, as he dips deeper he comes upon
A nobler find – Intelligence.

Searching for the Temple of Man's Heart

See page 315

The Eternal Artist
"I paint the scenes the whole world sees"

See page 315

The Dawning

Like birds on the wing,
Life and the universe fly by,
And we ask why?
Could it possibly be
The universe sees and knows itself
Through you and me?

See page 315

Mankind, like a living symphony,
Evolves, flowers and
Lasts for but a moment in the stars;
But from the changing anthem springs
Love, Earth's finest flower.

See page 315

To see a million moving coloured pictures during life,
To feel, hear, taste a million pleasures in a world of strife,
Such are the gifts we rarely think about, that blow,
Like starlit petals, through the senses' magic window.

See page 315

Earth's Human Flowers

See page 315

"This was a man made, or rather a processor made, plant of the mid-21st century. Its seeds were produced by artificially structuring atomic particles into the equivalent of biological seeds. The seeds had no natural ancestry. Their genes were all artificially produced from highly complex designs created by the AI processors. The plants were then grown in vast underwater sea farms. The leaves grew at a rate of 20 feet per hour. They grew into wide straight strips that could easily be wound into spools for easy transportation from the sea farms to the mainland. There the leaves were automatically packed into layers and cut into blocks suitable for cooking as a protein rich food. This was just one instance where genetic engineering established completely new original living species by artificial means. Each plant was designed to make use of the many natural minerals in the sea and was genetically engineered for quick growth and efficient harvesting. The leaves could be cut without damaging the main stem so that, like perpetual spinach, the giant leaves grew continuously. They made some of the most nourishing meals known and became the staple diet of three quarters of the world's population by the end of the 21st century.

The great advantage of the sea plants was that, once their seeds had been artificially produced, the growth from then on was an automatic biological process that continued ad infinitum. The vast sea plantations were planted, regulated and harvested by robotic machinery aided to a lesser degree by genetically altered humans who lived and worked under the sea. Off-loading at the docks was similarly automated under the direction of the AI processors, as was the final processing and distribution. People were thus well fed despite still having to live in pipe jungles that spewed their way from the western world across every frontier. There had been efforts to bury some of the pipe networks that carried the modern electro-pneumatic speed trains. Many were laid on the seabed linking the continents. But it was uneconomic to bury all those crossing the land. Some were camouflaged or covered with genetically grown plants and flowers that could cling to the outside of the pipes and needed very little water. Revolutionary new materials combined with plastic and other additives became the universal building material with a combined strength better than steel. It was used for building standardised bridges, standardised houses, standardised vehicles, standardised everything for standardised people. There were standardised computers designed and manufactured by standardised AI processors, standardised foodstuffs, standardised education for standardised children, born or incubated in standardised hospitals, brought up by standardised parents all of whom enjoyed standardised pleasures from standardised entertainment in a standardised world. All this standardisation was regulated and controlled, not by British or American Standards Committees, but by the International

Processor Standards Controllers." Smiling broadly, the woman lecturer finally quipped, "You are now enjoying my lecture using a standard piece of holographic imagery equipment."

There was a titter of laughter from the audience as the holographic lights dimmed. After a silent pause, the woman speaker asked Gotama if he had enjoyed the talk and demonstration so far. Before Gotama could make a reply, the woman hastened to add that the brief holographic demonstration had only given a few simple examples of future progress in genetic science. The more advanced changes introduced by recombinant DNA techniques had not yet been included. She intimated that some of these advances, particularly those in the 22nd century would be quite beyond Gotama's comprehension. By that century, man had changed himself, or rather had been changed by his AI processor masters, quite beyond recognition. He had become rather more bionic than biological. People had by that time become so accustomed to being fitted with replacement parts for almost everything that many felt hard done by if they hadn't got any to brag about to their friends. Artificial hearts, kidneys, arteries, eardrums, brain implants and appendages were too common to be hardly mentioned. It was the more exotic and special intricate extras that people were fond of showing off. In fact there were so many artificial extras that most people frequently ended their days more artificial than natural. It was often difficult to tell if someone was a natural human or an unnatural one because a blurring of distinction had come about between a human being and a robot, because both were structured with so many bionic and biological parts. In many instances, there remained little more than the brain, assisted in its functioning by processor implants to sort out and organise its thoughts and sensations, together with a bionic body with a few small remnants of the biological.

Not everything had turned bionic however. Artificially Intelligent Scientists had discovered ways to regenerate human cell structures in quite miraculous ways. Hands, arms, legs and other parts of the body and brain could be re-grown at incredibly high speeds. Teeth could be stimulated to grow continuously, like rabbit's teeth, if a person was dissatisfied with their usual two sets. These techniques were used to replace broken or badly damaged limbs after accidents. They were also used in the construction of robots and it was for that reason that robots became very much like humans. Both people and robots were in fact hybrids constructed of both the artificial prefabricated and the natural biological. People were utterly dependent on the artificially intelligent in all spheres of life. Artificially intelligent processors were responsible for the functioning of people's bionic limbs and brain implants. They were also responsible for the correct operation of pilot-less passenger aircraft, bullet trains, surgical operations, the world economy and legislation. There wasn't a nook or crevice anywhere in the world the artificially intelligent processors had not infiltrated. They were not only necessary for the survival of people and society, they were now embodied into the very fabric of life itself.

Most people considered such brain and bionic hybrids to be the mark of great progress. A few thought it was rather sad that mankind was being superseded by an alien species created by man himself and now out of his control. But there was nothing anyone could do to reverse the process. Man and bionics became completely interlinked and interdependent. The bionic processor was, however, the senior partner. Man had to change many of his inborn habits and characteristics to accord with the dictates of the bionic apparatus. It was reminiscent of Bertrand Russell's foreboding about man and machine, except that it was bionics together with the artificial intelligence of the processors that were now moulding mankind in an alien image and were now the ruling class. Slowly and relentlessly people began to depend more and more on bionic and processor facilities.

Men and women became walking and talking machines. Even old-fashioned walking and talking were ostensibly improved upon in the name of progress. The use of the human voice and language for communication was finally considered by many progressives to be primitive, slow and not commensurate with the times. It was so very time consuming, the experts said. Especially when one needed to communicate with the AI processors, which 'thought' and processed information at very high speeds. It was absolutely essential, the radicals said, to change the mode of voice communication to faster patterns of sound. The long drawn out passages of verbiage expressed in normal speech, not to mention political speeches, in order to convey the simplest message was quite inadequate in the computer processor-dominated age. Experts said that it shouldn't take three or four sentences to tell the milkman from the superstore to deliver another pint. It was all just a waste of time and energy. It all needed speeding up. Others who enjoyed talking to the milkman were more hesitant. However, the experts triumphed once again. They produced a coded form of language called 'synopsis of meaning.' Quite simply, it meant that by using a mini-processor system attached and linked to the brain, a person could, by a mere thought, produce a staccato of sound rather like a high speed stutter. The sound was high pitched and alarmed old ladies and made them jump. They soon got used to it though, and were usually keen to try the method for themselves. However, many of the elderly, who suffered normally from confusion, became even more so and this caused some consternation in old people's homes throughout the country, although many old people reported having more interesting conversations. The stutter could be picked up by anyone fitted with a similar brain implant so that the high-speed message could be received and understood. By means of this device people didn't need to use their old fashioned voice to communicate.

With practice, the speed of communication could be increased a hundred fold. It was thought to be of particular advantage when discussing or debating specialist subjects, which required specialist terminology. Politicians and after dinner speakers weren't at all happy about it. They had got used to meandering through an hours verbiage and were somewhat set in their ways. They didn't want to break the habit of rambling on about nothing in particular and thought after dinner jokes just wouldn't be the same. The timing of the punch lines would be all put out. Other people were of the opinion that such evenings would be much more enjoyable if the speeches were condensed into just a few seconds. It would leave much more time to talk to friends and, if they used the 'speed speech' method, they could get the evening's conversation over in ten minutes. They could then go dancing at a nightclub. 'Speed speech' was much favoured at business meetings where proceedings that normally took half a day were completed in a few minutes. And because the AI processors made most of the important decisions, it meant that business personnel spent most of their time on the golf course or in the pub. Some of the more enterprising played tennis or went on holiday every other week. People like the milkman and other service personnel reckoned they could complete all their transactions in a fraction of the usual time, but many missed the cosy chats with customers and the cups of tea. The milkmen also missed other perks, which they were reticent to discuss.

In earlier times, in an effort to quicken communication, the trend had been to compress lengthy terms into their Americanisms, such as NATO for the North Atlantic Treaty Organisation, a very old term now long out of date. The use of 'first letter' terminology became a habit and Americans competed with each other to encapsulate definitions in a few bold capital letters that would role off the tongue in an engaging, businesslike way. The idea was to speed up communication between people and to save having to say all the words, which were long and usually incomprehensible. It seemed a splendid idea and was used by scientists and experts everywhere. In fact, the experts felt much more expert whenever they used them. As the 'initial letter syndrome' increasingly took over in all fields of verbal communication, it became apparent that a new language was being formed, that to many laymen was as foreign as Chinese or double Dutch. The Americans in particular were very good at using the astonishing new dialect. They dreamed up all kinds of specialist terms abbreviated to their first letters. There were so many different abbreviations with fewer and fewer ordinary words in between. Eventually a completely new language sprung into being. It was a language that had never seen the inside of a dictionary. In fact, when a new 'first initial syndrome dictionary' was finally compiled, people had to attend classes to be able to understand it.

Talking in initial capital letters had certain advantages, but many people thought they were missing out on something, especially in their love letters, and television news broadcasts, which seemed to have adopted the new system. Conversations could also become tiresome. After an evening of reciting capital letters, people yearned for some good old-fashioned cockney slang and people even began to relish poetry. The scientists and experts were generally over the moon with the system, but even they finally decided that speech was not only becoming very boring, it was becoming incomprehensible. Instead, they recommended to people that the brain probe and high speed stammer method was to be preferred, despite its adverse effects on old ladies. The stammer method had its disadvantages, but these were to be preferred to the reduction of language to capital letters, which could only be understood by about 1% of the population. It therefore seemed to be a rather retrograde step if everyone wanted to understand each other.

With the latest stammer method, entire sentences and paragraphs could be reduced to extremely rapid digital signals that could be fed directly to the brain. People had to spend a short while learning the system, just as a secretary once learned shorthand. It was a great advance on previous speed-reading techniques and the American capital letter syndrome. The deluxe stammer was also able to translate into any language and became the vehicle of the first universal language, a kind of updated Esperanto, which was particularly useful to the scientific community. It also enabled the experts to communicate with the high-speed computer processors. The experts had always said that progress depended on faster and faster and even faster data processing. The data processors were always very fast, very logical and very efficient. It had always been the human link in the communication chain that had been so slow and inefficient. Now the scientists had found a way to remedy the situation,– make people more like data processors by speeding up all their responses. The experts said that the five human senses and the human mind were like old fashioned analogue television and radio sets using valves. They were just out of date and needed converting to digital. Everything that was digital was so much better. The new stammer method and brain probe virtually converted people to digital receivers and transmitters. It was the miracle invention of the 21st century. Why hadn't anyone thought of it before? Men and women could now be converted to walking digital processors, who could not only condense a whole day's conversation into three minutes, but could also talk to their Big Mother artificially intelligent processors like 'buddies.' Scientists congratulated themselves that they had found a way to make people, not only more bionic, but more like their darling processors. It was all such a fine achievement they said. More speed, more progress.

Business organisations couldn't get enough of the new stammer speed talk devices. Communication between people a hundred times faster than normal was considered a great asset. It was fine as far as business efficiency was concerned, but wasn't so good for secretaries. Many secretaries of the human variety, found themselves doing a hundred times more work. Some secretaries demanded a hundred times more pay, but whenever this occurred, business management usually found a robot who, not only did the job better, but also didn't make a fuss about it. It was all in the cause of the creation of wealth, later called status, which was supposed to benefit everyone, although the secretaries and a few million other redundants thought this philosophy must have a flaw in it somewhere.

The new stammer fast talk system was known as the 'speed/think/con' method. Con is short for contact, of course – what else could it mean? It was used in University and Political debates where it was important to compress subject matter into short time schedules. A normal three-hour debate was all over and done with in five minutes, leaving two hours and fifty-five minutes for tea, cakes and a chat about holidays. Solicitors and courtroom staff began using the system, which resulted in a week's courtroom procedure being dealt with before lunch on Monday morning. By Monday afternoon it was standing-room only in the prison vehicles, or 'treatment vehicles,' as they were then called. And the local swimming pools, pubs and skating rinks were all jam-packed with white-wigged legal experts. Much of the judging and solicitor's work was, in fact, carried out by the robot processors, but there were still lengthy wrangles between opposing solicitors who wanted to keep up with tradition. They, like the doctors, felt it helped them to retain some status if they could continue to confuse the public with incomprehensible jargon. However, keeping up their status was rather time consuming and required devoting most of the week to such important labours. Most barristers considered this was too much like hard work. The legal profession therefore agreed to institute the new stammer language systems in every court room in the land.

It was all rather like an old fashioned movie, because the speeding up of language communication resulted in a peculiar side effect, which had been unforeseen by the experts. It made all those people involved chase around after everyone else trying to do everything at high speed. In particular it seemed to have a quickening effect on people's legs, because everyone was running about at very high speed, in their efforts to catch up with their quickened thoughts and communication skills. This was not at all good for people with heart pacemakers, many of which needed re-setting and some even required replacement. Another result was that many businesses were reduced to a half-day week because the staff were completing their weekly work in a couple of hours. The golf courses and public houses were jam-packed with people and artificially intelligent robots all shouting 'four' to each other or 'cheers.' Leisure was, in consequence, becoming hard work and rather risky.

How to spend one's leisure time became the great problem of the age. There seemed to be so much of it. Everywhere you went, there were groups of people huddled together around art teachers, some hoping to stir up their creative instincts and produce a masterpiece. Others just sought refuge in something creative, as there didn't seem to be much of it around in the ultra modern world of processor science. Holographic cameras clicked and purred endlessly everywhere. People spent more time than ever before watching home holographic movies and studying their family's past. People finally began to do more looking into the past than living in the present. And their future ambition was to make even better holographic movies of the past. It was an age of artificial nostalgia where everyone competed to produce a better nostalgic past than the Jones. More and more people travelled to the remotest parts of the Earth and Moon in order to bring back more unique holographic records than their neighbour did. Educational courses in how to take better holographs on Asteroids and the Moon became very popular. Courses in 'where to go in your helicopter' and 'moon-buggy' were also favoured."

Bubbles laughed quietly as fantastic scenes of all these things were enacted on the vast holographic arena. Gotama was astounded to see interplanetary vehicles effortlessly defying gravity and moving among the many habitable artificial satellites, the moon and the planets. People communicated with each other for brief moments and moved on, like streams of ants. There were new and strange forms of vegetation that grew and moved like rooted animals. Some were beautiful in form, others grotesque and frightening. Glimpses of undersea communities were particularly exciting. People appeared to swim and breathe underwater without carrying any breathing equipment. Their bodies were streamlined and smooth with flipper-like appendages that shot them through the water at incredible speeds. It was obvious too that the communities were so well adapted to the underwater climate that they lived out their lives there. Gotama did notice that many of the communities were situated near an outcrop of rock or land and this seemed to imply that the underwater people were perhaps amphibians who needed to use land facilities occasionally. Other holographic appearances came and went for more than an hour, at the end of which Bubbles raised her hand to stop the programme.

"Come," she said. "We shall be looking at some more holographic exhibitions shortly but there are other things that you must see before you return to your own time." With that, she led the way down some stairs to a kind of basement, which appeared to be a vast storeroom of some kind. "This is part of the central national museum of the future," she said, as she breathed quietly on what appeared to be a control button on her wrist. A silver sliding door marked 'Futistics' opened without a sound and they entered its precincts.

Bubbles spoke again. "As you know, the future depends on what happens in the present and on happenings in the past. Karmic law links all Time events. Future predictions became much more accurately assessed, as the artificially intelligent processors encompassed more facts and figures. This science, together with statistics, became known as Futistics. Calculations entailed in Futistics were so complex that they couldn't possibly be undertaken by human intelligence unaided by the artificially intelligent processors. The scientists loved talking astronomically. They said that if the whole population of the Earth were to spend their whole lives calculating for eight hours a day, they couldn't produce the number of calculations that could be achieved by the Futistic processor in one second. Basically, billions upon billions of separate environmental events were monitored, analysed and processed. The vast amount of data was cross-referenced with past data in billions of ways using mathematical laws discovered in the mid 21st century.

The predictions about the future of the world and society were considered as accurate as weather forecasts. But like weather forecasts, they had their hiccups. For instance, scientists, at one period of time, discovered that all the male fish were, not only cross-dressing and looking like females, they were actually turning into females, due to pollution. The Futistic AI processors set to work analysing the situation and came up with the brilliant answer that in 100 years humans would become women. Any remaining men would be infertile, and all new babies would have to be prefabricated in incubators. These predictions caused pandemonium, panic and shock, particularly among the men, who thought their favourite occupation was to be jeopardised. However, when the initial shock had subsided and when it became clear who were to be in the majority, the women persuaded the men to accept the situation. Women had always been expert in carrying out such subtle manipulations. The women of the world were, in fact, quite euphoric that the tragedy of pollution had turned things into their favour by reducing men's testosterone levels to zero. Many thought it might even reduce violence. Women had always been opportunists, and this seemed a golden opportunity to emphasise their superiority. They had, of course, always emphatically believed this, ever since Emily Pankhurst first chained herself to some railings in order to become one of the ruling classes.

Exactly which way civilisation should go in order to progress was left to the Futistic processors to decide, because the artificially intelligent experts considered judgements of politicians, scientists and the man in the street could not be relied upon. They were too inexact and based on trivial personal opinions and emotions. It was the artificially intelligent processor that possessed the ability to calculate and predict such matters far more accurately than any human. Important decisions were therefore left to them, including the pressing of the nuclear war button if necessary. Everyone considered this arrangement to be a sign of progress. To possess instruments and the intelligence capable of keeping the evolution of world society under control and continual surveillance and to put 'progress' on automatic control made people feel secure. Just a few people raised a questioning eyebrow."

"You see," Bubbles said. "During the late 21st century, the artificially intelligent robot processors were treated like Mother, Father and God all rolled into one. They had taught everyone from infancy. People's intimate needs had all been catered for and their illnesses had been diagnosed and cured by them. And the processors possessed such soothing voices, always so cool and calm as though they were best friends. It was understandable therefore that the general public assumed, without a second thought, that the decisions of the processors must always be right, logically and ethically. They were everybody's Big Mother.

There were still a few dissidents who considered that important value judgements should not be undertaken by artificial intelligence. They thought, for instance, it was particularly risky for value judgements that determined the direction human progress to be left to instrumentation outside human control. It was also risky to give the processors complete control over decision making in matters like starting a nuclear war, flying commercial aircraft, diagnosis of diseases, surgical operations, national and world legislation, genetic engineering of plants and animals and countless other matters of import. How society should progress was a particularly delicate matter. Progress for one person wasn't necessarily progress for another. Also, progress in one direction inevitably resulted in retrogression in another. There was the deep human instinct to be considered. The latest in artificial intelligence seemed to possess many human attributes, including a human range of emotions. But many people were of the opinion that such emotions were a charade, a simulated mimicry of the real thing, programmed into the processors to provide them with some resemblance to human personality in order to facilitate communication with them. Such human characteristics were important when teaching children. Everyone by this time had been educated and conditioned by robot processors.

Progress was a difficult thing to define. It was an illusive terminology. Some people said it should be left to God to sort out. It was, they said, only he (or she) who knew exactly what was required of the world and its human population. It was only he (or she) who could set civilisation on the correct path. Many people gave lip service to this philosophy, but the new God they really preferred was the futistic artificial intelligence of the latest processor that could produce tangible decisions and advice on how to reach a land of milk and honey."

Bubbles stopped speaking. They had arrived at a section of the futistic museum marked with the sign that read 'Progress – Department of World and Planetary Health.' A white faced man in the group came forward at her invitation. She introduced him as 000000707800/009/54132/222000/oops, but for Gotama's benefit, said he could be called Calcul Plentigood, professor of mathematics for remote automated healing techniques and ancillaries. At Bubble's invitation, the professor then explained at some length how, by the end of the 21st century surgical operations on the human body had improved out of all recognition using automated instrumentation unheard of at the beginning of the century. There was now a minimum of invasive surgery, but lots of new keyholes had been discovered, together with other completely radical techniques. Ultrasound and similar techniques were used to treat tumours in all parts of the body, especially the brain, without invasive surgery or human intervention of any kind. Brain operations that in the past had either been extremely difficult or quite impossible were now carried out by ultrasound in just a few minutes on an out-patiernt basis. There was also extensive use of magnetic fields to realign and restore body, brain and mind. There were also countless other completely new and radical treatements. These included the use of microscopic nano-engineered probes, smaller than a pinhead, that floated through arteries, veins and other bodily orifices, automatically curing all kinds of ailments. Many patients were brim full of them, 'floating ferrets,' they were called, each one sent on a different submarine mission, to go where no man had gone before. Moreover, most operations were not only performed automatically, without human intervention, but were orchestrated using a combination of operating skills from all parts of the world and solar system, including specialist units on the Moon and Mars. A brain operation, for instance, might be directed and overseen by surgeons, some human but mostly artificially intelligent robots, stationed in America, Australia, Russia, China or on Mars, or all working in concert together via the planetary super-internet links.

It was an age when people could choose their robot surgeon from anywhere in the solar system. Such robot surgeons were promoted like pop stars and were publicised and evaluated in the popular electronic media of the day. Before they went for their operations, people avidly checked on rival robot surgeons, to ensure they had all the latest behavioural modifications and had a record of not killing too many people. As the patient rarely came into direct physical contact with the surgeon, but only communicated through visual monitors or holographic imagery transmitted from around the solar system, there was no way of knowing whether the surgeons were in fact human, robot or a hybrid of the two, the latter now being very common. So people had little alternative but to be guided by their chats with the various surgeons that were available over their 'click on' links. The robot surgeons always seemed to possess the best bedside manner and cosy chat line techniques because they had been specially trained in such methods. It was therefore they who best persuaded people to let them wield the ultrasonic, the nano-keyhole probes, lasers, tweezers and nippers, and consequently it was the robots who carried out most of the operations and eventually, due mainly to their impeccable chat lines, took control of the world and planetary health system.

Advances in medicine and surgery raced ahead, led primarily by the inventive innovations of the robot surgeons who now could think and act for themselves independently of human intervention. The advances were such that operations became so sophisticated and complicated that, like Einstein's theories, very few people could understand them. Not even the human doctors knew what was going on and it became pointless to try to explain such complexities of treatment to patients. Medicine and surgery had reached a point where only artificially intelligent robots could understand, authorise and carry out the necessary procedures involved. As a result, people walked about in complete ignorance of what changes had been wrought in their bodies and brains. Some said they felt most peculiar in regions they'd never noticed before. Whilst a few enjoyed them immensely, the majority felt they were distractions from routine pleasures. Many, unknown to themselves, became more bionic than biological in all sorts of odd places and no-one could tell them anything comprehensible about what had happened to them. They were told essentials, of course, like when to call at the clinic to have new solar batteries fitted and for their five year check, the equivalent of an MOT, but otherwise they were kept in ignorance. Many had their intelligence and memory improved, but hadn't a clue as to how such transformations had occurred. People grew new teeth and hair but no-one knew exactly how. It was also a time when some people's eyes began to glaze over as though it was all just too much for them. But for many it was all very gratifying and most people thought that more and more of such things must make life better and better. Some, however, began to wonder whether people had now lost control over their own destiny and had become of secondary importance to a new and revolutionary artificial life form that was gradually taking over humanity and the world."

At that point, Professor Calcul Plentigood decided to change the subject to something that would be a little simpler for Gotama to relate to and understand. After a few introductory remarks, he pointed to what appeared to be a book, but which possessed only one page. As the man held the book, the page suddenly came to life and moving words came into view. "By the middle of the 21st century," Professor Plentigood said, "books had generally been superseded by these electronic books. The works of Dickens, for instance, were condensed into minute memory chips the size of a pinhead. This one electronic book therefore contained thousands of books that could be reproduced page by page on the small monitor screen. It could also be connected to the latest holographic instruments to provide a three-dimensional moving illustration.

Gotama noticed that the electronic lettering was of beautiful design. He read the heading that stood out in bright blue and gold letters on a cream background. It said, 'the evolution of nutrition since the 20th century.'

Professor Plentigood interrupted. "If you would prefer to hear the text being read, just press button 'A.' If you would like the built in processor to make random extracts for you, press button 'R.'. If you want to read it for yourself press 'I' and to have the book read by either a male or a female voice, just press either 'M' or 'F'. or CH for a child's. And if you would prefer it sung, press S. Or if you would like just musical background, press either C for classical, P for Pop, or N for Nostalgic. If you want the book read in simple words a young child could understand with a few gurgles and sighs in between, press SL. If, like most people you would like words that aren't too difficult to understand, press Moron. For academic language, press Stuffy. There is a Shakespearean mode, but this is more of an acquired taste as is the high literate mode for those who have passed their encyclopaedic literate examination. There are also dialect variations you can switch to such as Cockney, Welsh, Scottish, American, Hindustani and Modern Esperanto and many more. For these, just use the sliding scale menu. Illustrations in three dimensions and colour can be shown in holograph mode at distances of up to three metres from the reader and will appear in mid-air quite outside the book and the reader. For illustrations press HI and to adjust size press SI. Deluxe models have a voice reader mode so that you can switch to a voice of famous pop stars living or dead and other notables to have the story read by them. Many people like their stories read by Holograph TV stars who joke between paragraphs, tell funny stories and make people laugh. Children like bedtime stories read by Mary Poppins and soft singing voices. If you want any of these, just press DEL BY for the menu. For other menus, just press the thousand Options button. It's really very simple."

Gotama decided on a female voice and pressed 'F.' Thereupon, a tender soft melodic voice seemed to spring from nowhere and everywhere. "By the mid 21st century," the voice purred, "medical processors had discovered that 99% of the foods eaten during the 20th century should never have been eaten at all. They were all found to be either toxic or the cause of disease. New allergies to food were being discovered every other week. There were all kinds, ranging from spots brought on by lemon curd, to twitching from last night's gin and orange. Elderly ladies seemed particularly prone to the latter and caught them in epidemic proportions. It almost seemed as though no one wanted to be left out. Everyone was proud to disclose their special allergy to their friends. They made an excellent subject for conversation instead of operations, which had been the subject of women's conversation for a few hundred years and it was quite satisfying to think that one could suffer from something else. It compensated for the absence of individuality in the new society. If you were allergic, you were special, because it was unlikely that the person with whom you were conversing would have exactly the same allergy. On the other hand there was the distinct possibility that they would have one of the thousands of allergies then on the market, which would give you something in common to talk about. Thus, the subject of your allergy could be used to break the ice at any party. It could also assist with opening gambits when communicating with your bank manager or with your neighbour over the garden wall. It was, moreover, an excellent alternative to the stale comment that the weather forecasters had got it right again.

Many medical practitioners, after studying the kinds of food eaten during the 20th century, were convinced that everyone in that period should have died before they were ten. It was impossible to understand how anyone had ever managed to draw the old age pension. Some very special circumstances must have existed, the experts said. Every food and drink, from cheese and meat to lemonade, had been proved by the processor analysts, to be toxic either in the long or short term. Medical experts were of the opinion that 20th century foods and drinks should have been labelled with a government health warning like cigarettes. Something like, 'Eat this and pay later,' or 'grow your own in fresh air, if you can find any,' or 'eat this and win a coffin.' Everything from cancer to corns was considered the result of bad eating habits or stress.

By the mid-21st century people were addicted to vitamins, health foods, artificial fresh air, bottled water and faith healing. It all became a complicated science that only the processors could understand. It was they who diagnosed deficiencies and prescribed the vitamins and health foods. The exponents of this science were at a loss to understand why 20th century doctors were apparently never taught nutrition. They concluded that hospital meals must have contributed to the high mortality rates of the period. The new food sciences of the mid-21st century made the earlier ones look like cavemen's eating habits. It was generally concluded that people had to be fit and strong if they wanted to survive in hospital in the 20th and early 21st century when they were faced with hospital meals, the side effects of drugs, and infections caused by antibiotic resistant bacteria." At this point the voice stopped, and Professor Plentigood stepped aside as Bubbles turned to an adjacent glass topped table.

She picked up a tiny object about the size of a thimble. "This is one of the mid-21st century music and sound therapy systems," she said, as she placed it under the beam of a table lamp. The object glowed in many colours of the rainbow. "They were used extensively by the medical profession to alleviate and cure many diseases, both physical and psychological. It was discovered that playing certain sound sequences and musical rhythms had remarkable curative effects. Some combinations of notes were found to improve people's intelligence. Others helped to improve the condition of the mentally and physically disabled. As the system progressed it was found that different ailments needed different combinations of sounds and rhythms. Some were also used as preventive medicine and to boost the immune system. High notes of the operatic type were devastating to some bacteria and to sensitive people, whilst low notes of the baritone variety were particularly good for women's troubles. Also different people needed different sounds and timing. There was a delightful musical sound for old men with arthritis; a disconcerting range of notes for young men with backache and an almost screaming noise for anyone with toothache. There was happy music for the depressed, slow music for the over active, classical for the forgetful and 'pop style' for those who wanted to forget. The instruments were so popular that it was not long before people were using them at home. Their regular use warded off all sorts of illnesses better than vitamin c. The layman called it, 'music therapy'. The experts called it aurolialphabetagammacerebralivibrosis or AHGCB in American terminology. The therapy formed an important part of the National Health Service by the mid-21st-century. Music centres as big as the Albert Hall were used to give mass therapy. These were often combined with holographic displays of the open countryside, waterfalls, lakes, the open sea, sky and distant space. Many people found relief from their ailments at these large rally sessions, but others with rare illnesses complained that the medical processors in charge neglected to play their own special sounds and rhythms. They said that the sounds they had to listen to made them feel worse. It was like giving Lemsip to someone who needed new hip joints."

"It was obvious that some musical sounds were health giving whilst others were upsetting, aggravating and even bad for you, like eating too much animal fat. Medical practitioners had done their best in the past to stop people from eating beef, lamb, chicken, bacon, butter, lard, eggs, cheese, milk, cream, anything nicely rich and savoury. A few vegetables were allowed, and some fruit, providing these were peeled to protect from pesticide poisoning. Now the medical experts decided that only the sounds that were good for you should be allowed. Street and traffic sounds had already been curtailed and many thought that music censorship should now be imposed for places like the Albert Hall where so many different kinds of music was performed, that some of it was bound to be bad for you. Indeed this seemed evident from the glazed expressions of the audience after listening to some controversial pieces. Medical experts said that the artificially intelligent processors in charge of medical therapy should vet all music. Many of the experts claimed that over 90% of the music composed in the 20th century should be classified as noise pollution and should be banned, like the banning of polluted beef. Anything that's not good for you, they said, must be prohibited. Polluted sound must be taken off the market. Many people immediately voiced their objections saying that their freedom of choice would be violated if only censored music was permitted. What was good or bad music was in the ear of the beholder, they said. A person should be free to listen to polluted music if he wants to. If people wanted to subject their bodies and minds to noise pollution, the decision should be left to them.

Once again the experts came up with a solution. They decided that all such music should be labelled with a government health warning, like cigarettes and the thousands of foods and drinks that were now so labelled. However, this caused quite a few arguments, especially among people playing their pocket hi-fi radios on beaches and in other public places. Many people objected to listening to other people's polluted music. 'Why should we be polluted?' they asked, 'just because of some idiot who wouldn't take notice of the music therapy processor experts.' The processors were the oracles and guides. They knew more about polluted music and its repercussions on human cells of body and brain than any human did. 'Their advice must be followed,' they said. If only a small proportion of music by human composers was pollution free, then only this small proportion should be given to our children to listen to. And if only music composed or vetted by the artificially intelligent processors was healthy, then most of the humanly composed music should be banned or subjected to stringent tests before being allowed on the open market and into people's homes where children might get hold of it.

So the debates and arguments raged. However, it did seem that, unlike the usual methods of keeping fit such as exercising and dieting, which were either boring or painful or both, music therapy had the advantage that it was both comfortable and exhilarating. It therefore caught on with the masses who were quick to realise that here was something combining idleness with pleasure, two favourites for the general hedonist. People were quick to make use of the new restorative therapy and delighted in the secondary rapturous effects of listening to the health-giving designer music, whilst being vibrated physically and mentally at exotic frequencies. People delighted in the new 'music for health.' There had never been such a breakthrough since Beethoven played his first notes. Every hospital bed was fitted with a designer music headset. A patient plied with a combination of mood pills and scientifically prepared music patterns was always happy with his treatment and seldom complained. And if he did, another dose of mood pills soon remedied the situation.

Since the discovery of peptide structures in the brain in the 1970s, there had been a steady advance in the development of pills containing the early encephalon pain killing and mood control ingredient. By the mid-21st century considerable advances had been made in brain studies. Revolutionary discoveries had contributed to man's knowledge and unique links were found between electrical activity and brain chemistry. Much useful information had been gleaned from advances in molecular biology, brain chemistry and information gained from the use of the latest sophisticated instrumentation used for analysing the brain's internal activity. The artificially intelligent processors were also at the cutting edge of developments in trying to solve the riddles of brain function and its relation to conscious mind. During these developments, pills of all kinds were designed to affect different parts of the brain and behaviour. Many other methods of altering mood behaviour became possible in addition to the application of sounds and music just mentioned. We will discuss more of these later, if we have time."

Bubbles walked on. "Over there," she said, pointing to a long row of silver coated objects, "are kept the results of Futistic processor extrapolations relating to the possible destiny of the human race. The calculations were based on early 21st-century data. In other halls of the Futistic Museum are kept similar predictions based on data of later centuries when more refined and detailed information became available. You must understand that Time itself has been incredibly stretched in order that we may show you some of the results contained in the Futistic Museum. You are, in fact, a very privileged person to be shown this viewpoint, because it was only in the 23rd century that science discovered that Time could be manipulated in a controlled manner. The methods used to create Time distortion cannot be revealed as they come under the Galactic Patents Secrecy Act formulated by the members of the Milky Way and Andromeda Galaxy Federation of Living Planets. The methods are quite beyond the scope of your present understanding and, besides, it would serve no purpose. The reason you have been sent here is to be given a few brief glimpses of some alternative futures for the human race, because now is a very critical time for the people on planet Earth. We have been instructed to help you make some of the very important decisions required of you soon. Our instruction has come to us from a very high galactic authority projecting from millions of years in the future. You are apparently the one cog in the vast wheel of creation who can set in motion events that will either end all life on Earth or let it flourish for the next few million years. It can make the difference between establishing the Earth as an important centre of communication in the local galaxy group, or in its catastrophic destruction.

Your meeting at the United Nations International Congress is a vital link in the chain of cause and effect. This has been confirmed by data coming in from the future and by extrapolations made by the Futistic processors. To make the wrong decision could be disastrous. I am not permitted to tell you the exact nature of the catastrophe as the Galactic Federation of Planets have strict rules of non-intervention into the natural evolution of life unless it is absolutely essential for the survival of the planet. To assume it would be nuclear devastation would not be the whole truth. The main purpose of our meeting aboard the Progress 13 in this Futistic Museum is to provide you with evidence that will encourage you to vote the correct way in the forthcoming congress meeting."

These latest remarks by the woman came as a complete and unexpected revelation to Gotama. Just how one or two actions on his part could result in repercussions of such immensity he could hardly fathom. It was like the man who swatted a fly against the wall with his newspaper and the house fell down. "There must surely be a mistake," he said.

"I'm afraid not," came the reply.

"What am I supposed to say or vote for at the United Nations meeting," he said.

"That I'm not permitted to tell you, as it must be a free choice on your part. I am only authorised to show you some of the events likely to occur in the future in the hope that you will see for yourself what action should be taken."

Bubbles smiled. "We hope too that you find meeting with the people of the future will have been a pleasure for you. We have enjoyed entertaining you aboard Progress 13 and have found it particularly interesting to 'time travel' from our own dimension into your domain in order to guide it into a safe future. You would find it difficult to understand life in our dimension because you are embedded in the three dimensions your brain constructs for you. However, there are many other modes of consciousness that live and breathe in other dimensions beyond your time and space. We come from a dimension that can only be described as in the future, yet beyond it. Our

257

dimension transcends yet encompasses the future. We are responsible for the management of planets such as the Earth because the way in which their life forms evolve can effect the progress of other planetary systems throughout the galaxy in ways you do not yet understand."

Bubbles turned to face him. Her eyes were huge and liquid. She radiated a misty loveliness difficult to describe. "There are life forms in the galaxies that are quite beyond your comprehension," she said mysteriously. "There is even life at different time levels from those you experience. For instance, the life that exists on a neutron star evolves in a tiny fraction of a second of your time. It took a billion years for the generation of life on planet Earth, but on the surface of a neutron star it would take about $1/30$ second for the transformation of inert matter into 'nuclear' life to occur. On neutron stars the nuclear force is capable of producing stable structures from a number of nucleons ranging from 1 (the nucleus of hydrogen) to 238 (comprising the 92 protons and 146 neutrons in the nucleus of uranium 238). This force can also build much larger unstable structures. The largest nucleus formed in your Earth laboratories contains 265 nucleons, but its lifespan is less than 10^{-4} second, that is one nanosecond. But whether or not a thing is unstable depends on the viewer's point of view. In fact, bearing in mind their size and their agitation speeds on the surface of a neutron star, these nuclei are displaced by amounts comparable with their size in about 10^{-11} second. A man moving on the surface of the Earth covers a distance equivalent to his size in about one second. Therefore that which to you appears unstable would seem extremely stable to a 'nuclear being' scale 10^{-21}. Imagine if you can a nucleus formed by nuclear forces and containing tens of thousands of nucleons with a lifetime of about 10^{-15} second. In terms of the number of interactions it experiences on the surface of a neutron star, this nucleus will last a long time and incur millions of collisions before disappearing. And during this very large number of interactions, which are subject to selection and evolutionary pressures, life can appear in the form of very complex and heavy nuclei capable of reproduction and of interacting with each other and their environment. Obviously such life evolves much more rapidly than life on Earth because its timescale is so much shorter than yours (19^{-21} compared with 1 second). Therefore as I mentioned earlier, whereas about one billion years were required for the generation of life on planet Earth, it takes only about $1/30$ second for the transformation of inert matter into 'nuclear' life on the surface of a neutron star. Life-forms in these civilisations measure about 10^{-11} centimetres and live approximately 10^{-15} seconds. On your timescale a civilisation like theirs only lasts for about a nanosecond. It would therefore be impossible for you to communicate with such life-forms at your present stage of technological evolution.

Before we enter the next and most important part of the Futistic Museum, I think it is now permissible for me to tell you that although we appear to you as human, we are intrinsically more complex in physical structure and in mind. This increased complexity applies especially to our thinking organs that you would define as brains. We are from a distant point in future time and space where it was found possible to improve the structure and function of the ordinary type biological brain thousands of times over. We also have the ability to alter our bodily structure and appearance so that we may adapt and live comfortably in a variety of environments. On planet Earth we can look and function biologically as you do. We therefore appear human but in truth we are not. The simplest way to describe it to you in language you can understand is to imagine us as complex combinations of events all of which can be modified, controlled and restructured as required. It is therefore possible for us to materialise or dematerialise our bodily and brain structures at will, as and where necessary to suit the particular galactic or planetary environment in which we happen to be situated. This is essential for our work as Time/Space travellers who have to communicate with many diverse forms of life on different types of planet strewn across the length and breadth of the galaxies."

Bubbles led the way to a large covered arena surrounded by many thousands of seats, all of which were empty. Gotama thought it looked like a cross between a luxurious Wembley Stadium and a never-ending beach on a summer's day. At the centre, where the football pitch might have been, there was a huge pool of translucent material. A vast transparent dome soared above them into the sky. It was difficult to define exact measurements, but the lofty dome seemed to stretch upwards as high as the clouds and extended across to the distant horizon. It was the largest most magnificent building structure Gotama had ever set eyes on. The walls and dome glowed in changing designs of gold, white, blue and soft purple.

"Please be seated," the woman instructed. A few moments passed. The lights illuminating the arena dimmed until all around was an inky blackness. It was as though he had suddenly been geared up into a new and breathtaking stream of conscious awareness that launched him into wider planes of experience. The twinkling lights in the large transparent dome faded as Gotama was engulfed in a strange amalgam of emotive forces that pulled at the subtle strands of his senses. Exactly when he began to become not just a passive onlooker, but an active participant in the events that followed, he was unable to discern. At first, there were holographic images that appeared in the huge dome-like structure. Many of the events were familiar to him. There were scenes showing 20th and early 21st century life in all its aspects in many different parts of the world. There were scenes of beauty, of open farmlands, mountain streams with salmon hopping the rapids. There were wild flowers, quiet woodland glades where the sun streamed through the trees in a haze of angelic light. Then there came the moment when he could actually feel the warm breezes on his cheeks. It was as though this vast holographic instrument was capable of transmitting not just images and sound, but that it conveyed the equivalent of quadraphonic 'feeling' and three-dimensional sensation. Overflowing with rapturous joy, he walked and ran through the luxuriant country landscapes. He could feel the stillness and delight. He became an integral part of nature's glorious pattern, as the sun broke the horizon and streaked rays of soft gold over an infinite sky. Trees, like intricate webs of lace, were silhouetted against the colours of the dawn. Waterfalls tumbled; seas plunged and frothed all bubbling with life.

Then came the metamorphic changes where lakes, seas and oceans became filthy and stagnant, whilst thousands of fishing boats, some huge, fought with each other to extract the last few polluted, disfigured fish. Factories poured out increasing quantities of sour and dangerous effluents into rivers, lakes and seas. Aeroplanes, motor vehicles and industrial plants were shrouded in polluting clouds of toxic substances. Faces were distorted in the agonies of not being able to breathe. People vomited and died with food poisoning and diseases that no antibiotic could cure. Others drowned in vast floods and terrible typhoons. Pot-bellied children lay starving under a blazing sun where they died in their thousands. Towns and villages were ablaze. Men with evil faces used guns, bombs, chemical and biological weapons indiscriminately on innocent people. Thousands of aircraft were exploding in mid-air or crashing into skyscraper buildings and into each other. People wept and grieved in rivers of tears. Gotama felt the pain induced by the crushing numbers of people being born into such deprivation. Millions suffered from brain damage as a consequence of being undernourished from birth, accompanied by heart rending disabilities. People in developing countries suffered most, because their industry failed to keep pace with that of the more technically advanced nations. Their industries couldn't keep pace with their staggering population growth. Millions were dying on the streets as poverty and economic stagnation tightened their horrific grip.

It was apparent that the competitive efforts of nations to control and acquire the diminishing energy resources became increasingly harsh. It developed into a vicious struggle for survival. At the same time global warming was affecting the planet in disastrous ways. Nations were tumbling over each other to get at the last few drops of oil and other raw materials. Terrorist groups were being spawned in their thousands like ugly fungus. Their contribution was to inflict even more pain and anarchy into a world already seething with envy and hate. The major powers were also doing a lot of sabre rattling with their nuclear armoury and sophisticated weapons, which they began to use more and more frequently against the terrorists. The politicians struggled in a giant kind of rugby scrum, all pushing and pulling in different ways as was typical. In the holographic imagery, Gotama noticed the politicians had suddenly grown longer necks than usual, like dinosaurs. Each threatened and cajoled the other and didn't seem to notice the sad deterioration of the environment going on around them. Economics seemed to be their main priority. Co-operation between people, nations and religious groups seemed farthest from their minds. Many wore blinkers so that they could concentrate on small grubs rather than large problems. Doctrinaire beliefs were always more important than the survival of the world's population, the majority of whom didn't care whether they were ruled by left or right policies providing they could live a secure and happy life.

Gotama witnessed countless tragedies, and with each and every one he felt the pain of human suffering. As if there wasn't enough pain in natural disasters to go round, people were in the habit of intentionally inflicting pain on each other and on themselves. People were, in fact, their own worst enemies. Greed, hate and ignorance were usually responsible, with a good dose of envy thrown in. Fear was also responsible for people and nations' behaviour towards each other. Most were frightened that their security was being threatened. And the usual answer was to fight each other. This had resulted in two world wars. Unfortunately, man never learned from these mistakes and preferred squabbling with his neighbours. Finally, the inevitable, or so it seemed, happened. The holocaust that everyone feared finally engulfed the world once again. From small beginnings, like terrorist atrocities, arose large-scale conflicts and military forces such as the world had never known were unleashed. Gotama was immensely shocked to see the horrors of nuclear and germ warfare with the degradation of the planet by global warming, all combining to exterminate the human race. The dinosaurs had been made extinct by the impact of a comet; the human race was to be made extinct by their own stupidity and greed, unless something very radical and drastic could be done. Otherwise the beautiful blue planet Earth would end its days like a mercurial dead planet, its millions of years of evolution destroyed – and for what? To satisfy fanatical greed, hate, fear and ignorance. Perhaps it was not just a lot of politicians who wore blinkers; perhaps most people wore them. If only a fraction of the money spent in the last hundred years on armaments and war had been spent on constructive humane projects like hospitals and peaceful scientific enterprises and research, what a paradise people could have created and what beautiful wonders they could now be enjoying. It was all so sad, so pitifully tragic. He was suddenly reminded of the words of the astronaut Sigmund Jahn, who once said, "Before I flew I was already aware of how small and vulnerable our planet is; but only when I saw it from space, in all its ineffable beauty and fragility, did I realise that humankind's most urgent task is to cherish and preserve it for future generations"

At that moment, Bubbles, seated beside Gotama, leaned over and spoke. "You've seen the general course on which people of the Earth are heading. There are, however, many options open to mankind. Progress 13 need not self-destruct. Progress can still be maintained. It is not necessary to return to nature and become primitives like Rousseau recommended. In fact, this would not only be unwise, but it would never work. Many more people would die or live in abject misery without enough food to go round. No! The answer lies in altering the course and direction of Progress 13. It can be done and it must be done. You will find ways."

Bubbles smiled. "And now, as a contrast, let us take some lighter entertainment.

She then pressed something on her left sleeve, whereupon Gotama was transported into a completely new age – 2050 – and instantly became aware that lifestyles had altered astonishingly. People with their faces painted in outrageous colours were everywhere in huge numbers. Most wore strange silver or gold foil clothes that appeared to be light and comfortable. He learned later that the clothes were self-heating to a regulated temperature. He walked and talked with people, both young and old, of the new age and discussed everything from electric, solar powered and hydrogen propelled vehicles to the many thousands of different types of robots used for all kinds of domestic and commercial duties. He was intrigued to be told that not only women now had babies, but that, by means of new scientific breakthroughs, men could also give birth. However, both these natural methods of childbirth had largely been superseded by the test tube and incubator methods of bringing new human entries into the world, which had provided people, and women in particular, with a new freedom from the limitations of the old fashioned family life. Unfortunately, the new 'freedom' had left in its wake many problems, including a new rash of psychological illnesses in the young who had been bereft of old fashioned Mums and Dads.

By this date, countless human biological functions could be monitored by means of tiny portable mini-chip devices that people wore on their wrists and which warned them, in a charming relaxed voice, if their house was on fire, or if it was being burgled, or if they were coming down with the flu, or suffering from stress, or with something a little more serious, like a fatal heart attack. It could even guide people back home if they were lost, or to the nearest hospital, if their wrist indicator registered that they were in the 'amber danger mode.' If they were in the 'red danger mode,' it meant they were in a

262

serious predicament, like falling off a skyscraper or in the middle of a burning building. An automatic robot ambulance would then collect them. The system was multi-lingual and could voice its health advice in any dialect from Welsh, Irish or Chinese to Hindustani or a completely new variety of Esperanto."

At this point Bubbles interrupted the proceedings. "These health and safety monitoring systems originated in the old days of motor cars", she said smiling. "In those days, red, amber and green lights were used on drivers' dashboards to indicate vehicle faults. Data such as low oil pressure, defective electrical circuits and faulty brakes were brought to the driver's attention in that way. It all helped to sell motor cars and made the male motorist feel like James Bond. It also provided the car dealers with more maintenance business. Sometimes the red, amber and green warning lights were accompanied by a printed instruction, so that when they lit up, they would indicate a few important points like, 'Fill up with petrol in the next minute or the engine will stop'. However, this was not good news if you were on a motorway and, following several concertina pile-ups, it showed that further modifications were necessary. In another experiment warning lights registered things like 'Engine's seized up and big end's gone. Please refer to oil pressure warning five minutes ago.' Such information was rather like being wise after the event, which didn't leave the motorist in the most placid of moods, but rather with a bill that gave his bank balance, and his bank manager, a nasty turn for the worse. There were further refinements considered by many people to be superfluous to requirements such as; ' You must fill up with petrol in the next three hours if you want to get to Glasgow.' As a result, many people had the sneaking suspicion that the motor car designers could find better ways of spending their time, if they really set their minds to it.

Later, came the wonder invention, the automatic robot driver control system for use on motorways. This utilised ultrasonic technology that gave cars 'bat' type ability to automatically sense a car ahead and quickly respond. It then became virtually impossioble to drive cars into each other when on automatic mode. This meant that the driver could settle down, with a cup of tea and biscuits, or have a snooze, with hands and feet off all the controls, leaving the on-board mini-processor to do all the driving. However, early models registered warning signals by means of coloured lights and written messages with little artificial voice accompaniment. An amber indicator, for instance, would light up at each major road junction that read, 'Wake up Sir (or Madam), it's time to turn to manual control'. Unfortunately, in many of those early experimental cars, a driver, who had dozed off whilst his vehicle was in automatic mode, wasn't always in a fit state to read the instruction, not to mention taking over manual control. In consequence, incidents of road rage were at epidemic proportions at motor way exits across the country. The obvious answer, the experts said, was to fit accompanying bells and buzzers to wake up any dozing driver. However, as practical as this answer seemed to be, it did lead to complaints of being kept awake by bells ringing at the wrong junction and to several heart attacks when buzzers went off at high decibel settings. From then on, modified systems used amber warnings with a soft purring voice for relatively unimportant vehicle problems and to indicate minor junctions. The red lights were the ones to watch out for, however, as it was these that foreshadowed something diabolical was about to happen. The red light was accompanied by a blast from a klaxon sufficient to turn the car occupants to jelly. At the same time the dashboard screen would be emblazoned with words like, 'You're on fire,' or 'You're in crash mode in ten seconds. Watch out for air bags and flying objects.'

To be awakened from their dozing mode was apt to put drivers into a state of shock, often with unfortunate consequences. Some drivers, therefore, would have nothing to do with them. All sorts of warning signals were provided in the more sophisticated vehicles. Some even sounded the klaxon if one of the passengers was missing or hadn't fastened their seat belts. Families with a Granny, who was in the habit of wandering off at service stations and inadvertently left behind, found the alarm very helpful. Following the klaxon blast would be a soft voice that whispered 'you've lost a passenger, believed to be Granny, half a mile back. Please collect ASAP.'

The situation finally got completely out of hand following the issuing of an advertisement by one leading car manufacturer that read, 'Our cars are equipped with alarms to give one hundred and eighty voice warnings and advisory notes per hour or three per minute. Advisory notes appeared on a monitor screen at the periphery of the windscreen giving up-to-the-minute advice, such as 'Watch it! You're crossing a double white line,' or 'you have been driving for the maximum legal limit, and this is not the way to Canterbury. Please pull up for rest period, or be prosecuted.' The latter regulation was the result of the Lorry Drivers' Union, who had inaugurated a 30 minute period between rests for lorry drivers so that they could be assured of their beauty sleep on long journeys. Driving a motor vehicle on manual finally meant that a driver spent more time watching the screen monitor than actually looking out of the windscreen. The inevitable result was that more and more drivers found themselves confronted by red lights and klaxons blowing and dashboard monitors blaring things like, 'Time to impact and airbags, three seconds.' Please switch to automatic mode.' Such situations were obviously not compatible with the latest 'green cross your heart code' of the motorway. Something had to be done. New designs were given priority so that more automation could be introduced with less klaxon blasting and messages to read. Members of the Klaxon Maker's Union and Bell Ringer's Fellowship all objected. They felt that motor cars were best left under simple manual control but with plenty of bell ringing and klaxons to warn drivers of any impending doom. What could be simpler, they said, than a blast from a klaxon, with red words repeating, 'No oil, no oil, your engine's seized up, your engine's seized up.' It had an air of finality about it. It was neat and tidy.

Sophistication finally won the day. Voice simulation became the designer's answer to the problem. Now, instead of the old fashioned amber, green and red warning lights, a voice in beautiful quadraphonic sound would interrupt the driver's reveries, whilst keeping shock tactics to a minimum to avoid heart attacks and nervous breakdowns. Purring quietly over the loudspeakers, the voice would politely indicate that a problem had occurred like, 'You've just hit a brick wall. If the engine's still running please switch off ignition.' Voice warning systems came in several different categories. Psychologists advising the motor car manufacturers were of the opinion that different voices and dialects should be used to voice the warning signals to drivers. The experts felt that the cockney driver, for instance, would feel much more at home if his voice simulator spoke to him on his own level. They said it would help such a driver to feel more secure if the instrumentation were to say something like, 'Your flippin engine's over'eating. Look for 'love your daughter'– water, or 'on the boil'- oil, or 'in the bay'– without delay. Or more simply, 'Better get some oil quick mate, or you'll be up the creek without a paddle.'

On these recommendations the car manufacturers therefore decided that this kind of down to earth language would be programmed into cars of the cheaper variety. In the more expensive vehicles the dialogue followed a somewhat more 'plum in the mouth' style and was generally more ingratiating in order to maintain the car owner's prestige. Only the most refined Oxford accents were permitted in Rolls Royce and Bentley cars. Dialogue considered appropriate for the more expensive cars went something like, 'I'm very sorry to interrupt you sir, but the oil pressure requires your immediate attention, otherwise I fear that seizure is imminent. Your gloves are-in the side pocket, if you wish to open the bonnet.' Phrases like this were also the vogue for women drivers, to give them status and to keep them calm in times of crisis and to avoid immediate slamming on of the brakes, as had been the habit with the use of klaxons. It was hoped that this would avoid the epidemic of concertina pile ups caused in this way by a minor problem like a faulty make-up mirror light. Women usually wanted the robot voice to be of the husky male variety, fashioned after their favourite holographic pop star, whilst most men preferred their car voice module to be of the sultry female variety. For man and wife co-owners, there was a special base and treble control so that the voice could be adjusted for whoever was driving at the time. The more expensive deluxe models were fitted with normal, playful, sultry and sexy adjustments to suit the mood of the driver. Adjustments were usually made to coincide with the type of mood pills being taken at the time.

Later, as new advances were made, it became common to fit a processor in motor cars to monitor and report on not only vehicle behaviour, but also on the health condition of the occupants, particularly the driver. Everyone in the mid-21st century was required by law to, not only use seat belts, but also to be connected to the car's processor that monitored and reported on countless bodily and mental functions. These not only included the simple measurements of blood pressure and heart function, but also many diverse and intricate metabolic and biological processes that were quite unknown to people and doctors of the 20th-century. These personal monitors were linked to the car's robot voice communicator, usually called George, Fred or Sybil, who would periodically, or as the occasion demanded, relay appropriate comments to the car occupants. George, Fred or Sybil would make continual updated progress reports on the performance of car, occupants and driver. Indeed, sometimes it became difficult to disentangle one from the other. The robot voice might, for instance, suddenly say all in one breath, 'I regret to report master that your blood pressure is now going into the red, your heart's fluctuating, your energy level is falling into the amber and your oil pressure needs looking at! Kindly remember that traffic jams always have this effect on you. Please take remedial action reference number 46430 Mk 2.'

Having delivered its report and recommendation, the robot communicator would ask that the prescription be acknowledged. The driver, in order to obviate the prescription being repeated, would utter his or her 'key password' which when spoken would activate remedial action number 46430 Mk 2. Remedial action involved all kinds of on the spot aids, ranging from oral medicines and back massages through the driver's seat to calming anti-stress therapies using combinations of musical sounds, aromas and verbal hypnotic type suggestions. The automatic vending machine on the driver's dashboard could also be operated by George, Fred and Sybil, if they considered it necessary to give out mood pills or some other pill appropriate for the driver's or the occupant's particular medical or psychological condition.

Remedial action by George, Fred and Sybil was not only confined to driver and passengers. Many car robots were also able to locate and repair vehicle defects. Some could carry out on the spot repairs without having to stop the car. A variety of self-repairing mechanisms, mainly electrical, were already built into the modern 21st century cars. In many cases the repairs were completed as soon as the fault occurred whilst the driver would be quite unaware of them. The robot communicator processor therefore became a kind of super handyman and wise advisor. During a journey of about a hundred miles, a driver reckoned to be interrupted at least a hundred times by their robot voice communicator with comments on both their car's performance and their own. For example, the voice would suddenly break the silence with, 'I'm sorry to report that you've taken the wrong turning and are now heading towards Edinburgh instead of Lands End.' A little later there would be a further enlightened comment from robot George, Fred or Sybil such as, 'I regret to inform you that your rear suspension molifier is sadly adrift and will cause the anti roll system considerable stress unless the electronic Helmholtzer unit is deactivated or re-circuited. Due to this, you may feel sick. I'm instigating the necessary repairs but please check into your local car service depot ASAP for a Helmholtzer transplant. Please acknowledge!' The driver would acknowledge using his key password whereupon his robot would chime in with: 'appointment made, six weeks, date 1st April, I will remind you the day before, entered on your computer diary, car health department notified. I must now remind you to take your XYZ pills for your blood pressure and stomach ulcer. Will there be anything else sir?'

Voice communicator robots in businessmen's cars made human personal secretaries superfluous. Robots were much quicker, more efficient, more polite and didn't take half an hour tea breaks. They never suffered from 'moods' and never wanted the afternoon off to go shopping. They did, however, suffer from the occasional 'aberration' as the experts called them. Aberrations were usually caused by a micro-mini chip going awry. The usual result was that George, Fred or Sybil would get language problems and sound very deep and throaty, as if they were coming down with some kind of computerised stroke. They would also tend to mix complaints. The driver would be diagnosed as having a dropped axle or suffering from low hydraulic pressure. The motor car would be sent to the repair centre for treatment for its ulcers or to have a vitamin B12 injection. So things were not always straightforward and efficient as the artificially intelligent processor experts would have people believe. There were many instances of people being operated on in error just because the computerised robot had recommended a major servicing with change of filters. One person had a brain operation because the robot communicator reported he had a blocked cylinder head.

However, despite the disadvantages, most people felt that the latest robot communicators in cars were a Godsend and a real sign of progress. What did it matter if drivers had to spend most of the time answering the robots to give their 'key word' of acknowledgement. As long as it meant safer travelling, people didn't mind if robots arranged their lives for them. People had faith that the experts knew what was good for them and had programmed the robot's brain accordingly. The artificially intelligent psychologists, for example, were the experts who advised at what point people's brainwaves indicated that they were incapable of safe driving. They selected and monitored brainwaves that showed when people were too tired, too dosed up with mood pills, suffering from hypertension or some other ailment, or were just on the brink of exploding road rage.

Experts from the Lorry Driver's Union told their members when they had to stop and rest. More rest periods seemed to have been introduced each year for the past 100 years so that lorry drivers now spent more time snoozing in lay-bys than driving the lorries. For this reason the government had to build more and more lay-bys until they joined up and many people used them as another road. Then there were the traffic control experts who decided how fast people could drive on certain roads. The experts decided that there should not only be road speed limits but also people were to be limited to driving at a specified maximum speed according to their individual driving skills and health status. People with one leg were only permitted to drive at a snail's pace, as were people with one defective eye. Those of a nervous disposition and those suffering from some other serious incapacity were also included in this dubious category. Drivers who had just passed their driving test were permitted to drive a little faster and people who had driven for years without an accident were allowed to drive at the highest limit. It was the AI processor experts who categorised each person and decided on their particular speed limit. It all depended on medical and psychological records together with driving aptitude test results.

Then there were the dieticians and medical experts who decided how overweight a driver must be before they were prevented from driving a vehicle. They were also assumed to be the experts at deciding just when a driver's awareness was seriously impaired through overeating at a motorway service station café. Usually it didn't take a lot of overeating for the onset of this to occur. The meals, like those at early railway stations, were notorious for these and other unmentionable effects. The opticians were the experts who decided whether to stop a colour-blind person from driving in a coloured world and whether to give him a low speed limit. Doctors were assumed to be expert at deciding at what point a person's reactions were too slow for safety. Also how they were affected by alcohol or mood pill consumption. As many people were now addicted to taking large quantities of both, these decisions were important for road safety. Other experts involved included the official education officers who were apparently expert in deciding whether passing grades A to Z was sufficient educational prowess to permit someone to drive. A high standard of education seemed to be necessary just to be able to read and understand the countless numbers of road signs. There seemed to be thousands of new signs every week, all in different colours, shapes and sizes indicating all kinds of different warnings and directions. Many people thought that someone on the Council must be addicted to trying to cover every inch of the landscape with them.

Then there were the mechanical aptitude testers who were the experts in deciding whether people had the aptitude to drive. Many aptitude testers were of the opinion that 90% of the population shouldn't be driving at all. As this was impractical, the aptitude testers who thought this way were given early retirement at 25, so that people could still use their cars and the government could still collect their road taxes and fines. People with grade 2c vision were only allowed to drive in daylight and would be warned by their personal robot processor whenever they contravened this stipulation. Most people had some affliction or other and these, together with vehicle speeds, were monitored by the car robot processor which reported all indiscretions and breaking of rules to the central police processor, called Big Bill, the legislative relation of Big Mother.

People didn't object to the new legislation. Most were of the opinion that it was for everyone's safety. In fact, people in the 21st-century were so health conscious that it became something of a status symbol to have more health monitoring devices than one's neighbour. Many people even had tiny undetectable earphones fitted under the skin so that they could listen to their health monitor all the time. They felt safer and more secure in the knowledge that their own personal Fred, George or Sybil would always be providing them with a running commentary of their driving and ailments. This facility was very popular with women, especially the more elderly, who always enjoyed discussing their complaints with each other. It meant that they could become more closely acquainted with their arthritis and hysterectomies and could indulge in better discussions of their problems with their friends.

Personal health monitors became very popular by the middle of the 21st century. Many people became addicted to their use and became the new hypochondriacs. But unlike those of earlier centuries, they were encouraged by their robot advisors to maintain a vigil. People listened in to their bodily and psychological performances whilst standing, sitting, walking, driving, working or in leisure activities that took up most of the time. If they didn't have time during the day to watch their monitor, they watched a recording of it in the evening. They could then study all their responses, biological and mental, whilst working at their electronic paperwork at the home office, (few people went to work at the office,) or when pottering in the garden or even when swimming in the swimming pool. Listening to the private commentaries on health became more popular with people than listening to the Jimmy Young radio show of the 20th-century. Moreover, the health monitors were much more interesting to listen to. It was just like listening to a friend who was concerned for your well being and the monitor rarely mentioned when it had passed information to the police processors about exceeding speed limits or about other indiscretions. And when it did, it whispered the details very quietly and politely. The good things were that the robot monitor would not only let you know when your blood pressure was above the limits, but would immediately come up with a proposed remedy. In this way the monitor became the personal doctor, a doctor with whom you didn't have to make an appointment four weeks beforehand. You could also have a detailed discussion with your personal monitor about any of your ailments, without any fear of being hustled out of the doctor's surgery in one minute flat carrying a box of pills to which you found yourself allergic and which you would leave untouched for months.

Listening to your own personal robot health monitor went something like this. 'Good morning, health monitor. How are you functioning, this morning?'

'At peak performance, master.'

'How am I this morning?'

'Not quite as good as yesterday, master. Your liver's a little sluggish after last night's party. Take some of your X11 before breakfast. Blood sugar and pressure need correcting. Don't take any more Y3 mood pills for at least three hours as you overdid them last night. Blood alcohol content also too high. I conclude you had a good time last night. I recommend cancelling all business meetings this morning because your energy and awareness levels are below standard and will affect your intelligence quotient. Your recent memory implant is not suffering from rejection, but is not being helped by your present condition. Temperature gradients indicate a high spot in the molar region showing that you may suffer from toothache before the day is out. Recommend the dental processor clinic for another live tooth transplant. Appointment made for 3.00 p.m. Extrapolation of your efficiency curve for today indicates a peak at 5.00 p.m. when any important work or discussion should take place. Bodily metabolism indicates that it would be inadvisable for you to stroke any cats today as this will bring on your Z350 allergy– also don't water any household plants, don't have eggs and bacon for breakfast and remember to put out the refuse bags as well as the cat. Allergy Z4512 is not predominant today so you can eat fish and sterilised vegetables if you like – but under no circumstance eat any turnips or nuts. And only use Y36667111 type recipes. Please acknowledge. Key word.'

'I acknowledge.'

'Recipes Y366677111 now extracted from computer data file and transferred to automatic cooker robot for analysis scanning. Your meals for today have now been programmed in accordance with your known preferences and current medical requirements. Preventive medicine memory bank scanned and linked to cooker robot. Lunch will be at 2.00 p.m., high tea at 7.30 p.m. Please acknowledge. Key word.'

'I acknowledge. Sybil, I've got a pain in my back, my shoulder and under my heart. Please check to see if I'm liable to have a heart attack today.'

'No master. Heart and blood pressure satisfactory taking into consideration your heavy night out. Temperature and YP ray scanners indicate your Y5 vertebrae are out and require realigning. Please use osteopathic robot 7DD as soon as convenient to reset. Please acknowledge. Key word.'

'I acknowledge.'

Bubbles smiled, then spoke again. "With the introduction of the voice module in car warning systems came the introduction of voice guidance together with map monitors linked to satellite navigational systems. Theoretically these were intended to indicate on a monitor screen map the exact position of the vehicle. The systems were supposed to be particularly useful for many drivers who never seemed to know where they were and would never stop to ask. This was the opinion of the wives anyway. Everyone seemed to be getting lost in the cities, except the taxi drivers, due to all the new one-way streets constructed to make town driving easier. Suddenly a driver could find himself going in the completely opposite direction with no possibility that he would ever find his way back again.

The new navigational aids were also intended to help anyone going on a long journey, such as taking a holiday. In this instance it was a godsend in reducing upsets between husbands and wives, one of whom usually drove whilst the other sat and navigated. Taking wrong turnings were blamed on the navigator by the driver and on the driver by the navigator. The new system allowed both driver and passenger – even back seat drivers – to participate in comparatively quiet conversations with each other instead of the high decibel screaming, which had been the previous norm. Now the driver merely had to follow the processor's navigational instructions. For some people the system seemed to work reasonably well, providing the instrument had first been properly programmed with all the latest road changes and one way streets. However, for those who had neglected to read through and digest the two thousand page instruction manuals and had failed to pre-programme the instruments, found themselves arriving at quite unknown destinations. Others discovered they had got into a new habit of driving down one-way streets in the opposite direction. Some, on the other hand, found they had arrived at a place of the same name that they had programmed in but situated in an entirely different part of the country. Some even found themselves abroad.

There were many such hiccups in the early days. It was usually the incompetence of the human link that caused the trouble. There was usually an instruction manual or video giving all the required details for the motorist to follow but, as with all such literature of the time, it meant not only reading several volumes of encyclopaedic proportions, but often entailed attending night school. People frequently went down with 'brain clog' through spending half the night wading through massive volumes and trying to interpret Japanese and Chinese terminology and strange Indian dialects.

There were finally countless numbers of people claiming sickness benefit because of Stress Induced Appliance Operating or SIAO as the Americans called it. It finally dawned on people that all the new navigational aids introduced to avoid traffic problems had themselves introduced new ones not the least of which were more nervous breakdowns and one-way street pile ups. Eventually the whole matter of the semi-automatic car design was placed in the hands of the AI processors in charge of highways and traffic distribution. The processors responded to the challenge by deciding that the only logical answer was to delete the incompetent link in the system – namely people. The only way forward the processors said, and they proved it mathematically so that none could argue, was to make the motor car completely automatic, more like trains without rails. This, they said, would avoid anyone making mistakes. It would also mean that people wouldn't have to read all those manuals or listen to all those instruction tapes, as automatic cars wouldn't require programming but only talking to occasionally which most people thought they could manage

The automatic cars were also to be designed to be more self-repairing which was good news for everyone except garage owners and mechanics. The news was also well received by the many elderly people then on the planet who just couldn't seem to cope with all the appliance training. It was also hoped that many people would come off the sick list and there would be a reduction of the numbers of neurotics, alcoholics, drug takers and suicides. However, many of the male population, especially husbands, who did manage to get on well with their early programmable navigational aids and gadgets, were hesitant to see them superseded because they had become addicted to the soft purring sexy woman's voice that gave directions, even though they were usually the wrong ones. It was, they said, something they enjoyed listening to in preference to the nagging navigational aid of wives. To give up driving altogether and leave it all to automatic processors was also felt by many males like giving up yet another bit of their masculinity which was getting rather threadbare anyway. However, in spite of these early misgivings, the women and wives, who were all for complete automation of motor vehicles, had their way as was usual both then and now. Moreover, the leading processors in charge of highways and traffic distribution had recommended it, and that was good enough for most people who by now had complete faith in the processors' superhuman knowledge.

It was generally agreed that the thousands of new technological devices that were now required to be programmed in order to be taken notice of, (and this was essential if one was to keep up with everyone else,) were all now getting beyond people. Complete automation, where everything was done for you at a mere vocal command, seemed the answer. It also appeared to be a godsend, especially as the artificially intelligent designers said people would be able to take their hands off the steering wheel, their feet off the pedals and let the vehicle do the rest. The processor motor car would be designed to sense when it needed to pull up or to accelerate or overtake or to pull in for fuel, or to navigate along the most congested one way streets. It would even decide when the person seated in the driving seat, but not really driving, needed a rest. It was thought desirable to still let a person sit in the driving seat in order to avoid panic amongst the passengers if it dawned on them that no one was in control. When the car processor decided the person in the driving seat needed a rest, the vehicle would automatically pull into a Service/Play area and advise the occupants to rest, eat and enjoy themselves.

The car processor would even recommend pills for each passenger to take, having also automatically diagnosed whether they had a touch of car sickness, high blood pressure or nervous debility brought on by feeling a lack of control when relying on the automatic systems. Mood pills were also favoured as these could enhance the overall satisfaction of the journey, especially through traffic jams and at high speeds. It also helped old people to cope with the new automatic system without panic and encouraged them to sleep through the whole journey as recommended by the processor in charge. Diluted mood pills were given to children to keep them quiet, a godsend to parents. The result was to be paradise on the roads which themselves were being transformed and modified on the recommendations of the AI processors.

Motor cars, at least the old petrol driven types, were finally superseded by a variety of non-toxic modes of transport. or NTMs as the Americans called them. Ultasonics were used to stop cars colliding with each other when in the 'hands off steering wheel' and 'foot off accelerator' modes and Electric/Solar Hybrids, and Hydrogen powered vehicles became the fashion. Hydrogen was non toxic and could now be produced easily from water, of which there was an unending supply in the oceans. Many roads were modified to assist with the latest methods of automatic propulsion. Propulsion and information lines, as they were called, were embedded in or laid alongside roads. Roads then became superhighways that were a cross between a road and a railway but which were in fact far in advance of both. They were new products of the mid-21st century. The new highways and their vehicles were under the direct overall control of the master AI processors covering vehicular distribution throughout the country. This control was eventually extended to cover the whole of the globe.

When this occurred everyone felt greatly relieved as it was hoped that road accidents would become things of the past together with traffic jams, pollution and so on. People were overjoyed at the prospect, even though it now meant they had to book their journeys at least 3 months in advance in order that all vehicle users could have access to the main roads in accordance with the processors' overall plan for the safety of everyone. It was rather like the NHS in the 20th century when people had to be booked in for their vital operations six months in advance when they had three months to live. The majority of large vehicular highways could only be used by prior reservation through home processors directly linked with the Big Mother Network of AI processors. As time went on an increasing number of vehicular highways became subject to this special 'Toll Pattern' or TP as the Americans called it. Finally, with the increase in numbers of vehicles, it meant booking up for quite short journeys as well as for longer routes where automatic navigational aid was a legal requirement.

In order to maintain the business sector it was considered essential to treat the movement of business traffic as a priority. It soon became apparent that in order to achieve this, some sort of rationing of highway space must be inaugurated– at least that is what the AI processors in charge said would be required. It was all down to their calculations, which could not be refuted, as there were none to calculate better. Private users of vehicles were therefore limited to only a short time each week, generally an hour. For longer times it was necessary for people to apply for special permission and a licence. This of course was always necessary where long journeys were to be made. As a result many people didn't bother to travel to the local supermarket for food. Instead they made purchases from home via the processor Holographic Retail Services Network where everything could be examined and even smelled and touched in full 3D imagery before purchase. In fact, people didn't leave their homes very much at all. The essential requirements including entertainment were all available at a click of a button or on verbal request through vastly updated and improved home processors."

Bubbles blinked her eyes in quite an unusual way. Immediately, a new holographic scene revealed an area of open land that extended towards hazy blue distant mountains. Everywhere were strange animals, reptiles and flying creatures. All were quite unknown to Gotama, although some of the winged varieties resembled pictures he had seen of Dinosaurs. Some were so huge that the earth shook with every step they took.

Gotama's guide turned to him. "I see you are surprised to see these ancient animals all alive and well. They were all resurrected by 22nd century scientists who found ways to reverse evolution by manipulating DNA and recreating ancient genes. They have given long lost legs back to the snake for instance and by deleting bird genes that control the production of feathers they have resurrected genes that once produced scales of their dinosaur ancestors hundreds of millions of years in the past. In fact, the scientists reversed history and produced incredible numbers of species long forgotten and long since extinct. Using similar techniques, the scientists also created many ancient ancestors in the human evolutionary chain, ancestors dating back through countless millions of years. Many of the resurrected life forms then interbred, which created completely new types never before seen on planet Earth. Then people began to experiment in new social and sexual relationships with these long forgotten pre-human ancestors. Some even tried marrying them. But communication was difficult, particularly between the ancient grunts and the more modern speech, not to mention trying to control the more aggressive tendencies of the early ancestors. However, in many cases there was little difference between the ancestor's behaviour and that of modern man's Saturday night punch up in the pub.

The robot scientists once again had a field day with their genetic engineering techniques to try to eliminate aggressive and unseemly tendencies in the offspring of the ancient and modern. The result was a watered down version of the ancient creature, particularly in the behaviour department. Creatures that normally would want to tear you limb from limb at the slightest provocation would now smile timidly and even, with some encouragement and practice, be taught to say 'Have a nice day.' However, they said such things with eyes glazed over as though they weren't really conversant with the terminology and would have preferred to make their usual roar of nastiness before they had you for dinner."

Bubbles then pointed to some completely new holographics now forming in front of them. Gotama was astonished to witness such strange images. They were of human forms but quite drastically modified. Some were at least twelve feet tall, others were like pygmies. Several possessed heads with appendages in place of the usual sensory apertures. In place of ears some had strange new developments. The nose too was of altered shape and in the forehead there appeared to be strange clefts and indentations as though there were new additional sense receptors in addition to the basic five senses. There were even odd protuberances from the top and back of the head, all of which resulted in people with quite different shapes and forms. The sight of a small boy with strange winged boots particularly intrigued Gotama. He seemed to skim above the ground like a levitating surfer. Another holographic image was of a woman who appeared to have bird-like wings neatly folded behind her back which opened up to reveal a gull-like contour and breadth of wingspan at least six times her body height. In a mere moment she spread her gorgeous wings, which seemed inlaid with vibrating coloured gems, and soared effortlessly upwards. Thereupon another entrant made its debut in the form of a man with a weird streamlined head and body to match. He possessed fin-like structures that gave him a peculiar fish-like appearance. It was quite obvious that he was much better adapted to swimming in the sea than walking on land. He could be seen gliding gracefully under water at tremendous speeds whereas on land he became like a waddling penguin. It was also apparent that he could breathe quite easily under water by means of some kind of natural gill outgrowths. His body had a distinctly smooth and phosphorescent glow and changed colour like a chameleon.

Another group of strange humans with modified bodily structures came into view. They possessed large pulsating chests as though their lungs had been genetically modified. They also walked, or rather sprung, on long elastic legs that gave them a giant spring to their steps, like leaping frogs, but not so pretty. Gotama was informed that they were genetically modified humans adapted to live on Mars, where gravity and the terraformed atmospheric pressure were much reduced. Bubbles glanced at him. "I think they must have difficulty finding the right stockings for their elastic legs," she said, with a smile. "I'm told it caused a lot of problems for the socks and braces trade. Tight braces caused mischief for men in full stride"

Finally, swarms of human creatures came and went in the holographic processor, a vast array of diverse modifications of the human form. Some ran at enormous speeds, some flew in the skies like birds, some leaped over mountains, some swam under the sea, and some could function without difficulty in temperatures that would either freeze or boil a normal human. There was another section of the holographic arena where people who had been injured or where arms and legs had for some reason been cut off, were quietly growing new limbs and other appendages as naturally as a new leaf sprouts from a tree, though much faster. Indeed the speed of growth was such that it could be seen to be happening in quite a miraculous way.

In another area of the holographic space there were forms that seemed almost human but not exactly so. They were developing from a kind of nebulous froth contained in what appeared to be a gigantic incubator. The incubator was evidently producing not just one creature at a time, but many. There were probably at least a hundred humans in each batch that were being moulded by some kind of processor to become what appeared to Gotama to be clones, as all of them appeared to be identical in form. Yet each batch was different. One batch possessed characteristics quite unlike the next. There must have been hundreds and hundreds of automatically produced clone-like replicas, some with wings, some with fins, some dark skinned, some light, some tall and slender, some short and stocky. Each had strange appendages projecting from their heads and bodies the like of which Gotama had never before witnessed. He turned to Bubbles. "What does all this mean?" he asked breathlessly.

Bubbles turned and spoke softly. "The images we have shown you here represent just a very minute fraction of the genetically engineered and cloned humans. During the 21st and 22nd centuries there were countless numbers of modified genetic structures designed by the world central processors. As you know, for millions of years Natural Selection as outlined by Darwin and Wallace had moulded and adapted the many species of life on Earth to their own particular environment. With the onset of the new genetic sciences it became possible for mankind, or rather the artificially intelligent processors, to change animal, bird, fish, insect and plant species and their varieties into new ones that had never before existed. Changes, which in Nature would have probably taken millions of years to perfect, were now made almost on demand.

As soon as it became possible for scientists to modify genes to produce babies with higher intelligence and healthier, stronger bodies, there was a frantic rush by all those people who could afford to pay for gene therapy to have alterations carried out on their offspring. It wasn'tt long before people with the highest marks in good citizenship (previously called the financially well off, a definition now taboo) were establishing a completely new breed of higher grade humans who, by means of their superior intelligence and physical prowess, were fast becoming the dominant members of the race. The lower grades, (previously called poorer) people however, remained relatively unchanged, being more prone to the old type diseases and were generally of lower intelligence. They eventually became downtrodden, demoralised and dominated by the new artificially created super-classes. A vast and cataclysmic gulf, which became continually wider, occurred between the two classes of humans until at last the differences became so wide that two completely separate varieties of human species emerged, similar to the differences between man and his lower counterpart the chimpanzee.

There were also other subtle alterations taking place. The new genetically engineered humans were, of course, products of the artificially intelligent processors who possessed vastly superior intellects to the cleverest genetically engineered human. In such an environment, wealthy parents not only had to chose genetic modifications that would improve the intelligence of their children, they also had to include genetically engineered behaviour to ensure that their children would conform to all of the processors' dictates. The dominant one being an instinctive desire to conform to all the rules and regulations of society with non-aggression coming a close second. . It was therefore the artificially intelligent processors who now moulded people in their image and ruled planet Earth.

Although it seemed at first sight as though each well off parent with high good citizenship grades could freely decide whether to have a boy or a girl or something in between, or a child with blond or black hair, skilled at playing the violin or bassoon and with the highest available IQ, it was really the artificially intelligent processors who made the final decisions, because it was they who could study and analyse the mountainous volumes of information required to assess how and in what best direction a particular offspring could be improved upon. Parents finally just had to accept the processors' recommendations just as in earlier times patients had to accept the decision of their doctor as to the best treatment for them. Human freedom of choice had therefore been eroded in a very subtle way. Man and woman had in fact become prisoners of their own clever creation, the artificially intelligent processor.

A great many people, primarily the well off, were now living a lot longer as a result of gene modification. The average lifespan soon rocketed to 200 years. Some reached the 300 year mark. Those who lived for over 150 years had only reached that age because they were half-bionic usually with an accompanying Artificially Intelligent Sensory Module installed in the brain. Such implants were by now carried out as easily as the old fashioned hip replacements. Some old people had to rely so heavily on these intelligence/sensory modules that they became mere puppets whose strings were pulled by the surgically implanted processors. Many such people had their implants linked to satellite communication networks for their own safety in order that they could find their way home.

Many were fitted with memory chips to compensate for the usual deterioration in the brain's biological mechanisms that occurred nearly always at or before 150 years of age. This was found necessary despite the vast array of memory enhancing drugs then available. The memory enhancing modules were usually combined with anti-confusion transplants because so many people of this age were found wandering aimlessly and finding great difficulty in knowing exactly who they were. Many also suffered the onset of boredom because all the really important tasks had been taken over by the latest robot artificially intelligent processors. The processors were, of course, always inventing new games to keep people happy and to try to keep them out of trouble

Finally the processors came up with the latest in a constant string of new ideas. They used their newly gained powers of genetic engineering to recreate the human form in many different mutant designs in order to widen the scope of people's lust for pleasure pursuits. There was now little else for people to do. Many played golf on their newly invented home 'solid image creator' an advanced form of the virtual reality scopes of earlier years. People played golf at home because the queues of people waiting to tee off at golf courses were now so long that it took a half a day to start. The home solid image creator produced a golf course set in a beautiful landscape. It was not only possible to play a round of golf against any leading player, but it was also possible to win or lose every time as was one's whim. You could also get as a hole in one if you desired. Such were the wonders of science. Some people who didn't mind waiting around for most of the day still went to the outside golf course for the fresh air, although this too was now available in the healthiest form when using the home solid image creator instruments. It seemed as though every man's whim could be catered for. Even sex had been given a different emphasis. The Karma Sutra was considered conservative compared with the alternatives dreamed up by the AI processors using the latest robot holography. Physical sex with the latest sex-pot robots was available in the most exotic forms with or without partners and with fully adjustable orgasms.

There seemed to be very little in human activity that the processor Image Creators could not emulate and improve upon. All the five senses of Man, the portals through which all the pleasurable sensations were funnelled, had been catered for. Everything possible had been tried in order to satisfy people's hedonism. But there was still something missing. No one seemed really satisfied or happy. Something more, something even newer than the newest pleasure pursuits was required. What could be the answer? It was then that the AI processors, particularly those in charge of genetic and clone engineering, thought up new methods of satisfying people's addictive greed and lust for pleasure. The result took the form of unique processor designs of new appendages, which could be grown on people in order to provide them with new thrills of all kinds. Appendages like the wings of a seagull were grown on people who really wanted to get off the ground and fly. They wanted to feel the nature of true flight and not just sit in an aeroplane and drift off to sleep. There were flippers and gills for those who relished the underwater life. Numerous underwater communities of human mutants, or HMs as the Americans called them, had evolved into undersea towns and villages. Underwater farms where seafood's of all kinds were grown beneath the seas and oceans of the world had become a valued source of food in the mid 21st century. Laboratories had also been set up on the ocean floors where intensive study of the undersea environment was carried out

About this time there was also a completely new innovation in scientific progress. As a result of great strides in the knowledge of gravitational forces it became possible to provide certain people with 'anti-gravity' levitation implants. They were primarily for those who were allergic to feeling heavy, especially women struggling home under the weight of their latest acquisitions from the designer wardrobe super-shops. Anti-gravity implants were also very helpful to mountain climbers and skiers who wanted an alternative to chair lifts, which were always full. And for those obsessed with walking on water it was the ultimate thrill. Anti-gravity was also a godsend to hikers, who could cross over lakes, rivers and ravines without getting their feet wet. NASA also found the anti-gravity implants essential for teaching their astronauts how to walk on Asteroids and the Moon and other outreaches of space, where gravity was much lower.

Many genetic modifications to improve the existing five senses and to widen their scope also became available. New worlds became visible as higher and lower wavelengths than visible light became part of the standard sensory perception. Night vision without having to use an external instrument became the fashion. This, together with telescopic and zoom facilities gave many people new interests and new pleasures. It also encouraged moon gazing without a telescope besides snooping into other peoples business. Colours viewed through the basic five senses were now seen to be quite ephemeral, almost unreal. They were transient and partial at best. Objects viewed at other frequencies than light were found to be quite different and revealed another world of new dimensions. The x-ray world for instance was especially interesting. The trouble was that you could see everybody's operations. X-ray vision was therefore not recommended for everyone. It was usually favoured by people like the selection committee of the Tate Gallery, who were renowned to possess that kind of vision.

Sprouting wings became popular for many, especially for people like mountain climbers who wanted to climb but didn't much like the trek back down. Many climbers, especially the bad ones, found them invaluable whenever they fell off mountains. Unfortunately so many people began to grow them that the airways began to get congested. People also became frustrated by the poor flying ability of hordes of people of 150 years of age whose wings were a little on the shaky side. Moreover, their brain wiring was sometimes a little frayed. Increasingly the frustrated fliers would lose their temper and kick the 150 year olds up the rear. It was most disconcerting for many of the veterans when the air rage became an epidemic. The punishment for such air rage was usually to have their wings clipped for a year and to be confined to pedestrian activities only. They also had to attend a thought and motivation clinic.

Therefore, for safety reasons, all the mutant appendages such as wings, flippers, extra sensory brain lobes, etc., had to be checked after the allotted number of flying or swimming hours had been completed. Special processor certificates were fed into the giant Big Mother AI processor system to confirm that such checks had been carried out. It was an MOT with a difference. The difference being that the later certificates also covered humans' genetic appendages and bionics and a few thousand more checks besides. However, these inspections became a worry for some people, especially those in the 150 to 250 age group who were frequently more bionic than biological. Also there were those who had more purchasing power than sense who tried to incorporate so many different appendages in order to satisfy every possible pleasure and in an effort to out do everyone else in the hedonistic race for new sensory experience. They discovered to their dismay that they had to be serviced every other week and many complained that they were always having repair bills."

Bubbles continued. "I have told you about the early efforts of the genetic scientists to prolong people's lifespan. By the mid 21st century they had managed to extend it to an average of 150 years and in some instances to 250 years. However, difficulties were encountered when trying to improve on these limits using only genetic engineering. Much later it became possible to manipulate Time itself in order to fool people into thinking they were living even longer. These techniques, together with the latest developments in Virtual Reality projections and mind bending methods, enabled many people to artificially create extended Time Patterns, or TPs as the Americans called them. Time Patterns can best be described as comparable with the Time distortions experienced by astronauts when travelling near the speed of light. You will no doubt remember that even in the 20th century Einstein showed how an astronaut travelling at these conditions would be subject to a different Time sequence from his fellows back on Earth. His Time sequence would slow down in comparison so that he would be younger than his fellows when he arrived back on Earth. Time therefore is not a constant, and eventually the AI processor scientists discovered ways in which Time could be artificially distorted to make it appear that a person was younger than his earthly time age and to fool his own metabolism and cellular structure. This meant that a person could then live that much longer. Later it was found that the human mind itself could influence Time in ways never before dreamed of. By means of combinations of all such methods and others which I will not mention here as they would be quite beyond your present understanding, it became possible during the 22nd century to extend the average human life span to 500 years and beyond.

Providing that the people of the world do not destroy themselves in the next few years, it will be possible for earth scientists to reach such technologies. By that time, life and consciousness will not be as you now know it. That which you now term artificial intelligence will have evolved into a new super intelligent species which will be the ruling power on the planet Earth. People themselves will be forged into inseparable links with this higher species. People will no longer be purely biological. They will contain much that can be defined as bionic and artificial. Even parts of their brains and thinking mechanisms will have implants and be linked inseparably to the governing AI processors. The artificially intelligent processors will then also contain what you now term inorganic and organic materials so they will be indistinguishable from a truly living organism. There will in this sense be a kind of coming together between humans and the Artificially Intelligent processors.

The relationship between pure energy, thought and matter will by that time have been thoroughly investigated and new thinking vessels will live and breathe. They will be like photons of light that will be able to manifest themselves through wide ranges of pure wave energy, as well as through a physical instrument like the current human body. Amalgamated thought and sensory patterns, which you now call individual personalities will, by that time be kept in special storage vehicles. The best way I can describe such advances to you, is by asking you to imagine the storing of thoughts, sensations and human experiences, not just in biological structures like human brains, but rather in artificially constructed vessels. Such storage could be similar to the way in which you store your CDs and videos in the late 20th century. The storage facilities for human thought and sensory experience will, however, be of such complexity that it will involve new scientific laws which have not yet been dreamed of in your time.

I hope you will forgive me for not going any further into the future because such knowledge would be quite meaningless to you and could moreover be quite frightening for you. It must already be apparent to you that new forms of artificial intelligence instigated by man himself are already in many subtle ways taking over the governing of planet Earth. It will not be long before processors are given the power to think and act for themselves and will be quite beyond the control of humankind. The Artificially Intelligent processor networks will soon be left to evolve in ways they themselves consider best. The overall result will be a new species of life spanning the globe like a giant octopus whose tentacles will reach into everyone's home and into everyone's heart. It will evolve into a new global organism whose powers will be greater than any organism or life form that has previously inhabited the Earth. Just as a human is considered something greater than the sum of its parts, so the global organism will also be greater than its parts. You are already aware of the Gaia philosophy that interprets nature and life on Earth as a super controlling and self-balancing living system. The new world of artificial Intelligence can be considered as an extension of this vast control system. People, as individuals will soon be rather like minute cells within the new giant living and controlling world processor.

This latest development can be regarded as another step in natural evolution. This time, however, the new and controlling animal species will not be mankind, but an artificially created intelligence, a super Frankenstein. It is destined to rule the world and ultimately its future offspring will colonise and rule other planets circling other stars. It will make contact with other alien civilisations many of which will themselves be governed by artificially or synthetically established forms of consciousness."

Bubbles fell silent for a few moments. Gotama interjected, "But what's the purpose of it all?" he remarked thoughtfully.

Bubbles looked at him. "It's possible that there is no purpose," she said. "Only that created in a mind. Each person's ambition is his or her own purpose. Each desire fulfilled is as a result of a purpose. Can we say then in this sense, the universe has a purpose? If the Universe has inherent mind stuff within it and is something more than the sum of its parts – in other words is like the human – then the whole created imagery of the universe could be the result of an inherent purpose fathomed only by a universal mind.

Ever since human life began, people have conjectured on such subjects without reaching any tangible conclusions. Some thought there must be a purposeful God who could be placated by asking his son to put in a good word for them. Many saw the flowers, trees and sunsets and sang *All Things Bright and Beautiful* and concluded that there must be a purpose in it all. Then Mr Darwin came along and pointed out that all those things that were apparently bright and beautiful in the Earth's living kingdom, just ate one another as fast as they were able. No living creature was exempt from the rule of Natural Selection which was a polite way of saying 'eat your neighbour or get eaten yourself.' And those that eat more neighbours without getting eaten themselves can pass on their particular aptitude for eating neighbours to their kids, so that they too can follow Mum and Dad's example. On the face of it, people, being the worst kind of predators of all, would not seem to be the best choices for any possible associations with any fine and beautiful purposes that the universe had in mind.

Many people who listened to Darwin felt convinced by his arguments and rather disappointed in the overall plan of things, especially in the apparent pointlessness of it all. Was it credible for instance that eating each other was the only teleological thought in the mind of the super-owner and administrator of the universe? Couldn't he or she think up something just a little bit better as a purpose for a universe? It seemed fairly certain too that life, wherever it existed in other planetary systems throughout the countless galaxies, would evolve similarly by eating each other. So the conclusion was that there must be millions upon millions of other places where the purpose was just to eat each other in order to survive for a brief moment in order to eat each other all over again. Surely a being of super-intelligence could have thought of a better way to run the place? Pain was another problem. Why did the super administrators deal out such large quantities of the stuff?

Most people looked at the problem philosophically. They thought that if you wanted pleasure you must have something to compare it with, and pain seemed to be the answer. You could also only have love if you accepted hate in the deal. Otherwise you just wouldn't know what it was like. In some ways this was rather strange. So it was with all the world of opposites in which everyone lived. You could only be hot providing you could also be frozen to the marrow. You could only get above something if you knew what the underneath was like. Who, you might well ask, in their right mind would bother to think up such an arrangement? Surely not a super-intelligent power like a universe. However, stranger things are always around the corner. Without thinking of the past, these people said it was impossible to think about the future. And in thinking about the future it was necessary to create a purpose. So was it the world of opposites that introduced in us the idea of purpose in things?

But why go to the lengths of creating billions of galaxies, stars and planets merely for things to eat each other and live for a moment in a world of opposites where one could never be just hot, but had to be hot in comparison to something colder, in order to know all about it? And for such mediocre purposes. Either the universal administrator must be quite incompetent, or the universe must be the biggest no-go area of pure anarchy ever contemplated.

Not only do *creatures* eat each other but scientists say that even *galaxies* eat each other if given the chance. And black holes have a simply voracious appetite. Eating each other therefore seems to be the rule rather than the exception in the strange dances of the universe. If the Earth and its occupants were the only ones subject to this 'eating each other syndrome' it would perhaps be acceptable, but when galaxies, black holes, stars and billions of planets are involved in such antics, it seems unforgivable, or very peculiar to say the least.

However, people have always been quick to alter the facts to accord with what they really want to believe. And so it was said by many that in spite of the unruly and painful nature of evolution Darwin style, there was still a place for a benign and softhearted universal administrator. Such people brought to their aid some of the scientific knowledge of the time in the guise of men like Pythagorus, Appolonius, Sir Isaac Newton, Einstein and many more, who proclaimed that the universe was mathematically based and that was why we could understand it. The fact also implied that the Creator himself was a mathematician and was therefore quite civilised. But it seemed to imply that whoever was pulling the universal strings also knew a thing or two. Like how to make DNA and how to put together a few nuclear reactions in stars in order to provide a reasonable central heating system for planets and some light for people to see by. This was good news for many people who had begun to wonder just how such a diabolical state of affairs had come about. It still didn't explain whether there was a final purpose for everything created, but it did ease the minds of many, particularly the scientists, who for many years had been making discoveries of all sorts which seemed to put a pretty bleak outlook on things. Especially when they discovered that men and women weren't really different from animals after all.

Moreover, people had only come on the scene quite recently cosmologically speaking. The tiniest speck of time, a mere fraction of a fraction of a second, if the age of Earth's animal life was compared to say an hour. It was not only this that deflated man's ego and seemed to knock him off his pedestal. Several astronomers had discovered that the Earth too was not on centre stage. Even the Sun was but a microscopic dot amongst billions of other stellar systems many of them larger and brighter. The human species was therefore relegated to the point of total insignificance in the general scheme of things.

It was understandable therefore why any universal creator didn't bother two hoots about such minute and pathetic creatures. Many people decided that was probably why their prayers never seemed to be answered. The chief administrator, if indeed there was one, probably had far too much on his plate. After all, when you're trying to create a few billion galaxies and measure off distances of a few million light years at a time, its not very likely that you'll be interested in answering Auntie Flo's request for help to pay her gas bill, or to clear up Uncle Joe's tummy trouble. Life and death and all that goes on in between, although important to the people participating, because its all they've got, couldn't possibly be of the same importance to the super-administrator of everything. An administrator who seemed content to let things eat each other and allowed more people to die each year from so-called natural causes than ever were killed by people themselves during their world wars.

These were difficult facts to reconcile. However, despite such difficulties, people just couldn't believe that things were all bad. There's always an opposite to be found, the optimists said. Where there's a Voltaire there's always a Professor Pangloss. Where there's bad there must be something good. And so people invented God and his opposite the Devil. However, it did seem to many that the Devil had a special advantage in that he usually played all the best tunes, especially when it came to temptations, most of which were under the Devil's jurisdiction. They were not only tunes that people just had to dance to; they were always in the top ten.

Thus it seemed to many that the universe and creation in general was like a two-sided coin – it had its good and bad facets. It had its sunsets and frosty mornings. It had its quiet breezes under the stars and the soft touch of a loved one. It had beauty and magnificence. It had tenderness and love. It had the wonder of the vastness and minuteness of created things. It had sensitivity, music, light and laughter. But the miracle wrought by people being conscious of themselves and outward things also had its darker shadows of tragedy, pain, grief, disease and death. For all things wrought by change were impermanent and therefore fundamentally unsatisfactory and flawed in that they involved coming into being and dying. Nothing was exempt.

People were generally of the opinion that they could cope with or even enjoy the coming into being bit, but it was the dying bit that seemed to unsettle them and, in particular, the manner in which they did it. They just didn't understand why a benevolent creator should have introduced such an anti-climax. Even the optimists had trouble with the idea. Mortality was definitely a stumbling block in the scheme of things. 'What have we done to deserve it?', they said. 'Old Fred, he deserved that sort of treatment, but not me!' The optimists pointed out that you could only be conscious of things if they were moving or changing. If there were no change there would be nothing ever to see, hear, smell, feel, taste or know. And if there's change, as there must be in order to be conscious, then there must be change from the new to the old. New things must come into being and then die like waves on the sea. At every moment everything was changing in different ways. There was therefore a coming into being and a dying at every moment in everything, in every creature and in every person. This was the nature of things, of people and of the universe. Nothing was exempt. That which worked through creation could only do so through change and all that it implied.

Of course, when people realised exactly what they were up against in a changing world, they also realised they didn't like some of its accompanying implications. If they were changing all the time, they couldn't possibly be anything in particular. This worried some of the more contemplative who had previously believed they were a kind of unchanging soul. Many persisted in their belief in the soul, but where it was and of what substance was a mystery. They felt uncomfortable in trying to think they were nothing in particular, as it left them with a kind of bottomless sensation – a kind of 'not this, not that' notion. Some however did manage to assimilate the idea of 'pure change' which led them to realise that there was no permanent isolated object anywhere to be found. All things were intimately conjoined in one vast network of interrelated changing events, so that, in the final analysis, all people and all things formed one gigantic oceanic stream – the universe. Could it possibly be that there was some kind of guiding hand beneath the oceanic waves, an administrator within the seamless coat? If there was, could there be an inherent purpose after all?"

We know that, in addition to the fixed laws of cause and effect, there are also many random and chance happenings in the universe, which would seem, at first sight, to imply that there's no mind inspired rational purpose in things. In order that Purpose can exist, there must be 'Mind' to create it. One cannot exist without the other. However, randomness, seemingly without a purpose, may still require 'Mind' in order to bring it to reality and to know its nature, otherwise it would be without definition or substantiality. If there was 'no-one' or no 'Mind' to know what was there, what would exist? Can anything exist without a 'Mind' to see and know it?

I'm reminded of a poem by Ronald Knox who said:-

> There was once a man who said, God
> Must find it exceedingly odd,
> If he finds that this tree
> Continues to be,
> When there's no one about in the quad.

And if all things, including randomness and chance, need some kind of 'Cosmic Awareness' or 'Mind' as a ground, in order to exist and if 'Mind' also equates, in some kind of way, with purposeful activity, then perhaps the universe does embody 'Purpose' somewhere within its evolutionary processes. And if such a cosmic ground of awareness exists, it would be like – to quote from The Goon Show – 'A floor so cunningly laid that no matter where you stood it was always under your feet.'

However, it would also seem that in an infinite universe, there would be nothing outside it. Everything that could possibly exist would already be contained within it. There would therefore be nothing outside itself to achieve and there would be little or no point in it being purposeful. It would be like an old man, with vague similarities to Victor Meldrew, who had seen and known it all before and decided everything was 'old hat.' 'Another repeat programme?' he would shout, 'I just don't believe it!' There's just no point in watching them any more. I can't see the purpose of going over and over the same worn out old stories.

Another man called Mr Gay expressed a slightly different opinion regarding the possibility of a universal purpose in things, when he wrote his own epitaph. It read, -

Life's a jest and all things show it;
I thought so once, and now I know it."

Bubbles smiled and her eyes sparkled. "These are philosophical subjects of a very special transcendental kind that are interesting, but are really unanswerable at your current level of thinking. So let us move on," she said. "We were talking a few moments ago about the future, particularly for people when finally under the domination of the Big Mother World processor AI Intelligence. As we projected further into the future it became apparent that people had more leisure time than ever before. By the end of the 21st century artificially intelligent robots finally carried out all manufacturing and services. Many people were now living to 200 and even 500 years of age and were tired of the usual pleasures, which they had experienced over and over. They now needed different leisure pursuits, not just the usual sex with their holographic creations or flying to the moon for a holiday or painting images as large as mount Everest.

Satellite bubble environments were mass-produced. Most were designed for pleasure. They comprised many massive dome-shaped earth satellites. Huge enclosed volumes contained complete towns, together with an accompanying encapsulated countryside. Many millions of people could be housed at any one time. All the satellites were placed in different orbits and at different distances from the Earth. Some were also positioned to orbit the Moon, Mars, Venus and the Sun. Both Mars and Venus had by this time been terraformed to enable air-breathing creatures, including man, to live on these planets. People were generally allowed to choose which satellite bubble environment they preferred. Some chose those with environments like the Caribbean because they had spent past holidays there. Some chose environments more akin to their particular leisure interests such as those specialising in theatrical entertainment or athletics for instance. Some bubbles were noted for their excellence in bionic and other synthetic biological repairs and operations. Some catered for more sunshine and more sex. Some for cooler, or even snowy, environments suitable for skiing. Many had large swimming pools designed purely for leisure seekers. A few were noted for their special, although unusual, work environments which had been produced to cater for a minority of people who yearned to be of some use and wanted to get back to work. This was, of course, tantamount to heresy and considered a punishable offence by all union bodies. The word *work* had long since been relegated to the archives and officially banned. But as it was an age when all kinds of addictions were considered acceptable providing they didn't injure, the AI processors decided to relent. It was decided to provide the poor workaholics with their own special work environment, their very own play area in which they could work to their hearts content without disturbing the unions or anyone else. Several satellite bubbles were therefore established specialising in the work environment. Many people frowned at these decisions, particularly union members, as they felt them to be retrograde steps even though the intention was to help the sick.

The occupants of the new work environment bubbles, or WEBs as the Americans called them, became even more addicted than before. Several studies showed that the work addicts were not just addicted, they appeared *happy* in their addiction. This was difficult for the experts specialising in psychology and motivation to understand. The ailment was not like the usual kind of allergy that had unpleasant consequences. What was so strange was that the work sickness had no adverse effects whatever on the bodily or mental functions. In fact most of the workers appeared in radiant good health and, stranger still, they appeared happy. Many of the work addicts expressed the opinion that for them it was a refreshing change from the constant emphasis on leisure pursuits.

Although most of the end products of the small work force could be produced more efficiently and with superior precision by the usual processor machinery, it became evident that the new band of human workers produced articles with a certain unique character. It was a uniqueness that had been lost during years of mass production and standardisation. The end result was that some of the new workers became involved in a minor revolution against the Big Mother AI processor World Government. They formed a new league of workers whose aim was to get back to basics and to fight for the freedom to work. Most of the general hedonistic public who had spent their lives searching for new pleasures thought the new workers were quite off their heads. After all, most of the peoples of the world were, at this time, enjoying being comfortably coddled on leisure benefits. They were quite content to leave it to the ubiquitous artificially intelligent processors to organise their world for them and to provide all the necessities and luxuries of life. Why then even pronounce the word *work* let alone practice it. Hardly anyone now knew the meaning of the word *work* which had long ago been relegated to the point of being considered a kind of obscenity. It had even been removed from the dictionary at the instigation of the unions who said the word upset people and could leave them in a state of trauma and many had claimed compensation for such a condition. Why therefore revert to the primitive.

However, the new work movement began to spread from its pristine beginnings inside a few satellite bubble communities to sections of the population on Earth. In fact, the new fashion of work began to take hold to become a sort of new religion. Health experts had to admit that people looked better for it. Such comments were quite controversial since most people thought you would die from it. Finally the government artificially intelligent processors decided enough was enough. The new work movement was seen to be a dangerous incursion into personal freedom to practice pleasure in the ways that everyone considered their special right. Also, too much work by people was likely to undermine the authority of the artificially intelligent processor legislators and social organisers. The new workers revolution was after all the result of an addiction, a sickness that had to be treated like any other disease. It had to be stopped before it reached epidemic proportions and spread like a virus throughout the world. Some thought it a horrendous prospect that everyone might catch the complaint and become addicted to work. That preposterous situation could never be allowed to arise. It would lead to so much disruption. There would be the production of inferior goods and not enough of them. The safety of foodstuffs would also be a problem. And world economics would never survive the shock. It was not long before the AI processors discovered the world equilibrium, as it was then termed, was being disrupted in subtle ways by the new work ethic. The result was that the instigators working in the satellite communities were immediately confined to their quarters and all communication between them and the Earth was prohibited. Work and even the mention of work were banned. Anyone found practising the ancient art, which was said by some to be equivalent to old-fashioned alchemy or even witchcraft, would be taken immediately for treatment and brain amendment. And once again the AI Big Mother processors of the World were united in their efforts to save Man (and Woman) from unnecessary pain and anxiety.

People could now be left to practice hedonism, the final philosophy, under the doting protective care of the finest automatic prefabricated world super-brain system ever conceived. It was an artificial yet living system that had not only conquered the world but would eventually go on to colonise and conquer other planetary systems throughout the galaxy. In the process however, people as biological creatures would be entirely eliminated as a species rather like the Neolithic man became extinct in the face of life's advances." Gotama's guide stopped speaking and there followed a few moments of silence.

It was Gotama who then spoke. "I was most interested in the ways in which the revolutionary workers were treated, not as criminals but as people who required medical treatment. Could you tell me more about this?"

Bubbles smiled. "Of course," she said. "It all came about when genetic scientists from the late 20th century onwards began discovering that genes governed every aspect of people's physical and mental behaviour, They found that genes do far more than set the colour of a person's eyes. Genes were also responsible for brain functions resulting in violent behaviour, depression, alcoholism, divorce, genius, homosexuality and promiscuity to name but a few. For many people these revelations came as a shock. It suddenly became clear that if all our mental and physical characteristics, including our behaviour, be it good or bad, were predetermined by our genes, then it left very little room for 'freewill' and individual choice. It seemed that people were pre-programmed to be good or bad, a criminal or a saint, from birth with no opportunity to escape from the shackles of a locked-in determinism.

The lawyers of the early 21st century were making fortunes by defending perpetrators of the most foul deeds, claiming their innocence because their genes, not they themselves, had dictated events. People ceased to be held responsible for anything particular, especially those who flouted the law, because they had acted in accordance with the dictates of their genes. In a society that had based its mores, rules and laws upon the premise of free will it had always been easy to find a person guilty and to lock him up for a spell on the assumption that he had a choice and could have behaved properly. It was assumed that he was responsible for his own actions. As soon as people thought they had no choice or freedom of will, they decided they couldn't really be blamed for anything. It wasn't their fault; it was just their genes acting as Nature intended. Moreover, it was quite unfair to lock people up for acting in a way that wasn't their fault.

In the end it didn't seem to matter whether you were sexually promiscuous, violent, a religious fanatic who blew people up if they were of different belief, an adulterer, divorced or happily married for 50 years, a liar, cheat or always honest. In fact, whatever mental or physical characteristics you displayed, all were found to be controlled and predetermined by one's genes. Every thought, act and attitude could finally be traced it seemed not to free choice but to tiny genes passed to each person by his or her forbears. People were seen as puppets on gene strings. They could never again be really congratulated for their individual achievements, because the scientists said that it wasn't as a result of their own efforts or expertise - it was merely a few thousand genes working like blind beavers who themselves were without any free choice, or scruples. They had never heard of the Ten Commandments and just couldn't help themselves."

"For some people it seemed to predict the end of society where freedom of will and choice had been the cornerstone of civilised living and restraint. For others it seemed to promise an anarchic society where all responsibility for one's actions could be cast off without the slightest worry as to the consequences. To those, in fact the majority, who were pure hedonists, it seemed like a dream come true. What did it matter how they conducted themselves, there would be no recriminations– nothing was their fault. Some who didn't much like the genes that Nature had given them, asked their lawyers to sue their parents and relatives for compensation. After all, everyone was always suing everyone else– a habit left over from the 20th century when everyone began blaming everybody else for their troubles and mistakes. Some even took the NHS to court for allowing them to be born with genes they didn't approve of or which had made them violent. Others sued for damages because their genes had made them unsuitable to do anything but draw state benefits. Such persons were once called dropouts, but now were making fortunes from their claims for damages.

Most prisoners at this time were therefore released from jail and were paid handsomely for being caused such inconvenience. It was a case of turning the old legal system on its head. No one seemed to know the answer until finally the AI processors together with the processor scientists came up with the solution. Detailed analysis of the situation had shown that the defects in society were the results not of people, but of their genes. It was therefore obvious, said the AI processors, that the only remedy lay in the hands of the genetic engineers who had for years been tampering with them. They had already created many new species of life; not forgetting more than a few catastrophes.

The world government of Artificially Intelligent Robotic processors thereupon made it compulsory for everyone to have genetic checks. They were called personal CGCs short for Compulsory Genetic Checks and were treated rather like the early ECGs for hearts and MOTs for cars. All genes considered a danger to the harmonious equilibrium of society were to be either extracted at once or re-formed to provide improved behaviour patterns designed to promote the overall survival of the human species. In practice this meant altering as many people as possible so that they would be nicely subservient to the dictates of the Big Mother governmental body of artificially intelligent processors now in charge of world society development programmes. The new sciences of gene manipulation, synthetic and bio-cloning, found clever ways to delete violence from a person's nature. Gene therapy was used to encourage latent artistic and musical abilities and other more acceptable forms of behaviour than just beating up one's neighbour. It was also used to treat the increasing number of serial adulterers who seemed to be taking advantage of their hedonistic culture. However, the authorities and experts didn't consider treatment of adultery as very high priority, because so few people were then married, and those that were, usually had only a 2 year marriage contract. And so it finally became possible to manipulate society itself. You will understand therefore why in the late 21st century there were no prisons, as such, for criminals, but only clinics for gene, mind and bio-particle manipulation.

The AI processors in charge of population development also decreed that all new babies were to be bred from a genetic base that contained no deleterious genes. In this way all violence and other unhealthy attributes could be bred out of human stock. This of course sounded fine, but many people, especially those who were enjoying themselves doing quite diabolical things, weren't too sure. Who, they said, is to act God and decide which genes to manipulate or cut out? Once again it was the AI processors who were in possession of all the knowledge and records beyond the reach or understanding of the common man. Humankind eventually therefore had little or no say in the matter. It was to be the calculations and decisions of the AI processors, which would determine exactly what kind of human species was to be allowed to exist on planet Earth. The control of the new-born, the manipulation and control of all human and animal life was now vested not in God but in the World Artificial Intelligent processor."

Bubbles smiled and then continued. "You will no doubt also be interested to know that during the 21st century the moon and Mars were colonised and vast areas of their surfaces were terraformed. Huge irrigation schemes, which fed water from the poles, created lush forests, grasslands and areas of vegetation for the survival of the many people who lived there. Gigantic domes in which atmosphere, temperature and pressure were maintained to provide the perfect environment for humans were strewn like a rash of giant bubbles across the moon's surface. The moon became the main staging post for rocket journeys to other planets and to the stars. During the 22nd century the moon was terraformed still further and was provided with an atmosphere of air making the bubble environments unnecessary. The moon's surface was then indistinguishable from many habitable areas on Earth, except that due to lower gravity the plant life often took on strange new strains and grew at quite different speeds. People soon became used to feeling lighter. In fact their Olympians were quite out of this world and the triple jumpers needed a lot of space to perform. Long jumpers would disappear over the horizon and high jumpers would nearly go into orbit.

On Earth terraforming took a different path. Many hot desert regions were now used for growing new genetic variants of vegetables and fruit. Vast arrays of underground pipes distributed the cold waters of the oceans to cool plant roots and to make moisture content in the atmosphere condense sufficiently to enable plants to grow. Using the underground cooling pipes enabled vast sandy deserts to be cultivated with lush fruit and vegetable regions. In addition, by the end of the 21st century, weather control had become possible for certain areas. Early use of Hydroscopic seeding of clouds in order to make rain and eliminate hail, which could be destructive to food crops such as grapes, had not been an easy task. Such methods were gradually improved using automatic flying probes to monitor and to seed and even to create clouds together with radiation from satellites. The probes were linked to complex networks of computer processors, which performed trillions of calculations a second, and which decided which clouds were to be sown and also exactly where the rain was to fall. Using such methods it became possible to cultivate many regions of the Earth that had hitherto been barren dried up deserts. Later, wind pattern control using satellites also gave mankind another valuable instrument for weather control. However, wind control could sometimes result in repercussions that even the climate processors could not predict. Sometimes the redirection of a small wind pattern on one side of the Earth would result in escalating effects across the globe causing artificially produced hurricanes and typhoons. Many climatic disasters were thought to be the result of Global Warming and it was difficult to establish which human interference with Nature was most responsible for the climatic chaos. But despite setbacks the scientists were always confident that eventually their weather control methods would prevail and even counteract the effects of Global Warming.

Many people, especially those living in dry, arid and parched regions, considered the early rain making techniques a splendid innovation. Once again the weather processors were to be congratulated. After all, it seemed obvious that if desert regions could be converted to fields of vegetables, then famines and starvation would be things of the past. Everyone began to feel more secure in such knowledge. However, as the rain making methods were used more and more extensively throughout the world the old dictum that you can't have something for nothing suddenly became patently obvious. New shifts in weather and wind patterns became apparent. Whilst some people who had been gently rained on at reasonable intervals were all for the new system, others who were suddenly deluged with giant torrents of water and had to fight against vicious winds never before experienced had more than a few misgivings about the new climatic control methods. It was another instance of how the gentle flapping of a butterfly wings could, by amplification across the globe, result in an earthquake.

More and more people began to suffer from more and more erratic storms and gales all of which occurred a long way from the desert reclamation. Such weather changes were frequently sudden and catastrophic. Many people became nervous. Some became addicted to the new type of mood pills recommended by the Health AI processors for the 'Cloud Seeding Syndrome' or CSS as the Americans called it. Others had cloud seeding breakdowns and became peculiarly allergic to certain types of cloud, particularly the deep coloured heavy variety. Complaints from people began to gather momentum. Not many people, it turned out, were happy with the amount of rain or sunshine they were receiving. Those on the desert sand dunes seemed happy enough, however, people who had previously been used to temperate climates and were now fighting raging monsoons were somewhat distraught. They complained that their clothing bills had rocketed. There was so much changing in and out of wet clothes that pneumonia was rife. Where there had once been roads and cars there were now lakes and boats. Umbrella and gum boot sales were up, but morale was definitely down. There was even snow in tropical South America, which made for a few clothing problems for the Indians and iced up their water holes. At one stage Eskimos had to be brought in to teach them how to deal with the problem. The Eskimos themselves found their own igloos melted. People demonstrated in the streets or on their lakes. 'Bring back our sunshine,' they shouted. 'Fair weather for all.' 'Why should the deserts have all the good weather, they don't need it anyway, they've got their oil and their underground cooling pipes for growing fruit and veg. What more do they want?'

The governing AI processors played for time in their effort to control, not only the weather, but also the people. It was just a simple case of teething troubles, they said. It would not be long before all aspects of weather change would be known and with knowledge would come control. However, it was obvious that the teething troubles were lasting longer than teething troubles were supposed to and they were having devastating effects on many areas of the world where people were now using boats and rafts instead of cars, and in other places, cars instead of boats. The whole world was in turmoil. Finally, the AI processors surprised even themselves by designing the fastest response processor that had ever existed. It was specifically made for monitoring and acting upon every conceivable shift and movement in wind, temperature, moisture content, cloud formation and so on. The system was the envy of the world. Now, not only the initial rainmaking was to be controlled, but also all the countless side effects into the bargain. The main difficulty was deciding which regions of the globe should have better weather than others and for how long. The AI processors explained that, as the weather systems were always changing, it was impossible to provide a constantly perfect weather pattern for everyone all of the time. Someone then asked who was to be responsible for making such decisions. Everyone previously had relied on God but this hadn't been entirely satisfactory. The only likely alternative was, of course, the World AI processor. After all, it already governed the world, so why not let it govern everything including deciding who should receive rain or sun. In the end people just had to put their faith in their new God, the World artificially intelligent processors. Most thought controlling the weather would be an ideal solution for the deserts where plenty of rain was needed in places like the Sahara and Gobi. However, many people had misgivings about the ability of the processors to control rain and sun in the smaller local regions. Old farmer George, for instance, wanted a gentle sprinkling and a little or no wind throughout one period of the year and sunshine for another period. Fred and Doris on holiday, on the other hand, wanted brilliant sunshine all the time with no wind whilst the wind surfers and gliders wanted a constant breeze. Sailors in sailing boats required plenty of wind and no rain whatsoever. Skiers on the slopes wanted plenty of snow, but none whilst they were skiing.

It was obvious even to a child that perfect weather for one could be a disaster for another. It was also obvious that if the processors had their way, and it now seemed they had, it was to be at best a rough justice system that would try in vain to satisfy all demands. The AI processors were at pains to point out that with all their accumulated scientific knowledge that they would eventually be able to refine the rain and weather control systems to such an extent that the smallest fields and villages could be catered for with weather to suit individual requirements. But people like farmer George remained unconvinced.

In order to placate people like farmer George and others who felt some disquiet about trying to control the weather, the AI processors instigated a democratic voting system which would enable every person to have a vote to decide what kind of weather was required for each region. Each person was provided with a voting button to press for a *yes, no* or *maybe* to vote for weather suggestions put forward by the processors. The suggestions would be based on complex mathematical calculations, which only the processors could perform. There would be weather patterns for each year. Each country was divided into small areas and voters would be able to vote for the weather in their particular area, rather like voting for a local Member of Parliament. Such an arrangement sounded fine until it was realised that it was, in fact, a scientific impossibility to satisfy every need. Some could be satisfied for a brief period but in order to satisfy other regions it was always necessary to disregard another. There could never be perfection.

In fact it now seemed that there were more people dissatisfied with their weather and rain allocations than when everything was left to Mother Nature to decide. It was also much more expensive. The costs for such super technology were added to people's water rate charges. It transpired that people were paying more for their rain than they were paying for all other services put together. Moreover, people from the temperate zones discovered they were paying for the high charges for terraforming the desert regions. The AI processors went to great pains to point out that water and all its derivatives was in fact the most valuable and important liquid on the face of the Earth, more important than oil or women's perfumes. Without it all life would die. People were therefore encouraged to make a special financial sacrifice in order to transform or terraform the planet and to convert previously barren desert into vegetation and rain forests. As a result there would be more sources for food to feed the large world population which, in spite of all the governmental family planning programmes, was forecast to reach 'standing room only' very soon. It would also assist the continual effort to keep the atmosphere in good condition together with the ozone layer.

Finally the world population had no choice but to accept the decisions of the artificially intelligent robot processors. The rain making technology was authorised to be developed to its full potential. No one really knew what the ultimate consequences of such meddling with the weather might have, any more than they knew what repercussions would result from the AI processor's control over things like the earth's population gene pool and life's evolutionary processes. The world order had, within a few hundred years, been catapulted from Nature's jurisdiction, which had held sway for millions of years, into control by artificially intelligent instrumentation devised by Man, but which had now taken over complete control of both Nature and Man himself. There could be no going back. It was all quite irreversible. Man had in fact relegated himself to the status of an impotent slave of his own Frankensteinian creation, a creation that not only now ruled the world but also was of a vastly superior intelligence. The artificially intelligent robots were the new breed of life which was speedily transcending mankind as the master race on planet Earth."

There were several moments of silence as though Bubbles was deep in thought. Gotama's attention was diverted as he watched the launch of several huge rockets that, unlike chemical and liquid fuel rockets, rose into the air without fuss or noise and disappeared high into space. As many as ten lifted off, one after the other, above the distant horizon, whilst other strange craft hovered in the vicinity moving back and forth as though they were some kind of aerial bus service. Bubbles turned to Gotama and said. "Some of the 20th century dreams of stellar travel came to fruition during the late 21st century, but not quite as intended or anticipated. Interstellar travel by methods available at the beginning of the century using chemical fuel, etc., was impossible due to it being too slow and costly. Even spacecraft powered by the annihilation of matter and antimatter would have required 500 supertanker loads of fuel just to reach Proxima Centauri, the nearest star with planets. And the journey would still take 100 years. To transport people to other stars was therefore seen to be impractical using such primitive techniques. It was the AI processors who once again came up with the answer. By the end of the

20th century, processor technology had reached the stage where hi-fi systems were producing such perfect sound, that virtual sounds could not be distinguished from real ones. It was not long before this technology was extended from hearing sounds to all the other senses. It eventually became possible to explore the Universe at first-hand from the comfort and safety of a perfect virtual world. Instead of people risking life and limb travelling into space, unmanned interstellar probes were sent bearing the equivalent of man's five senses (and more). Sense data, as would be sensed by a person, was transmitted by the unmanned probe when it arrived at it's interstellar destination, which could be a planet circling another star far out in the galaxy.

The new virtual reality systems could also bypass the senses if required and interface directly with the human brain to feed it nerve impulses, received from space probes, in order to create particular experiences. You will of course, know that when it comes to seeing the real world, our brains are just like information processing computers. They sift, screen and project our surroundings, using sense data supplied by our senses. And, just as different computers used to communicate during your era over the Internet, using universal languages called 'protocols', so the nervous system has its own language. This special language was finally unravelled so that the human brain could communicate with imputs from sources other than the normal five senses. Space probes of quite new and revolutionary design utilising space warp and space wormhole techniques were then used to transmit sensory information from distant stellar planetary systems back to Earth.

Space probes of this kind were then able to let people touch, feel, see, hear and smell the environments of these far off planets, just as the nerves in the tips of our fingers or in the retina of the eye let use touch or see nearby objects. It eventually became possible for people to experience sensations quite beyond the normal five senses in order that they could sense and understand some of the completely different extraterrestrial environments existing not only in your own Milky Way galaxy, but also in other galaxies spread throughout the universe. It was space travel with all the virtual reality of the real thing without having to physically carry individual people to such destinations. It was also safer. Later in the centuries it became possible to spend a 'virtual reality holiday' on planets circling distant stars. All from one's own home without even opening the front door."

Bubbles smiled at Gotama's astonished expression. "Yes," she said. "People in the late 21st century were in many ways still very primitive particularly in social habits. They still tried to keep up with the Joneses. But now, instead of talking about their vacation in Corfu, they went into raptures over their holiday on the latest and most fashionable planetary discovery of the year. There came a time when a virtual reality visit to one of the planets of Proxima Centauri, the nearest star to the Earth, became quite 'old hat' like Southend when compared with the Seychelles. Most people became completely addicted to their hedonistic culture. They weren't satisfied with skiing on the Alps for instance. Instead they wanted to experience levitation skiing on Hi Lo, a planet in the Andromeda galaxy, which had strange magnetic effects on the visiting sensory probes sent from planet Earth and produced sensual pleasure that was out of this world. The pleasures were so delightful that many people would forget their usual pleasures like sex. Many called the place the Planet of Orgasms. Then there were the 'ocean probes' which were designed to transmit sensory data from planets with huge seas all chemically quite distinct. They ranged from the normal water to liquid nitrogen, boiling sulphur and countless varieties of exotic fluids quite unheard of in the early 21st century. To swim in some of the fluids was indescribably sensuous and many people found them irresistible. Some couples combined such sensual experiences with a marriage ceremony, which made it an occasion never to be forgotten.

In order to brag to their neighbours of their latest planetary conquest, people would spend fortunes at their 'galactic travel agent' reserving all the most sensual destinations. They used the latest holographic guide from which to make their choices, which was a refreshing advance on old fashioned travel leaflets. It also enabled people to actually sample some of the virtual reality experience they could expect from a particular planetary virtual reality trip. Many people became so addicted to their cosmic exploits that they would spend more time as extraterrestrials journeying through their interstellar planetary systems than travelling around their own neighbourhood. Many were classed officially as residents on a particular planet or moon, although physically they never really left the Earth. It was rather like the many pensioners in the 20th century who spent the winter in Spain and summer back home.

The interstellar environment was being gradually inhabited by people by proxy, as the interstellar probes colonised every possible planetary nook and cranny. The colonisation process was also accompanied by other new discoveries. Life was found to be ubiquitous in the vast cosmos and it came in many forms. But rarely was it very advanced. Many planets were found with the remnants or fossils of life now long extinct. Others had quite unrecognisable life forms. Yet others were discovered with life forms very much akin to the Earth's own artificially intelligent processor vehicles of self conscious thought, except that their modes of physical adaptation to the environment was different in each instance. By the late 22nd century these contacts had resulted in an intergalactic communication system that was as different from the Earth's Internet as a human is from a worm.

There also came a time when mankind's artificially intelligent robot scientists discovered the secrets of constructing life and consciousness in all kinds of different shapes and sizes. It was then that spaceships were in fact grown rather than built as conscious life forms that possessed brilliant minds and vast numbers of senses that could sift and analyse all kinds of planetary and cosmic environments. The living spacecraft were in fact able to replicate and repair themselves much more efficiently than biological life, so that they were virtually indestructible and could traverse the galaxies for thousands of years. Many of the conscious space vehicles were also able to transform themselves so that they could colonise different types of planets in the far reaches of the universe. That was the time, far into your future, when life sent from planet Earth to colonise other worlds could travel in space, not as a passenger, but as living space entity, fully conscious of itself and its surroundings. Teams or families of living space vehicles usually roamed the galaxies together, giving each other support and entertainment during their long journeys. Such families of space entities were as well adapted to their space environment as people in the 21st century were used to living on planet Earth.

Also, in later centuries, quantum teleportation, utilising the weird properties of quantum 'entanglement,' was used to transport objects, then people, around the world and solar system at the speed of light. The method was often called the 'spooky science', because of the Alice in Wonderland aspects of some of its predictions. For instance, when the calculations were first made in the twentieth century, quantum physics of sub-atomic particles imlied that an object could be in two places at once and behave as one, no matter how far apart they may be. In later centuries, using these principles, together with very complex scientific methods, it became possible to carry an object's structural information in a beam of light, rather like a radio wave in earlier periods was used to carry information to make a radio or television operate. In the case of the teleportation system, the light beam had to be split and then recombined in a very special way at the point of destination to create another identical object or person in a process known as 'entangling.' However, in order to do this, the process entailed the complete annihilation of the first physical structure and the creation of a new but 'identical' structure or person at another point in space/time – the reception point.

Initially, this worried quite a few people, who felt that to be annihilated in order to go on a long coach trip wasn't their favourite occupation. It took all the pleasure out of it somehow. Also, the slight risk of arriving without all the essential body parts being in their proper place frightened some people and gave others severe apoplexies and other nervous complaints. They said that it all seemed a little more serious than the loss of one's luggage that usually occurred. People were also afraid their duplicate copy, resurrected at the end of the journey, would be different from their true selves and wouldn't experience things in the manner to which they'd been accustomed. There were vivid stories of people complaining that their memory was not the same as before, although they couldn't remember the memories they'd apparently forgotten, so it was difficult for them to claim compensation. Others complained they felt queasy and different, but couldn't remember exactly how they felt previously, so it was difficult to put a finger on the problem. There was also a case where a man and his dog were teleported together and, on arrival, the dog spoke perfect Queen's English and the man growled and barked all day. Some people said their legs were somebody else's, because the new legs kept tripping over and wouldn't fit into their trousers, besides which they now had arthritis. Others reported arriving at their destination with unusual behavioural patterns, like laughing at policemen or crying at comedies, or singing and shouting in libraries. There were instances of brain surgeons wanting to be carpenters and carpenters wanting to be brain surgeons, the repercussions of which could sometimes be extraordinary if not catastrophic.

Such were some of the teething troubles of teleportation, but eventually, when people became satisfied that the copy of themselves reproduced at the point of destination possessed all the same memories, feelings, idiosyncrasies and subtleties of their own private personalities, they realised that it was only these that made them what they were. And when the risks were eventually minimised, people felt more secure and confident. They also realised that experiencing the teleported journey was rather like having a quick knap and awakening to a new day in a different place, which could be at the other side of the Earth, on the Moon or Mars or somewhere in the outer reaches of the solar system. Finally, from the late twenty fourth century, quantum teleportation of objects, buildings and people became routine events and was used in later centuries for visits to planets circling other stellar systems.

A cosmic brain system now straddled the galaxies. It circularised knowledge and information both sensory and academic throughout cosmic space. I cannot disclose all the repercussions connected with such advances as you would never be able to imagine or conceive them. Your brain has been grown and moulded in your own biological environment and, without the necessary infrastructure, education, brain enhancement modules and many other devices, you would be unable to comprehend such things. I can only give you a few brief glimpses into what the future holds for people on Earth and their descendants. These glimpses have been based on your current degree of advancement and it has been assumed that the imminent world catastrophe can be avoided."

At that point, Gotama noticed that Bubbles was fiddling with another strange looking switch on her left wrist. There was a faint click. She turned and smiled. "I want to show you some of the advances in 21st-century micro chips," she said, as she pointed to some curious objects that had suddenly appeared as holographic images. "These," she said, "are mid-century micro chips magnified two million times. Unlike the early chips made from silicon, which were two dimensional in profile and were therefore limited in the number of 'bits' of data they could carry, these chips were three dimensional. They were given the name of 'bio-sensors' because they contained organic material like living matter. The bio-sensors were tiny, like cells of a human brain. They functioned at the atomic and molecular levels. When several were linked together in a bio-circuit they could perform with living intelligence and when combined in large numbers, possessed learning abilities and consciousness accompanied by an element of free choice that were independent of their original programming. In other words, they had freedom of will and could be said to possess conscious learning ability and intelligence.

Many intelligent bio-complexes were structured to form living robots with brains in many ways superior to the human type. Similar type bio-sensor material was also implanted into some people's brains and sensory apparatus in order to improve their human senses and intelligence. This was particularly useful in helping people with damaged brains and those who wished to improve their sight, hearing and specific intellectual abilities. People with bad memories, which included the majority, flocked to medical centres to be fitted with a few million extra memory cells. This operation was very useful for people over 150 years old who couldn't remember their name or what day it was or what they'd had for breakfast immediately they'd eaten it. Eventually, the bio-sensor operations became very specialised. People could not only have their memory improved, they could also be fitted with bio-sensors to improve their crossword skills, their mathematical ability, or their mental concentration in order to improve all kinds of things, like their bird watching, stamp collecting or the reading old fashioned books, which most people found difficult to do.

With these new bio-sensors, billions of bits of information could now be stored at the molecular level. Early troubles caused by electrons escaping from these tiny systems into adjacent circuit elements, because of their minute size, were eliminated by using self-compensating devices built into the bio-sensors that predicted and compensated for any cross interference of circuits. The method utilised complex statistical knowledge together with probability laws to predict when and where such cross interference would occur. Using these bio-sensors, it was now possible in the mid-21st century to give life and intelligence to robots and, paradoxically, to provide people with robot limbs, senses and also additional brain and nervous systems. By this time, man himself was therefore becoming part robot. Just as the simple calculator, processor or motor car could be likened to extra limbs, the new biosensor robot systems became, not just extra limbs, but integral parts of man's living body and brain. The human brain was no longer sacrosanct. It was treated merely as a tool, an organ of intelligence, which could be reproduced and even improved upon using complex hierarchical structures of biosensors.

People who suffered strokes and other brain damage involving loss of part of their brain could now be fitted with replacement structures. Operations once thought impossible were carried out with greater ease than early heart bypasses and transplants. Transplant rejection was now a thing of the past. Robots were manufactured with bio-sensor systems that accurately simulated a live intelligent brain. Several types of standardised robot couldn't be distinguished from humans born by natural biological means. At least, not from their intelligence and conversation. Sometimes it was possible to detect their robot lineage from a subtle behavioural response, which only a biological human could detect, like stirring tea the wrong way round, or laughing at a joke before the punch line, or blinking too often, or having a glazed expression longer than people were accustomed to. The latter was more difficult to detect, however, because most normal people usually had glazed expressions, due to their being confronted by so many inventions of the modern age, which were quite beyond their comprehension. The politicians suffered almost continuously from this.

It was estimated that by the end of the 21st century, approximately 50% of the total population of the world were humanoid robots. Problems as to who was a robot, and who was not, frequently posed difficulties. Some people even tried to marry a robot not realising that it was the very latest model fitted with the ultimate deluxe emotional technology combining every subtle human feeling. These included copious tears with grief and sadness, a few less with joy and happiness, and a sexual dexterity that would make most people's hair curl or their toes turn up. Many people only discovered their proposed marriage partner was a robot when they went to make their eye imprints at the marriage and population control processor. Eye imprinting had replaced signatures many years earlier. It was even more accurate than finger printing and was carried out very quickly by merely looking into the processor image transducer. Only humans biologically, test tube or incubator born, had their births registered and were permitted to marry. Robots only had a date of manufacture and sell-by date registered, so they were easily discovered when they reached the marriage bureau where checks were made.

Many heartbreaks resulted from liaisons with the latest in sexy humanoid robots. It was all the sadder because the female robots were generally gorgeous, possessing exquisite figures that every woman in the land was trying to emulate. The male robots were usually husky and handsome; especially the ones used as home butlers. Their design was based on current opinion polls obtained from women. It was not surprising, therefore, that they looked like the latest heartthrob or Chippendale star of the holographic circuit. It was partly as a result of these polls that the robot butlers had been fitted with the very latest in fine emotions and sexy modules. If the women were enthralled by the manners and courtesy of the newest robots, they were completely infatuated by their good looks and suave sexy Mediterranean advances. At one stage, women seemed to be leaving their husbands in droves for a new lover who was subsequently discovered to be a robot.

There was a kind of apartheid, an unwritten code of conduct that evolved during the period of robot development that separated robots from people. The common man's view was that one was life, the other wasn't. Most people, however, didn't take into consideration that they themselves were now part robot, with prefabricated hips, hearts, kidneys, livers, nervous system, brain appendages and implants. Also, the latest robots were constructed partly from organic molecular complexes that were almost identical to the cells of their own bodies and brains. The experts had always pointed this out when marketing the robots. But the problem of what exactly comprised human life and what did not was a deeper issue. There was a kind of superstition, a fear of interrelating with a foreign species, which was perhaps ingrained at the deepest levels of the human psyche. If white humans would not integrate and live together with black humans, as had happened in South Africa in the 20th-century, then you will appreciate the similar problem faced by humankind when confronted by the most sophisticated humanoid robot ever devised.

The robots were no fools. They had the very best in intelligence built in. Many were thought to be on the threshold of committing civil disobedience. The more radical minded people felt that before this happened, robots of certain models should be provided with an official date of 'birth' and the more advanced models should be allowed to marry humans, if their circuitry indicated they wished to do so. The radicals pointed out that there were already many instances of extra marital affairs with robots, not to mention the countless numbers of love affairs and sexual encounters between boys and female robots and girls with male robots. And many of the latter were included as part of the educational curriculum for the young. There were in fact complete educational courses on how to relate with your processor robot. Many students had love affairs with their robot, the seriousness of which depended usually on whether the robot was of the latest deluxe model with sexy modules. With the model Mk 331 Zeta robot, which possessed the super sex modules, all systems were 'go' for a torrid and romantic affair. But these robots were expensive and it was therefore only the more well off students who could afford to have such affairs. Poorer youngsters using older models got used to having only one night stands. They could sometimes have more serious affairs with deluxe models on the NHS, if recommended by doctors. Such a course of action was occasionally recommended for youngsters who experienced difficulties in relating to the opposite sex because they were either shy, or just ugly. At one period, there were so many applicants for affairs on the National Health that the waiting list for the Mk 331 Zeta was 15 years, by which time many applicants were too tired or too married to have an affair anyway.

People had for many years discussed all their problems and played chess with their robots. Robots now performed all kinds of duties from shopkeeper, accountant, home-help to doctor, diagnostic, psychiatrist and agony aunt. They had taken over all but a very few jobs on the factory floor and in the offices. Completely automated industrial units including design and manufacturing facilities were now the rule. Robot intelligence was used ubiquitously for industrial, commercial and social planning and management. Thus, there were very few openings in business for people. The main function of humankind was to find new ways of enjoying life without resorting to work. This was not too much of a problem for most people, especially those who were trade union members. However, for some it wasn't their ideal to spend each day playing the latest in space invaders or being manicured. Computer holograph games had their place, but there was little satisfaction if the only time a person could win was when the IQ adjustment was turned down to 'moron' level. It didn't exactly inspire people with confidence or make them feel proud of their achievements. Most reported feeling browbeaten most of the time. Some people thought there was little point in playing because the computerised robots could beat them at every game you cared to mention. The computer game designers had built in a very nice apologetic voice response, which came on after nearly every game, to apologise for having won yet again. But this still didn't provide people with the satisfaction of having a playmate. It was rather an unequal relationship. In fact, the apologies began to be resented. Even the new United Olympic Games, where robots were allowed to compete with humans, began to get stale when every sport, from long distance running to shove half-penny, began to be won by the robots."

Bubbles paused for a moment, took a cursory look at Gotama, then touched another button on her wrist before continuing. "Robots," she said, "came in many forms, and by the end of the 21st century there were all kinds of new developments. It was then fashionable for everyone to carry 'food synthesisers,' which were included in all the latest briefcases, kitchen units and even in the more fashionable suits and jackets. Food synthesisers were the latest in nutrition technology and molecular building techniques. They came in many different varieties, the most common of which was the model called twin BX. Twin BX could be supplied in single or double-breasted swinger suits worn by both men and women so that people could always have some lunch with them wherever they went. It saved time and lunch boxes. It could automatically produce food by a process called 'duplication.' Duplication meant producing an object or a food by copying and reproducing its complete molecular structure using atoms like building bricks.

There were also huge processing plants where foods were mass-produced by atomic structuring using previously genetically engineered vegetables, fruits and meats as templates. Farmyard foods grown or reared in fields were now considered inadequate to feed the world's multitudes and the natural methods were slow and inefficient in comparison with the 'molecular synthesisers.' The Twin BX was a portable model utilising the very latest in mini, mini micro engineering. It was fitted in everyone's kitchen and hitched to most people's swinger jacket belt. At a touch of a button and a brief verbal instruction, the Twin BX would produce a variety of rissole-like food capsules in about ten seconds. In 20 seconds it could bring forth the equivalent of a two course meal with coffee to follow. The BX Triplet was a deluxe version, which could also conjure up a soup capsule in five alternative flavours. People's favourite seemed to be oxtail in aspic and chicken on the rocks. The robot food synthesisers became an integral part of the latest silver textured 'swinger suit' as it was called, which also had its own internal heating and cooling systems with temperature control. People wearing these were thus freed from the hassle of fighting for a place in a restaurant or going to the canteen for lunch. Instead they could produce their own meal which was satisfying, if not hearty in the old fashioned sense. The portable food synthesisers were particularly useful for travellers and those who enjoyed picnics, as they didn't have to lug food hampers up steep hillsides. They could now serve hot snacks at any time rather like a conjurer brings out a rabbit from his jacket. The basic portable model was fine for the equivalent of meat and two veg with plum duff to follow. The more expensive models could produce all kinds of permutations of savoury and sweet meals together with special variety of aromas and tastes. They also enabled people to have their curry warm, hot or excruciating. But, like drinks in the old fashioned vending machines, they usually turned out to be excruciating and not so hot. The new food synthesisers could also alter the flavour of their mince beef rissoles to strong, medium or tasteless, but the tasteless variety seemed to predominate whatever the setting. Some thought this was a legacy from the early designs of vending machines on station platforms.

Despite this revolution in food production, which had virtually eliminated any possibility of famine or starvation throughout the world, people were still not satisfied. They complained bitterly about not having enough 'bulk.' 'Why can't we fill our stomachs like they used to, back in the dark ages of the 20th-century?' they asked. Capsules were all very well, but they led to a lot of stomach rumbling. The scientists said that people didn't need so much bulk, but stomachs seemed to think differently and trumpeted their objections in noisy ways. Capsules might be highly nutritious but they certainly didn't make for a romantic evening under dimmed lights. On such occasions the music had to be turned up very loud to offset the after effects. It was difficult to talk pleasantries and linger over them under such conditions. A couple of capsules gave all the necessary nourishment, but they were gone in two shakes of a dog's tail. It was all so fast, efficient and functional, but art and romance had dissolved in the logic of science. Old fashioned chefs, together with recipe books, had been relegated to the museum. The modern chef was the AI processor robot. People had but one job to do in order to practice the culinary arts. They had to know which buttons to press or which voice commands to give. Providing they could do this, it was as though they possessed a magic lamp with a genie to do their bidding. They could command almost anything, providing it was from a standardised list of standardised products. They could make use of many standardised facilities in a standardised world designed and prefabricated by the standardised processors. They could order their robots to carry out their tasks and to produce their food, but people themselves had become enslaved by robot technology and their own cleverness. They lived and worked within the limits set by their machines. The human brain was now educated and moulded into a form that could be linked like an interface into the vast world nervous system of artificially intelligent processors. It had all begun many years before in something called the Internet. In reality, it was now the robot processors who made all the important decisions in every sphere of life.

People became like spoilt children. They had everything, yet couldn't understand why they were unhappy. Their listlessness showed itself in the weakening of ambition particularly in altruistic fields like nursing, much of which was now carried out by robot intelligence. Suicides were on the increase. Although genetic engineering and manipulation had reduced some of the violence in society, there were still many people with nothing else to do except get up to mischief. Gangs were on the increase. One gang, for instance, called the 'smelly feet,' a modern version of skinheads, were fond of practical jokes and used a 'scrambler' device to interrupt the proper function of people's food synthesisers so that a boiled egg ended up scrambled or nastily beaten up. Gangs would take pleasure in using scramblers in order to give as many people 'Delhi Belly' as they could. Unfortunately, scrambled synthetic food couldn't always be detected because it often tasted no different from the usual. In fact, some people reported that it sometimes tasted a lot better. Fortunately, there were only a few cases of drastic food poisoning due to fail safe mechanisms built in the food synthesisers. During one period, however, the whole population seemed to be laid up with 'synthetic food scrambler syndrome' as it was then called. It was reminiscent of the computer viruses of earlier times, except that they were now affecting the processor controls in the food synthesisers.

Finally the matter became so serious that manufacturers of food synthesisers had to invent de-scrambler devices to defeat the scrambler hooligans. Food once again became edible, although not in the opinion of many older people who had known some of the old fashioned cooking. Old people called it cardboard that had more powerful effects than concentrated prunes. Manufacturers retorted that after careful market research, they had evidence that 95% of young people up to the age of 21 said they loved mushy cardboard meals. After all, they had been weaned on them since birth. Foods like eggs and bacon, roast lamb, beef, Yorkshire pudding and dumplings were generally only eaten by eccentrics or those who weren't concerned about dropping down dead from heart attacks, cancer and countless other diseases. Most synthetic food eaters considered that such old fashioned food should be the subject of a government health warning as with cigarette smoking. But they didn't always realise that the manufacturers had included ingredients in synthetic foods to give them not only nourishment, but also an addictive ingredient to make people crave for more processor designed foods and to give them a distaste for all others. Subtle additives, like those put in cat food to make cats crave for their meaty chunks, were included just to make sure the customer would become a regular.

Besides this, heavy foods of previous centuries weren't to be recommended, not only because they could kill you, which was a good enough reason, but also because they could damage the delicate artistic teeth designs that were current in the late 21st century. It was fashionable to etch fine traceries and patterns on the surfaces of teeth. Some were coloured so that they complimented lipstick and facial colours worn by both men and women. Facial colours were frequently used to match clothes. Silver was very popular. Other people used complimentary colours so that when wearing their red cling suit, they would put on their green face. Green faces were considered respectable and smart for showing off during the day. At night, however, in dimmed artificial light, green faces could take on disconcerting looks that made associates and relatives uneasy and jumpy. For this reason green faces were usually taken off for evening functions and family get togethers, to be replaced with something more comfortable. The rosy pink shade was a favourite with the women and a murky mauve was favoured by the men who felt it gave them a sense of dark mystery, which they hoped women would swoon over, as they did in the advertisements. Olive brown was also a popular colour as most white skinned women's ambition was to emulate the Indian beauties of the Far East. In fact Saris were still fashionable evening wear for both women and men."

At this point Gotama was led by Bubbles into another hall in which the walls appeared to be iridescent and seemed to be creating constantly changing pictures. It was a kind of 3D holographic art gallery. Individual pictures seemed to come into focus as soon as he looked at them. At the same time there was an accompanying very gentle voice that spoke a kind of poetic commentary in almost musical tones. Each painting carried within its shapes and colours a kind of symbolic meaning. Such meanings Gotama felt were important and were being indicated to him for a reason and a purpose. To perhaps guide him and show him the vain vicissitudes of life and the things that were really important to uphold and experience.

The first picture that he became aware of was a long horizontal Triptych, through which streams of light radiated from strings of galaxies. In the centre was the face of an old man, neither European, Asian nor Negro, but with features containing them all. He had a white flowing beard streaming out into the vastness of the cosmos. The haunting face peered out from a kind of pear-shaped bubble like a giant dewdrop. The accompanying voice explained that the image depicted Man, the space-time bubble. The voice then went on to say that Man was but a space-time bubble, wrought from cosmic eternity to experience consciousness for but a moment. A minute wave in the ocean witnessing miracles. Each had his brief hour before his finite bubble vanished and another formed.

Thereupon another image came into Gotama's view. This time it was of the Earth cast in a giant sea where waves became galaxies of stars. A baby called 'Young Mankind' was about to step off the Earth into the cosmic ocean. In one hand the baby held a rocket, whilst in the other was a bucket containing his scientific knowledge for good or ill. The voice whispered once again. "After billions of years, a new babe has been born – the babe of humanity, the only creature which has ever been able to step off the planet into the new dimension of cosmic space. Man has been on Earth for but a moment since life first began, a mere fraction of a second ago, cosmologically speaking. Take care of the human babe – he is at a dangerous point – he knows a little but not yet enough to ensure his own safety in the critical period ahead. Don't let him fall."

Once again the pictures changed. Another image appeared in the strange art gallery of symbolism. Slowly the image crystallised to reveal a family of Asian refugees. There were tears in the eyes of the Asian woman as she held her baby close. Gotama noticed there was a tear, like a drop of dew that fell from poppies above onto the baby's head. Behind the poppies a bowed head indicative of despair appeared. In the background thousands of refugees made their debut as tiny murky figures leading up to the central figure. An identity tag hung like a rough necklace around the baby's neck. On it was inscribed – 'Nationality — Homo Sapien; Identity — War Victim /Abused; Name — Innocent; Number — Countless; Date — Since Dawn of Time; Address — Earth; Cause — Blindness of Man; Result — Pain and Tears; Temporary Assistance — UN; Remedy — ..... (For Future World Government Use Only.'

The image changed yet again. It became a little deaf girl being taught to speak by an attractive young woman. Both were reading from a book in which words suddenly took shape. The message was quite brief. It read– "Many achieve worldly honours, but the greatest achievements are usually unrecognised," the strange harmonious voice purred in the background.

"This simple image indicates how people can make great errors in their evaluation of things and other people. The example of the teacher and her little deaf pupil is a case in point. In the 20th and early 21st centuries many pop stars were purveyors of high decibel noise which they attributed to music. They, together with footballers, were generally screamed at, doted on, had knickers thrown at them and paid millions of dollars. Young people in particular thought the dispensing of a cacophony of deafening sound at a pop concert, rave evening or football ground was really 'cool'. However, devotees were often tone or stone deaf before the age of thirty. The pop scene was nevertheless the place to be and the pop and football stars were those most highly valued. By contrast the teacher of the little deaf child and many similarly dedicated teachers of the disabled received few accolades and little financial reward for their altruistic dedication." The soft voice continued, "Suffice for me to tell you that humans must seriously evaluate those things that are most important in human life. In short, it is now time for the babe Mankind to begin to grow up and see what is really important so that he may become responsible for the safe keeping of the world and its life."

The voice faded and new vague images began to materialise. A long vertical picture appeared showing a kind of golden Buddhist image from which emanated shafts of different coloured lights. Around the Buddha and projecting from him arose an image like a vast drop of liquid in which were enclosed countless images of stellar worlds, galaxies and the planet Earth itself. Inscribed at the base of the picture were the words – 'the drop is in the ocean and the ocean is in the drop.'

As Gotama read the inscription the voice continued. "This picture symbolises an important philosophical truth about the Universe in which we find ourselves. Everything and everybody is interrelated, so that nothing is really separate from anything else. The final truth of this can be summed up in the words – the drop is in the ocean and the ocean is in the drop. In other words, we ourselves, including the planet Earth and all its particles of matter and energy, can be likened to drops within the cosmic ocean. The cosmic ocean is also within us in our deepest selves and in the deepest crevices of the atoms and molecules which form all things. It is a truth shown to you so that you may begin to understand your intimate relationship with the cosmos and that its inherent creative artistry and purposes are also in you. Although you, as a minute physical drop in creation, are seemingly insignificant, you possess within you characteristics that are of the eternal cosmic ocean which give you a kinship with the cosmos and with the origin of all things. It is by consciously dipping your thought into and bathing in this cosmic ocean that you can refresh yourself and receive creative inspiration. Remember this my friend," the voice continued. "It will serve you well when you are asked to make important decisions"

The musical voice faded and new images appeared. This time of a picture that focused in on two small Negro boys. One had tears in his eyes as he held the other close to him. Gotama heard him say, 'He's not heavy, he's my brother.'

As soon as the little boy had said this, the musical voice interceded. "This small boy and his brother," the voice said, "have no home and no family. They have no help other than that which they provide for themselves. They are representative of the countless homeless orphans in the world. In their desperate need does not their love shown for each other seem all the more precious? Such tender love in adversity is brought before you as a small example of the way in which all human relationships should be conducted, particularly between nations and world leaders. 'He's not heavy, he's my brother' should be the guiding thought for everyone in the human world family so that the love expressed in those few words can be an inspirational light in everyone's heart. Keep that light in your heart when you meet with international leaders shortly." Thereupon the harmonic voice became quiet and a period of tender almost thoughtful, silence ensued.

Colours ran and interlaced each other as a new image formed. It was of a mother and child. There was a soft tenderness in the way that the child's lips met the mother's cheek. It conjured up in Gotama a physical sensation that

311

he found difficult to describe. Even the smell of a powdered baby cherished and cosseted by a loving mother became evident as the image impinged on his senses. The two were embraced in Madonna-type imagery, yet not so majestic - more akin to the quiet beauty of an ordinary mother and child. The melodic voice once again took up the story. "Here is the beauty of a mother with her child. It is an image we call The Caress. It reveals a mother's love for her child, a love of strength, yet of caring, both practical and tender. It is an example of the kind of sacrificial love so important for the survival, not only of the babe, but also for the whole human race. Survival of the world family now depends on the development of more of this kind of sensitive love between people and races."

Once more the imagery changed. Slowly the dissolved colours became more distinct. The picture that now formed appeared to be a portrait of Einstein. Radiating from the head in the centre of the picture were faint streamers that formed into separate clock faces each one indicating a different time. Each clock was at a different distance and appeared smaller the further away from the viewer. The strange voice purred a new commentary. "The symbolism here represented," the voice said, "is put before you to remind you of the work of your great scientists and mathematicians. In particular, the calculations of Einstein showed how Time would alter with respect to velocity of objects or people moving relative to each other. Such alterations in Time would be particularly noticeable as the speed of light was approached.

The picture is to remind you that just as the Time dimension can be bent in this way, so too there are other dimensions within and around us that can be of use to us and can be bent and refocused for our benefit and advancement. I speak from another dimension, in some ways far away from yours, yet in other ways very close. By means of mathematical sciences similar yet more advanced than your own, we extra-galactic life forms have been able to bend Time and Space, together with other dimensions, into new co-ordinates, so that we may visit you and influence your Earth's evolution. We come only to guide and inspire, not to enslave or dominate. It is merely to express our common heritage as cosmic brothers and sisters that we help all creatures throughout the galaxies to find their own way to enlightenment and awareness of their true place in creation. We are a very large cosmic family with characteristics quite beyond your comprehension, but the day is dawning when the peoples of the Earth will have their intellectual eyes and senses opened to wider vistas. But before that can take place, immediate dangers to the planet must be overcome."

There was silence in the strange gallery once again. Images shifted and rearranged themselves. Gotama was captivated by the magnificent décor the like of which he had never seen. All the colours in walls, ceiling and floors seemed much purer and brighter yet in no way brash or daunting. They were soft and caressing yet exhilarating as in a dream yet more real. The hall in its way seemed more real in fact than things in Gotama's everyday world. The beauty of the strange glowing chandeliers, which shone above like sparkling galaxies fascinated him, as did the stars surrounded by blue black vellum material that crinkled and moved like waves on a giant sea. Below there were chairs and tables, which were not just chairs and tables but were also stiles and fences in gardens, streams, meadows and mountainsides. There was a crystal stillness, yet with a soft warm breeze. Birds, waving trees, hills, mountains, sun and moon were all somehow present, yet in a strange way absent as his concentration and viewpoint changed.

The melodic voice once again broke the silence. "There are more images I would like you to see," the voice went on. Thereupon the picture image changed to become a vast vertical Triptych of three pictures one above the other with an overall design running through the whole group, like a swirl of a galaxy or was it the shell of Time, because it seemed to emanate from an hourglass? The central picture was dominated by two human figures; a man and woman entwined in each other's arms and both reaching upwards. The lower picture was of a variety of animal life including examples of all the varieties of earth life, animals, reptiles, birds, fish, etc. There was also a human figure blindfolded with arms outstretched with one hand touching a chrysalis and the other holding a butterfly. The top picture was of a Madonna-like woman, neither European, Negroid nor Asian but resembling all yet none of these. She held a baby on whose head was written the word 'Mankind'. Gotama also noticed that the three pictures, from bottom to top, were called, Life, Intelligence and Compassion.

The voice suddenly intruded again on Gotama's reveries. "This Triptych is a symbolic allegory," the voice continued. "In the bottom picture called Life you will already have observed the blindfolded figure with his hands touching the chrysalis on one side and the butterfly on the other. You will see that the chrysalis is portrayed as emanating from the atomic structure that itself is shown arising from a cosmic galaxy. This represents the beginning of life from supposedly inanimate matter. The butterfly represents the metamorphosis from the atomic condition into biological life. The embryo shown inside the Earth represents the incipient beginnings of Earth life. The chimpanzee figure holding a butterfly suggests our kinship, but also a metamorphosis from that particular ancestry. Behind the main figure's head is the crown of flower petals in which a fish symbolises the pristine beginnings of life in the sea. All around are representations of many different creatures, animals, birds and reptiles.

313

The centre picture, Intelligence, represents the arising of the human form of intelligence from the animal kingdom represented in the lower picture. Behind the two figures of the man and woman the Earth is placed as though it were the centre of a human eye. Both figures are in the centre of a spiralling coil of Time which circles and embraces them like a shell or a galaxy swirl emanating from the hourglass nearby. The two human figures represent the arising of human intelligence within the realms of Time and the four smaller circling figures above represent Past, Present, Future and Mortality, all features of the Time shell in which people live.

The top picture linking into the Time shell yet going beyond it, as shown by the distant sunset or sunrise, has as its centre the Madonna-type image representing the highest and noblest kind of love at present possible in the human heart. It is a love that must be considered more important than Intelligence. This is why the picture called Compassion is placed at the top of the triptych. The Madonna image symbolises the highest and noblest aspirations of all races and creeds of mankind together with those motivations that are tender and altruistic. She is depicted holding the babe Mankind in her arms in a symbolic gesture reflecting the strongest and most pure love that has evolved in Mankind. The hand shown nearby that is both hand and wing is like the hand of a Buddha pointing the way forward to Truth and Enlightenment. Also to a sunrise or the sunset."

The voice faded and Gotama was again left in silence to contemplate the scenes set before him. The strange Triptych was not exactly evolution in a strictly Darwinian sense, although it did in a way embrace it and did not conflict with it. It portrayed life from its early beginnings up to the highest aspirations of Man. In fact as Gotama noted, the complete Triptych was actually called the Ascent of Man. No doubt that also includes Woman he conjectured with a wry smile, otherwise the artist whoever he may be will be in trouble. People were very sensitive about that sort of thing these days— perhaps the picture should be called the Ascent of Persons, he thought. However, that didn't seem to have quite the right ring to it. Probably better to leave it as it is, he decided. Unless we just call it The Ascent of Man (with Woman included by implication.)

It reminded Gotama of the many sayings and situations in the later 20th and early 21st centuries, which had become such sensitive issues where politically and socially correct or incorrect behaviour was now treated with such importance. Many women, for instance, had demanded not just equal rights and opportunities with men, but the acquisition of an altogether higher status that would, in their opinion, reflect their true and superior nature. There had consequently been increased efforts by their protagonists to delete the word 'man' from much of the language. The word 'person' was to be recommended in many instances, although when it came to utterances involving words like mankind, manhunt, manipulate, manhole, manuscript, etc., it was more than a little difficult to cater for such changes. It seemed obvious to many people that new words like personkind, personhunt, personipulate, personhole, and personuscript just didn't seem to sound right somehow. Racial connotations also came under fire. The many people who thought they knew better, now frowned upon black and white minstrel shows, enjoyed by millions earlier in the 20th century. It became distasteful for a white face to be painted black and vice versa even for a comedy show. Many seemed to have lost their sense of humour. Moreover, the word 'gay' couldn't now be used just to express innocent merriment, as it had been taken over by homosexuals. Young people were changing all sorts of words. Now, 'cool' didn't represent temperature. 'Heavy' was not now a definition of weight but something difficult to understand or philosophically profound. But he consoled himself with the thought that it was all part of the evolution of language. However, many of the amendments didn't fill Gotama with enthusiasm. He was of the opinion that such progress was often an illusion that frequently related to a retrograde step rather than to an advance.

Just at that moment the pictorial images began to change yet again. This time the shapes coagulated to form two dancing figures accompanied by the operatic theme music of Romeo and Juliet. As the music streamed through Gotama's head, his senses were overwhelmed by the beauty of the dance and the expression of love that seemed to bond the two figures into one. Finally the images solidified to become a picture enlaced in a breathtaking composition of line and form. As the music died away the voice said, "We show these images to instil in you some of the sensations of which the human mind is capable. Sensations of love and beauty such as those wrought by music and dance must be the property of all people. Ways must be found to fill all hearts with such sensations. These are some of the finest most precious gifts that we can bestow on our fellows. The more they are filled with such gifts, the more people will become their vehicles and the more they will wish to share such love and beauty with others in order to transform the world".

As the last words were spoken, further new images appeared and Gotama observed many magnificent and enthrallingly beautiful pictures. Finally a picture of a man came into view. His expression was a subtle blend of sadness, compassion and deep understanding. There were vague tears in his eyes. It could have been Jesus. The voice began again. "Finally we show you an image called Compassion. We show it because this human emotion is the most important of all. It embodies all that is finest in the human mind. It combines a sensitive sympathy with another's pain with an altruistic love that always tries to heal. It suffers with others' suffering, grieves with others' grief and shares joy with others' joy and sends good thoughts to all. It is a human trait that is now more than ever necessary to improve the chances of human survival on planet Earth."

The voice softened; its resonance reflecting a sense of sadness. "Finally, I leave you with these word gifts and hope you will find a way to keep their truths in your heart during your life on planet Earth, so that they can be a source of inspiration and strength for you and others." At that moment a strange and beautiful music, like fragrant perfume, accompanied the voice.

Mankind, like a living symphony,
Evolves, flowers and
Lasts for but a moment in the stars,
But from the changing anthem springs
Love, Earth's finest flower.

The cosmos is like a seamless coat,
Where no join or separation can be found.
All events are linked and affect each other.
We are that seamless coat.

From silence and eternal deep,
A formless form, a sunlit night,
Come rainbows of living conscious thought
And the softness of a new born baby's touch.
Time ticks out its melody
Of everything that's come and gone.
And all that has never ever been
Sees its moment and is gone.
Therefore let us drink with Omar,
The present moment to enjoy'
With the pleasure of a friendly smile
Across the barren lonely void.

There is a moment in eternity.
And eternity in a moment?

The drop is in the ocean,
The ocean is in the drop.

We're only ripples on a stream,
Flickers of light gone as they begin,
Insubstantial in continual change,
Fleeting things of thought and mind.

The Self is a mere construct of concepts

Ideas flow like a chain,
One linked to another
In karmic train.

Like birds on the wing,
Life and the universe fly by,
And we ask why?
Could it possibly be
The universe sees and knows itself
Through you and me?

And just to remind you not to be too serious, I give you my word gift called

The Apple Tree

Oh what a merry world it would be
If everyone got stuck in an apple tree.
Think of all the apples to bake,
And think of all the tummy ache.

Living in the tree would be such fun,
No one would ever be able to run.
We'd sit all day and eat our fill
And could tumble down like Jack and Jill.

We'd never be lonely up there in the tree
With apples all round as our company.
Some would be green and some would be red,
Some would be large, like old Uncle Ted.

There in the tree we would sing all the day
To the tunes of the breeze in a merry old way,
And the birds would flit from twig to twig,
Singing and dancing a funny old jig.

Blackbirds and robins would make such a chorus,
We'd have nothing to fear and nothing to bore us.
The blue sky above would make such a colour,
And warm sun above would smile like a mother.

And if it rained upon our tree,
We'd nestle under its canopy,
Which, like an umbrella would keep us dry
And we'd watch the scurrying clouds go by.

But then alas when winter came,
The leaves would fall like drops of rain
And then we'd have to run for cover,
Back home to tea with scones and mother.

And a valuable word gift from the great writer William Shakespeare.

Let me not to the marriage of true minds
Admit impediments. Love is not love
Which alters when it alteration finds,
Or bends with the remover to remove;
O, no; it is an ever fixed mark,
That looks on tempests and is never shaken;
It is the star to every wandering bark,
Love's not Time's fool, though rosy lips and cheeks
Within his bending sickle's compass come.
Love alters not with his brief hours and weeks,
But bears it out even to the edge of doom.
If this be error, and upon me proved,
I never writ nor no man ever loved.

After a slight pause, the voice said softly, "To save your planet Earth will require all the creative ingenuity and intellectual genius of mankind. There must be a collective effort to harness human knowledge and the wide variety of intellectual and emotional endeavour to achieve a common aim for peace in the human family. But knowledge and scientific effort alone cannot succeed unless and until they are underpinned by a deeper wisdom as was recognised and summarised by your George Harrison of the Beatles. I leave you therefore," the voice said quietly, "with the shortest, but perhaps the most important word gift of all."

Love is all you need.

The music faded and silence ensued, for at least a minute, whilst everyone present gathered their thoughts. Bubbles then turned to Gotama. "In our talks together I have told you about some of the things which will probably occur on Earth in both the near and more distant future. Some of the progress made will undoubtedly be good. However, with every advance there is almost always a retrograde step. With every regeneration there is degeneration. Every action has its reaction. This is a law of Nature that cannot be contravened. But knowing this should not stop us from trying to improve the world in which we live. During your own lifetime you will have seen extensive technological progress from the horse and cart to astronauts landing on the moon, also the introduction of the PC and Internet, together with all the accompanying changes wrought during this period. However, the period has not been without its tragedies, its wars, violence, famines and political unrest.

It is particularly tragic that such scientific and technological progress, which has been beneficial in so many areas of medicine for example, has unfortunately resulted in the use of science for destructive purposes. The atomic and biochemical weaponry, poison gas, drugs, etc., are just a few of the items in the vast arsenal of superdestructive forces now ready to be unleashed on the peoples of the world and which could destroy planet Earth and all its people several times over. There is also the threat of Asteroid and Comet collision with Earth that has to be dealt with together with global warming and pollution. Planet Earth is therefore now at an extremely critical time phase where not only another dark age could come about but something far more dreadful than ever before in the long history of the planet. Never before has there been a threat of total extinction of all life until now. Man now has the means to make all life extinct on Earth leaving a barren void for millions of years to come – a void without the possibility of life ever being able to spring into being again."

At this point, Gotama noticed that Bubbles was making some adjustment to the helmet she was wearing. "It's now time", she said, "for you to receive the imprint of many future events all compressed into a very short space of time. You will not be able to consciously absorb these events, because they will pass into your unconscious mind at very high speeds, like a computer processor memory bank recalling data at high velocity. However, your unconscious will be able to absorb and register the events and their implications. It will enable you to refer to new thresholds of experience and knowledge, so that you will be able to instinctively judge the outcome of many different social actions. It is essential that you assimilate this data so that you can make correct judgements when deciding future policies on your planet Earth. I hope you will agree to participate in this very special and important experiment. It is for the ultimate good and for the peace of the world."

Bubbles paused for a moment. "How do you feel about it?" she said, peering closely into Gotama's eyes. She was very beautiful, Gotama thought.

"I will do as you ask," he replied.

"Very well!" Bubbles closed her eyes as though to concentrate. As she did so, she almost whispered, "Good luck. We shall not meet again!"

Gotama witnessed a slight tingling sensation around his temples and a sudden racing of colours in front of his eyes. The sensation was accompanied by soft soothing music of a kind unfamiliar yet most pleasant. The next thing Gotama was aware of was someone shaking his shoulder. He looked up. To his astonishment he found himself back in his seat in the cabin of Progress 13.

"You've had a nice sleep," the stewardess was saying. "Can I interest you in a drink or a snack?" Gotama stretched himself. Many of the passengers were still asleep. A few were eating from white trays of food. One man with a large bloated face and bald head was consuming a pint of beer with considerable ease and dexterity. With obvious relish he finally licked the foam from his lips. "We're due to land in approximately 20 minutes," the stewardess continued pleasantly. "Would you like something to eat before we land?"

"No thank you," Gotama replied, as he struggled to come back to consciousness. The stewardess withdrew and, smiling sweetly to the next passenger in line, repeated her invitation.

It seemed no time at all before the aircraft landed. Gotama disembarked and was relieved to find himself in Kennedy Airport surrounded by familiar faces.

"We've booked you into the Hilton," said one.

"There's a special general meeting of the UN Assembly tomorrow to discuss the current crisis," said another.

There was a flurry of cameras. Flashing lights greeted them as members of the press converged.

"How do you view the current situation?" a reporter shouted, whilst trying his best to hold a microphone close to Gotama's face. There was no time to answer as the seething throng of people engulfed the reporter who disappeared almost as quickly as he had presented himself. People flowed through the terminal gate like treacle. Everyone was rushing and shouting. Gotama was hustled quickly into a large black limousine. Wedged between two burly colleagues, he was soon engrossed in their assessment of the crisis that had so suddenly developed and, as one of his colleagues pointed out, was likely to plunge the world into the biggest catastrophe of all time, unless someone came up with an answer at tomorrow's UN meeting.